ADIAMANTE

>>> <<<

L. E. MODESITT, JR.

A TOM DOHERTY ASSOCIATES BOOK
NEW YORK

ADIAMANTE

Edited by David G. Hartwell

Cover art by Kevin Murphy

A Tor Book
Published by Tom Doherty Associates, Inc.
175 Fifth Avenue
New York, NY 10010

Tor Books on the World Wide Web:
http://www.tor.com

Tor® is a registered trademark of Tom Doherty Associates, Inc.

ISBN: 0-812-54558-3
Library of Congress Card Catalog Number: 96-16114

First edition: October 1996
First mass market edition: March 1998

Printed in the United States of America

0 9 8 7 6 5 4 3 2 1

For Carol, as always,
and for Jim Harrison, for inspiration

If the conversation had been offline and spoken, neither of which was possible within the working systems contained in the adiamante hull of the *Gibson,* the words would have followed old patterns, patterns based on the spoken words that seldom echoed within the bulkheads and networks of the Vereal ship.

"Are you certain?"

"It's Old Earth, all right. The geography is within parameters," answered the cybnav, but since all the crew members—especially the line marines—were cybs, her tag on the net was nav, navigator, subcommander, or, less frequently, her given name.

"The DNA has the same base across all the samples," added the environmental officer. "And there was no hostile reaction to the samplers."

"They were scanned," interjected the weapons controller.

"I don't like those terms—base, within parameters. Does the DNA match or doesn't it? What about the geography? A planet doesn't change that much in ten thousand years, does it?" asked Commander Gibreal, knowing the answer, but seeking, as do all those of human DNA-type, confirmation of the obvious.

"There have been what look to be deliberate genetic manipulations, some subtle, some not so subtle," signaled the envoff to the *Gibson*'s commander. "Certainly not enough to account for the reputation of the place as the planet of death."

"What about viruses, bacteria, that sort of thing?" Gibreal knew the answers, again, before he received them.

"The former colonies were pretty clear about that. So were their records. Whatever the effect was, it wasn't anything known to their medical science. People died in full clean-suits and armor, in extreme trauma, and without any form of radiation, or any other trackable internal or external cause."

"Of course, there aren't any real records or tissue samples left." Gibreal's words smoked across the net with the bitterness of aqua regia. "What some people won't believe. Healthy bodies just don't die."

"What about telepathic auto-suggestion?" asked the envoff.

"Another rumor lost in time. No one's ever been able—not even the demis—to master telepathy. Anyway," added the commander, "that was thousands of years ago, and the old colonies have sent traders and envoys without harm for generations. They don't stay long, but their technology doesn't approach ours—or that of the old Rebuilt Hegemony." The commander snorted soundlessly, and his disgust colored the net with brown and the unsmelled odor of animal defecations. "Technology? Structures?"

"There aren't a lot of visible structures, except for those hundred or so energy concentrations—and that mass of ruins east of the mountains in the middle of old NorAm—that's what the records call it." The nav projected laffodils across the web with her words.

The laffodils wilted under the image of a blazing sun. "No other ruins? Just the one set?"

"There's the Great Wall—but we knew about that—and the non-talking heads. There may be smaller sets, but nothing else that exceeds two hundred meters."

"Two monuments, one set of ruins, and one-hundred-plus energy concentrations—that's it?"

"Within the system parameters so far, ser."

The sense of exhaled breath flooded the net, and the nav winced at the gale that whistled through the circuits.

"What are the energy concentrations?"

"They look to be a combination of transport hubs, service maintenance and manufacturing centers—with some transient housing."

"Everyone's there?" Gibreal's words lashed like a laser along the net channels. "The whole population within some hundred enclaves?"

"Not a chance. There's almost an energy web across the planet. It's hard to tell, but there seem to be a lot of independent energy generation points."

"So they've really regressed, have they?"

"Decentralized, anyway," temporized the nav, rubbing her forehead and blinking back the water jolted from her eyes by the violence of Gibreal's slashes through the net.

"Do we go in openly?" Gibreal's lashed words honed back toward the weapons officer.

"Why not? If they're hostile we can flatten those centers, and that should leave them helpless." Weapons projected fire and flames, and the ice of the de-energizers. "It looks straightforward enough."

"It won't be," countered the nav. "They ruled this part of the galaxy once. You saw what their fleet did to Al-Moratoros."

The image of the satellite of Moratoros three flashed across the net—a shining polished sphere, lifeless after more than scores of centuries, a sphere bathing an uninhabited planet in brilliant silver moonlight.

"That was then; this is now. They're coasting on the glory of a technology and power that's long since faded. The asteroid cities are dead, and the atmosphere of Mars is leaking back into space. No society has ever maintained its power for that long."

"Not even us." No one owned to the thought that crossed the net.

"We've regained our heritage," the commander added, "and we've avoided them for too long, just because of something that happened millennia ago." The commander flicked his order at the comm officer. "Send the signal."

The same message went out in multiple forms—beginning with complex variwave, then comm laser, UHF, VHF—all using the old protocols from the days preceding The Flight.

It was a simple message.

"The Exploration Fleet of the Vereal Union greets you. We request the opportunity to meet with the appropriate authority to discuss resumption of contact between our peoples. Please respond."

Less than a stan passed before the variwave response came.

"This is Old Earth, Deseret station. . . ."

As the transmission echoed along the net, the cybcomm and MYL-ERA ran the analysis.

"A high power, tight beam transmission," observed MYL-ERA, her net projections cool and sharp-edged, without emotional overtones.

"They know where we are."

"Not that difficult."

"In less than a standard hour—to receive, analyze, discover, find us, and frame a logical response?" asked the comm officer.

"A high degree of efficiency," agreed MYL-ERA.

"Too high," muttered the comm officer offline and under her breath. "Far too high."

"Still the same old demis, as arrogant in their knowledge as draffs are immobile in their ignorance," added Gibreal.

Neither MYL-ERA nor the comm officer responded.

<<< II

I sat at the circular cedar table I had made nearly a half-century earlier and stared out across the piñons, looking beyond the mist at everything—and nothing, as I had for a string of uncounted mornings.

The age-polished timbers still lifted the steep-pitched ceiling above me, and the wide windows still admitted the light, and the white, hand-plastered walls held still held that light.

I sniffed, catching the faintest of familiar scents, and I swallowed and looked back at the piñon-covered hills to the northwest.

Morgen was dead, and there wasn't much more to be said. Nothing changed that—not all the linkages we had shared or the ability to block her pain, to enjoy the last days as she had grown weaker. Nor had all the rationalizing helped, not about how much longer she had lived than could have any draff or cyb—not that Earth had any cybs left since The Flight.

She was dead. A half-century together had not been enough. Her soulsongs were not enough. If only athanasia were possible, athanasia of the body and not just of songs so painful they ripped through me, so beautiful that I still listened—and wept within myself, if only. . . .

Yet I did not wish to follow her—and I did not want to remain, either. So I watched the piñons, my thoughts floating out with the greedy jays, the spunky junkos, and the perpetually frightened jackrabbits. Beyond those more traditional auras loomed the darkness of the vorpals and kalirams and the protective emptiness of the sambur.

In that limbo, because I could not or would not decide, I answered the inlink when it chimed in my skull.

"Ecktor."

"Crucelle. The cybs are back. I thought you might like the charge." Crucelle's thoughts were clear, with the practice of centuries, along with the pulsed information on the cyb fleet, the dozen shielded ships that glittered power in the underweb and overspace and the multi-form transmissions that they had beamed at each locial point on Earth. Behind the information was the slender red-headed presence of Crucelle himself, a formal red-bronze dagger of a soul, and behind Crucelle was the ever-hovering soulshadow of Arielle, swirling stormangel on his linknet.

"Me?"

"Someone has to be Coordinator." The thought words reflected the tempered and honed edge of a formal blade: seldom used, but always ready.

I understood the unpulsed thoughts. Someone . . . and Crucelle had Arielle. Rhetoral had Elanstan. Even old Mithres had Dmetra. Coordinators took the risks. And with Morgen gone, I could certainly afford the compensatory time that would follow, assuming that I didn't follow the unwilling precedent of many Coordinators.

"And I'm that someone?"

"I could ask around. . . ."

I understood that as well. "The cybs? Might as well be me. Thanks."

"Thank you."

"Hello, Arielle," I added as Crucelle finished.

"I told you he would accept." Her words carried the whispers of the winds, winds that could have dwarfed the great storms that still swept the mighty west ocean. Winds, not the singing bells of dawn and twilight that I needed. "He needs a challenge bigger than his pain."

Crucelle snorted, or that was the sensation that I received. "You did; he does, and he will."

"Have they said what they want?" I ignored Arielle's netflashed smile.

"Not yet," answered Crucelle, his phrases as precise as though transmitted on a print screen. "They're scanning the locials, almost as if they can't figure out why we have so few discernible instances of technology. We have a little time before responding."

Arielle storm-ghosted out of the shadow-link with the hint of a wink and another smile as I thought about the cybs.

"They're after revenge, obviously."

"Elanstan opts for conquest, but I'd picked revenge," agreed Crucelle. "In what form, though?"

"Revenge isn't revenge if the victim doesn't know it. That's why the call."

"They could be cautious."

"What did they ask for?"

"Here's the whole transmission." With the short message also came the information on the multiple sending methods, including those that had scrambled more than a few draff datanets.

"Just a meeting . . . requested with the hint of immense power. Twelve ships each two klicks long, each with an adiamante hull." I found my lips pursing, and recalled Morgen's phrase about sealed lips being unable to kiss. I shook my head.

"I felt that headshake." Crucelle laughed. "Clearly, the mythology of death hasn't stopped them, unlike the released systems."

"Of course not. They're brilliant, rational cybs, and they haven't changed in millennia."

"There aren't as many of us now as there were then," Crucelle reminded me. "Twelve adiamante hulls indicates there are more of them and a significant technological and industrial base. You don't create adiamante in a small locial. What do you suggest?"

"Agree to their meeting to begin with. Let me think about the rest of it."

"You're hoping to find another way?" Even his question was formal-dagger sharp.

"Who wouldn't?"

Who indeed wouldn't? If Old Earth indeed needed to return to being the planet of death, the costs on all sides would be high, perhaps too high. That was always the risk posed by the Construct. I sighed as I broke the link.

<<< III

The morning after Crucelle linked, I was up early, as always. With Morgen's soulsongs soft-pealing through my mind, I wanted to hold her, talk to her, not to her images. Words and songs and memories . . . they were better than the emptiness of nothing. I did not call up a full-body holo, nor had I ever, especially not since her death. Life is whole-body, not net-images, and that was something the old cybs had never understood—and something I feared had not changed.

Nor had I opted for deep-soul thought-reality, for I was too much an intuit to accept such a shallow construct, and too rationalist to let myself be deceived, no matter how welcome such self-deception might be.

Instead of continuing with memory, I turned on the burner for the kettle, a small luxury, and ate a pear, one of the last ones off the tree in the side garden, firm with a hint of tartness in all its aeneous glory. Then I toasted another slice of heavy homemade bread. The maize was holding out, despite my increased appetite for carbohydrates, and that was fine. Between the firin cells, the solgen, and joba stocks, I had plenty of power.

Then, again, between the cybs and the duties of being Coordinator, the power stocks for the house were scarcely likely to be a problem. Coordinator duties carried both a comptime burden and a hefty admin offset credit—and every bit of that offset was usually earned. I shook my head.

The kettle began to boil, and I brewed, in the old-fashioned way, a cup of tea, wondering absently if tea would outlast all our heritages and worries. Then I sat and ate and sipped my way through two cups, letting the steam wreathe my face between sips as I held the cup two-handed below my chin. The crunchiness of the few sunflower seeds in the bread was another reminder of . . . what? I wasn't feeling that philosophical, but they tasted good.

Coordinator? Against the largest fleet seen since the Rebuilt Hegemony? As Arielle had said, it was definitely a challenge, but not bigger than Morgen's death—just different, and my loss made me the best candidate. Wonderful.

I ate a second slice of toast before I left the table and dressed for exercise: yet another form of escape from reality, an escape created by seizing the moment so tightly that the reality of the past faded—while I ran, at least.

The sun hung unrisen below the eastern mountains as I stepped out of the house into the gray light. From one of the top branches of an ancient piñon on the southeast side of the long hilltop, the golden eagle—the one with the self-concept/image of "Swift-Fall-Hunter"—flapped into the dawn, then glided into the shadowed silence of the west gorge over the scattered meleysen trees that remained. Although the dwindling meleysens continued to clean air and ground and spread their pervasive faint orange perfume, the scent usually didn't reach the house.

As Swift-Fall-Hunter vanished, I smiled and stretched each leg in turn, placing it on the waist-high pile of hand-sawn deadwood, gradually stretching and leaning forward, avoiding any rocking motion. I had left the bow saw inside—no wood gathering when I needed to think. Besides, I had enough deadwood, and Morgen had been the one who really liked the fire in the antique cast-iron stove that dated back centuries or longer.

The breeze carried the scent of cedar and juniper and piñon, the air barely damp from the quick evening rain of the night before. A light dusting of snow had covered the higher mountains to the east, and to the north the Esklant Peaks glittered white, as would the hills around me before much longer.

I finished stretching, straightened the loose sweat clothes, checked the razored blade in the sheath, and walked along the path toward the western end of the ridge. A brilliant blue piñon jay squawked, then a second, and both flapped upward, followed by the rest of the small flock, as they swirled downhill to light on another broad-branched piñon, high enough that they would not be easy prey for a vorpal.

After a quick glance back at the thick brown walls that merged with the hillside and the one partly open window, I began to run, letting my mind free-associate on the thought of the cybs—of the coming meeting in Parwon.

As always, the lines of dialogue spooled through my nets, almost independent of moving legs and breathing.

Dialogue line one: The cybs seek an undefined goal, probably revenge cloaked in something, and are human enough to make it nasty, if given a chance. Old Earth has no ships with adiamante hulls—or any other kind of warship hulls—just twenty to thirty million talented demis. What do the cybs want in their revenge? Symbolic atonement? Destruction of Earth's remaining demis? Acknowledgment of their superiority and that they were treated wrongly?

What would Morgen have said? Enter soulsong one:

> "My songs for you alone will flow;
>   at my death none but you will know
>   cold coals on black stove's grate, ash-white,
>   faintest glimmers for winter's night. . . ."

Dulce, dulce, with the smoothed gold of a perfect pear, the gold hair of mountain dunes at twilight, and a funeral bell across the hills of Deseret.

Fighting the images, the ghost sense of silky skin I could no longer touch, I ran harder. I used all my other senses, full-extended, because my eyes blurred and burned, and I skittered thoughts toward the cyb-ships, the twelve adiamante hulls, hard and black in the void-wrapped nielle, that darkness deeper than black.

Downhill to the right, a jackrabbit thumped and jumped sideways behind a cedar, another ancient twisted trunk that felt as though it dated to the Rebuilding. Above, Swift-Fall-Hunter circled, his eyes on the jackrabbit.

Dialogue line two: Are the cybs people or aliens? Does it matter? No matter how deeply we feel, nor how much we try to develop a picture of an alien, or a concept of one—those concepts and descriptions are just humans masquerading as aliens . . . unless you believe that intelligence, as we define it, has as its goal survival—in which case there are no aliens, only humans with different shapes.

The jackrabbit darted to a halt under a piñon beside a washed-out scrub brush, and Swift-Fall-Hunter circled to the east on wings that spanned more than four meters. The golden eagle sought other prey, gliding silently over the valley that had once held, among other things, a long-ago town. Now only scrub and cedar rose from the red clay.

I kept running, westward, away from the vanished town and away from history.

Dialogue line one: Morgen, morning, morning in my twilight, what would she have said? Certainly something to the effect that revenge is human, all too human, and therefore a fitting vice to be overcome, except she would have said it, thought it, more gently . . . something like, "The cybs have human vices, too, Ecktor. . . ."

Not like that, either, I realized, as I started down between the hills, concentrating on putting my boots evenly between the rocks and depressions. Not even with the net and her songs could I construct what she might have said to the unexpected, like the return of the cybs.

Some demis run naked and barefoot, but that takes bodymods, even if they're natural calluses, and that was carrying naturality to extremes—something I tried not to do. I could sense my oxygen demand rising, both physically and through the selfnet. My lips curled, and I forced my legs to stretch out despite the discomfort.

Dialogue line two: No aliens—not even the cybs? Next you'll be saying there's no difference between virtual-net real and whole-body real.

Conthesis one: Is there a difference between reality, symbolic reality, and representative/virtual reality? One might as well ask whether there is a difference between women, pictures of women, and mannequins dressed as women . . . or soulsongs of beloved women.

. Soulsongs of beloved women . . . beloved woman. . . .

I ran with the breeze, breathing heavily, setting each foot in harmony, mind out ahead and scouting the trees and the path, relaying the information to my body. The scent of the meleysen leaves to the northeast drifted into my nostrils, and I stepped up the pace.

Conthesis two: I don't have one.

As I panted up to the top of the next hill to the west, the breeze strengthened, cooling me, and bringing the slightest acrid scent of a distant vorpal. My hand touched the knife, and my lips curled, but no vorpal would come after me, not with my luck.

As I kept moving across the hilltop, dodging rocks and cedars and junipers, the coolness did nothing to unscramble the thoughts and emotions within.

Fine excuse for a demi I was, unable to break free of the hold of the past, the hold of the memory of floral essence on bare skin, the hold of. . . .

Too bad the cybs had forsaken integration in favor of crystalline clarity. I almost laughed at that, and had Morgen been there in more than soulsong, I would have.

Instead of staying on the path, I turned due south and darted this way and that downhill and through the piñons, trying to avoid any spot where I might have run before. The soil wasn't cryptozoic, even away from the meleysens. It just hadn't ever been that fertile, although it was richer under the trees and around the pale blue-green of the sagebrush. Lava takes millions of years to degrade in a dry climate, and the sagebrush hadn't been working on the black stone anywhere near that long.

I kept running, and the pressure of the physical shut down my internal dialogues.

When I slowed to a fast walk near the top of the next rise, I was breathing heavily, and sweating. Through the trees to the north, I could see the grasslands and the hummocks of the prairie dog town, rising above the chest-high and browned grasses. Swift-Fall-Hunter circled, then passed on, looking for easier prey.

The sourness of my sweat and the panting confirmed that I'd neglected my physical condition more than I should have. With the slowing down, something from a pile of rocks caught my eye and senses—rather, the absence of something did.

Under another old and twisted cedar, among the lichen-covered dark gray rocks, lurked a chunk of darkness—a blackness that swallowed light, that turned seeking eyes from it: a curved fragment of black adiamante. I squatted, letting my fingers ease the adiamante up.

How long had it rested there, impervious to age, to deterioration, to anything but the mighty lines of force that had sheared it into a smooth-sided and round polygon whose exact dimensions still eluded the eye?

I lifted the adiamante, a relic of the great confrontation between the demis and the cybs that had led to the Rebuilding. Neither warm nor cool to the touch, neither seeking nor releasing heat, the smooth blackness—heavier than hardwood, lighter than iron, and stronger than anything made by man before or since—lay in my hands.

After a moment, I replaced it in the rocks and straightened up. Adiamante—harder than the diamond from which its name had been derived, and virtually useless except in a handful of applications like armor and spacecraft hulls . . . and, I supposed, swords, except no one had ever squandered that much energy to forge an adiamante sword. Once formed, you couldn't mill it, work it, or change it, and only a gigawatt laser, a sun-fired particle beam, or a nucleonic knife could cut it.

And yes, it had taken a full asteroid complex to create it. I supposed the complex was still out there, beyond the night, fusactors cold, waiting for the resurgence of the Rebuilt Hegemony that could never come, or some future rebuilding of Old Earth necessitated by the workings of the Construct—and my failure. I shivered at that thought.

Under the tree lay a fragment, a faraway meteoric fragment that had dropped from the sundered skies of The Flight. I let it lie, wishing the cybs had been wise enough to let the hard fragments of their past lie. But, being cybs, that was exactly what they could not do, not when for them net-reality was equal to whole-body reality.

After a few moments of deep breaths, I began to run again, back through the trees, away from the adiamante. I circled slowly north and uphill, back toward the past.

As I stopped outside the house, close enough to hold the comment, I pulsed a link to Crucelle, who answered as though he had been waiting.

"Any further thoughts?" he asked, red-bronze mandagger waiting for use.

"The ell stations . . . they need to be powered up. Isn't that Elanstan?"

"I'll tell her," Crucelle volunteered, and I let him, shaking my head at the thought.

"Me, too," he answered my unspoken concern. "There's no guarantee that we could put Earth back together again. We almost didn't last time, and the Jykserians weren't nearly so strong."

"Letting them destroy the locials? Would that be enough?" Arielle's storm-currents pulsed darkangel-like.

"That wouldn't give them enough revenge, I suspect," I pulsed, sensing Crucelle's nod even before I finished. "People who feel they're right, and who've been humiliated . . ."

"They'll want to reduce us to a bloody pulp?"

It was my turn to nod.

"So what do we do now?" he asked.

"We'll need to concede whatever it takes to get their marcybs . . ." I stopped. "No . . . that will just encourage them to act immediately. Give them full access to the locials. Treat them as honored guests, but not too honored, as if they were not quite equals."

"That's true enough."

"That's also the problem. They're sitting in orbit with enough power to make a large mess, and they're looking for an excuse to do it without any understanding of the repercussions."

"I think they understand," interjected Arielle. "They

just don't care. If we use force to stop them, then we fuel another millennium of cyb-based technological development. At the end of that development, they'll have developed devices that will nova an entire system, or worse. If we surrender, they'll find an excuse to commit some range of atrocities or try to sterilize the whole planet. The Construct forbids either, in any case."

"Like the way the Construct forbade what our forbearers did to Al-Moratoros?"

They both winced. That memory had not faded, though it was not ours, nor our doing. And that wince said all there was to say about why we wouldn't break the Construct, no matter what the cost.

"Either way," Arielle concluded, "that's our payback for using power in forcing The Flight."

"Thanks, Arielle," I flipped back.

"You are most welcome, puissant mage Ecktor. And Coordinator," she added ironically.

I continued to concentrate, but nothing new or original came to mind. I finally concluded, "We're still left with the fact that Old Earth is the planet of death where only demis and draffs can live. Proving that could be hard, if they still fit the typical cyb profile."

The sense of a nod followed from Arielle, along with a sigh and a frown. "That's going to be hard. I'd estimate a twenty percent mortality, maybe as high as fifty percent for those in direct contact."

I sent back a shrug, not a disinterested one, but a resigned one. So far, I didn't have any alternatives.

For a moment, stillness dropped across the net like a niellen shroud, and I could understand that.

"You're breathing hard," Crucelle finally responded.

"I ran a while."

"How far? How long?"

"Not quite thirteen klicks . . . in half a stan . . . but I'm not in shape, and I was scrambling through the woods." If

I had been in better shape or followed the path, I could have done close to twenty klicks in the same time.

The dialogue box in my head pointed out that while I could run from grief, running wasn't going to solve the cyb problem. It hadn't millennia earlier, and it wouldn't now.

<<< IV

"Two before upper entry."

The warning clipped across the lander's net, and the nav checked her restraints.

"It's all superstition," snapped Commander Gorum, his words strong enough to flex the net. "That's why I'm here. To show that it's just that. To look at Old Earth and its demis logically and factually."

"To send down the head marcyb does seem like over-kill," pointed out the second pilot.

"Someone with an overview has to see these people—if they're still people—before we act. That means me or Gibreal."

"Marines are more expendable. Not much better than marcybs." No one owned the thought, cold and direct.

"There's not likely to be any expense." Gorum laughed. "Besides, Henslom or Ysslop or any of the majers could do the job. The demis retreated from all the systems of the Rebuilt Hegemony. As soon as one system revolted, and then another, they just folded. Then they created this myth of Old Earth as the planet of death as a last defense. Because the demis still had a fleet then, everyone bought it. It was a handy excuse for the old colonies—they didn't have to fight a war that would have been costly. So they went along with it. There aren't any medical records that show anything because nothing really ever happened."

"What happened to Old Earth's fleet?" asked the lander's second pilot. "It was never broken."

"Same thing that happens to all old fleets," answered the marcybs' chief. "Fell apart and disappeared. You don't maintain weapons, you don't have them when you need them."

"What about the shuttle craft we spotted?" asked the nav. "The one heading for that asteroid in the stable orbital position?"

"What about it? It's a nickel-iron asteroid. Energy dead even on EDI levels, both underweb and overspace . . ."

"Al-Moratoros," snapped the nav.

"That was at least two millennia ago. At least."

"And that asteroid up above us had to have been moved there."

"Old technology," answered Gorum.

The net crackled, cutting over the interchange, and pins shot through the net and the cybs as the lander slashed deeper into the ionosphere. Except for the static, the net was still.

<<< V

I should have run up to Parwon to watch the cybs bring down their welcoming groups in landers. You don't land a two-klick-long interstellar ship on a planet, not even a cyb-ship with an adiamante hull. In the shape I was in, I didn't even try to run the distance. I should have, but I didn't.

I rolled out the small flitter from the hangar attached to

the back of the house, then ended up spending more time on maintenance than it would have taken to run up and back. A strand of sandy hair on the second seat didn't help my mood, but spending more effort on cleaning the already spotless turbine exterior did.

The flitter was one of my luxuries—hydrocarb fueled, and that meant a special refining module for the joba processor—plus a few stans a week doing screen-pushing at the Deseret locial to compensate for my toy and the technology that supported it. Plus growing the joba, and that meant regular flights south to the Fireo Desert.

The flitter itself wasn't especially advanced—deployable rotors and turbines integrated into a lifting body—but it was dependable.

After a last check, including the knives and the rest of the survival kit stowed under the seats, I pulled on a one-piece coverall over my browns, donned the lightweight helmet, and strapped in. Again, I could have had a flitter with automated restraints and a full-sound-insulated hull, but that would have had me working half my life at Deseret in arduous heavy maintenance.

Under the timeless *thwop . . . thwop, thwop* of high speed rotors, I held the flitter steady on the ground cushion, then dropped the nose fractionally, letting the flitter build up speed as I eased it down the lane that ended in the dry snye of the creek. Before the point where the snye joined Kohl Creek, the lifting body was functional, and I turned the flitter northward, crossing the higher grasslands and the prairie dogs and flicking a pulse through the transmitter to Deseret station to lock our track into the traffic scanning. There was another new burrow complex on the north side of the prairie dog town. Before long the mountain vorpals would be raiding again, and the kalirams would be waiting for the vorpals' return.

For all my maintenance efforts and dependable technology, the faintest scent of hot metal and lubricants tickled my nostrils. So I cracked the vent valves, and the whistling cold air removed the odors, and most of the heat, from the two-place cockpit.

I leveled off in the green zone, high enough to allow the safety seats to work with the rotors deployed, and *thwopped* northward. The trip was too short to retract the rotors and go high-speed, as I would have on a trip to the Cherkrik ruins or the Ellay locial.

No more than ten klicks north of the house, splotches of snow showed on the north sides of the cedar- and piñon-covered hills. A small herd of sambur grazed in one of the fire-meadows, and, despite the stolidity of composite and metal around me, I sensed a cougar slipping through the piñons toward the ruisines.

The sambur scattered at the sound of the flitter. Beyond the fire-meadow was a large stand of meleysen trees, thriving as they detoxified yet another remnant of either the Chaos Years or the decades that precipitated The Flight.

Then the flitter *thwopped* over a stand of ancient cedars, their age seeping into the cold blue sky, and left sambur and meleysens behind.

Parwon was less than fifty klicks north, but even the lower meadows on the south sides of the hills around the locial, and the shaded spots in the lanes, bore traces of snow.

After pulsing the station, I linked momentarily with the net, and began the descent. I could have flown the easy way, linked with the pilot module, but I used the old-fashioned stick and collective controls the whole distance, though I did have to link in the overrides for safety purposes on the approach. The transnet didn't even flicker— that's how smoothly I slipped the flitter onto the apron beyond the tower, and that smooth an approach would have been hard even for a demi whose collateral was transport.

The wind gusted around me while I secured the craft. I peeled off the coverall and folded it onto the seat before I sealed the flitter and walked across the permacrete toward the white spire that rose out of the oval locial landing building.

My eyes flicked up, along the invisible approach beam that the landers would follow down.

Cybs. Why now? Were they really bent on revenge, or was I projecting the face of a grim history on people who might be far different from those who had forged that history?

The rushing sound of a shuttle penetrated my introspection, and I glanced toward the slender tower that contained the beacons and a single controller. A second craft—a standard magfield shuttle version—settled right before the tower as I neared. The door dilated, and three figures stepped out: Crucelle, Arielle, and Rhetoral—a redhead, a dark brunette, and a blond. Rhetoral was the blond, tall and imperious, a genetic throwback in appearance, and, unsurprisingly, very much a rat-comp. If Crucelle was a formal dagger, then Rhetoral was an ancient longsword.

After the three cleared the shuttle, the pilot air-taxied the flitter toward one of the north hangars. Arielle led the way as the three walked toward the tower.

We met by the east portal.

"Elanstan?" I asked Rhetoral. Elanstan was his soulsymb and had hair so black it was almost nielle—that was what I remembered, anyway. They were almost as close as Morgen and I were—or had been.

"Bringing up the ell stations." He winced.

So did I. Although they were maintained in standdown, the ell stations hadn't been used since dispersing the Jykserian Armada. Despite their pleasant appearances and their all-too-human origins back with the ancient Longships of NorAm, the Jykserians had minds as alien as any found among the stars—or on Old Earth. Had that outlook been created by radiation? Or by economically influenced genetic self-selection? They had wanted to trade for technology and refused to understand that some knowledge was not for sale.

Of course, once again, we—our ancestors—had paid a heavy price, but not so heavy as the Jykserians. Unfortunately, the cybs of the Vereal Union appeared to have higher technology and a grudge, and we had the Construct, and the interaction could easily lead to catastrophe for us all.

"Who else?" I asked.

"Some of the senior locial coordinators will be at the Hybernium to add presence." Rhetoral grinned, a smile warmer than his cool appearance.

We had learned over the generations. Too many apparent functionaries, and those who visited Old Earth received the impression that we lived on past glory. Too few, and the impression was contempt. The senior coordinators swelled the ranks, offered historical observations, and were excellent listeners.

"Why—besides pity—did you outlink me for this?" I asked Crucelle.

"Because there are only a handful of comp-intuits. You're rare, and the Council thinks the combined outlooks will be needed."

"So do I," added Arielle, midway through Crucelle's words, her smile flashing in my eyes and through the close-link, her dark eyes both warm and concerned, yet behind that concern was the cold rationality of a first class rat-comp, and the power of the untamed storm.

Rhetoral just nodded, pale blue eyes as cold as the snow on the mountains overlooking the locial station.

Wondrous! The three of them had put Old Earth's future on my shoulders as a rehab project.

So I was rare? Rare, like an extinct ratite lost in the Die-Out, one of the ones too fragile for the DNA to fossilize and too unknown to mixfill a genesplice. Rare, like a comp child born in a draff family. Rare, like an emote from a long line of rat-comps.

Rare, like all of those, that was what Crucelle had said—and so had my old tutor Mithres. I was rare, a dual mind, comp-intuit, and that was why I was all mixed up. Of course, my emote scale was below demi-norm, and that bothered my mother, but Morgen had had more than enough emote-intuit for the both of us.

"Here they come, ready to reclaim their heritage—as if they knew what it was." Crucelle's words were dry, and underscored by the rumbling whistle as three black dots grew into smooth and ponderous wedge shapes that bore down on the locial from the north.

As I watched the three heavy landers caress the permacrete and roll ever more slowly toward us, I scarcely felt rare, only old—not that any of us, even Morgen at the end—looked old, except in the depths behind our eyes.

The landers were big—fifteen meters high and more than two hectometers long and massing who knew what—and black. Not the deep darkness of nielle, but black—plain, ugly black, black scarred by scores of atmospheric transits.

Once the orbit-to-ground craft had rumbled to a stop and a handful of cybs had begun to disembark, I walked across the permacrete toward the figures below the first lander's ramp, a perfectly human and normal set of motions that carried me toward the cybsens officers. I centered on the cyb with the most metal and one of the higher ENFs. The matched and glittering metal diamonds on each shoulder of the antique-appearing military blouse had to signify a certain position, as if any rigid structure ever conveyed anything meaningful except the ability to exert power over those lower in the structure. Power without morality is disaster; morality without power is useless.

The brown-haired and brown-eyed commander—over two meters tall—looked down at me with eyes as soulless as any mech processor. After a moment, he spoke in rusty Anglas, his voice with the raspiness of a netdweller who seldom exercised the joys of speech. "I am Commander Gorum of the Vereal Union. It is a pleasure to stand here on Old Earth."

"Liar," flicked the netline from Arielle.

"It's called diplomacy," came the silent rejoinder from Crucelle.

"I am Ecktor, current Coordinator." I almost choked on the title. "This is Crucelle . . . Arielle . . . and Rhetoral."

Crucelle bowed slightly, as did the others at their names.

"We greet you and hope your visit will prove fulfilling," I continued.

"You're as bad as he is," commented Arielle on the net.

"How might we help in your visit?" I added, ignoring Arielle.

For a moment, the commander paused, and I caught the pulses of information between him and the lander and the stocky brown-haired woman behind him and to his left, information boosted through the flat, short range net repeaters on their belts. Before long, I thought I would probably be able to decipher the protocols, but that would have to wait. I kept my expression one of mild interest as I waited for the commander's spoken response.

"Obviously, we have little data on what happened to Old Earth after our ancestors . . . departed, except for some vague details about the rise and fall of the Rebuilt Hegemony we obtained from the independent systems." The tall commander forced a smile. "More detailed information would be welcome. We would also like to see what we can of our ancient home."

"So you can figure out how to conquer or destroy it," came Arielle's netline comment.

"Millennia of information . . . that will take some time." I smiled, again ignoring, for the moment, Arielle's words, although I agreed with the thoughts behind them. "Perhaps we could begin at the Hybernium, with both refreshments and general background." I pointed out the structure, its dome visible. It was scarcely more than a few klicks from the old landing field we still maintained at the Deseret locial for the released colonies—and for the handful of strangers that had straggled in from across the stars after the collapse of the Rebuilt Hegemony, strangers arriving in everything from standard shift-jumpers to bussard ramfleets to solar scows. They all came, and looked, and departed—one way or another.

"You seek to avoid providing details?" asked Gorum smoothly.

"Ask, and you shall receive," I answered, disliking his extreme suspicion while understanding it. "But sometimes the details make more sense if there is a framework to which they can be attached."

Gorum inclined his head ever so slightly.

As he paused, I inquired, "Might I ask of your colleagues?"

The faintest frown flicked across Gorum's brow before he answered. "This is Subcommander Kemra."

The sandy-haired cyb subcommander nodded briskly. I concealed a wince, or hoped I concealed it. The woman looked far too much like the sister Morgen had never had.

"Careful," cautioned Arielle, net-voiced in silence.

"This is Officer Mylera." Gorum nodded toward the slender brunette with the slightly flat black eyes.

With relief, I turned to the modest appearing woman, without revealing that I had almost immediately determined that Mylera was MYL-ERA, the physical construct/extension of the Vereal fleet's net intelligence.

Rhetoral refrained from commenting, and I didn't have to worry about Crucelle or Arielle.

"Majer Henslom and Majer Ysslop." The two marine officers glanced at me with the same flat eyes as MYLERA's construct, but their blankness came from wariness and training, unlike the blankness of their troopers. A quick comm burst flicked between them.

"Greetings, majers," I answered, bowing slightly.

"Greetings," answered Ysslop, the voice polite and even.

All I got from Henslom was a curt nod, and a sense of chill as his eyes focused on me, as if to freeze me in his personal databanks.

Out of the five, two were information specialists of one sort or another, I suspected, and three were cyb military—a fair indication of what we faced.

"It is a pleasure to meet you all," I said.

"Might I ask, just for the record," interjected Gorum, "who speaks for Old Earth."

"Ecktor does," Rhetoral said, with a cold smile in my direction, a smile that made him seem as antique as the slender longsword he personified.

"Thank you."

"Any others in the landers who might wish refreshments or just to stretch their legs are certainly welcome to join us at the Hybernium. We have more than adequate transportation," I offered.

"Thank you."

Again came the sense of a shared net-like conference before Gorum added, "Perhaps a few others would benefit from your hospitality."

"They would certainly be welcome." Welcome: as if the greeting reception were almost like an ancient pavane, stately and formal, except the dance would be for information.

Nearly twenty additional cybs, all junior marine officers, climbed into the electroshuttles. That left close to two hundred of the marcybs on the shuttles, with a few officers, but since I was being diplomatic, I didn't mention their presence to Gorum or his officers. The four of us and the five senior cyb officers took the last shuttle. Major Henslom was the last to board, and his eyes had never stopped scanning the locial station, as though he had measured it every way in which he could.

The veridium-tinted vehicle slipped along the curving lane silently, past the mulched and bedded gardens covered with smatterings of snow, past the long administration building that looked like an antique submarine rising out of the sea of browned grass.

As the shuttle glided up to the Hybernium's wide and open porticos—empty of people in the chill—Subcommander Kemra asked, "Why is the structure called the Hybernium?"

"It memorializes the dangers of the long winter," answered Arielle.

Ancient chronicles were more her specialty than mine, and I remained too absorbed in more personal recent history, an absorption not aided by the subcommander's visage.

A puzzled look crossed Subcommander Kemra's too-familiar face and vanished. "Why is it here? Because this is where visitors land?"

"Actually, there's one at every locial," I said.

"Locial? Is that another name for your small cities?"

"A locial isn't really analogous to a city," I tried to explain. "It's a regional locus for services and support systems." With that, I could almost sense the mental click in the Mylera construct. "This is the Deseret locial, but the center area is called Parwon."

"You have considerable housing in such locials," said Mylera. "But the power usage reflects a higher per individual consumption from single units outside your locials."

That was probably so, since most draffs lived in locials or near them, but I avoided a direct answer. "Generally, there are economies of scale in the locials."

"Do your more affluent individuals live outside the locials?" pursued Mylera.

"There's probably a greater percentage outside the locials," I agreed, "but it takes certain necessary skills to live outside a locial."

"The Hybernium," came the words from Dvorrak, loud enough to halt the conversation. Dvorrak was a painter, old-style, but he worked as a shuttle driver for his comptime.

I nodded to him as I stood on the pavement and the others stepped down. He smiled sadly, then eased the shuttle back toward the underground maintenance bay.

After leading the way up the hardened Navaho sandstone steps, I stopped at the top of the wide stairs and pointed at the inscription over the main entry portal: "Lest we forget the lessons of the Long Winter, and the longer spring . . ."

"We have no record of a long winter." Mylera's voice was nearly flat.

"It was the result of the events that led to The Flight."

"The Flight was more like a forced exile," pointed out Gorum, "and all too many cybs did not survive the freezers."

"Perhaps," I acknowledged, "but thousands of millions died on Old Earth."

"I see no graves or memorials," said Mylera flatly.

"If we had attempted such, we would still be erecting them," Rhetoral commented, "and all of Old Earth would be little more than a cemetery."

"Or a crematorium," added Arielle. "Your forebearers loosed the small stars and the deathsmoke."

The commander started to speak, then closed his mouth with a snap.

I stepped through the open archway.

The first three holos—each taller than the cyb commander and twice as wide—showed scenes from Ellay, Hughst, and Londn, captured in full depth and color right before The Flight. The one from Hughst depicted lines of cybs marching toward a line of antique ground-to-orbit shuttles, shuttles almost as large as those cyb vessels we had greeted. Behind the figures rose lines of smoke, and the haze of death that covered the blood-red skies that had been the visage of heaven for all too long.

"Why are these here?" Gorum snapped, turning from the holo at his elbow.

"To remind us of what led to the Long Winter," answered Arielle, her spoken voice gentle, but her dark, almost black, eyes hard.

"Let us go on," suggested Subcommander Kemra.

Frowns crossed all of their faces as they passed the next set of images, where the ice and snow covered all but the tallest of the ruins, those buildings half-melted like wax, then frozen there.

The other cybs had already arrived, and, according to their orders, had gathered in groups like ravens, each group encircling one of the senior locial coordinators to pick away information as if it were carrion flesh.

"Your images are disgustingly vivid," complained Crucelle over the link.

"Sorry," I apologized silently.

At the table covered with pressed and pale green linen in the center of the receiving area were bottles, open and closed, containing a range of beverages, crystal goblets, several insulated containers filled with ice, and plates with fruits, nuts, cheeses, and crackers.

Santucci, one of the senior locial officials, stood near the west wall before the long case that held the replicas of the original *Paradigms,* but her eyes were glazed over, and I could sense she had called up the image of Duffery from the memory chip in stone beneath. He'd died in a climbing accident several months before Morgen, caught off-guard by a kaliram. It's so often the stupid things that are fatal. I swallowed as I watched, then turned away.

Crucelle looked at me again, pulsing as he did, "You get to make the welcoming speech to this lively crowd."

I nodded.

I only had to clear my throat slightly, and, suddenly, everyone was looking in my direction, as if each had been waiting for just such a moment.

"Welcome to Old Earth . . . except for those of you who were already here. . . . You just get to enjoy the refreshments."

Not much of a laugh, but there was some slight relaxation.

"We welcome those of you who come from the far Vereal Union. May your visit be both pleasant and enlightening to us both." I gestured toward the table. "Enjoy the refreshments."

Slowly, the hum of conversation rose again, and, as I turned, I realized that I stood alone. The closest individual was the cyb-construct Mylera, and I doubted that was exactly by chance.

I eased back to the table and chose a goblet of Earthflame. Only a handful of the clear goblets with the smoky red fluid had been touched, while the goblets with the clear white wines of Snoma had mostly vanished into the hands of cybs and demis alike.

The Earthflame seared my palate for a moment, and I let the liquid slip down my throat, with its olfactory hints of autumn leaves, fragrant coals, and ice.

Then I turned, glowing as I did because my browns contained lutinin-bearing cells, though the minute flares of light were just below the visual recognition threshold, a design developed to create a sense of glowing. So I glowed as I carried myself across the polished light-polarized

stones of the Hybernium, where each departed soul flickered pulses of reason from the chips imbedded beneath,
allowing any passerby to pause and converse—all net-to-
net, of course.

Someday there would be a chip for me, I supposed.
There was a chip for Morgen, in a stone on the floor to the
left end of the window that gave a panorama of the eastern peaks. I avoided that part of the Hybernium.

Santucci still remained fixed before the case, an example
of just why I avoided the north side of the long eastern
window.

I walked toward Mylera, the cyb-construct who glittered with a subdued harshness in the energy web as truly
as I glowed imperceptibly. She waited and watched, the
spider—or the spider's scout—waiting for the prey.

I bowed slightly as I stopped and before I spoke. "Officer Mylera, the commander never mentioned your duties
and functions."

"He did not," answered the cyb-construct, an apparently perfect biological replica of a cyb. "I am a liaison
and information specialist."

Like so many cub statements, it was true and mislead-
ing all at once, but I inclined my head slightly. "Your specialty?"

"Gathering whatever information is necessary." Her
voice was not quite so harsh as that of the true cybs, an
apparent contradiction that amused me.

"All information can be necessary at some time or another," I countered, my own net assessing the web that
surrounded the construct.

"That is certainly so," was the measured response.

No linkage pulsed from her, and I paused, after another
sip of the Earthflame, letting my ears detect what they
could, but Mylera's breathing and tension levels remained
relaxed, a certain sign that she was a construct.

Gorum linked with the subcommander beside him,

through the small repeaters, since their net did not function away from the landers. The words, low-powered as they were, were strong enough for me. "Involution was the destiny of the demis, involuting until their brains had navels and their navels brains."

"Yet each is said to have the ability to immobilize or incinerate a score of draffs," answered the one introduced to me as Kemra, the one who vaguely and disturbingly resembled Morgen.

I wanted to snort. We couldn't incinerate anything, not mentally. That didn't mean we didn't have abilities, but they certainly didn't include physical pyromancy.

Yet over my irony, because of the cyb's resemblance to Morgen, a fragment drifted through my internal dialogues, unbidden:

> ". . . golden autumn that will see no spring,
> for whitest flakes will gown my grace,
> and jewels of ice will frame my face . . ."

Kemra could have worn ice, so cold was her face, so frozen those green eyes, so chill her distanced words.

"Said? Rumors and more rumors," groused the heavily muscled cyb commander.

"You find them interesting?" asked Mylera/MYL-ERA, noting my abstraction and absent attention.

"Although they said nothing," I lied, forcing my concentration fully back within the Hybernium, "their posture reflects a growth of rumor, a rumor I am somewhat amused at."

"Most rumor has truth at its base," Mylera/MYL-ERA pointed out. "But a tense posture does not mean rumor."

"We try to avoid rumor and face what we believe to be fact. That can be difficult if rumors are more attractive than fact." I shrugged and lifted the goblet.

Mylera nodded, then added. "Since you are interested

in directness, I do believe the commander would like to discuss some . . . technical details with you."

Almost as she completed the statement, Gorum was at her elbow, the professional soldier's smile upon his lips, the kind of smile I wished to keep absent from Old Earth. "I could not help overhearing—"

"The opening you asked Officer Mylera to make?" I asked politely.

"Obviously, it was easier that way." He spread his free hand in a gesture meant to be disarming. The other held an untouched goblet of Whitespring.

Behind him Subcommander Kemra drifted toward us, also carrying a goblet of Whitespring, still untouched, the crystal rim shimmering and virgin.

"Technical details?" I asked.

Rhetoral drifted into our circle, far less obtrusively than had Gorum, a faint smile of amusement vanishing as he listened, blue eyes intent. His goblet of Whitespring was half full.

"Personnel details," Gorum corrected. "We would appreciate the opportunity for the majority of our crews to see Old Earth, but that would require some billeting space."

I nodded, waiting. Across the room, the cold Majer Henslom slowly studied the walls, detail by detail, as if committing the entire Hybernium to memory.

While listening, I could also sense Crucelle's efforts with the monitoring equipment, and Arielle's presence flitting across the upper net. I hoped they could get solid ENF records, and the information they needed—information we might all need before it was over. I trusted they wouldn't do something to alert the cybs.

"While we could create planetside quarters in some vacant place . . ." Gorum let the words trail off. He finally took a sip of Whitespring.

"There are no vacant places on Old Earth," Rhetoral said evenly.

"I find that difficult to believe." Gorum turned, and his hard eyes fixed on the rat-comp.

"It has been difficult to balance the ecology," Rhetoral pointed out.

"After so many millennia?"

"How much space do you need?" I asked to forestall the debate. One way or another, Gorum wanted enough marcybs on Earth to take over a locial. "Enough for fifty, one hundred, of your people?"

"You're going to let them have a guest quarter section?" asked Crucelle on the net.

"Of course," I snapped back, my mouth shut as I waited for Gorum's response.

"Our ships are large, and our time is limited," the commander temporized.

"Three hundred?" I asked innocently.

"Five hundred would be optimum."

"That will take a few days," I mused, "but we could clear a guest quarter bloc for them." Of course, the differential credit and compensatory time and other assorted incentives would take generations to balance out, but it was better than letting them drop heavy equipment or clean up an additional ecological mess.

"I would appreciate that," Gorum said evenly.

I met his eyes. "I understand."

"If we could look over the location later . . ." he pressed.

"All of the guest quarter blocs are quite convenient to all operations of the locial and the landing station." I smiled. "You may choose which bloc suits your people."

The faintest touch of a frown crossed Subcommander Kemra's brow, but the senior commander only bowed. "You are gracious and hospitable, and we are pleased to see that time has warmed your receptiveness toward those of our persuasion."

"Our hospitality, anyway." I offered an honest and rueful laugh.

"Are many on Old Earth like you?" asked Gorum more conversationally, as if all he had wished to accomplish was earthside lodging for the marcybs.

"Probably no more than all those in the Vereal Union are like you."

"I think that the commander was curious as to whether differing . . . outlooks . . . remained on Old Earth." The sandy-haired subcommander lifted the goblet and sniffed the bouquet. "This smells very good."

"It is. I tend to prefer the stronger reminisces of Earthflame." I took a sip, slightly surprised that my goblet was less than half full, and paused within myself, easing up my metabolic level, before answering. "We don't have any cybsensers, except those who visit. Otherwise, the range of 'outlooks,' as you rephrased it for the commander, is rather wide."

"That's a general statement," observed Gorum.

"We don't keep statistics on the inclinations and ability levels of everyone on Old Earth, Commander. You'll certainly see demis and draffs, and people who have inclinations in between, and people who have the inclinations of neither."

"Do draffs have demi offspring?" pursued Gorum.

"They always have, and always will—just as some demis have draff offspring. I am certain that you know the genetics as well as I do." I inclined my head to the subcommander. "Both of you."

"So why are there no cybs?" asked Kemra, her goblet still untouched.

"Being a cyb is not a question of ability, but inclination. You should know that as well." I paused, but only enough to signify that the subject was closed. "Where have you visited before this . . . pilgrimage to Old Earth?"

"A number of the former colonies . . . past members of the Rebuilt Hegemony."

"Did you see Sybra—the winter planet?"

"No. From our records, it is somewhat removed," answered Kemra.

"I understand there's so much ice that even from orbit it glitters."

"Have you been there?" asked Gorum.

"No. Few of us on Old Earth travel much any more, Commander. Would you care for more Whitespring?"

"Is that what it's called?" asked Gorum.

"Yes. It's one of the standard Snoma wines."

The commander and subcommander exchanged glances, and I got the *clicking* feel from Mylera. Wines hadn't traveled to Gates—if Gates were still the head of the Vereal Union.

I wanted more Earthflame, but refrained. Instead, I reclaimed a bottle of Whitespring and refilled the commander's goblet. The welcoming reception had hardly begun, and I knew it would be long—long indeed. Holding in a sigh, I smiled.

<<< VI

Society is based on morality.

Morality rests on consensus and requires the use of power to remove those who will not accept that consensus.

The continued existence of a shared morality rests on the forbearance of every single individual within a society from claiming the entire fruit of his or her labor.

A society's ability to achieve consensus is inversely proportional to the size and complexity of society, to the degree of technological advancement, and to the speed of internal communications.

The more complex a society's framework, the shorter the existence of that incarnation of a society.

Power cannot be maintained and effectively exercised without a moral structure accepted and practiced by all because power attracts the corruptible and because corruption destroys consensus.

Certain individuals are born incapable of forbearance; so are certain cultures.

Thus, continuation of society rests on: the willingness of each individual to accept the shared values of the society; the willingness and the ability of those in power to remove those who do not support the morality of the society; and the willingness of all to limit the size and complexity of society to the scope of consensus required.

—*The Paradigms of Power*

For a time that next morning after the ceremony at the Hybernium welcoming the cybs of the Vereal Union, I sat at the old cedar table, looking out at the light snow, sipping tea, and thinking about the cybs—and what they wanted.

Most of those who landed had been military, and their fleet was clearly designed for destruction and conquest. As Crucelle had seen, action along those lines was not likely immediately—not until the cybs were convinced they could act without undue costs or until we had been sufficiently humiliated—or both.

With a sigh, I slipped into the overnet, seeking Crucelle out.

"Now what?"

"Have they picked a guest quarters bloc? You did make me Coordinator, remember?"

"We're doing that now. They'll take the south bloc, it looks like."

I received the image of the larger bloc of low quarters midway between the station and the locial center.

"Rather luxurious for marcybs. They are what we calculated, aren't they?" Sometimes even a good comp-intuit needs reassurance, and I did.

"Fairly close. They've avoided genetic sympathetic resonance by ensuring a wide variation in base stock, but they're marcybs, all right. Neurotrained in every weapons system and standard tactics, then field exercised to a sharp edge. That's probably one reason they want them on the ground."

"It's hard to believe they'd go to such lengths." I gave a mental shrug. "But it doesn't look like they've changed."

"No. Wayneclint was too damned generous," Crucelle opined.

"The resonances?" I asked.

"We're working on it, but we've only got the theory. It's been a long time, and . . ."

The whole business with the marcybs was nasty and disgusting, but I didn't have much of a choice in options until Crucelle and his team were done, and there was no point in arguing over where a few hundred marcybs were lodged with twelve adiamante hulls orbiting Old Earth.

"Elanstan?" I asked, to change the subject.

"She's finished with the initial phase, but . . ."

"I know." And I did, even without the net equivalent of Crucelle's sigh.

"Rhetoral has gone to join her."

I understood that, too.

"Are you going to rejoin us this morning?" continued Crucelle.

"Do I need to?"

"Probably not."

"Then I won't. I'll be there later and when we turn over the space to them. I'm not going to have much free time after today."

"No," Crucelle pulsed back, "but, since you will be here then, I will leave such a happy event to you. K'gaio estimates that we'll have the area clean the day after tomorrow."

"That will wipe out a lot of back comptime."

"One of the few benefits," came back over the net, with the hint of a grin. "Oh . . . the Coordinator's office has been cleaned and refurbished for you. Your name is already on the door—in heavy metal letters."

I repressed my own sigh. The last thing I had wanted was to be the Coordinator.

"I heard that."

As I left the net, I refocused my eyes on the falling snow. A raven sat on the dead pine near the west end of the clearing. With a shake of wings and a spray of snow, he was gone.

With a last sip from the green mug, I stood, then walked toward the wide doors on the west side of the house.

The snow kept swirling out of the north as I pulled on the wool jacket and the cap knitted by Morgen's mother. She'd only died a year before Morgen, and I had more physical keepsakes from her than from my soulmate.

After stretching on the stones of the porch, under the overhang of the roof, I pulled on my gloves, fastened the knife in place, and glanced out into the flakes. Swift-Fall-Hunter was nowhere in sight, and the raven that often perched on the piñons when he was absent had not returned.

I turned and looked into the clouds that shrouded the Breaks. It was a long run up the canyon, especially carrying weapons, spectacular as the Breaks were. But the upper canyon was the home for both vorpals and kalirams, and I never felt totally safe relying just on internal defenses against either. Sometimes the vorpals hunted in packs—not that a lone one ever hesitated to take on anything that provided meat, from injured kalirams to unprepared humans, but the vorpals formed up in packs more when they raided the prairie dog towns.

I turned back to the west where a thin carpet of snow covered the open spots between the piñons and cedars, but the ground was dark under their branches.

Soul-song fragments cascaded through the silence, the notes within my brain, unheard by even the sharpest of owls on the stillest of frozen nights.

"My songs for you alone will flow;
at my death none but you will know

cold coals on black stove's grate, ash-white,
faintest glimmers for winter's night.
This moment is my last time to sing. . . ."

With her words and voice echoing in my thoughts, I
stepped into the ankle-deep powder and began to run. Despite the heavy boots, my feet still slipped on the slopes.

I ran to the northwest, down the long slope from the hill
crest out into the valley flats, past the creek and out into
the meleysen trees, where the warmer ground still melted
the small flakes and slowly built a ground fog that circled
up and around the meleysen trunks like the white mists of
spring and fall.

A jumble of white lay under the outer reaches of the
meleysen trees' intertwined outer branches, black-barked
beams that formed a thin canopy over the soft and hot-
leaved soil even in winter.

No mist rose from the white lines, as would have with
any snow that reached the ground unmelted. I refocused,
straining slightly, and nodded to myself as I slowed.

The twisted white bones under the cold-fluttered meleysen leaves might have belonged to a sambur, or some
form of ruisine, perhaps a white-tail, but no ruisine
healthy enough to breed true. The link-strength of the meleysens' orangish spice scent had been enough, and the
scent-trapped sambur had either eaten some of the thin
leaves in desperation, and died quickly—or starved.

The genetically flawed animals were few now, and I'd
only seen a handful trapped by the trees' power—mostly
jackrabbits, and those might have been natural off-sports.
The back net-records contained images of meleysen
groves strewn with white. I shivered, thinking that even
the orange spice couldn't have concealed that much death
stench.

In the windless chill, the heat from the trees was palpa-
ble, like a curtain, but heat or no heat, the jackrabbit prints

circled away from the grove, and I followed their tracks, swinging toward the north.

I began to sweat even more, from the running, from the wool jacket, from the ground heat of the meleysen roots, for a dozen reasons, but I forced my strides back into a longer pattern.

In time, the first of the hills leading to the iron mines—mines worked-out and reclaimed without visible evidence long ago—rose before me, a mixture of white slopes and dark cedars and piñons.

Sensing the ruisine trail, I turned, panting, and kept running, my boots jolting unevenly on the hard ground, the sweat pouring down my hot face and cooling as it flowed.

"This is my last moment to sing. . . ."

I pushed away the song and sent my perceptions out, trying to sense something—anything.

And I did.

Even from beneath the snow I could sense another fragment of adiamante, less than a dozen meters ahead and to my right. Adiamante—almost indestructible, shattered only by those forces that sundered both planets and the very ships that once sundered planets and their satellites.

My legs slowed, glad of the respite, as I edged toward the unmarked spot.

Had I really sensed it?

After brushing away snow and digging around, I found it—a small oval scarcely bigger than my fist, neither giving nor taking heat, neither holding or dispersing cold.

For some reason, I slipped it into my jacket pocket, trusting to my intuit senses that there was some reason for the action.

I turned back downhill, moving more slowly and cautiously through the increasingly heavy snow.

Dialogue one: Another chunk of adiamante. . . . Why now? Why had I been able to sense it—as opposed to sens-

ing eagles or ravens or jackrabbits? They were living beings, and that was something that adiamante certainly was
not. Coincidence . . . or a reminder that the hardness of
the past refused to stay buried or ignored? Or had I always
been able to sense the hard darkness of the past and refused to acknowledge it?

Dialogue two: Who ever looked for adiamante? The
fragments were useless, and painful reminders of the
lessons that had been so hard to learn, lessons whose existence the cybs still refused even to acknowledge.

Back on the flat, I kept running, heading southeast
back to the house, back to memories, and the netlink that
would update me on the cybs, and the twelve adiamante
hulls that orbited well above the heavy gray clouds of a
too-early winter.

<<< VIII

THE OLD DRAFF'S TALE

In the low and still-too-near old days before the small
stars scarred the fields to ashes, before the lands smoked,
and before the ice walked the world, there were many
types of fishes in the sea, and many animals that roamed
the forests and plains and hills, and birds with all colors of
feathers that roosted and perched and strutted.

But there was only one kind of human. Sometimes that
kind was man, sometimes woman, sometimes child, but
for all the names, they were the same. Some were taller,
and some were shorter, or thinner or thicker, and some
spoke Anglas, and some Nippin, and some Mandi. But
they were the same. That is, they all thought in the old-
fashioned manner, and their thoughts stayed inside their
heads.

.Their thoughts stayed inside their heads.

Yet into that low and not-so-far-off time were born the fathers of the cybs and the demis, the dreamer Krikwats, the doer Ibmer, and the mighty Gates.

Ibmer, with wire and diode and solder and chip, made the first cyb. It was not a good cyb, for it was of metal and ceramic and wire, and it was not really alive. It could count very fast and compare pictures of things, if a human fed those pictures into its head. And it was backwards, because it could only calculate. People could see its calculations, but it could see nothing that it was not told, and its calculations stayed within its metal head.

Its calculations stayed within its metal head.

Then came Gates, and he asked, "How can I make this cyb help humans?" Because no one answered him, he answered himself, and his answer was, "I will build something that will help the cyb think." So he did, and he built an invisible softweb that gave the first cybs commands on how to turn calculations into thoughts. At first, it took all sorts of different softwebs, and the way the metal cybs thought was very, very slow. Their thoughts were very, very simple and very, very strong, and those thoughts stayed within their webs and metal heads.

Their thoughts stayed within their webs and metal heads.

Then came the Interleavers, and they took the unliving cybs and made them smaller and smaller, and they extended the webs of Gates so that humans could think their complicated thoughts as quickly as the mechanical cybs could think their simple thoughts. Among the first was halfJack, and he died, and yet he did not, and his circuits wound through OldCity unto the generations.

Soon there was no telling where the thoughts of the human ended and the thoughts of the machine began, and the new human-cybs sent their thoughts along the wires and circuits and around all of Old Earth, and they began to insist that everyone send thoughts and ideas along the fibrelines.

They insisted that everyone use the fibrelines.

But some did not want to open their minds to all who prowled the circuits, and some could not, and still others said that the new-cybs were no longer even human. Others, such as the sons and daughters of Krikwats, used the metal cybs that spun thoughts on the webs of Gates to prod and peer within themselves, and they unwound their souls and the very cells of their bodies. Then they rewound them back into helices, but they rewound themselves tighter and straighter than they had been, and some of the thoughts and cells were left outside their bodies.

"Now what shall we do with what remains outside us?" asked the one called Neverte.

"Let us weave them into an invisible net to link us together," answered her sister Sebine, "for together we can sense what is happening before it occurs and hear what is said before the words are spoken."

They did, and, for the first time, their thoughts ran outside their heads, without wires and circuits and fibrelines.

Their thoughts ran outside their heads.

They were the first demis, and that was the beginning of the new world, and those who knew what had happened were few, and those who did not were many, and they were those who would soon be called draffs. And the thoughts of the old draffs, as is yet proper, still remained inside their heads.

The thoughts of the draffs still remained inside their heads.

Soon, where once there had been only one kind of human, there were now three, and fearful halfbreeds as well. There were the cybs, who wielded the fibrelines like whips, and the demis who walked free of the fibrelines but shared their thoughts beyond the reach of the cybs. And there were the draffs, who kept their thoughts to themselves.

There were hundreds of scores of demis, and millions of cybs, and millions upon millions of draffs in those days. And the demis planned and ordered, and the cybs organized and directed, and the draffs worked. Thus, the demis became as well-off as all the kings of the ancient days, and though the cybs were like lords, they were not happy.

"You have risen on the work of the cybs and shared nothing," said the cyb leader Greencross to the great demi Wayneclint. "You must divide your riches with the cybs."

"We have struggled strong and hard to obtain what we have," answered Wayneclint, the great coordinator of the demis. "We have toiled long and late into all the nights of the years, and we have improved the lot of all those in the world. We have reduced illness and made the wilderness bloom. We have reclaimed the sea. You have followed our advice and profited, yet you are not satisfied."

"We, too, have worked hard," said Greencross. "We have fired the fibrelines of the world, and our brains have burned to help you, but you are rich, and we are not."

"The draffs work hard, also," said Wayneclint. "Why have you not shared with them?"

"Because they do not fire the fibrelines of the world, and they do not burn their brains into the evening."

The draffs do not fire the fibrelines of the world, nor do they burn their brains into the night.

The more the two talked, the angrier and angrier that Greencross became, until sparks flew from his fingers, and the blue glow of power from the nets shrouded him, and he said, "If you do not share willingly, then you will share unwillingly, but share you will."

"Yet you refuse to share with the draffs, and you chastise us for failing to share with you." Wayneclint laughed, and his voice was gentle.

"It is not the same!" insisted Greencross.

Wayneclint smiled, but he said nothing, and Greencross became angrier yet.

The next day, Greencross decided to punish the demis for their arrogance, and he changed the moneynets so that no demi could obtain credits or coins through the bank-machines, nor would any of the doors to the cybs' buildings open to a demi, nor could the demis use the skimmers and flitters or even the undersurface ways to get about the great cities. Nor would the food stores sell them provisions.

For days there was confusion as the demis became hungrier and hungrier, and as their children grew weaker, and the smile across Greencross's face grew broader. And he waited for Wayneclint to share . . . and he waited, and his thoughts of victory crossed the fibrelines to all the cybs.

And his thoughts of victory crossed the fibrelines to all the cybs.

The draffs waited, their eyes turning to the sealed buildings of the cybs and back to the hills beyond the cities where the demis waited behind their walls.

Then, in a space of hours, the mindblazes began, lines of firepain that seared every cyb linked to the fibrelines. The cybs shriveled in pain, and they groveled, and they died.

They shriveled, and groveled, and died.

But before they died, they sent orders along the fibrelines, to the ancient war machines, to the powerblades hanging in the skies, and the mushroom-shaped sledges of death. And the small stars fell across the land and broke it. And the fields were carpeted with ashes, and deathsmoke rose from the ash heaps that had been great cities.

The very next morning, the doors to the few buildings of the cybs that yet stood flew open, where there were buildings still left, but none remained within but corpses. Even Greencross was a corpse, with his broad smile burned into his face, and over all the world there remained but scattered handfuls of cybs.

For every hundred souls that had been draffs, cybs, or demis, but a handful remained, and few indeed were cybs.

Then, before the ashes settled or the small stars ceased falling, Wayneclint gathered the remaining cybs and chastened them and stuffed them into the longships and cast them into the darkness of space. And he told those who remained on Old Earth, "Trust not your thoughts to the fibrelines or to the machines, for all who seek to chain humans with cybnets shall perish as these."

All who use cybnets shall perish.

And of the draffs of that time? Most died, and those who lived were those who kept their thoughts safe within themselves, and waited, as we still wait, our thoughts safe within us.

Our thoughts are safe within us.

<<< IX

I'd flown up to Parwon early that morning, keeping the flitter low over the valley under the high and featureless gray clouds. A few sambur had scattered at the sound of the rotors, but some had not, and that bothered me. Were my flitter trips too common, so common that they were accustoming the deer to the aircraft despite my attempts to vary my flight path?

Even after all my maintenance efforts, the odor of hot metal and oil crept into the cockpit, and I ended up flying in a flitter filled with very cold and fresh air.

Another dusting of snow covered the Esklant Peaks to the north, but the flattened mountains to the east of the locial center had no new snow. Some of the red rocks were showing through, as were the patches of darkness that represented the meleysen groves.

After securing the flitter on the side of the Deseret locial tower away from the two black landers where the cybs were already unloading, I walked the three klicks to center Parwon, at not quite a run, but more than a fast stroll.

The wind gusted out of the north, and the ground was hard underfoot. Two ground shuttles whined past me toward the landing station, and both drivers waved. Though I knew neither, I waved back and kept walking, past the nearly full-klick band of the low bungalows where the admin draff families lived, past the cinqplexes that housed the singles on compensatory duty of some sort, past the residential transient blocs, and across the park toward the Deseret admin building. Most of the functions were below ground, in spaces far larger than the three-story structure in the northwest corner of the park.

The shouts of children playing came from the school west of the admin area, and I smiled. Yslena had gone there, oh so long ago, before . . .

I shook my head. She had her own life, and that was what she had chosen, three continents away, although she was certainly warm enough when we netlinked, or got together all too infrequently.

The Coordinator's office was on the top level of the admin building. Outside the office was a cedar-paneled waiting room with two long wooden benches backed up against the inside walls. Guarding the door to the office was a cedar-framed and covered console station where Keiko sat. The faintest hint of flowers filled the space, though none were in evidence.

Keiko smiled as I walked in, though she'd certainly known the minute I'd touched down at the station. Her teeth shimmered white against her dark olive skin and black hair. Keiko was acting as the Coordinator's aide and receptionist—though Old Earth never had a Coordinator except in times such as these, or a receptionist. Certainly, she really didn't need the screen and keyboard input before her, but visible technology always seemed to disarm and reassure people, and we needed someone to remain as a link-point while the world unraveled.

"Greetings, Coordinator." Keiko's voice was deep and smooth, revealing nothing she did not want disclosed.

I tried not to wince at the title, and my eyes flicked to the closed door to the office, and the three-centimeter-high brass letters.

COORDINATOR

ECKTOR DEJANES

The letters were very shiny, like a vorpal's eyes, and about as soulless.

"The cybs have landed," she said.

"I saw them, and I probably should go over to the residence bloc—be a presence on site."

I opened the office door. An antique cedar desk, seemingly as broad as the landing dock of an equally antique battlecruiser, surveyed the seamless expanse of windows that overlooked the park and offered a panorama of the eastern peaks. The Deseret landing station spire was visible to the left side of that expanse.

I turned back to Keiko. "Later, I'll need a shuttle to Ell Control. Just me." I could have set up the arrangements, but Keiko was there, and before long I wouldn't be able to handle it all, not the way things were headed.

"Yes, ser. Is it safe to leave the cybs unattended?"

"It is right now. Before long, it won't be." My guts told me I needed to actually check out the feel of the ell station, although a cyb would have called making a non-computed decision illogical. But life wasn't yes-no, on-off. Life was shades of gray, and rainbows not in the order of the spectrum. Our bodies have always known more than our minds have acknowledged they knew.

For a few moments, I walked around the enormous office, past the low chairs and matching green upholstered couches, before eyeing the leather swivel.

A long black cloak was draped carefully on the coatrack in the corner by the door. I stepped back and asked aloud, although I could have used the net, "What's this?"

"It's a cloak. Arielle left it for you. She said you needed something dramatic." There was a slight hint of laughter in the smooth voice.

Dramatic? The cybs probably thought we were all too dramatic, dark villains of the evil past. I lifted the heavy fabric, my fingers sliding over the smooth red lining. It was dramatic all right—red and black. Fresh blood and cold dead ashes. The cybs would love that symbolism.

After resettling the cloak on the rack, I tried the swivel chair behind the desk. It squeaked as I sat down, and the odor of well-kept old leather rose around me, bringing back the sense of earlier times. I got up and tried it again. It still squeaked.

"Keiko."

"I've already asked for some oil from maintenance." She had: I'd caught the energy pulse of the request that she'd flicked off at the second squeak.

The desk had drawers, two on each side, and they were empty. They'd stay that way. Accumulating paper was hard on the ecology and hard on whoever had to maintain and read it. Besides, the growth of documents generally reflects the lack of trust in a society. No paper trail can make someone accountable. Only self-assumption can. Too many societies had used paper as a substitute for accountability. So far, we'd avoided that mistake. We'd made lots of others, though, and I wasn't certain that naming me Coordinator hadn't been yet another mistake.

Outside the wide windows, snow flurries swirled for a few minutes, then subsided.

With a sigh, I stood and looked toward the east side of the park, in the general direction of the residential bloc that the cybs would be occupying shortly.

"Don't forget the cloak," Keiko prompted. "Arielle said . . ."

"She probably said that the imagery was important, didn't she?" I retorted. Crucelle thought the straight demonstration of power was the key. They were both right, which was probably why they'd pushed my name through the Consensus as Coordinator. There have only been eleven Coordinators, and that's if you count the mythical Wayneclint. Maybe he existed, but we'd have had to invent him if he hadn't.

"Yes, ser." Again, there was the hint of laughter concealed behind the smooth modulated tone.

I took off my jacket and used the straps to fasten the cloak in place, not as heavy as it seemed. I hung the jacket on the wooden rack and headed for the residential bloc.

Keiko gave me a mock-militaristic salute as I left.

"You better be careful. I'll institute conscription, and send you after the cybs."

"I'll be right behind you, ser."

"Such confidence."

"We all have great confidence in our leader." The white teeth flashed in another smile.

I got the emphasis on "leader." That's the problem with being Coordinator. You're expected to lead from the front. "I appreciate it."

By then I was downstairs, but I could feel her grin over the net.

When I stepped outside the admin building, the wind was gusting and swirled the cloak away from my body, and it carried the odors of distant meleysen and not-so-distant snow. I resettled the cloak around me and walked toward the southern residence bloc and the cyb troopers. Despite the chill and the wind, I didn't even need to jump my metabolic rate; the cloak was warmer than I had expected. That bothered me, because it meant Arielle had made it to be used and worn. She was dead serious about my wearing it as a sort of badge of office. I trusted her comprehensive and calculated logic, but it underscored the nature of the Coordinator as not only leader but target.

I reached the residential bloc just before the ground shuttles arrived and had barely gathered the cloak back around me when out of the first ground shuttle stepped a dozen or more of the marcybs, their dark green dress uniforms crisp, matching dark green berets in place. None wore heavy jackets, just dress blouses that could scarcely have broken the wind, but the chill did not seem to bother them. Their eyes, no matter what color, were flat, like mechanical scanners that missed nothing.

None bore visible weapons, but each carried a large and long kit bag that could and probably did conceal complete ground combat kits. I had few doubts that additional equipment would arrive with each Vereal Union lander.

Studying each marcyb as he or she emerged was Majer Henslom, cold green eyes flicking from one figure to the next, occasionally nodding. The entire process was silent, and I could sense that a portable netlink had already been established in the housing bloc to supplement the personal short-range net capability of the belt units the marcybs wore.

They formed up in rows, by squads or whatever their organizational units were called, each with the nearest corner of a kit bag precisely fifteen millimeters from the toe of each marcyb's right boot. In front of the group, silent, stood Majer Henslom, waiting.

The other majer—Ysslop—waited by the doors to the residential bloc. Her eyes—I realized Ysslop was female— were colder than the intermittent swirls of snow. That I hadn't sensed her sex the first time I had encountered her indicated to me exactly how alien the cybs really were, or at least some of them were.

On the short side avenue—Frensic—a couple with a single child between them watched as the first group of marcybs walked briskly into the building. The woman shook her head, and the man looked at the cybs. All the cybs were short-haired, whether men or women, all with eyes that saw and did not see.

The draff couple shivered, and I understood why. Cold were the cybs, colder by far than the supercooled mechcybs that ran our own Old Earth, colder than the heart of an antique supercon line or deep space beyond the Oort. And hot was their hatred—hot as the gaze of a kaliram—and their scarcely concealed desire to wreak vengeance upon Old Earth.

Yet what could I do, under the power paradigms? We had retained the ability to apply force, but applying it in anticipation against the cyb-ships would be costly. More important, it would invalidate the Construct.

Then, I reflected with a twisted smile, allowing our destruction would also invalidate the Construct.

Another group of marcybs stiffened, then peeled off, and began to file into the residence bloc, their measured steps automatically transforming the building into a staging barrack.

I glanced back at the couple who had crossed Frensic and were walking slowly across the park toward the Statue of the Unknown, their breath trailing them like white fog. The dark-haired boy between them turned his head and glanced back toward the uniformed cybs, but his mother tugged on his hand, and he finally looked away.

The figure on the red stone pedestal could have been anyone. The sculptor had caught the agony of a soul caught in mindblaze and fire. I always had thought of the statue as the "unknown draff," and most demis did, but a good percentage of demis had died in the mindblazes, as well as cybs and draffs.

As another file of marcybs straightened, I swirled the niellen cloak back enough to reveal the red lining and walked through the irregular snow flurries to Majer Henslom.

He nodded, brusquely, as I stopped a good meter from him.

I waited, faintly amused smile in place, listening in on his tactical net.

". . . the local headhonch . . . scanning me . . ."

". . . be nice to him, Henslom . . ."

". . . silly in that black cloak, like a melldram hero . . . vacuous grin . . . what do I say . . ."

". . . less the better . . ." snapped a nearer transmission, probably from Majer Ysslop. "He can't be as vacuous as he seems, and that means he's dangerous."

"Him? I could take him apart in moments, even without weapons," Henslom net-answered.

"You might be surprised, one way or the other."

"Stuff it, Ysslop."

"Your farm, Senior Majer Henslom."

I wanted to sigh, even as I was willing to acknowledge Majer Ysslop's pragmatic insights. The more I heard, the more likely it seemed that nothing had changed over a millennium. Then again, despite all the growth in abilities, basic human emotions never changed. The bottom line was always force. The problem facing me was that the cybs didn't seem to recognize the difference between force and violence.

That was the basis of the SoshWars, back before The Flight. The Mascs relied on violence, and the Fems didn't understand that social controls represented force as surely as the violence of the Mascs. Even millennia after The Flight, the cybs seemed to carry some of the Masc heritage.

"Greetings, Majer," I offered verbally. "Is there anything else in which I might provide assistance?"

"Rations?"

"Food? We can provide supplies to the central kitchens, and cooks, if you like. Would that be agreeable?"

"The supplies would be fine." Then he added, in a transmission to the locial field—and probably from the lander to the orbiting ships, given the delay in responses, "No way I'd trust their cooks."

"They might make the food edible," snapped Ysslop.

"Enough!" growled a voice after a short delay.

"I will make the arrangements," I promised and offered a very slight bow before turning.

Behind me, the marcybs continued to march into the residence bloc. I waved down a shuttle. I didn't know the dark-haired driver, but she knew me. "Where to, Coordinator?"

"The landing field."

"The field it is, and we'll be picking up more of their greencoats."

"Greencoats?" I hadn't heard the term before.

"That's what Ser Dvorrak called them, and it stuck. He has a way with words."

I sat down, glad to be out of the wind. Even with the cloak, it took energy to stay warm in the cold. The shuttle was empty except for the two of us.

"Cold out there, and getting colder." The draff driver wore a heavy leather jacket with the golden kaliram fleece out. The jacket represented a very brave soul, a great obligation, or both.

"I think so."

She glanced at me, both in the mirror and the screen, several times as the shuttle whined back toward the landing field before finally asking, "Are they going to make trouble?"

"I think that's what's on their minds," I said frankly.

Anything else would have been untrue, and even a draff would have known that. That she was a shuttle driver trusted with carrying marcybs indicated intelligence, and that meant she was a draff by choice, not from lack of ability.

"Why don't they just have a nice visit and go back where they came from?"

"We're working on that." I shifted my weight on the seat.

"Good. Where do you want off?"

I looked for the shuttle, and finally located it about fifty meters east of the base of the tower. "By the tower is fine."

The driver nodded to me as I slipped off. I watched the ground shuttle whine northward along the landing strip toward the remaining marcybs that waited amid the scattered light flurries of white that blurred the sharp black edges of the landers that had brought the greencoats to Old Earth.

The craft that waited for me on the permacrete was as dissimilar to a cyb lander as a demi to a cyb. Less than thirty meters long, white, the top of the forward cockpit no more than five meters off the permacrete, the magdrive shuttle looked like a toy compared to a cyb lander. The side door slid open, and I stepped into the small cabin behind the cockpit.

"Coordinator." The short-haired redhead in the plain gray jumpsuit nodded. "I'm Lieza."

"Ecktor, Lieza," I corrected. "I'm only Coordinator for now."

The shuttle pilot smiled briefly as if to dispute me, but only said, "Do you want to sit back there or up here?"

"Up there, if you don't mind."

She nodded again, and her eyes blanked as she went fullnet. I took off the cloak and folded it into a square that I put into a locker before I strapped in to the other cockpit couch. As I settled in, I studied the display screens, far simpler than those on board the cyb landers, I was certain.

Appropriate technology is only one key. The cybs couldn't use magfield drivers, not even on their landers. Even if Gates had a magnetic field as powerful as that of Old Earth, and the cyb's home planet probably didn't, other planetary and solar magnetic fields vary, and there usually isn't enough power concentration in the outer fringes of most systems. Fusactors always work, but they're heavy and require a comparatively high amount of fuel. You can't take a ship underspace in high dust densities, and that means traveling outsystem before underspacing, and that requires concentrated energy generation systems—fusactors or the equivalent.

Magfield drivers tap existing energy flows, above and below the normspace web, whereas fusactors create an energy flow to be used.

After checking the door and seals, Lieza returned to the pilot's couch, and brought the taps on line, using the electric drivers in the wheels to propel us out to the end of the buried guideway.

While Lieza would handle the piloting, much as I would have enjoyed it, I did follow the linkcomm, the pulsed bursts so quick that even the best of the cybs' equipment couldn't have detected the communications, even had they known the method and the standing wave modulations.

"Deseret Control, this is MagPrime, ready to lift for Ell Control this time."

"Cleared to lift, maintain one eight zero until clear of the zone."

"Stet."

The modified mag-induction system that was far smoother than any of the alternatives had the shuttle's lifting body airborne within a few hundred meters, but Lieza held the shuttle down as the speed built, until we reached the end of the guideway. Then we angled up so fast that I couldn't have seen Kohl Creek even if I'd had one of the exterior scanners focused there.

The hint of ozone inevitably rose with the continued operation of the magfield shuttle, one of the few drawbacks for some, though I didn't find the odor objectionable.

"Clearing zone this time. Turning to ell intercept radial."

"Stet, MagPrime."

The magfield shuttle swept eastward, pressing me back into the copilot's couch. The hull insulation didn't totally damp the roaring whistle that continued to build, and static crackled through the net as we climbed, not with the sudden acceleration of an old-style rocket but with a continuous two-plus gee force that lasted far longer than the chemical rocket jolt.

"MagPrime, on Ell Prime radial. Ell Prime, do you copy?"

"We have you, MagPrime," answered Elanstan, sounding husky and full-voiced even on direct netlink despite the link static, a shield to accompany Rhetoral the ancient longblade.

"Stet."

"Take care of your passenger," linked Elanstan, thinking protection even to others, the dark-shield always, the shield to come.

"I'll take as good a care of this one as the last."

I had to grin, since Lieza's last passenger to Ell Prime had to have been Rhetoral.

"You can take better care of this one."

I grinned at that. Elanstan was somewhat possessive, near the end of the permissible range, since possessive tends to slide into control.

The net interference faded, and once we cleared the upper atmosphere, Lieza dropped the acceleration and switched the screens.

The main screen showed a dark blob that would have been hard to pick out had the shape not been enhanced by a soft yellow screen-highlighting. As the image grew, I had to admit, again, that Ell Prime didn't look impressive—just a three-klick chunk of nickel-iron filled with linked fusactors, shielded enough that the Vereal fleet's EDIs wouldn't show more than a satellite power system in operation.

"Just a chunk of iron. Right, Coordinator?"

"Absolutely. An observational station of no interest whatsoever." I tried to keep my tone light, since we certainly hoped the power of those shielded fusactors wouldn't be needed.

The far left screen, a representational screen, showed Ell Prime and the rest of the orbital asteroid stations in luminous blue, and the twelve orbiting adiamante hulls of the Vereal fleet in brighter green.

"There they are, our friends the cybs." Lieza's hands flicked, although she could have used the net, and the Vereal EDI readings appeared on the far right screen—each ship generating and using more power in hours than a locial used in weeks.

"Do they track you?"

"Every time."

That figured. The cybs were doubtless paranoid and then some, but they'd find little threat in one apparently low-powered asteroid station, or in the apparent navigation beacons on the other asteroid stations. When one sees limited technology in use by a rising power, one assumes greater technology is either reserved for warfare or still being developed, but when one beholds such limited technology in use by a once-great empire, one assumes that greater technology has been lost or abandoned. And that's usually the case. Usually, but not always.

The ell station image grew until it filled the screen.

"Ell Prime, MagPrime beginning decel and approach."

"We're standing by. Commence approach when ready."

Then I was pressed into the couch for what seemed a short eternity, followed by near weightlessness as the magshuttle slid into the locking tube without even a shiver—another advantage of the system—and we eased to a stop smoothly, but all the metal of the asteroid severed my netlinks. The small shuttle shivered with the hiss of forced warm air entering the landing-lock tube.

"Be just a moment, Coordinator," said Lieza warmly.

I unfastened my straps and stretched before standing in the enhanced point two gees of the asteroid station and reclaiming my cloak. I just draped it over my arm. Who needed a cloak inside an asteroid station? Getting rid of heat was usually a bigger problem than staying warm.

"All right," said Lieza, as she cracked the shuttle's lock.

The station air was warm, not unpleasantly so, but warmer than the winter air of Parwon, with the hints of ancient ozone and oil and metal heated and reheated for probably all too long. With the air came a resumption of the netlink, repeated by the ell station.

"How long will you be?" asked Lieza as she followed me out of the shuttle.

"I don't know," I admitted. "Hours. Not more than a day, I'd guess, but that just depends."

"Then I'll seal up the shuttle."

She linked with the ship's system, and the hatch slid shut.

As we turned, Elanstan stepped forward out of the main corridor into the light of the high-arched docking/unloading area. "Welcome, Ecktor." Her hair was as dark as the nielle of my new cloak. Her smile was warm, and she looked like a frail elf of ancient times, a frailness that concealed the power behind the appearance, the solidity of a shield. I almost laughed at my antique metaphors, but I preferred them to more modern ones.

"Thank you. I hope I won't disrupt your efforts."

"I'm glad you came." A wry half-smile crossed her face. "Not all Coordinators have taken their duties personally enough to inspect an ell station."

"Call it my intuit background. I can't factor in what I haven't seen and felt."

"You haven't been here before?" asked Elanstan as we took the main corridor toward the center of the station's mid-level.

"Not under these circumstances. I've done stand-down maintenance, but it's not the same thing. Power makes a difference, and that's something people don't understand." As we passed the first set of side corridors, dark and unused, I slowed, sensing the energy that flowed in and thought the solidity of the nickel-iron above and around us, tied into the underspace in minute filaments. "Where's Rhetoral?"

"He's in the center. I feel better if one of us is there." She shrugged her thin shoulders. "We've had the basic system fully up for only three days. The remotes still aren't operating on Delta and Kappa. Rhetoral just got back from putting Gamma on line." She turned to Lieza, then refocused her black eyes on me.

I grinned at the pilot. "You can tag along, or do whatever else you want to do. I'm just poking and prodding."

"Sleep sounds good to me," Lieza admitted. "In this line, you take it when you can get it."

"You know where everything is," said Elanstan, "better than I do."

"Let me have a few minutes' notice, Coordinator. That's all." Lieza gestured down the glowstrip-lit passage. "We're going the same direction."

According to the schematics, Ell Control had been laid out on three levels—upper, mid, and lower—that sliced through the middle of the asteroid. The locks were on mid-level, on what corresponded roughly to the "equator," although the asteroid was shaped more like a loaf of bread, and the locks were where the heels would have been.

Every twenty meters, or so it seemed, we passed a door—occasionally sealed hatches, but usually just doors. I couldn't sense net-based operations behind the doors, but if the records were correct, Ell Control had once been the central operations focus for the starfleets of the Rebuilt Hegemony, and had hummed with activity. Those years were long, long past.

We slipped down the corridor in gentle and near-effortless movements, our lightened steps whisper-echoing on the hard permaplast that coated the smoothed metallic ore beneath. The walls were similarly coated, and our words echoed as well as our steps, almost like ghosts of a far-distant past.

I tried not to move too quickly. Weight might be twenty percent of normal, but mass and inertia remained, and trying to stop in low gee had broken all too many limbs throughout the history of satellite installations. Plastic-coated nickel-iron remained hard in low gee.

"Are they still cybs?" asked Elanstan. Her voice sounded preternaturally loud in the silence, and she lowered it as she added, "The way the legends say?"

I shrugged and, not being quite reaccustomed to low gee, nearly lost my balance and careened toward the corridor wall.

"Careful," warned Lieza with a touch of concern in her voice.

"Hard to say," I answered as I straightened. "I have this feeling that they aren't going to see much besides what they want to see."

"Oh . . . that could be difficult."

That was the understatement of the millennium.

"Here's where I leave you two." With a raised hand in half-salute, Lieza took a smaller side tunnel that slanted at an angle of thirty degrees to the right off toward one of the quarters sections. While there were several hundred almost luxurious apartments there, not to mention the thousands of bunks in the lower-level caserns, only a handful had been used in centuries, although all were maintained.

Elanstan and I continued moving along the main corridor toward the control center, past the closed doors that contained who knew what. I'd studied the layouts for quarters and systems, not the plans for the entire station. Finally, I asked.

"Are all those rooms empty?"

"Mostly. There are several dozen storerooms with enough dried and sealed food to feed a fleet for a decade, if you want to call fortified and enriched sawdust dating from five millennia back 'food.' "

"It's still nourishing?"

"The ancients were good at preserving just about anything, except taste and themselves." Elanstan tossed her head and her short niellen hair sprayed away from her face.

Ahead, I could see an area of brighter lights.

"That's the central hub," Elanstan pointed toward the increased illumination. "We're stopping here." She touched the lockplate for a hatch on the left side of the corridor, and I followed her through the adiamante-armored double locks.

"I thought you'd be here." Rhetoral rose from the central console as we entered and the inner door hissed shut behind us. "Do you want the board? Or do you want something to eat first?"

"Both. A quick scan of the board, then some food, and then an in-depth immersion."

"Typical intuit," laughed Rhetoral, through the net, his amusement enhanced by Elanstan, and even by Lieza, from wherever she was.

"Damned comps," I complained, even as I eased into the control chair and spread my senses through the local net.

The upper channels and the outer beam guides felt chill, sluggish, but that was to be expected. We couldn't heat the unused components too quickly, not with decades or more between power-ups.

My mental fingers flipped through the maintenance files. A minimum of another two days before all the systems were close to optimality—except for Delta and Kappa. Even for the online systems, a week or more would be better. I'd suspected as much. We just didn't use the old systems that much.

Even through the multiple links, I could smell the age of the massive, web-linked, not-quite-in-real-space systems, and I wondered how long before we would again have to rebuild and reconfigure them.

My head swam, and little white spots danced across my mental screens.

"Ecktor!"

I broke the connection and looked up at Elanstan and Rhetoral. "How about some food?"

"It's about time you had something to eat. You look like a cyb ghost."

"That good?"

At least they grinned. But I worried. Twelve big adiamante-hulled warships was a lot for an ancient system—even one as well-designed and redundant as this relic of the Rebuilt Hegemony—and we needed every station, one to match each of the Vereal ships. I still wanted to do an in-depth, comp-like analysis, but that needed to wait for bodily maintenance.

"Once there was a complete recycled hydroponic biosphere here," said Elanstan, "but it would have taken so much effort to get it back in place that we didn't bother. What we have is pretty limited."

"Not so limited as starving," I quipped back as I stood.

My eyes watered, and a few more white spots danced across my field of vision.

"I'm not sure," groused Rhetoral, his blue eyes glum. "Goat cheese as solid as nickel-iron, dried fruits with the consistency of antique synthetic rubber—"

"Please," I said. I didn't want to hear his lecture about how the ancients had actually sweetened and flavored synthetic rubber and chewed it. Chewing the same stuff that you put on groundcar tires?

"We've got the old mess room operating," Elanstan said. "The hardest part was defrosting the water supplies."

She turned right when she left the control center, toward the central hub. I followed. Rhetoral sealed the hatches behind us. Despite the innate shielding provided by the bulk of a nickel-iron asteroid, the Rebuilt Hegemony had also encased the control center, the broadcast and reception nets, and the power and defense systems themselves in a double layer of adiamante—about twice the protection provided by the hulls of the Vereal Union's fleet. I could feel both Rhetoral's and Elanstan's links to the center, and their apprehension.

"Does one of you want to stay on the board?" I finally asked.

"No . . . so long as we're both in the hub area," she answered.

"Not so long as we've got the Coordinator with us," quipped Rhetoral.

"Thank you."

Fifty meters farther along we reached the circular chamber that represented the center of the station's main level. Eight corridors angled from that point.

I paused to study the diorama displayed in the arched dome. The holoed reality left me looking up at snow-covered peaks, and firs and pines that moved in the winds under a deep blue sky, as if I were in a deep mountain canyon.

The faint sound of falling water caught my ear, and I turned to study the line of silver that sprang from the dark rock. A hawk of some sort I had not seen—not that many hawks were left on Old Earth—circled a white throne peak plateau.

The heat of the sun beat down on me, and the scent of a river and pines wafted across me.

After a moment, Rhetoral said softly, "Amazing, isn't it?"

It was amazing, on two counts. First was the technical skill involved in creating such a vivid representation, and second was the ancient arrogance that full-body reality could be duplicated through mere technology.

"Yes, it is amazing." But I shook my head.

We continued straight through the hub another hundred meters along the corridor, where Elanstan paused and asked, "You haven't been into the mess here, have you?"

"No," I admitted. "This part was closed off the times I worked on the net antenna and the power systems."

She smiled and pressed the lockplate. "You might find this interesting, then."

Rhetoral smiled back at her, and I caught a shared sense of amusement that passed between them.

Again, after stepping through the locks, I swallowed. The walls of the mess were apparently paneled in polished dark wood, and rich green velvet hangings surrounded the windows that displayed a hillside vista of a city—but no city I had ever seen. Three tables were actually placed within bay windows that seemed to display a continuation of the city view.

Each of the dozen tables was preserved and polished wood, and the chairs were upholstered in the velvet-like fabric. I looked back at the lock, but from within, it appeared as a thick wooden door. My eyes traversed the room, taking in the hundreds of details: the pressed pale green linen tablecloths, the real silver utensils on the single table set for eating—the one in the middle bay window.

After stepping toward the table, I picked up a knife. It was cool, heavy, and felt like real silver. I fingered the cloth. Not cotton or linen, but something smoother, yet still woven.

"How?" I asked.

"Inert pressgas," said Elanstan. "The physics are complex, but it uses a convection system where the cooling of the gas to close to absolute zero creates heat and circulation. . . . I can't say I understand it, but all you have to do is seal the place, and start the system. Once it's sealed, it's good for twenty or thirty millennia."

My eyes drifted back to the center bay window that displayed the city and the harbor below.

"Sit down," said Elanstan. "You don't have to worry. There's a full-circuit net repeater here. We've checked it out."

At that moment, as I sank into the chair with the velvet-like cushioned armrests, I hadn't even considered the net repeater. My eyes went back to the window across the table from me, where a huge watership slipped out toward the sea toward a massive cable-supported bridge that crossed the mouth of the bay.

I recognized that ancient scene—pre-collapse Sfrisco— but only because of some holos of the great bridge that had been buried in the locial records. It had been years ago, before I'd even met Morgen, and I'd wondered then at the need for such a massive bridge. The bridge and the city were long gone. Between the faults, the small stars, and the sledges of death, the area's topography only faintly resembled what it had been.

Then the music began, and, once more, the sounds were something I had not heard before. Oh, we have pianos, and strings, and woodwinds—but no one put them together like that, and few play so well, and not in such unison.

My eyes watered.

"It's dangerous to experience this," Elanstan said dryly, seating herself in the chair to my right. "We might actually want to return to the high-tech days of the ancients."

I'd forgotten she was there, but shields don't glitter and shimmer, only protect.

"The sustenance doesn't measure up to the setting," Rhetoral added, setting two loaves of bread, a large wedge of cheese, and a bowl of mixed dried fruit in the center of the table. He turned back toward the dark wood counter on one side of the room, returning with three crystalline goblets and a pitcher of water and sitting on my left.

"Impressive, isn't it?" he asked after he sat down.

"I think dangerous is more appropriate," I said after I cleared my throat. "Luxuries are always dangerous."

The two exchanged glances.

"Ecktor, these weren't particularly luxurious. Millions of people could hear that kind of music or purchase furnishings like these," said Elanstan.

It was my turn to feel patronizing, but I tried not to sound that way. "I meant societal luxuries. What is the total resource bill if everyone, or even millions of people out of billions, can purchase hundreds of small luxuries?"

"Ecktor . . . this music was laser-printed on a plastic disc ten centimeters across. That's scarcely a huge resource bill."

I thought for a minute, but I had to access the net for the calculations, and I could see them both frowning as the silence drew out. "Let's say . . . one disc per year for every person on the globe. Before the collapse, there were eight billion people. If we assume that one of those discs weighs 25 grams, one disc per person per year requires two hundred thousand tonnes of plastic. That's a million tonnes of plastic every five years—just for a little music." I lifted the synthetic cloth. "How about one of these every two years for a family group—nearly one billion family groups getting a half kilogram of synthetic fabric annually . . ."

"Ecktor, it wasn't the luxuries that led to the chaos years and the collapse and flight," pointed out Elanstan. "It was necessities. Taking your own math—if you give everyone just one set of clothes a year, they would have needed to produce more than four million tonnes of fabric annually."

"But they didn't do it that way," I had to counter. "In NorAm, most people had ten to twenty sets of clothes, and with five percent of the world's people, NorAm and the IndBloc were using almost eighty percent of the world's raw materials at the end. That's the problem with luxuries. That's why we weight comptime so heavily for goods above midline."

"Something got lost here," Rhetoral said dryly. "I'm missing the point."

I had to think. What had my point been? Then I shrugged. "I can't think. I need to eat." I cut off a chunk of cheese and a thick slice of the heavy bread and took a bite of each.

We all ate for a while, and my head cleared somewhat. After several mouthfuls, I filled the impossibly fragile-looking and almost indestructible armaglass goblet and took a long swallow before setting it on the pale green tablecloth.

". . . earth's last reign and rain . . ."

Morgen's words danced in my thoughts, and I tried to fit it all together as I ate another slice of cheese.

"In non-Construct societies, luxuries become necessities," I announced. "Then they can't be denied, and the resource requirements override ecosystem balance requirements."

"Maybe . . ." mumbled Rhetoral through a mouthful of bread. "Have to think about that."

"It doesn't matter," said the dark-haired Elanstan. "We have to get the system running, and we can't produce these any more, and I'll enjoy them while I can."

"She has something there," I said to Rhetoral.

"She usually does."

I studied the window, where the huge ship had almost disappeared beyond the Sfrisco bridge. The whole setting still left me unsettled, as if it were a window on the past that I found hard to believe had ever existed.

I looked from the routinely exquisite automated workmanship of the goblet to the tasty rich bread and the strong and tangy cheese and then to the silky tablecloth.

We'd opted for solid basics, but I could see the appeal of luxuries. I smiled wryly. Then, the bridge, the city, and the ancient ship all were gone, and had been for millennia. Only a few time-preserved relics remained, and those only because of the Construct.

Morgen had been right.

> ". . . and though the sun will blaze our tears,
> our joys will last the endless years."

In the end, only what each of us could hold endured, and only while we endured.

<<< X

The cross-connection of the main net conference aboard the *Gibson* provided the officers with a backdrop of flickering flames and muted red lights.

"Why did you pick the inferno idea?" asked Commander Ideomineo, the executive officer.

"Because hell is preferable to where we are right now," snapped Commander Gibreal, each word a fiery bullet.

"Toil and trouble . . ." The words whispered from nowhere.

"Status," continued Gibreal. "The demis have already billeted a full armed company of marcybs. Their leader watched the billeting, without any reaction of the sort that would be expected if they were fully knowledgeable. Majer Ysslop believes this Coordinator Ecktor is aware of the weapons already landed. Majer Henslom disagrees."

"Trust Ysslop." The veiled words appeared from nowhere.

Lightnings rattled the net, and, in his seat, Commander Ideomineo rubbed his battered forehead.

"Subcommander Kemra?" asked Gibreal.

"We can detect no overt buildup or change in global power sources or distribution, with one exception. The demis seem to be making an effort to rebuild their satellite navigation system," observed Kemra. "They still have two stations that aren't online."

"Would it help in a ground war?" asked Gibreal.

"Would it help? Would it help to have a system that could probably drop an HE warhead on the focal point of a laser? Or a hovertank?" Gorum's sarcasm oozed both heat and the redness of blood across the net.

"It wouldn't take that long to knock out those beacons," noted Gibreal.

"Longer than you think, ser," answered the weapons officer. "Every one of those stations is buried inside an asteroid—a big lump of solid nickel-iron. They probably have retractable backup antenna grids—maybe even use the whole surface as a broadcast web."

"So . . . that would make the nav systems an early warning device as well?" mused Gibreal. "Not quite so open and trusting, are they?"

"They are demis." Kemra's words were edged in frost,

and cold fog drifted across the net, hissing as it struck the flames and hot rocks.

"Analysis?" asked Gibreal.

"The demi leader showed a marked physiological reaction to Subcommander Kemra," announced MYL-ERA.

"It wasn't significant," observed the nav. "Certainly not statistically significant."

"Perhaps not," reflected Gibreal. "But, according to the construct's measurements, he was the only one who showed any reaction. Any insight would be better than none."

"Just blast the place," snapped Weapons.

"Our mission was also to reclaim any advanced technology possible." Gibreal's words held the chill of absolute zero. "It's hard to reclaim what you've destroyed, and I'd just as soon not be the one to make such a report to CybCen."

"You need a navigator. No one else . . ." began the subcommander.

"Majer Lyans has almost the same qualifications as you do, Subcommander. And their leader, Coordinator, whatever they call him, isn't likely to entertain the majer. So you must." Gibreal's words slithered across the net with the fanged ominousness and sibilants of the legged snakes of Gates.

"Just because I resemble someone who triggers a reaction?"

"What else do we have to exploit?" Leering image of a naked woman with spread legs.

The flash of power and lightning rumbled the net, and three overrides tripped.

"Imagery was excessive," announced MYL-ERA over the speakers. "Overrides tripped. Repairs are commencing."

"Touchy, isn't she?" rasped Ideomineo in his seldom-used voice to no one in particular.

"Conference ended," muttered Gibreal. His fingers went to his temples, and his eyes glittered in the privacy of his stateroom.

Subcommander Kemra unclenched her teeth and massaged her forehead, her eyes flickering aft to where she knew the weapons officer lay dazed. "Teach him . . . teach them all."

<<< XI

A cold mist drifted out of the north as I hurried down Jung toward the admin building, glad that I had landed at the locial before the weather closed down. I still hated letting the system control the flitter: the sign of the true demi, I supposed, worried about systems controlling people. Of course, cybs didn't believe in people, and put more faith in systems.

I wiped the dampness off my forehead as I crossed the park. To my left, across the browned grass, droplets of water had beaded up on the statue of the unknown draff. I hoped I didn't end up like him, but there weren't many guarantees the way the cybs were behaving.

"Coordinator?" asked Keiko's smooth voice through the net.

"I'm coming. I'm coming."

"Majer Henslom is here, waiting for you."

"What does he want?" Whatever the cyb majer wanted, I wasn't going to like it.

"He says he has something to discuss with you, not with your lowly subordinate." The hint of a white-toothed smile followed the words.

"He didn't say that."

"He might as well have." Keiko laughed, a laugh unheard by Majer Henslom.

"I know. They're worse than Coordinators."

"Not much." The laugh was more pronounced.

"I'm crossing the park now."

When I got to the admin building, I hurried, but not to the extent of taking the stairs two at a time.

Henslom was waiting, in greens so smooth they could have come from an antique metal press. I inclined my head to him and gestured toward the office. "Come in, Majer."

He stood stiffly on the other side of the broad desk as I peeled off my jacket—bison leather.

"Sit down." I motioned to one of the green chairs and dropped into the swivel. It creaked, as I expected. "What can I do for you?"

Henslom sat as stiffly as he had stood, at attention on the front half of the chair, watching me as if I were some demon from the past.

"Coordinator Ecktor . . . the majority of our troopers have not been planetside in months. Some have not been off their ships since we left Gates." Henslom's voice was harsh, as if he had been told to ask me. He would have rather demanded. "We appreciate your assistance in billeting the first five hundred, but we have several times that number of troopers."

I fingered my chin. "We're a small society, Majer. I don't see how we could billet another five hundred troopers—that was what you had in mind, wasn't it? Not in the Deseret locial. We might be able to work something out in Ellay."

"Ellay?"

"That's the locial west of here, about thirteen hundred klicks. We could probably open another residence bloc there in the next few days." I spread my hands. "It's not as though we had large empty dwellings or antique hotels. The residence blocs function more as temporary housing, and some sections are like guest houses for people visiting friends or family, but we don't travel that much here. Coming up with space for a thousand extra bodies in one locial isn't that easy."

"We could bring down temporary billets," said Henslom flatly.

"That's not feasible. We're still trying to get the ecosystems balanced."

"A few thousand people couldn't do that much damage." His voice was disbelieving.

"We'd rather not risk it. There's a great deal you need to find out about Old Earth before you make statements like that. Remember, unlike Gates, Old Earth suffered unbelievable ecological damage. We're still expending close to sixty percent of our societal resources on ecosystem maintenance or rehabilitation." I paused, then added. "Reforestation was an early and comparatively easy accomplishment, but even after all these millennia, in some areas more than ten percent of the trees are meleysen groves."

Henslom looked blank.

"Sorry. Meleysens are bioengineered trees which detoxify soil. They literally die and decompose once there are no unnatural chemical organics and certain heavy metals left in an area."

He still looked uncomprehending.

"Majer," I said softly. "Think about it. If more than five millennia after reforesting was initiated we still have ten percent of some forests with areas of high toxics levels, just how stable is the ecology? We still have unbelievably high mutation rates in many species, and some totally new species that have evolved."

"I see," he said. I could tell he didn't.

"I'll begin arrangements to vacate a residence bloc in Ellay. We'll try to have it available in three days."

"I had hoped—"

"Majer. We have to move several hundred people." I forced a smile. "Is there anything else you need?"

"Your head . . ." That was subvocalized, and I ignored it.

"Not now." Henslom stood. "Thank you. I will tell Commander Gibreal that we can land another five hundred troopers in Ellay. He will be pleased. We can work out more arrangements later."

"Let me know what you need." I wasn't promising, just saying I'd listen if asked.

I got the barest of nods.

After the majer left, I linked to the net and tried to connect with Locatio. I probed his index, but there was no response. I hated using the voice-storing feature, but sometimes there was no option. "Locatio, this is Ecktor. The cybs have requested additional earthside billeting for their marcybs. In order to ensure continued harmony as the cyb visit to Old Earth progresses, I'd like to request that you make available a five-hundred-person residential bloc for that purpose. This will have to be done by the day after tomorrow. You're authorized to grant comptime credits, temporary housing upgrades, whatever is necessary. Thank you."

Then I went out and told Keiko.

"How many marcybs do they have stacked up on those ships?" she asked, black eyes glancing toward the hall and the open staircase down which the majer had departed in his stiffly fluid strides.

"Five thousand, I'd guess, from the design and comparative analysis."

"Enough to create a mess, but not enough to take a planet."

"They don't want a conquest," I pointed out, "but a reason to slag Old Earth. It's hard to avoid giving them that reason."

"That's an understatement."

I yawned.

"Do you want some tea?" she asked.

"I could use it, if you wouldn't mind."

The office seemed empty, but it was immense enough that I could have had the entire representative Committee of the Consensus around the desk and it still would have felt empty.

The park was filled with gray mist, and droplets formed on the outside of the office windows, then condensed into globules that ran down the glass in random tracks.

"Your tea, Coordinator."

I tried not to jump. So distracted and unfocused had I been that I'd not even heard her enter. "Thank you."

"They don't make it easy." In a black jumpsuit and with her black hair, she was probably the cybs' nightmare version of a demi. She nodded in the general direction of the south residential bloc where Majer Henslom's marcybs were boarded. "That's why you're Coordinator."

"Such a vote of confidence."

"No one has ever been that fond of whoever was Coordinator—not until much, much later."

"Like I said . . . a great vote of confidence."

She smiled briefly, then left, her steps silent and graceful.

A faint trail of steam wafted up from the pale brown mug that sat on the middle of the desk.

After drinking half a cup of Keiko's royal blend—that was enough to wake up a hibernating bear—I connected into the uppernet and pulsed a link toward Ell Control. "Elanstan?"

"She's on Kappa, Ecktor." Somehow, Rhetoral felt more tightly wound, and I could almost sense the chill of angry blue eyes. "Do you want me to twist the link there?"

"No. That's fine." I tried to keep my words easy. "How is it going?"

"The rest of the system is warming, slowly. The online stations will be above ninety percent by tomorrow."

"That says you've still got problems with Delta and Kappa."

"Elanstan says Kappa will take three or four days. She's not talking about Delta. I suppose you want everything on line tomorrow?"

"We have some time, but I had to agree to vacate another residential bloc. This one's in Ellay."

"Do you think it's a ploy?"

"No, Henslom was told to ask me. He didn't want to. The cybs haven't quite figured out how to proceed. I think they expected outright hostility, and our welcome has upset some of their notions."

"That won't last long." He laughed harshly.

"You're right, but I'll take all the time they'll give us. Keep me up to date."

"We will."

After the link cleared, I swallowed the rest of the royal blend, too quickly. Then I walked to the window and stared southward across the park, where sunlight was beginning to break through the gray mist. Patches of blue appeared in spots, especially to the south.

"Ecktor! Some Coordinator you are!"

The words burned through the net, jolting me upright in the green swivel that squeaked sharply with my startled movement.

"You didn't even have the courtesy to consult with me before this . . . the request." Each of Locatio's words burned like red-hot iron spears.

"It wasn't exactly a request, honored Consensus representative," I offered smoothly.

"I know that! You're the Committee's representative, not its dictator!"

I swallowed before answering. "Under the Coordinator's charter, there are no limits on my actions, except my immediate removal. The Committee could probably even send me to one of the swept isles, Locatio. But a Committee can't respond fast enough, or assess the changing situation. I did what I thought best." Maybe so, but I was beginning to sweat as I responded. Had I done right?

"Letting another five hundred of those monsters back on Old Earth? Displacing hundreds of our people? Without even consulting those most affected?"

"Guilty as charged—except that I have to consider the alternatives. Crucelle's team hasn't come up with a viable blazelink. The satellite system isn't fully on line, and there are twelve adiamante hulls in orbit, and each one generates as much power as all of our locials together normally. I'm trying to purchase time as cheaply as possible. Do you have any other ideas?"

The silence stretched across the link. I wiped my forehead.

"It's still high-handed. Couldn't you have at least said that you'd let them know?"

"The one advantage we possess is myth—the myth of demi unity and decisiveness. If I wander around like a demented cleft cow, I give that up."

"You have an answer for everything, Ecktor."

I wished I did.

"I'll be talking to you later."

The faint hissing vanished with the link, and I rubbed my temples. Talking with Locatio in person was difficult; linking was almost impossible.

A knock on the half-open door got my attention, and I motioned Keiko in.

"While you were on the net, the majer sent a force leader over here. They're not happy with the food supplies. They claim they need more animal protein." Keiko rolled her dark eyes.

I frowned and went into the logistics net, trying to track something I thought I'd seen. After a timeless instant, I found it. Keiko was still there when I shook my head. "There." I passed the data to her. "The midplains bison herds are above eco-norm. See if the Kaysta locial can cull what we need."

"I'm glad we're not in Afrique. You'd have someone culling rhions." This time, she offered the thought without a smile.

I winced. Rhions made vorpals look small and mild, but rhion meat was good.

"Coordinator . . ." The smooth oiliness of the netlink betrayed K'gaio's presence even before her signature-link identified her. "Locatio just contacted me."

Keiko nodded to me and slipped back out of the office, graceful and silent.

It had to be the middle of the night in Kelang, but K'gaio was as unruffled as she always sounded or appeared. That might have been one reason why I wasn't comfortable with her. No one was that calm all the time, and I wondered what inner fires stoked her.

"I could sense the firebolts from here," I offered with a laugh.

"He was somewhat agitated, and he asked me to intercede on his behalf, or, more properly, on behalf of the Ellay locial."

"I'm in a difficult position, K'gaio," I pointed out. "There are twelve adiamante hulls in orbit, jammed with weapons reminiscent of the Rebuilt Hegemony, and our system isn't fully operational yet."

"Do we really know that they have such capabilities?"

"They have enough power generation ability to move those hulls from star system to star system. They've got portable net capabilities, and multiple comm systems and channels. I wouldn't want to assume that they don't have matching weapons capability. Would you?"

"No. When you express it in that fashion, Ecktor, I can understand your concerns. Still . . . it might be useful to know more . . ."

I smiled. "I agree, absolutely, K'gaio. That's why it's important to let them put more troops on the ground, and to keep them separated. We're far better off with five hundred marcybs in Ellay and five hundred in Deseret than with a thousand in one locial."

"You continue to convince me that you are the right person to be Coordinator, Ecktor. You may tell Locatio that we have spoken." With that, she was gone, leaving me with the dirty work of relaying her messages to Locatio.

My stomach growled, confirming the fact that I hadn't eaten since right after dawn. Keiko smiled as I left the office and headed downstairs to the small cafeteria.

Two draffs in blue singlesuits looked away as I stepped inside the archway and toward the serving bar. I tried to ignore the low-voiced comments as I took a basket of greens, with cheese.

". . . Coordinator . . . say . . . lost soulmate and doesn't care . . . what cost . . ."

". . . nice enough . . . when . . . on comp-duty . . ."

". . . better tech than any cyb . . ."

"Cyb type came out of his office . . . looked like the Coordinator had chewed him up like a vorpal would . . ."

". . . hope we don't get . . ."

As soon as I gave my code to the terminal, I left the cafeteria and took the basket back to the office. Keiko shook her head.

"Everyone's speculating," I explained.

"We don't have Coordinators that often."

"It's not as though I'm Wayneclint."

"You're the first since him who's had to deal with the cybs," she pointed out.

"Could I have some more tea?" I asked, imposing more than I probably should have.

The rest of the afternoon went better, or at least more smoothly, despite the endless linkages on the logistics for clearing the Ellay residential bloc, the repeated questions about the bison requisitions, the maintenance queries about Elanstan's authorization to requisition all manner of electronics and subchip assemblies, not to mention several dozen less pressing items that got to me simply because, as Coordinator, I represented a new and higher authority to which more routine matters could be appealed. I turned them all back, because that wasn't my business, but even denials took time.

Late that afternoon, as I took off into the wind, heading north, the dark snow clouds were rolling southward toward Parwon. I turned the flitter south, rotors *thwopping* their way through the cooling skies, glad to be away from the locial, if only for a few hours.

After another light dinner, I decided that I needed more exercise, something to get my mind off both the past and the rapidly approaching future.

The gray of twilight had begun to fade into the faded nielle of early evening as I trotted westward under a moon that would likely be covered before the evening was fair begun. A few tattered leaves fluttered from the limbs of the three pear trees at the western end of the garden, and something small and furry scuttled through the leaves under the spreading piñon that marked the beginning of the endless hectares of restored lands.

The rustle halted with the soft *whuft, whuft* of wide wings. Downhill and to the north passed a great spotted owl, her two-meter wings partly folded by the time I saw her outline vanish below the tree line. Exit some rodent, probably a giant field mouse.

I laughed softly and stretched out my stride, letting the cool air flow past my face. It had been a long day, and Locatio's inane protests had been the worst part.

I didn't run all the way to the meadows. Even had I been in good shape, just to get there would have taken most the night. But the meadows were on my mind. I'd studied the reclamation records for the area around the house, years back, just out of curiosity, and had been surprised to discover that at some ancient time, there had been a massacre—not of Amerindians, but of old Caucasians, something less common among such sites. Not much had been left but bones bearing the marks of firearms, but there had been plenty of bones—and remnants of a monument, but the inscription had been weathered out of existence and the rec teams had reconstituted the stone.

Morgen had claimed the place had a haunted feeling. I'd always felt melancholy there, and the cyb arrival triggered something. Were we to be the attackers or the victims? Either choice meant deaths.

My steps had shortened, and I forced my stride into a longer pattern as I paralleled the dry depression to my left.

A dark tower of fur growled from the hill to my right, three-plus meters of young black bear, and I growled back, the kind of growl that acknowledged her claim, presence, superiority, while skirting the area. Over any distance I could have outrun her, so long as I didn't get within the first fifty meters where her sprint could have caught me, but there wasn't much sense in provoking anything. Besides, the bears pretty much kept the vorpals away in the hilly areas that weren't out and out mountains. And the young female on the hill probably was more interested in plastering shut the giant bumblebee-hive entrances with the mud she slopped from the rivulet running from the spring.

I didn't know what plants the bears plastered inside the hives, but whatever it was, the bees would eventually abandon the hive and leave the honey. Most bears cultivated a few hives that way, and one sometimes took a few pears from the tree at the end of the ridge, but only on the side away from the house, and only when I'd taken the flitter.

Sometimes I wondered if they'd eventually inherit the earth—if we managed to leave them an earth to inherit.

I kept running, more slowly now that the moonlight was fading as the first tendrils of the clouds seeped southward across the sky and across Luna herself. When I got to a clearer spot on the trail, I squinted, and sure enough, could see that thin and short black line on the moon's surface that was all that remained of the ancient linear accelerator that had stretched for more than two hundred klicks.

I studied the piñon forest gently rising in front of me, then shook my head and turned back toward the house, trying to ignore the fatigue in my legs and the numbness in my soul.

<<< XII

Outside the windows of the Coordinator's office, the snow had stopped falling, but the sky remained gray. Gray, like my mood.

Delta and Kappa stations remained inoperative, despite two more shuttles full of equipment and a half-dozen technicians. Elanstan and Rhetoral sounded haggard and stressed. Ingehardt from the NorAm maintenance depot had called me again, and he sounded haggard and stressed, and wanted to know if Elanstan's priorities for immediate shuttle lift were *that* urgent. His voice got even more ragged when I told him that if he could find a way to do it faster, he'd better.

Cyb commander Gorum sent a written message confirming Henslom's request for billets for another five hundred marcybs, and asking us to consider another five hundred after Ellay. I'd forwarded that through the link to the representative Committee of the Consensus, indicating I would stall on the third increment.

"Ecktor?" The persistent voice bored through the uppernet.

"Yes, Locatio?" Leaning back in the swivel, I waited.

"We're still having trouble . . ."

"So am I. I don't have answers from Crucelle. We can't get the necessary system equipment aloft to the ell stations, and the cybs are already pressing me for more planetside billets. No, I'm not granting any more yet."

"I told you this would happen. You give in to them—"

"I never wanted to give in. We're not ready. Do you think I like this charade? We have to show some sign of cooperation because they're looking for noncooperation as an excuse to power up all that destructive hardware."

"Ecktor? Can't we have another day?"

"No." He might get it, but if I told him that immediately, he'd just be asking for another day by tomorrow.

"K'gaio won't like this."

"I've already talked to K'gaio, and she told me to tell you that she felt I had a lever on the situation. Link with her if you want."

"She said that?"

"Absolutely—in her very polite way."

"Why did you contact her? That's a way of circumventing the Committee."

"Locatio, she linked with me—at your request. I made no effort to contact her."

With the momentary silence, I added, "I'm doing the best I can under the circumstances, and I appreciate your cooperating under difficult conditions."

It took more pleasantries, but I finally disengaged without giving in, and without telling Locatio that Crucelle still hadn't given me an answer on the ENF resonance issue. No sense in having Locatio linking to us both.

The problems wouldn't have been even fly bites for the

old Rebuilt Hegemony, but the economic and social pressures created by the conflict between power and the principles of the Construct had forced the implosion of the Hegemony in a handful of centuries. The Construct was unforgiving, and so were the Power Paradigms. Of course, the cybs hadn't managed to figure those underlying principles out yet. No culture does when it's young, and when it's old enough to understand it's usually too late. We'd been lucky—lucky, and willing to pay the very high price. At times, I hated the Construct, but it had one big thing going for it. It had worked for a long, long time.

"A cyb subcommander to see you, Coordinator." Keiko's words came through the net, as smooth and polished as always. "A Subcommander Kemra."

Kemra—the cyb officer who resembled Morgen. She was all I needed.

"I'm here." I stood and walked to the half-open office door.

"Coordinator." The sandy-haired woman in the dark green uniform of the Vereal Union stopped more than a meter short of me, not surprisingly since the cybs like more physical space than most cultures. She inclined her head stiffly.

"Subcommander. Please come in."

She did, and I closed the door, then motioned to one of the upholstered green chairs. She took the one facing both the door and the windows, sitting down somewhat stiffly, though not in the rigid way Majer Henslom had. I eased into the chair at the other end of the low table and studied the cyb. She still looked far too much like the sister Morgen had never had.

"You're the navigator?"

"I'm Kemra."

"What do you want?" About some things, I've never been good at saying nothing.

"Information. Background on what's happened on Old

Earth. A general feel for your culture." Her voice was harsh, husky, almost hoarse, because she spoke so little.

I nodded and asked, "Why you?"

"Why not? The Fleet doesn't need a navigator while it's in orbit." She shrugged, and the gesture was half-familiar.

Why her? Had the cyb construct picked up my reaction? Probably, and that showed just how dangerous the cybs were, despite their arrogance. I forced myself to wait.

"I studied old Anglas, and nav work isn't exactly solar-flash right now," she concluded in a professional tone, one that would have done justice to Majer Ysslop.

She didn't want to be in the office, and that bothered me, although I certainly understood the feelings. I didn't really want to be in the office, either.

Still, pleasantries were necessary, and I linked to Keiko. "We need some of the Selastiorini, fruit, crackers, something to go with it. Two glasses."

"So friendly already?" Keiko asked, the hint of raised eyebrows following the words.

"Quite formal," I pulsed back.

"I can barely even sense your netlinks," Kemra said.

"I asked for some refreshments, that's all."

Another swirl of snowflakes fluttered past the windows, and Kemra shivered slightly. I was more than warm enough.

"It's cold here."

"Colder than Gates?"

She pursed her lips. "Not necessarily. We have cold polar regions, but all our populated areas are in warm temperate areas."

"We have locials in warm temperate or tropical locales. It's just that Deseret isn't one of those. Some of us like the seasonal changes. If someone like K'gaio becomes Coordinator"—I shrugged—"the welcoming locial would probably be Kelang. It's warm and damp there."

"How did you get to be Coordinator? We really don't

know anything about how Old Earth's society has evolved. It's been a long time." Kemra tried a smile, and I wished she hadn't. She was worse than I at dissembling.

Keiko knocked perfunctorily at the door and entered with a tray containing a bottle of chilled Selastiorini, two glasses, sliced winter apples, and alternating thin white and red cheese wedges. Even carrying all that, her steps were graceful and silent, her black hair perfectly in place.

I stood. "Thank you."

Kemra also stood and nodded.

Keiko set the tray in the middle of the table. "It wasn't a problem at all, especially for such a distinguished guest." She smiled charmingly, the way I wished I could, and I could tell she didn't like Kemra at all. With a nod to me, Keiko slipped out of the office and closed the door.

Since the wine had already been uncorked, I poured two glasses of the Selastiorini, and handed Kemra one.

"What's that?"

"Wine," I answered, recalling that she had not even touched the Whitespring at the welcoming reception.

"Is it poisonous?"

"Hardly. Ethyl alcohol content is about twelve percent, and the various side-contaminants make it flavorful—to those who wish to taste it." I took a small sip.

Her face went blank—a blankness that signaled a retreat to the hard-wired nets and the repeater or data bank worn on her wide uniform belt.

"Wine—that's something we lost in The Flight—the grapes, not the techniques," she said after a moment, the expression/possession returning to her face. "A small amount won't affect me . . ."

"And your net will sense if you have more than a small amount," I finished with a smile.

"Your aide out there doesn't like me."

"Most people on Old Earth are wary of cybs," I pointed out, "just like you're all wary of Old Earth."

"It's not that." Her eyes were direct, too direct, too like Morgen.

I forced a shrug.

"You never said how you became Coordinator." She took an infinitesimal sip of the Selastiorini.

"It's simple enough. The Consensus chose me."

"What is the Consensus exactly, some sort of representative body?"

"That's close enough, although . . . that's not it exactly, either. Locials and regions have Consensus representatives, and the representatives are the ones that make the choices." I wasn't ready to explain all the checks and balances, and the exponential compensatory time required. I almost shuddered at how many years it would take me to work off having been Coordinator. Then I took a small sip of the wine.

"Did you seek the position?" she probed.

"Hardly. It's not the sort of position anyone seeks— and anyone who did would be suspect."

"How do you get good leadership if no one wants the job?" She sneaked another sip of the Selastiorini.

"Fear." I laughed. "People accept the positions, if they're good, because they fear the alternatives if they don't do their best. It doesn't always work, but it works better than anything else we've tried." I decided against mentioning that Coordinator was a sometime position. This time, while waiting for her response, I put a wedge of the red cheese on an apple slice and chewed both slowly, letting the two tangy tastes and differing textures blend together.

Kemra took exactly what I did, but only nibbled at the edge of each, and we sat in momentary silence. The sky lightened as the high clouds outside thinned, and I saw the sunlight on the top of the eastern peaks, but only for a moment.

"It's hard to believe that you've eliminated the power-hungry in your society," she finally ventured after licking her lips and moistening them with another small sip of the Selastiorini.

What she meant was that the cybs continued to think of the demis as power-hungry. That meant more trouble because the entire chaos that preceded The Flight occurred because the cybs had possessed an inflated image of their own indispensability to society and the universe.

Hell, no living creature is indispensable to anyone or anything—except to himself or a newborn offspring.

"We've managed to deal with the problem," I finally answered.

"We'd be interested in the details."

"It's simple enough. We developed a philosophical credo and applied it consistently. We accept that morality, power, and consensus are the underpinnings for any society and work to maintain all three in balance. Trust and mutual respect are, in a way, the mortar that hold the other three together."

"Every modern society has tried that, and most have failed," the cyb navigator pointed out.

"Actually, if you look at history, you'll find that most gave lip service to them, but few ever applied them. The problem with most past societies was that they insisted that either control or freedom was the paramount requirement of society, and neither works."

"Still the same old dictatorial demis, I see." Her tone was ironic, rather than bitter.

"Hardly." I forced a laugh. "We offer great freedom. We just don't place it first. The first freedom in primitive society, after all, is the freedom to starve or die. Most cultures rejected that freedom. They also rejected the freedom to kill others." I took a sip, a longer one than I should have, from the goblet. "Yet they proclaimed freedom as the central tenet of their cultures. The first goal of a culture is survival, both short and long term. A culture that is too permissive or too restrictive cannot survive, nor can a culture that cannot agree on its morality. That's where we started." I set down the glass.

"Is this great philosophical credo set in print some-where? It would be . . . interesting to study, if it isn't too technical."

"We call it *The Paradigms of Power.* There are seven or eight paragraphs, that's all. I'll get you a copy in the next day or so." I wasn't about to give her the *Construct,* be-cause the cybs would have totally misunderstood it. I could have had Keiko get a copy of the *Paradigms* while we were talking, but the more I could stall her, and the cybs, the better, because we needed time to get the full sta-tion system up and running. The defense system would work without the Delta and Kappa stations, but both the strain and potential casualties would be higher. Besides, the more time the cybs spent on Old Earth, the greater the possibilities of avoiding actual armed conflicts. At least, that was what Arielle calculated. I wasn't that con-vinced of the comps' analyses. My own intuition said the cybs wanted an out and out battle no matter what. Either way, we needed time.

"You don't have one nearby?"

"The *Paradigms* were developed centuries ago—actu-ally longer. While it's accessible through all the nets, hard copies take a bit longer. We avoid paperwork, and there's actually not a printer in my office."

"I suppose it's in everyone's interest to take some time in feeling out the situation."

I grinned. "Absolutely."

She took another small sip of the Selastiorini. The level of the wine had hardly dropped at all, and her dry lips had barely smudged the rim of the goblet. "Why do all the Old Colonies call Earth the Planet of Death?"

"That dates back to the Rebuilt Hegemony, when Old

Earth was more . . . uncontrolled than it is now. That's one reason why we left the Cherkrik ruins."

"Those are the ruins on the other side of the mountains northeast of here? From when do they date?"

"From the period of The Flight. It's still sobering to tour them."

A long pause followed, and her eyes glazed. I could pick up the general sense of a relayed conference, including disagreements, but I couldn't catch the details, and I had a hard enough time looking blank as I strained to cross the barriers between the net systems.

"Could I tour them—say, tomorrow?" The green eyes remained hard.

I frowned for an instant. "If you wish."

"We can take one of our landers."

That was a bribe of sorts, letting me have a chance to see their technology, and an implied and false hint of co-operation, but I smiled. "Fine."

"You never did answer my question about the Planet of Death."

"I guess I didn't. Our forbearers used their abilities to create an impression that prolonged habitation on Old Earth wasn't healthy for those not born here." I laughed. "We've never bothered to correct that impression, since sometimes it still isn't."

"Why isn't it?"

"The ecological balance is both more fragile and more hostile than would have been the case without the disruptions of the time of chaos. Making the environment less hostile would increase the fragility, maybe push it into a degrading spiral. So we live with it."

"That's a general statement. How about some details?" The green eyes flashed, with an impatience similar to Morgen's, though Kemra's words were far harsher than Morgen would ever have used. The similarity/dissimilarity contrasts were disconcerting.

I swallowed another gulp of wine, and refilled my goblet, tweaking up my metabolic rate before answering.

"I don't know what your records show about the ecology of Old Earth," I began, ignoring her impatience, "but generally, that ecology was diverse and complex. Take predators. NorAm had a range of predators, large cats like the present cougar, amphibian predators, canine-related—"

"Canine?"

"Ancestors of the dogs." Dogs were extinct, a casualty of the modified Thimeser virus that wiped out wolves, dogs, coyotes, and even some of the rodent species like beavers. "That left a lot of ecological niches, and there were mutations that stabilized before we really got the meleysen program going. So our biggest predators are the bears, vorpals, the kalirams, and the cougars, and they're all—except maybe the bears—a lot nastier than anything that preceded them. The bears are just smarter. We've seen a gradual increase in size among a number of the arthropods, and the rodents that survived are also bigger and tougher, and nothing seemed to stop the snakes. Scorpions and red centipedes attack in groups or packs, and they can be fatal unless you're carrying antidote kits." I didn't mention that such fatalities referred generally to drafts and outsiders.

"Perhaps a visit to the ruins will be even more useful than I'd thought." Kemra's fingers touched her chin, one gesture I didn't recognize. After a pause, she cleared her throat. "Unlike some of the other demis, almost back-to-the-soil types, you seem to like technology—or not dislike it," she said. "Don't you fly a flitter?"

"I have a flitter." I wondered where they'd dug that up, although it wasn't a secret. Maybe she'd just been on one of the cyb landers when I'd touched down at the locial.

"Why don't more people?"

"It's time-consuming."

She shook her head, as I knew she would. "Air travel of almost any sort is faster."

"We compute total time in all uses—manufacturing, maintenance, net support—and then require comptime in locial support." I grinned. "It's amazing how much technology proves not to be time-saving when the user has to pay from his or her own time and resources."

Kemra frowned.

"A great deal of time-saving technology is designed to save time for the user, but not for all of society. Some technology is necessary—medical devices, emergency transport, food processing—but a lot is just metal gadgetry for those with resources and power. We've made an effort to downplay that."

"Even you?"

I lifted my goblet. "I've been spending five to ten stans a week pushing screens and handling routine maintenance here at the locial. If my balance gets too low, I'll do satellite maintenance. That's all work that has nothing to do with being Coordinator."

"You can't tell me that compensates for all your personal technology."

"Probably not," I admitted, "but the system seems to work."

"You sound suspiciously like an ethizard."

I winced. An ethizard was the last thing I was or wanted to be. People who live their lives strictly by ethics are even worse than people who accept becoming Coordinator. "I'm scarcely that pure."

"No." And she laughed, actually laughed. "You couldn't be Coordinator."

I rose. "Speaking of which . . ."

"You need to do some Coordinator-type work." She also rose and smothered a cough. Her voice was even more hoarse.

"Your voice could use a rest," I suggested. "When would you like to depart tomorrow?"

"Ten hundred local?"

"That's fine. I'll meet you at the locial tower." I walked her to the door and opened it.

Keiko was studying an almost blank screen, then looked up as Kemra walked past the console.

The navigator then turned back to face me. "Good day, Coordinator. I will see you tomorrow."

"Tomorrow," I agreed.

After Kemra vanished down the wide old-fashioned beam steps, Keiko raise her right eyebrow, and both dark eyes fixed me. "Did I hear something about a ruins tour?"

"You did. I'm trying to buy time. They're even supplying transport on one of their landers."

"Don't you worry about that?"

"Personally, yes, but kidnapping or killing a Coordinator would certainly qualify as an attack under the Construct."

"For your sake, I hope they aren't that dense."

"You and me both." But I had to wonder. It might be a lot better if the cybs did kidnap or kill me—better, at least, for Old Earth.

I walked back into the empty office with the door open behind me. The clouds had dropped over the mountains again, leaving the day as gray as it had begun, and I needed to get a progress report from Elanstan. And talk to Locatio or someone about the arrangements for the Ellay locial. And check with Crucelle and Arielle about the marcyb vulnerabilities and the marcyb officer profiles . . . and . . .

A swirl of snow flicked across the south window and was gone. I looked at the tray on the table and took a deep breath.

<<< **XIII**

Finally, after another quick meal snatched from the cafeteria and vorpaled down at my desk, I managed two linkages with Elanstan and Rhetoral, with one to Ingehardt sandwiched between. But Delta and Kappa stations were still not on line, and wouldn't be. Elanstan was holding something back, but I couldn't tell what.

After the second link with Ell Control, I walked back to the window and stared into the late afternoon, down at the browned grass of the park, then toward the white spire of the locial tower.

I took a deep breath and mentally reached for the link again.

"Crucelle?"

"Yes, Ecktor?" I could almost sense the warmth in his green eyes, even over the net.

"This is your very friendly and very worried Coordinator. What can you tell me about the electro-neural-resonance of the cybs and marcybs? Are they the same? Is a repetition of the pre-Flight blazing possible?"

"I can answer one question so far. We're having to operate at a distance, remember. We don't exactly have a co-operative subject in a laboratory."

"I know that, but you've been around them. So has Arielle. You had the whole welcoming reception for data collection."

"Ecktor . . ." There was the impression of a sigh. "We have a great deal of data. We also have a great deal of garbage. Making sense out of it is something else. We also are having trouble with the equipment in the residential block—enough that I can say that there's a significant ENF differential between the marcyb troopers and the officers."

"So the marcybs are constructs?"

"They're totally biological, but there have been some significant changes. We're working on it. That's all I can say."

"Ecktor," added Arielle, "it isn't easy. We're skirting the Construct to do this, because this kind of observation implies mistrust, and that doesn't make it any easier." The stormy darkangel projected currents of frustration and determination.

"I understand. Let me know."

For a time longer, I stood at the window, enjoying the almost imperceptible flow of cold air off the glass as I watched draffs and demis walk the paths of the park below. One or two looked back at the admin building, but most just walked.

Thrap.

At the tap on the door, I turned. Keiko stood there, trim, muscular, black on black.

"I'm leaving now, Coordinator, unless there's anything else you need."

"I'm sure there is, but I don't know what."

That got a brief and white-flashed smile.

"I'll leave it on the system. I'll probably go straight to the tower tomorrow for the ruins tour. If anything should happen, let K'gaio know, and dump the entire Coordinator bank on her. She's stand-by Coordinator."

"I hope nothing happens."

"So do I."

She inclined her head and was gone.

Next came what I'd put off—a system-by-system check of the maintenance status of the locial hardening and defense emplacements and systems, beginning with Deseret.

When I reemerged from the maintenance net an hour

later, I'd noted and flagged more discrepancies than existed in routine reports, and the extra comptime for the supervisors involved wasn't going to set well. Then again, unnecessary casualties wouldn't set well, either.

I took a deep breath and slumped back in the green swivel. It squeaked loudly enough that I winced, then took another deep breath.

The sky remained gray, with swirls of intermittent snow. My soul remained gray, with swirls of intermittent ice. Before long Parwon would darken, its lights almost the only sparkles in the night for klicks and klicks—the individual illuminations of isolated demi households lost in the vastness of Deseret.

I was hungry, and I didn't want to cook. I also didn't want to eat cold cheese and bread, my usual escape from preparing something.

So I closed up the office and walked down the steps to the main level. The wind swirled around me as I stepped from the admin building into the incipient twilight and headed west toward Dhozer's. A scattering of wet brown leaves lay across the tan grass of the park, and the air smelled of damp leaves, evergreens, and soil.

Two couples walked ahead of me, conversing, while two young girls walked in front of them, sometimes skipping, sometimes lagging until the adults almost walked into them. Then the children would skip ahead, only to repeat the process. The six of them turned right, crossed Jung (the street that bordered the front of the admin building), and strolled down the walk beside Hammurabi Lane.

Dhozer's wasn't much more than a converted cinqplex seven hundred meters from the admin building. According to Dhozer, most of his food was "authentic Graecian." While it was tasty, I had my doubts about its authenticity.

A gust of colder wind whipped through my hair as I reached Dhozer's, foreshadowing the clear if colder weather headed our way. I stepped under the overhanging eaves. The pair of bronze urns and the shielded tapers flanking the dark carved front door were the only indications of a commercial establishment.

I was earlier than most diners, and Dhozer greeted me himself.

"Ecktor, or is it Coordinator Ecktor now?" His short-cut black hair curled in ringlets, and set off his pale olive skin.

The restaurant smelled of wood smoke, cooking oils, and spices, and the warm air inside was humid, a relief after the cold damp outside. Metabolic control doesn't always make you *feel* better.

"Ecktor is fine. It's better for longevity."

"Who wants to live forever?"

For someone who hadn't been too sure about living at all, I realized with his comment that living forever sounded better than the alternatives faced by most Coordinators. "That's not a problem. Coordinators don't," I answered with a laugh.

"Then you should try the braised stuffed lamb. I don't make it that often, and you should taste it."

"I'll think about it." I got the corner table, warmed by the wood-burning fireplace. Despite Dhozer's suggestion, the lamb was out. The last time I'd had lamb—and it was costly, since sheep have to be raised close to the locials and put in barns at night—I'd felt stuffed for days.

His daughter, nearly Yslena's age, brought the crusty wheat bread and the olive oil and filled my glass with the pine-flavored wine that I couldn't believe had lasted for millennia. Why would anyone contaminate wine that way? For all my complaining, though, I had to admit it went with the food Dhozer served.

Idres looked at me.

"I'll have the dolmades and the soup."

She nodded and slipped away, and I dipped the bread in the balsamic vinegar and olive oil mix. While the ancient

Greeks may have marinated and stuffed grape leaves, I doubted that they used fire peppers, brown rice, and ground bison to fill the leaves. Then again, who would question Dhozer? Most of what had been Greece that wasn't underwater was still being recovered. Not many of the ancient Greeks or Mohammedans had survived the Chaos Years, when no one cared how many different ways they killed each other or what they did to water and food supplies.

Dhozer used more spices than I had in all my cabinets, but I didn't use more than we'd been able to grow, except for salt and black pepper, and that amounted to a double handful at most. Eating at Dhozer's was a luxury, because diners paid for it essentially by trading compensatory service time. Some draffs, especially, piled up comptime just for such luxuries.

The problem with having currency is that any society that controls it eventually debases it and taxes it. Any society that doesn't control it will still have it evolve, and then the currency becomes pegged to outside influences—like the scarcity of precious metals, colored seashells, or large circular rocks with holes in the middle.

Our compromise was simple. We tied transactions to real goods and services. I had a comptime balance on the screens. If I provided an hour of administrative screen service, I got five credits. If I provided an hour of something like comm satellite maintenance, I got forty. The credits came from the system, not from the recipient. Likewise, for each hour I used the flitter, I lost twenty-five credits to the system, and that didn't count fuel or parts, or the time and skill for repairs I couldn't do myself.

Of course, the system depends on honesty, but in the end, any system does, and we just threw out those who proved they were dishonest. Surprising what that does for honesty.

"You did not want the lamb?" asked Dhozer, appearing silently by my shoulder.

"Too rich," I said, after finishing a bite of the warm and crusty bread.

"The dolmades are good." His tone implied that they weren't nearly so good as the lamb.

I waited.

"What will the cybs do?"

"I don't know." That was true, but not good enough for the restauranteur.

"What do you *think* they will do?"

I took a sip of the retsina, a small sip, before answering. "They want revenge for The Flight. They have not indicated how they plan that."

"Always the Construct, is it not?" he asked with a sigh.

"Always."

"A pity."

"Yes." I thought so, too, but not so much of a pity as having no Construct.

He nodded and refilled the wine glass, although the level of wine had barely dropped, and then slipped away.

My eyes flickered to the replicated bronze shield and crossed spear, and then to the black and white crater that had never been used for wine.

Dhozer had reclaimed some of his heritage, and I wondered how much the rest of us had lost. Were we better off without the legends and myths, and the bloodshed out of which both had grown? But the myths hadn't died away, except among the older demi families.

When I was young, we'd lived right outside the Bouthba locial on the ocean, where it rained all the time. At the times when the northeast rains poured down, my mother told stories, just like all draff mothers did, I thought. My father had often smiled, not an unsympathetic smile, while she told of strange little people and pots of gold at the end of rainbows. But there had been a darker side to some of those stories, too.

Once my mother told me an old, old story about Lyr, an ancient Sidhe god. She said that she told me because, before there were demis and cybs and draffs, there were legends and myths, and that some of those myths were real. She never said which were, and when I asked her, she'd only answered that they all held truth, and that I'd have to find out which held which truths, because once I was a demi, I'd have to understand. She knew from the beginning where I was headed.

I didn't remember much of the story about Lyr, except three things. First was that he was the god of the sea with horses like sea-serpents that pulled boat chariots through the storms. Second, was that he wasn't a big tall god, and he looked like a little old man. Last was that he went out of his way to put down heroes. I wondered if that part got added because my mother didn't care much for heroes.

"Storms on the sea—they don't care whether you're a hero or a coward or a draff or a demi. When the clouds clear and the sea is flat, none leaves footprints. Nor does Lyr. The gods of the land, they tear up the ground and leave mountains and hills and canyons, but for all the violence on the sea, it's unchanging. The only thing the sea changes is the land."

Now, Yslena was working for Lyr, so to speak, and my parents had been dead for a decade, and Morgen was gone, too. Time was like Lyr, too, I thought as I took a sip from the refilled wineglass. Not many left footprints on time or on the water.

Idres brought the salad, with the strong-tasting goat cheese and the tangy dark brown olives. I wondered what cow cheese might have tasted like, but there were so few cattle left that I'd never had any.

"Do you think they will try to destroy all the locals?"

Dhozer appeared and added a touch more wine to my glass.

"They could; they could try anything."

"A pity they have learned so little." He replaced the olive oil and vinegar with a fresh dish, and added another quarter-loaf of bread to my basket.

I nodded as I took another bite of salad.

"You should try the leklavi."

"I should eat the dolmades before I consider something that rich," I countered.

He smiled as he headed for the door and a new customer, a thin, dark-haired woman.

In the end, I didn't have the leklavi, and I left early, still feeling stuffed. I didn't need to complicate things by waiting until I was totally exhausted before taking the flitter home in the dark, instrument beacon or not at the house.

<<< XIV

THE CONSTRUCT

> Mutual individual respect and self-respect must be maintained, since the greater the mutual respect between individuals and the respect for the role of each individual within society, the more stable the society.

> Because society is based on trust, trust cannot be withheld on unfounded suspicion.

> Threats are a form of mistrust; so are unprovoked violence, use of physical force, and manipulation of another. Failure to be trustworthy requires removal from society.

Attempts to redefine principles into written rules of conduct reflect mistrust and are doomed to failure.

Direct statements of individual desires are not forms of mistrust, but no individual or group of individuals is bound or required to fulfill another's desire.

Society may agree upon mutually restrictive and/or coercive measures, but only so long as such measures have commensurate impacts upon those who develop and impose such measures.

<<< XV

The previous day's clouds had lifted, and as I landed and air-taxied the flitter to the base of the Deseret locial, a glance to the east showed that the warmer breeze out of the southwest was strong enough at the higher altitudes to lift plumes of snow off the eastern peaks.

After shutting down the turbines and flight systems, I'd barely lifted the thin case containing the copy of *The Paradigms of Power* and a general recent history of Old Earth off the second seat of the flitter when Kemra waved from beneath the nose of the cyb lander, a boosted hydrocarb monster that had to gulp kilolitres of fuel on every hop.

After sealing my comparatively minuscule flitter, I linked with Crucelle and Keiko and walked toward the cyb craft. I wore a winter jacket, not the black cloak. The ruins would be cold.

"Any reports to you from Elanstan?"

"Kappa's up; Delta's a mess." Keiko's words were quick and crisp, as efficient as she always was. I'd have bet she was wearing black again.

"The cybs are using solar arrays to charge what seem to be firin cells," Crucelle reported, each word precise. "They are pulse-mapping most of the locials, and they did a survey flight over the earth side of the moon. They spent a lot of time in the equatorial belt."

"They target anything there?" I asked, trying to recall if we had any sealed installations or depots there, although I thought most were in higher lunar latitudes.

"They covered the whole surface," he answered ironically.

"That Commander Gorum was here already, asking for hydrocarb fuel to their specs, suggesting that it would be a nice gesture since they were transporting you to Cherkrik," added Keiko.

"Hydrocarb fuel won't hurt, if we can refine any in that volume," offered Crucelle.

"What he wants has the same specs as what the Coordinator's flitter—or anyone's—uses. The volumes are something else again."

I shrugged as I walked, keeping my mouth shut and answering on the netlink. "See if you can work it out, Keiko."

"What's the point of all this?" asked darkangel Arielle, slipping into the net like a sudden storm.

"Stalling them until they see the error of their ways," I answered. "Or until we're ready to convince them."

"They're thinking the same way, with all the power recharging and troop drops." The darkangel offered a snort. "They want to force the error of our ways down our throats with supercharged particle beams or de-energizers."

"You have a better idea?" I asked Arielle.

"You're the Coordinator."

That meant she didn't.

"Crucelle? Make sure that the old hardening systems are operational."

"Great suggestion for our morale, mighty Coordinator," offered Keiko.

"Coordinators have to be honest."

"Don't be quite so honest with the subcommander. They're still playing your memories," assessed Keiko, accurately . . . but painfully. Then, I suspected one of the reasons she was my assistant was because the precise—but caring—Crucelle was looking out for my welfare.

"Don't I know it," I admitted, my eyes focusing on the sandy-haired cyb waiting ahead by the lander ramp, clad in a midweight green wind jacket that would not be heavy enough for our destination.

"Remember that," added Crucelle, not quite able to hide his concern.

I downlinked and smiled at Kemra, ignoring the junior officer standing slightly behind her. "It's a much better day today."

"Yes. Our observers say it's clear over the ruins as well."

"But cold."

"The way you're dressed means I'll need a heavier jacket."

"Probably." I extracted the thin folder from my case. "I remembered your interest in the *Paradigms*. There's also a relatively recent, and mercifully brief, history of Old Earth since The Flight."

"Thank you." She took the folder, but did not open it, and turned to the officer behind her. "Are we ready, Kessek?"

"Yes, Subcommander."

She motioned to the olive-black ramp, and we walked up it into the main cabin, where rows of empty acceleration couches filled the dim space. The lander could have easily carried two hundred marcybs, loaded like livestock or cordwood, which was about the way the cybs regarded them.

"We'll go forward." Kemra did not look at me.

Forward of the bulkhead and through a heavy hatch was a smaller compartment, containing a mere half dozen almost luxurious couches, three against the fuselage on each side. In the middle was an open space, but the lines in the deck gave the impression of a large extendable table of some sort.

"Take any seat."

I sat in the left forward couch-seat. Unusually supple, it was covered with a black synthetic leather. Kemra sat in the forward couch on the right side.

Behind us, the ramp whined up and into place. Then Kessek closed the hatch separating the troop compartment from the officers' space, and without looking at either of us, marched forward into the cockpit, closing a second hatch with a dull thud.

Deciding to take the risk, I let my net-enhanced senses probe the lander as Kessek began his checklist for lift-off. Fuselage—enhanced metalite-boron-composite. Propulsion—fan-ram-scram screamers, with magboost. The magfield boost surprised me a bit. The delta wings contained antimatter pellet launchers, although I couldn't sense any pellets. That wasn't surprising, given their weight. Also concealed in the wings were two pair of heavy-duty, high velocity slugthrowers, with plenty of ammunition—the nasty osmiridian-depleted uranium tipped stuff. The guns were just for emergencies, since the lander's real military purpose was destruction of wide areas of landscape, presumably inhabited areas rather than hardened military targets.

Lovely people, the cybs.

A thin whine grew into a larger whine, and the lander began to move. I tapped the locial control frequency and got Kessek's transmission.

"Deseret locial, this is lander one. Ready to taxi for departure."

"Lander one. You're cleared to the north end of radial two zero zero."

After a moment, another transmission—net-to-net—followed. *"Gibson,* lander one lifting for the ruins with the subcommander and the demi Coordinator. Interrogative instructions."

"That's negative, lander one. Follow observation plan."

"Stet."

The lander kept rolling northward.

"What do you think?" asked Kemra, the slightest gleam in her eye.

"It's a rather impressive way to transport two individuals."

"We'd like to impress you," she answered.

"I gathered that." Mere size and brute firepower weren't that impressive in demonstrating technological prowess or sophistication, but they were successful in suggesting what the cybs had in mind for Old Earth.

Kemra fell silent as the lander began to accelerate, the whine of the fan turbines turning into more of a thundering rush as the lightly laden lander angled into the sky, almost as steeply as a magdrive shuttle. Before long Kessek reconfigured the engines into scramset, and the external sound bled back into a dull rumble.

The blank oblong on the bulkhead in front of Kemra shimmered, then began to display a panorama of the terrain in front of and below the lander; the white-covered mountains and darker valleys northeast of Parwon.

Kemra glanced at the view for a moment, then opened the folder and read the sheet that held the *Paradigms.* Finally, she looked at me. "That's it?"

"I didn't say it was complicated. Principles usually aren't." I offered a smile. "In the beginning, the implementation was nastier than a pack of vorpals. Sometimes, it's still a problem."

"In what way?" She closed the folder and brushed back a lock of short sandy hair, an unfamiliar gesture.

"The whole issue of power. Some people won't accept society's values except at the focus of a weapons laser. Others never will. If we overuse force, then no one will accept the society. If we don't use it, we have no society."

"Nice generalizations. What about some specifics? Cases?"

"You sound like a true rat-comp."

She raised both eyebrows.

"Rationalist comprehender. The facts, please, nothing but the facts." I shook my head, trying to ignore the distractions of the lander's noisy net and the rumbling of the engines. "At first, children were the biggest problem. How do you deal with them? They're innocents, relatively. Wayneclint's successor, Terese, decided to finesse the issue. She gathered a Consensus on a replacement birth policy and enforced it with reversible female sterilization after two children."

"Rather chauvinistic. How could she enforce that?"

"Easily enough. Anyone who didn't comply lost their children, got forcibly sterilized, and dumped on one of the swept islands. That's where we still put malcontents."

"That's barbaric."

"Let's see," I answered. "It's civilized to let a society overbreed and destroy the ecology, raise interpersonal tensions to the point that violence is endemic, and stretch resources to the point that all too many children are ill-fed, uneducated, diseased, and without any hope of ever reaching their potential? Or would you prefer millions of abortions? That happened, you know, before the chaos. But it's barbaric to require people to limit their offspring?"

"What if a child dies or something?"

"Reversible sterilization," I repeated. "How do you handle the problem? By expansion? Or by market forces?"

"Market forces?"

"Economics—only those who can afford children can have them . . . or some variant."

"Cybs are rational enough that we don't need such brutal measures."

I nodded. Simple enough. If a cyb couldn't access the net, and use it proficiently, then access to partners was nil. Likewise, a common net meant everyone knew everything—which was a different form of consensus, power socially imposed. Plus, the cybs had never had to deal with a large population of draffs, and that made matters easier.

"How do you know what I'm talking about?" Kemra asked.

So I told her what I'd been thinking, and her mouth opened and then closed. "I never said that."

"It's basically true, isn't it?"

"You make it sound so . . . compulsive."

I forced a laugh. "Your society has survived. That means you have to follow most of the *Paradigms of Power*. You may have a different morality and a different way to apply power, but it's the same in the end. Survival means acceptance of a desired moral structure and the use of some sort of force to maintain it against any small minority that would undermine it." I shrugged.

"What about large minorities?"

"If you won't or can't enforce or adapt the morality to reduce discontent, you'll have some form of civil war, societal breakup, revolution, or all three."

"I'd like to think about that." She looked toward the screen before and above her.

Self-delusion about the applicability of the Paradigms is also an all-too-human trait. We all like to think that we aren't slaves to belief and that we aren't governed by power, or fear of power, but most of us aren't that altruistic, especially deep-down. Shared morality is a way to survive, and it's hard to overcome our basic genetic hardware. Some never do.

Instead of resuming the conversation, Kemra opened the folder again and began to read the history I'd provided. That might not prove any more palatable to her than my observations on the cyb society I'd never even seen.

Before long, the desolate ground appearing in the screen indicated our approach to the ruins.

Kessek was smooth. I had to hand him that, the way he greased that big lander right onto the Cherkrik locial's strip, even in what seemed to be a stiff crosswind.

The front hatch slid open, and Kessek called back, "I'm lowering the ramp, Subcommander. Do you have any idea how long you'll be?"

Kemra looked at me.

"If you want an in-depth look, it'll take a minimum of two hours, and maybe four."

"At least three hours, Kessek," she answered.

"You can close up and come with us," I offered. "Or relax in the locial tower. There's a small café there—no charge to visitors."

"You can have the ruins," the pilot answered.

Kemra opened a small locker on the bulkhead before her and withdrew a belt and a handgun. "I assume you don't mind. You had mentioned the ruins are wild." She crossed to another locker and extracted a heavy jacket that was slightly too large for her. After stripping off her lighter jacket to reveal a set of informal greens and donning the greenish-brown heavier jacket, she transferred a pair of gloves from her wind jacket to the new one.

"Hardly. I'd made arrangements for defense also, but the handgun is fine."

I followed Kemra out of the lander and down the ramp into the cold and bright sunlight in front of the white tower that fronted the only occupied structures in hundreds of klicks.

"Could I tour the ruins—tomorrow?" Such a simple and meaningless demand, but there we were at the Cherkrik Station, the only station on Old Earth not serving a populated locial.

A gust of wind lifted white dust from the equally white permacrete, and the wind's faint whistle and the cooling of the lander's engines were the only sounds. The large blood-red inscription emblazoned on the side of the tower facing the landing strip remained the same: "Lest We Forget . . ."

With only a glance at the inscription, Kemra turned back toward the ramp, olive green-black metal, her net crackling around her. "Going offnet now . . . place is eerie . . . can almost sense old nets, old energies, and the damned ruins stretch for klicks and klicks."

An assent flicked back to her from the lander pilot.

"Are we ready?" asked Kemra.

"Coordinator?" Standing by a vivid green electrocart was a dark thin woman in a trim gray singlesuit.

"Yes," I answered, both verbally and net-net. "I'm Ecktor. This is Subcommander Kemra from the Vereal Union."

"It's good to meet you, Subcommander. I'm Dienate, Cherkrik local logistics officer." Her brown eyes turned to me. "Here's the cart you requested. It's fully charged. The provisions are in the front locker."

The cart wasn't much more than an electric drive system powered by fuel cells and a backup battery, four seats in two sets of two, and a windscreen.

"Thank you. The lander pilot may need some refreshments. . . ."

"We'd be happy to oblige. It's always good to see a fresh face, especially in the cold months." A crooked grin creased her face, showing brilliant white teeth against her near-black complexion.

"Thank you."

Kemra echoed her thanks, and Dienate nodded and smiled. I walked over to the cart and checked it out. Two rifles were racked in the electrocart, both slugthrowers, with the simultaneous twin-magazine option, either of spray-shells or solid-expanders.

"I can see you haven't given up heavy weapons, even on peaceful Old Earth," the cybnav said sardonically. "Do you arm troops with something even heavier?" Kemra's hand strayed to her holstered handgun, a slugthrower rather than a dart gun or a stunner.

By then, I could catch her words reverberating on her self-net before she spoke them, but said nothing until after her last word. No sense in alerting her and giving up that minimal advantage.

"We have a few of these for defense," I said. "But we don't have troops the way you do. Hop in." I didn't want to talk about weapons and the way we handled defense, especially not before she'd really seen the ruins, and not after her quick dismissal of the warning inscription.

". . . probably have more than we've ever had," she sub-vocalized.

I forced a smile. It could be a long tour, even if it were short.

After a quick check of the emergency beacon, and to make sure Kemra was seated securely in the right hand seat, I used the floor throttle to ease the cart across the dusty permacrete. The little four-wheeler whined westward on the slight upgrade past the tower and along the lane that separated the dozen small dwellings from the three shop buildings. Each dwelling had a walled rear yard, mainly to protect the gardens and fruit trees from the climatic extremes, and the occasional vorpal.

Fifty meters of flat and cracked permacrete separated the rear walls of the houses from the beginning of the ruins. I turned the electrocart left on the former groundcar highway and we bounced southward, the landing field to the east and a mixture of roofless ruined structures to the west, interspersed with low hummocks where houses built of wood or other degradable materials had once stood.

Small piles of frost and snow lay in the shadows on the north side of the ancient remnants, but even by winter's end the accumulation would not be that great.

A few stick-like dried weeds rose from cracks in the ancient surface, and an occasional low bush protruded from the frozen dust—probably creosote or something even tougher. Nothing else grew, and all the old trees, except for the handful of mutants on the other side of the Barrier, had long since died and crumbled into dust.

The ancients had left the area too dry and too infertile for grasses, and we'd halted the ecobuilding efforts at the perimeter of the ruins to preserve the devastation. Some things cannot be explained, but have to be experienced.

With a disinterested expression that never varied, Kemra just looked as the electrocart whined southward. Once we passed the end of the locial's landing field, the roofless ruins and low hummocks appeared on both sides of the ancient byway.

Less than half a klick south of the locial field, I slowed the cart and eased it across a narrow metal span that ridged a crevasse in the old road. Beneath the replacement span, the dark line of the bottom of the crevasse was a good two hundred meters down.

"Was this caused by . . . weapons damage?" asked Kemra.

"No. Much of the subsoil here is hydrostatically unstable clay. There are some faults nearby, and the ancients diverted water from a number of mountain rivers. Then they used a good fraction of that water to support an artificial garden-like ecosphere—grass, trees. Of course, the water eventually lubricated those subsurface faults, and that transformed the clay into the equivalent of jelly." I shrugged. "Some of the damage happened long after these were ruins, but the fragmentary records that survived show some occurred while people were living here."

Kemra fell silent again as the electrocart began to climb a long and gradual grade. I halted at the top. From where we sat, on an ancient highway bisecting a barren space that might have been a park, we had a panorama of the ruins.

The rows of square-cornered houses, most still larger than ours—*mine* now, I mentally corrected myself—went on for klick after klick. Some few still had roofs. Some did not. Some had walls. Most had collapsed into heaps of plastic and other nondegradable rubble. Still others were but holes in the ground.

A shiny black line—the Barrier—rose above the ruins almost due west of us, but Kemra stared southward across the brown- and white-dusted desolation, looking toward the broken towers that still jutted into the sky like the decayed teeth of the past. Fragments of reflected light still glittered from some of the towers. Those on the north side slumped, half-melted, supposedly destroyed by an orbital solar array that had been blasted out of existence millennia earlier. The visible damage didn't include the toxins and nerve spores that only required water and organic contact to resume their search-and-destroy missions.

"Can we go there?" She pointed to the towers.

"Not unless you want to wear a full decon suit."

"You left them that way?"

"If we hadn't, who would believe that so much idiocy once existed? It'd become a story, then a fable, and would already be forgotten and dismissed." For a moment, I recalled my mother's stories—and that I'd forgotten many, demi training or not.

"Not if you kept it on your nets."

"Nets aren't the same thing. Some experiences require full-body reality."

She raised those eyebrows again.

I blushed. Morgen could do that to me so easily. "That's not what I meant."

Her face turned professional. "I'll try to remember that."

Did she have to alternate between being a good cyb and a flirt? Or was that the idea, to keep me off-balance? Was there any question?

So I just waited as the dead silence continued, broken only by the chill wind that blew across the open electro-cart.

"There must have been more people here than on some entire worlds," the cyb navigator finally ventured.

"The peak population for the entire complex was around five million, in an area that ran two hundred fifty klicks north-south and about one hundred and fifty east and west."

She frowned, and I could sense the mental calculations. "That's over a hundred and twenty-five people per square klick."

"Say a hundred meter square for each one."

She shivered. "That's hard to imagine."

"That was spacious compared to some of the ancient cities, places like Newyrk or Mexity. The towers of Newyrk were the biggest in the world."

"Why didn't you save them?"

"It was too dangerous ecologically. Too many rivers, and with the rise in the ocean levels, the poisons were having too great a negative impact on the marine ecosystem. Cherkrik is ecologically isolated, at least comparatively."

"How long does this go on?" she asked.

"We're a bit north of the middle of the ruins. So we could travel another hundred and twenty-five klicks south, and it would look pretty much the same—except for the towers there."

"Oh. . . ."

I eased the four-wheeler downhill, and we traveled on through stillness broken only by the whispers of the cold wind and the whining of the cart. A klick south of the rise where we had stopped, I turned west, in the direction of the Barrier.

Blackened swathes of vitrified material began to appear at irregular intervals through the ruins we were traversing, lines of black glass barely higher than the old secondary road the cart followed.

Finally, Kemra gestured without speaking.

"Orbital laser, powered by a sun tap."

I could sense her noting that bit of information for her records. Would she would ask whether we retained that technology or just assume that we did? There was one such system, stored at the depot on Luna, but we had no intention of reactivating it. It wouldn't cut adiamante.

The instances of black glass finally disappeared after another klick of whining westward. We entered the area where the buildings—built just before the Time of Troubles— were strong enough to resist time's erosion.

"These look much newer," Kemra observed.

"They're still millennia old—one of the last achievements of the ancients."

I eased the cart up beside a square structure comprised of gray building blocks, stopping on the south side in the sunlight. Each block bore a tracery of fine lines. At irregular intervals, holes had been punched through the synthetic stone, even though the hollows in the centers of the blocks had been filled with a cement that solidified as hard as the blocks themselves. Some of the holes were fist-sized, others almost large enough to walk through.

I flicked off the cart's power.

"Why are we stopping?"

"To give you a close look at the ruins."

"Isn't a ruin a ruin?" The words were not quite playful.

"Sometimes." I rummaged under the seat until I found the standard rock hammer, then laid it on the flat console top between us. After that I unstrapped the rifle, though I could sense nothing nearby. Most of the time the ruins were empty, since nothing grew in the center areas, and probably nothing ever would. Beyond the Barrier was another question, but I preferred being careful to being dead.

"Do I need one?" Kemra asked.

"One's enough here." With the rifle in one hand and the rock hammer in the other, I stepped up to the battered wall.

Kemra followed, and her gloved fingers ran across the stones of the wall.

"Take off a glove and touch it. The stone."

"It's just a synthstone."

"Not just. This building was built in the Time of Troubles before The Flight." I gestured around.

She peeled off a glove and touched the stone. "It's just stone."

"How cold is it outside? How cold is the stone?" I asked.

She nodded as she pulled her glove back on. "Almost a total nonconductor?"

"Pretty close." I pointed to a protrusion, a rough and almost needle-like triangle of stone jutting into one of the larger holes in the wall. Then I handed her the hammer. "Hit that. Knock it loose."

"I probably can't." She gave a hoarse laugh. "Not if you're asking me to."

I couldn't help grinning. "Go ahead and try."

She took a firm but not overpowering swing. The hammer bounced off the fragile-looking stone fragment without leaving a scratch behind. With a nod, she returned the implement. "What are the blocks made from?"

"It's called bortbloc. Call it an early and cheaper relative of adiamante." I stepped into the interior, dimly lit from the dozens of gaps in the wall, and red dust rose as I walked down a narrow corridor.

Kkcchhewwww!

"I'm sorry," apologized the cybnav. "It's dusty."

I bent down and picked up an irregular chunk of bortbloc. "Here. You were interested in it."

Kemra frowned but took it, slipping it into her jacket pocket. We walked back to the cart. The whole way I kept scanning for signs of predators, but didn't sense a thing. That was fine with me.

After replacing the rifle in its stand, I guided the four-wheeler back onto the ancient secondary road, still heading westward, past endless battered and holed structures, roofless and more widely and irregularly separated than those to the east.

Ahead of us, over the mainly roofless bortbloc dwellings, loomed the Barrier, its black surface smooth yet unreflecting.

"What's that?" Kemra finally asked.

"We call it the Barrier. It's the only visible adiamante structure left on Old Earth. The only intact one above ground."

"You have some installations below ground?" Kemra probed.

"There were some ancient installations that were covered by lava, and it wasn't worth the trouble to break them apart. They may give some far-future geologist great pause, assuming there are any geologists in the far, far future." That wasn't the whole truth, and I wasn't required to offer that, since, again, it would have been close to a threat.

I eased the cart to a halt in the open space east of the Barrier, that long unbroken black wall that stretched for klicks. I couldn't sense anything living within at least a klick. Most predators avoided the Barrier—the stones still emanated death, although the systems had been depowered and removed millennia earlier.

"I'm hungry. How about you?" My question was rhetorical. The change in her circulation and skin color indicated a precipitous drop in blood sugar.

"Ah . . . something might taste good."

Dienate had been as good as her word about provisions. Besides the sandwiches, crackers, cheese, and winter apples, there was even a bottle of Springfire with two mugs.

"Elegant for a ruins tour," Kemra said after swallowing some of the Springfire and munching through half a bison and cheese sandwich. "Tasty, too. What's the meat?"

"Bison. Even with the vorpals and the cougars, they tend toward overpopulation. So we can cull quite a few without upsetting the balance much. Originally, or semi-originally, hunters were part of the natural balance. I asked for the cheese because some people find the bison too strong without the moderating influence of the cheese."

"You sound like a net engineer."

I'd done that, too, but admitting it wasn't wise. "Coordinators pick up things from everywhere."

"Including off-planet."

I shrugged, hoping the semi-flirtatious phrase was just gentle flattery. Rather than answer, I ate the other half of my sandwich in four bites. The cyb hadn't been the only hungry one.

"How did you get to be a navigator?" I asked, sipping Springfire kept chill by the wind and the ambient temperature.

"I always wanted to be one, and I was good with astrophysics. I qualified as a pilot, and, after a long time, here I am." She finished the crackers and the cheese I'd offered her.

"You're the most senior woman in the Vereal Fleet, aren't you?"

"Someone has to be. Most women don't like to specialize in abstract concepts and calculations. I do."

"We do tend to have fewer female rat-comps," I admitted, "but not nearly so few as the ancient theorists predicted." After a sip of Springfire, I asked, "What prompted the mission to Old Earth?"

There was a long pause before she answered. "A number of things. Curiosity. Wanting to know if the demis survived. And we were visited by a ship from one of the former colonies of the Rebuilt Hegemony."

In short, they'd reclaimed their technological heritage and discovered that the bogeymen of the far past had apparently crumbled. Yet they'd still sent twelve adiamante hulls. That alone showed how deep the fear and hatred ran.

I gathered the remains of our meal back into the bag, corked the half bottle of Springfire and put everything back in the locker. "Ready?"

"For what?" she asked.

"The interesting part of the ruins tour."

The cart rolled forward and eased through the gate. The gate: ten meters tall, imperishable and enduring, still glittering black and untouched except for the thin coating of white dust. From the guardhouse above pointed dual barrels of Sasaki cannon, and the cracked ceramic sleeve of an antipersonnel laser. The early demis had coated them with preservatives to maintain their legacy of menace. Those particular weapons were the only part of the ruins we had preserved, but I still felt the Consensus had been right in choosing to do so. I still supported it, although the bitterness over preserving just those few weapons had lasted for generations.

Beyond the gates were the plastic trees, now nearly eighty meters tall, their twenty-meter-plus trunks elbowing aside the curbs of the ancient parkways where they had been planted. They weren't real plastic, but I felt that way about them. They were firs genetically modified to manufacture a lignin-based plastic composite as part of their trunk and limb structure, and to extract water from the air. The original idea had been to provide an organic source of composite armor fibres, but the cost proved too high, and there was no practical way to harvest them. Each had cost the equivalent of three ground-to-orbit shuttles to create. They were virtually indestructible except to heavy weapons, direct fission explosions, or similar catastrophic applications of force. They continued to grow, if glacially, and were projected to be able to reach heights in excess of two hundred meters with roots twice that deep locked into the very depths of Old Earth.

The tips of their limbs quivered in the heavier wind gusts, and their natural appearance belied their unnatural birth. Of the old evergreens once growing in the ruins area, none were left, not even the trunks, except for one withered out-of-place bristlecone in the single park up the hill.

Kemra was silent as the electrocart whined past an intact and full-scale replica of an ancient castle, complete with four round turrets at each corner, and a dry moat.

Another half klick up the winding and smooth drive was a replica mosque.

As we neared the mosque, Kemra turned in her seat. "This is . . . different from the other ruins. They look like they were just abandoned. Why are these still complete? Who lived here?"

"I'll answer that after we tour the next dwelling, if you don't mind." I knew she did, but I was feeling difficult. She'd kept looking, but I wasn't sure she'd really seen anything except more ruined buildings than she'd ever thought about.

Past the mosque-like dwelling was the temple house. A long winding strip of adiamante-like pavement led toward the three-winged structure built of a light green stone that shimmered in the midday light, although in the shade, snow bleached whiter by the omnipresent dust lay piled against the north walls.

The cart whined to a stop opposite the short walk leading to the double stone doors.

Kemra took in the graceful columns and the transparent and indestructible armaglass between them. "This was a private dwelling?" she asked.

"All of them on this side of the Barrier were."

I climbed out of the cart seat and set the brake, then lifted one of the rifles. "I'd like you to look at this one."

"It's like a temple, or something from Hzjana."

"More likely, the one on Hzjana came from here." Not that I knew that for certain, but architecture on the former Colony Planets had to have some origin in Old Earth.

The carved stone doors, synthetic jade depicting a man kneeling before a blazing bush in the middle of hillside, opened at my touch. They always did, a testimony to the engineering and the balance. I'd also cleaned the tracks several years back, and that helped.

The polish of the entry hall's stone floor was muted by the dust, but remained as smooth and hard as it had for its builder millennia earlier.

Kemra glanced up at the ten-meter fluted columns. "A replica temple? From where?"

"From what I've been able to discover, it's an idealized version of something called Minoan, except the religious motif got confused."

Kemra paused. The mosaic on the wall facing the door depicted a naked, blond-haired, and beardless young man vaulting through the wide-spread horns of a bull in the middle of a banner-clad arena. There aren't many cattle left these days, but Wienstan told me they thought they had the bovine cleft-gene virus pinned down. So there might be a chance for them.

"The detail is amazing." Kemra leaned close to the minute colored stones, none larger than a half centimeter.

A wind gust swirled snow outside the north-facing stone doors, but not the hint of a sound entered the temple-like house, and the powdered dust by the doors didn't move a millimeter.

Kemra turned and scanned the entire lower entry hall. When she seemed almost finished, I shrugged and started up the left-hand set of stairs to the upper level. A landing nearly five meters deep overlooked and encircled the entry hall on three sides. There were wide squared lintels framing openings to each of the three wings on the upper level.

At the top, I waited for Kemra, shifting the rifle. I couldn't believe I'd need it inside, but in the ruins beyond the Barrier, you never quite knew. Besides, we'd have to return to the cart.

She paused and turned, looking down again, before giving the smallest of headshakes. "Where next?"

"The wings are similar. Each provided living space for an individual, or a couple, at most. The center wing is the most interesting." I stepped into the entry room, something once called a sitting room, although, eons ago, someone had removed all the furnishings in the house, or they had turned to dust and sifted away, or both. "According to what the researchers have been able to discover, this was just a room designed for sitting and talking."

The room was fully fifteen meters wide and ten deep, with recessed alcoves that had held artwork on each side. The floor was pale green and white polished marble, flat and smooth, with a repeating design of triangles.

Beyond the sitting room, past the square arch that had once held double doors, was a corridor leading to the bedchamber. On each side of the corridor was a bath chamber. I waited as Kemra inspected each. The one on the left held an oval marble tub large enough for four people, included a space the size of my kitchen just for a commode, and had enough closet space for a marcyb regiment. The bathing chamber on the right was similar, except that in place of the tub was an armaglass enclosed shower of equally heroic proportions.

Kemra looked through each, then rejoined me in the corridor. "You read about these, but . . . seeing something like this . . ."

"It gives you a different perspective."

I walked forward into the bedchamber, fifteen meters wide and twice as deep, a space almost blindingly bright. The side walls were comprised of fluted pale green stone columns joined by lightly tinted armaglass that ran from floor to ceiling. The end wall continued the same pattern, except for the set of carved stone doors centered there.

Kemra glanced around the empty chamber, saying nothing.

The right hand outer door groaned slightly but opened, and we stepped out onto the covered south-facing balcony, rimmed by a stone balustrade supported by miniature columns. From the balcony, the outline of the departed gardens that had encircled the forty-meter pool was clear. The pool was empty, the pale green marble-like sides still shimmering in the cold light, but snow and white dust covered the mosaics that had floored it. Once, from the balcony, the white-tipped mountain giants would have been reflected in the water.

"It's still beautiful." Kemra's voice was even more hoarse. "I can't imagine what it must have been like."

I could theoretically conceive of it, but the emotional impact was too much to dwell on, especially with my background. I looked toward the mountains instead.

"Why don't you live . . . I mean, with only ten million of you—couldn't everyone live like this?"

"This dwelling used more electrical energy in a week

than I use in a standard year." I forced a laugh. "And I don't lack for conveniences."

Her face tightened. "Has it gotten that bad . . . here?"

"We're cautious." I turned to look at her face, still bearing a quizzical expression. "Although we have a lot of hydrocarbon reserves, we try to restrict hydrocarb consumption to our renewable sources—things like the joba plants, the propylene harvests. For some things, you need more concentrated energy, and we still use fusactors, but we try to keep their usage to where it's appropriate." Like powering the satellite station systems.

Her eyes scanned the other structures, more than a dozen easily visible from the balcony, some larger, none that much smaller. Mine skipped over the replicas of ancient architecture I did not recognize and over the synthstone reproduction of an early starship. Beyond the silvered starship, the golden pyramid glittered in the cold sun, and I took a deep breath. Even for me, visiting the ruins was hard.

Unbidden, the words of a song, Morgen's song, glittered through my thoughts. . . .

> ". . . though buds blossomed too quick, too true,
> and words we whispered flamed in vain
> against Old Earth's last reign and rain . . ."

Dialogue one: Had the ancients been Old Earth's last reign, the fruit of the tree of knowledge that had fruited too soon?

Dialogue two: Get it together. Morgen had nothing to do with the ancients or the cyb at your elbow who's looking for any possible key to Old Earth.

"Is there more?" asked Kemra.

I flushed, realizing that I'd spoken some of the words aloud. "It's more of a private song. I'm sorry. I hadn't meant to speak it aloud."

For a moment, her eyes seemed different. "That's all right," she said, and cleared her throat, before half-turning and gesturing toward the remaining houses of the enclave. "How many of these?"

"There are more than five hundred behind this barrier. Similar enclaves existed in every major city, but this was the first and only one that had a barrier. That's why it survived, I suppose."

Kemra moistened her lips.

"There were gardens with flowers, thousands of different kinds. We only have a few handfuls of those left, although most of the wildflowers survived. That says something."

"There aren't many flowers on Gates."

That didn't surprise me, but I answered. "If you didn't think it would upset the ecology, you could take some clips, some DNA samples."

"How could that upset the ecology?" She laughed. "The early settlers terraformed everything. More than ninety percent of the flora has an Old Earth DNA base."

Her acceptance of the casual reordering of an entire ecology upset me, but didn't surprise me—not with the kind of "our might makes your right" ethic the cybs seemed to espouse.

A pair of broad wings caught the corner of my eye, and out of habit I focused on the eagle, trying to mesh, to follow. . . .

"It's beautiful. We don't have anything like that on Gates." Kemra's words disrupted my concentration, and I dropped my eyes and scan.

"He is," I answered, glad to change the subject. "He's a hunter, and hunters have to be functionally beautiful."

"Do you think he's aware of how . . ." She did not finish the sentence, then added, "Are they really aware?"

"He's aware enough." I studied the circling avian for a time.

"How aware, do you think?"

"Enough to have basic self-concepts."

"Oh?"

"If I've got it right, this one thinks of himself as something like 'Sky-Wing-Search.'" I shrugged.

A moment of silence followed, as I suspected it might.

"Careful!" came the faraway caution from someone monitoring me. Crucelle?

"Nothing else has penetrated," I pulsed back, but got no answer.

"How do you know?" asked Kemra.

I had to shrug again. "I couldn't tell you, exactly. It's more a matter of feel."

Her eyes traversed from my face to the sky and back to me. "Not exactly verifiable."

"No, it's not. I'm part intuit, and it drives the rat-comps crazy, the way . . ." I left off the part about how Morgen had done the same to me.

For a time, we watched Sky-Wing-Search as he circled farther and farther westward into the higher hills that fronted the mountains. Kemra stood as close to me as she ever had, lost in following the eagle, and something was wrong, something missing, but I could not place it.

"What's that?" she asked abruptly.

That she even saw the slinking black shape streaking uphill toward the old park that held the only few areas of vegetation in klicks—besides the plastic trees—indicated boosted vision and a few other improvements.

"Vorpal." I had the rifle ready, but the predator was headed away from us, and that was fine with me.

"A vorpal? It's gone. You keep mentioning them. What are vorpals?"

"Vorpals are nasty predators that evolved/appeared since The Flight. Cross the independence of a wolf with the intelligence of a high primate, teeth that make knives seem dull, and the mindset of a Uksorissan—something like that, anyway."

"You allow something that dangerous to run free?" Kemra seemed surprised, even after all that I'd already said.

"It's not quite a question of allowing. Old Earth has this tendency to adapt. I'm not sure we'd like the vorpal's successor."

Again, for an instant, another puzzled expression crossed her face, only to be replaced with the mask of mild interest.

I wanted to scream at her, to tell her to really look at what she saw, but that wouldn't work. History has shown that it never has, and that realization depressed me even more. I checked the sun and my selfnet. "We should be heading back. Your pilot will be getting worried before too long, and it would be better that he doesn't."

We left the Cretan home in silence, but as I reracked the rifle and guided the electrocart back down the drive, Kemra cleared her throat.

I looked at her for an instant, then waited.

"You said you'd answer my question."

"About who lived here? The demis, of course. This was the enclave where Wayneclint lived."

"And you leave it like this?"

"There are things we shouldn't forget, either," I said softly, remembering my mother's rendition of *The Old Draff's Tale,* and, later, my first visit to Cherkrik. "We, most of all. That's the reason for the legend on the locial tower."

We drove back mainly in silence, except for a few questions Kemra asked about geography and water supplies.

Both Dienate and Kessek were waiting at the foot of the locial tower.

"Thank you for everything," I told Dienate. "I especially appreciated the Springfire."

"I thought you would." Dienate turned to Kemra. "I hope you found the ruins as instructive as we do."

"They were very . . . interesting."

I couldn't help but catch Dienate's disappointment, although her professional smile never wavered. "I'm glad you found them so," she answered Kemra without even a flicker of anything besides politeness and warmth.

"Thank you," I told Dienate again.

"You're welcome," she said, adding net-to-net, "I don't envy you, Coordinator. She's like ancient marble, and if they're all like that, we've got troubles."

"We got troubles," I answered on the net, nodding as I did so, and turning toward the cyb lander where Kessek waited.

"So how were the ruins, Subcommander?" asked Kessek as we walked up the ramp.

"Ruins. Very instructive. Our friends"—she looked at me—"have some impressive history. You might have appreciated them."

"Ruins are ruins. You ready to head back?"

"Very ready." Kemra shook her head.

We settled into the luxurious couches in silence.

Later, as the lander leveled off and headed southwest, Kemra rubbed her forehead and looked toward me. "You don't make it easy, do you?"

"I'm not in an easy position," I answered truthfully.

"How long have you been Coordinator?"

"Since your approach to Old Earth was noted." Should I have not answered the question truthfully, I wondered. A few questions to draffs or others in Parwon would have revealed the answer anyway, and the last thing I needed was for the cybs to question my honesty.

"Why were you selected?"

"The Consensus thought someone unencumbered would be better able to devote full energy to the situation."

"I can't believe you're unencumbered. Is this some transition?"

"My soulmate died three months ago."

"And that makes you a candidate for planetary Coordinator?"

"The Consensus committee could change its decision at any time." I laughed. "Maybe they will." She was right, in a way, though, as the flashback in the enclave had demonstrated. I wasn't operating as clearly as I should be.

"You don't act as though you want the position."

"No Coordinator does."

That stopped her for a moment, and she moistened her lips and frowned, glancing up at the screen for a time, her eyes glazed, her attention on the net, seeking and scanning data on Old Earth. None of it was surprising.

I leaned back and waited, as I monitored her data requests.

"What's that?" She gestured to the screen and the evenly spaced hummocks centered in the plains north of the Esklant Crossing. "Some renegade draffs hiding out?"

"Hardly. Draffs don't live away from the locials."

"Why not?"

"It's a little rough out there. I've told you about the vorpals and cougars, and that doesn't include the giant scorpions, snakes, and some very intelligent bears. It's safer nearer the locials. Anyway, that's a prairie dog town."

"A prairie dog town? Rodents made that?"

"It's a prairie dog town."

"I don't believe it."

I shrugged. "It's true."

"Could you take me to see that? And Viedras—he'd love to see something like that—assuming it's real. Could you take us to see it?"

"Who's Viedras?"

"Our naturalist."

Obviously, the idea was to keep me occupied and out of

touch as much as possible while the cybs readied their attack. And she clearly didn't believe my statement that draffs didn't live away from the locials, but they didn't, except for those that didn't live long.

Crucelle was off-system. He did sleep, sometimes. So I netlinked Arielle, and backplayed the conversation. "Your thoughts, darkangel?"

"So complimentary you are, Ecktor. That scheming cybnav has definitely gotten orders to keep you on the go, and she likes you in an odd way, which means she's putting more into it than she has to."

"Thank you. Do you think the town will reveal too much?"

"It's more likely to mislead her and the cybs. I'd calculate that they'd think it would show how we've totally lost control."

"I can't say no."

"You shouldn't. Not to the town visit," Arielle answered.

"Thanks." I turned in the seat to Kemra. "We can manage something, I'd guess."

"Where were you?"

"I'm sorry?" I managed to look puzzled.

"Your eyes sort of glazed over for a moment. You were here, and you weren't."

Great! She knew we had something like the overnet, but I didn't want her to realize its range, not yet, anyway. "I was thinking about prairie dogs and what we'd need."

"Need? They're rodents, aren't they?"

"You'll need your sidearm and the equivalent of a rifle—slugthrower variety. We can provide them, or you could even bring a half-squad of your armed marines."

A faraway pulse from Arielle added to my concerns. "Ecktor, I told you she was more than a little interested. You're Coordinator, remember?"

"For rodents?" asked Kemra.

"You'll see," I promised both of them. Then I leaned back in the supple couch and closed my eyes.

<<< XVI

After my day at the ruins, I decided to spend the next morning in the southern gorge. If it had been earlier in the year, I would have gone up to the Breaks, but there was already more than a meter of snow there, and I didn't want to fight bodily chill when I was trying to lift soul-cold.

I lingered over a third cup of tea, running my fingers across the polished flattened oval of adiamante that I'd brought back from my run days earlier. No matter how I held it, the niellen-deep blackness never lightened. Nor did the adiamante ever seem warmer or colder, and not even a diamond could scratch it. I suppose that was the way we demis wanted Old Earth to be, unchanging and unchangeable. Not that there wasn't a reason for that desire, since most change, at least in the ecosystem, usually was for the worse, but we'd also learned that change was inevitable and unstoppable—except at a cost higher than we could afford to pay. Even before the end of the Chaos Years, most of the ancient coastal cities had vanished under the waves—those that hadn't been devastated by the reawakening of the ring of fire and the red mist.

As the sky lightened, I set the adiamante in the center of the table and swallowed the last of the tea. My eyes crossed the holo of Morgen that hovered above the corner table, the one she had carved over the years from an ancient and gnarled bristlecone root. Her green eyes still questioned.

Was I doing right?

How would I know?

I shook my head and stood. Unlike Morgen, who *knew,* I had to struggle and grasp up from more mundane roots. Had our fates been reversed, she would have made a better Coordinator, a far better Coordinator. But we don't choose our lots that way. With a last glance at the miniature representation of the sandy-haired woman in dark green trousers and tunic and a carefree smile, I headed for the shower.

No . . . the cyb didn't really look like her at all.

The weather had held, and as soon as I preflighted the flitter, I was headed a hundred klicks south. Although the cedars and bushes had reclaimed the land, the path of the old highway below stood out clearly, especially where the ancients had removed bluffs and mountainsides. For millennia more it would remain a half-hidden pointer southward. There just wasn't any practical way to undo all the massive mountain modifications undertaken by the ancients.

The smaller plateau above the river where I set the flitter down was a good thousand meters lower than the house, and correspondingly warmer and sunnier. The sunshine and warmth I needed. The combination of the cyb navigator, the job of Coordinator, and my own losses were going to leave me with years of compensatory-time debts—assuming I survived to pay them.

After a moment, I shook my head, pushing away thoughts of job and past, and turned westward. More ruins I didn't need. After checking my jacket, my high boots, and the two long belt knives, I pulled on my gloves and began to hike toward the rim, less than a klick ahead.

My boots automatically carried me around the sagebrush and the smaller cacti interspersed irregularly along the plateau. The sun warmed my back as I walked, and my lips whistled a tune I thought I'd forgotten.

As I skirted a larger cactus—the kind that looked partly like a palm—whose name I never learned, I paused as a jackrabbit bounded from one low cedar to another with a speed I envied, a speed probably responsible for the species' survival in a time of even swifter and deadlier predators.

Ahead lay the pile of rock that formed an ideal vantage point for the gorge and the twisting river that had formed it and that had survived the manipulations of man in the Time of Troubles.

The plateau was too flat and even to suit vorpals normally, but I still scanned for them, and left the straps on the knife hilts unsnapped.

I studied the rocks as I neared them, ensuring my gloves were on tight. The faintest of clicks, well-below normal hearing range, alerted me, and I skirted the dark flat rock. One of the scorpions flash-hissed onto the dark surface, twenty centimeters of clawed tail and venom, all appetite, but I left it alone. Killing it would only have ten to thirty others hissing out after me, and the one horde had to be the only one in a klick or so. The area woulnd't support more. Scorpion packs—that was another thing the ancients wouldn't have believed.

The pack meant that there were more than a few other invisible fauna, but concealment was their best defense, and I saw none of the desert prawns or the sliders or anything else that the scorpions usually hunted.

I bounded up the rest of the rocks, slowing as I neared the top, and halted abruptly short of the edge as I saw the heavy black horns and the golden coat.

The kaliram clicked its front hoof on the stones, and a section of sandstone broke and slid onto the sandy detritus, then skidded downhill. The kaliram's red eyes glittered, and I could sense the black cloud of confusion flashing toward me.

My mental screens went up, enough that I only staggered, although most draffs and even some demis would have been stunned or dead from the sensory impact thrown by a mature beast.

Downhill, the scorpions' hisses died away, but they were too insensitive to be much more than stunned.

I dug in my boots and hoped that the ram would get the message.

When I did not fall, the kaliram stamped again, and another flash of blackness speared toward me. Prepared as I was, I stood, marshalling my defenses.

I didn't need them.

After several moments, the golden-fleeced kaliram lifted his head and needle-ended black horns. The red eyes flashed, and the thick lips revealed the knife-edged teeth.

I watched.

The kaliram licked its muzzle, then turned, and bounded across the rock scree, surefooted as its vegetarian ancestors, then angled down toward the river below and easier prey.

I laughed.

After studying the silver stream below, and watching an eagle and a raven skirmish across the blue skies of morning, I turned and began to walk back to the flitter. Soulchill or not, I was Coordinator, and the mess in Parwon was still waiting.

<<< XVII

Barely after I'd gotten airborne on my way to Parwon, as I climbed past Kohl Creek and away from the house, Keiko net-linked. "That Major Henslom was here. He wanted to take all his troops on a recreational hike into the hills. He called it a hike. I suggested that I'd need to inform you."

"He can do it, but find an area that doesn't have any prairie dog towns, and no concentrations of vorpals or kalirams."

"Such as?" Keiko asked dryly.

She was right. There weren't many.

"How about due north of Parwon along the track of the old highway? Then run a flitter with a screamer over it before they set out."

"I can handle that." She projected competence, and a smile. "Now, about Locatio. He says he can't clear the Ellay residential bloc until tomorrow, and that other majer, Ysslop, said that you promised today."

"Remind Locatio the Consensus Committee will reduce comptimes, increase allotments, whatever is *reasonably* necessary, but it's a Coordinator-deemed-necessary requirement."

"I told him that."

"Then tell him that if he wants the cybs to fry his locial first, he can screw around all he wants, and I'll put his rebuilding priorities below everything else."

"He might understand that."

"Furthermore, tell him I'm a crazy, grief-struck widower who's likely to do highly unreasonable things if he doesn't cooperate. And that the Consensus Committee picked me because they wanted a crazy, unreasonable Coordinator. Oh, and tell him that K'gaio even wanted me and agreed to the schedule I set."

"He will understand that." A hint of a laugh followed, and I imagined white teeth against her olive complexion.

"Is that all?"

"No. That cyb subcommander sent a messenger to confirm that you're going to see a prairie dog town. They want to bring a full squad of marcybs, and two officers."

"Fine. A full squad won't hurt. I'll need the big mag-shuttle, though."

"I think I can arrange that." Keiko paused, as if going down a list. "And Miris—he's the draff rep to the Committee—wants to meet with you. Something about permitting the cybs on-planet violating the Construct."

I sighed.

"I heard that. He'll be here at 1400. Oh, the bison shipments arrived, but there's a problem of reallocation of the rest of the food shipments because of the cybs' protein requirements."

"Have we got enough for the next two weeks?"

"Yes."

"That can wait."

"And a number of other items."

"Closed net?" I asked.

"Naturally. We're still secure, but they'll wait. Just so you know they're waiting, Coordinator."

I knew. Even before I'd reached Parwon and landed my poor flitter, trouble was knocking on the net.

It got worse. I got from the landing strip into Parwon and into the admin building before it did. I'd just reached the top of the stairs and was walking toward the Coordinator's office when Keiko net-alerted me.

"Coordinator," linked Keiko. "There's a pair of draffs here, and one was assaulted by one of the marcybs."

"When?"

"This morning, on her way to work at the components assembly bloc."

I pasted an expression of grave concern, as opposed to the anger I felt, as I walked toward the two draffs on the couch. The woman's left cheek was bruised and the man glared at me as he bounded to his feet. She rose more slowly.

"What are you going to do?" he demanded.

"Find out what happened, first," I answered with a calm

I didn't feel as I turned to the woman. "Can you tell me exactly what happened? I know you told Keiko, but I need to know."

"Her name is Nislaki," Keiko pulsed me. "His is Kaluna."

Nislaki took a breath. "We were in the park. The greencoats were marching down Yeats, and then they stopped and ran into the park for some sort of group exercise, and one of them knocked down Divis—"

"Divis is our son," the man explained.

"—and I picked up Divis and asked the man who did it to be more careful, and he just hit me."

"He told her that she was useless draff baggage and to get out of the way," added Kaluna.

"Did their leader say or do anything?"

"Nothing."

"And then you came here?" I asked.

"We took Divis to my mother. She lives in a cinqplex on Edson."

Nislaki's deep brown eyes met mine, and I could sense her shock that such an incident could occur. If the cybs were successful, she'd be more than shocked; she'd be dead, or worse.

"What are you going to do?" asked Kaluna.

I looked at him. "What needs to be done."

They both looked away.

Keiko smiled, and gestured to them. "If you have any questions about what the Coordinator does, get in touch with me in a few days."

That was safe enough. In a few days, it was likely to be all over, one way or another.

"I know," Keiko agreed through the link. "But what are you going to do?" Today, she wore a gray vest of some sort, but still black trousers and a paler gray high-necked shirt.

"Have you get someone to contact Henslom and ask him to stop by," I answered as I watched Nislaki and Kaluna walk toward the wide stairs.

"He won't do that."

"I know, but first we ask."

She shook her head, and I wanted to shake mine, too. The cybs were trying to provoke us, and it would get worse. The problem wasn't one insolent marcyb, unfortunately. The line marcybs weren't insolent. That took a direct net order from Henslom or an officer.

I walked into the Coordinator's office. Although the sunlight poured in the south windows, I still felt cold inside. My metabolism was fine, and the temperature in the office was probably too warm, if anything.

At my request, Keiko had installed a standard compensatory-time visual screen and keyboard in my office, although I could netlink to it if I chose.

After dropping into the swivel chair behind the desk I really didn't need, I used the boost to link with Rhetoral. He was on Ell Prime, while Elanstan was on Ell Delta. "How is it coming?" I asked.

After the string of profanity, unusual for him, Rhetoral explained. "Someone falsified the entries. Delta was never time-proofed. They just flipped the breakers, sealed the hatches and left. We've got solid contacts welded in place, freeze-dried electronics, and the most obsolete mess you ever saw."

"Obsolete? You think they never used the system during the Jykserian incident?"

"They couldn't have. I don't know when the station was last operational. We're basically boxing it and replacing it bit by bit, but we don't have enough parts." Rhetoral had settled down, the longsword of his soul back in its scabbard.

"Lift them by magshuttle. Cannibalize a locial system." I called up the local system requirements and the cross-links and made a quick decision. "Either Thun or Machaga or even Chitta."

"Chitta? K'gaio would have a fit."

"Let her—unless she wants to be Coordinator. We're going to need every ell system we can muster."

"You sound so encouraging, Ecktor."

"I took their head navigator and chief spy through the Cherkrik ruins yesterday. Noting much—except she wants to see a prairie dog town."

I caught the sense of a low whistle before Rhetoral responded. "Wayneclint was right, it seems like. They really are slow on the nonlinear."

"Arielle still calculates, based on their reaction to the Hybernium, that they'll attack. Nothing less than a perceived unitary probability of their total destruction will change that decision. And we can't provide information on that level. That's a threat under the Construct."

"So why are they waiting?"

"They're still rebuilding power stocks and mapping, and I'd intuit that they don't have all the technology we do, and they'd like it. Call it greed." I paused. "I'll let the liocial admin offices in Thun, Machaga, and Chitta know that you've got priority lift."

"Thanks."

Then I looked toward the half-open door. "Keiko?"

"Yes, ser?"

"Come on in with your list. And shut the door."

She brushed a lock of dark hair off her eyebrow as she sat down across from me, her dark eyes deep with concern. "Rechar is taking your message to Majer Henslom. I told him to be careful."

I nodded. "What's first?"

"The number two big magshuttle will be ready at 0800 tomorrow. Lieza will be the pilot, and I'm waiting for a return call from Subcommander Kemra."

"Next?"

"Locatio got the bloc cleared, and the marcybs are settling in. He says you owe him."

"He's right. I do, if I live long enough for him to col-
lect."

Keiko gave me one of those level stares.

"Bad joke," I said out loud.

"You won't get out of comptime that easily, Coordinator."

Having heard of Keiko's handling of K'gaio—she was
as much K'gaio's representative as my assistant—I had
this feeling Keiko would drag me back from the dead to
make sure I completed my quota. She was competent
enough that she might actually manage it.

Keiko raised her eyebrows.

"All right. What's next?" I braced for the rest of her list.

After Keiko left more than forty minutes later, I looked
at the screen before me, since using the eye-resting screen
was easier for admin trivia than concentrating on holding the images mentally. And centralizing the record-
keeping certainly took less power and equipment than
holding open two-way transmissions to every demi-that
owed the system. Besides, that kind of link would have required personal comptime and just added to what I owed
the locial.

Even being chief negotiator, or spokesman, or whatever for Old Earth didn't relieve me, not in my mind, anyway, from my allotted compensatory-time. I reached for
the keyboard, then straightened. Much as I dearly wanted
to whittle it down, compensatory-time would have to wait
. . . a long, long time, the way matters were proceeding,
and by then I'd owe enough that I'd die with a comptime
debt.

"Crucelle?"

It took a moment for him to uplink, or break whatever
connection he had.

"Yes, Ecktor?"

"Start diverting locial critical production into the hardened stores."

"We started yesterday."

"You're more of an optimist than I am."

"That was Arielle."

"Our darkangel. Your darkangel," I corrected.

The screen beeped, and a flashing icon on the upper left corner of the screen coincided with the mental "power interruption" alarm that rang in my thoughts.

"Another crisis. Reads cyb all over it. Link later." I broke off and tried to scan the system.

Locial power systems were nearly foolproof and tamperproof, but outages did occur. The link had offered no hints, and I could sense the oversystem, outside the admin building, was still operational. I bolted upright. At the moment there weren't any other demis in the buildling, except Keiko. That didn't surprise me. There was no sense in being at possible ground zero when it wasn't necessary.

Standing at my door already, Keiko looked at me as I hurried out.

"I don't know, but it's here in the building," was my answer to the unspoken question. I don't know if I took the stairs two or three at a time, but I was on the main level fast enough.

Outside the screen room on the main level, I passed Vyldia—draff, but draff by choice, and bright enough. Her once-long blond hair was cut short, almost like a marcyb.

"Hello, Vyldia."

"Hello." She looked down, but I was already well past and heading for the closed ramps down to the mainboards and powerlinks. I slipped into the ramp well, lit only by red lights, and eased inside the door at the top of the ramp leading down to the first level, senses extended and hearing torqued up.

Breathing as quietly as possible, I paused inside the

closed door, and let my vision adjust to the dimness of the emergency red-lighting.

Silence—except for breathing on the main access bay in the middle of the net repeater filters. Silence, except for the muted click of a slugthrowers's lever being switched to shred.

I dropped flat and used the overrides to kill the emergency red-lighting as well—about the only vestige of net-control left to me in the building's powerless maintenance levels.

Rrrrrrrtttttttttt. . . . Projectile fragments sprayed head-high, then dropped to knee-high, uncomfortably close to my head.

As the echoes died away, I inched forward, hugging the right-hand side of the ramp and imitating a snake sliding down through the darkness toward its prey. I stepped-up hearing and metabolism.

Another click—signifying the magazine switch to solid projectiles—and another burst of solid slugs fragmented not that far overhead, as the cyb ducked out of the middle corridor and hosed the corridor again, the fragments imbedding in the receptive hard insulated finish of the corridor. If I'd been on the right side, I'd have gathered enough holes to qualify as an antique sieve or whatever.

When the pin clicked on the empty chamber, I *moved,* ignoring the pain and the knives of red that shot through me as muscles and nerves coordinated the step-up at the top edge of physical capability.

The cyb didn't even get his weapon up as a block before I reached him. Three blows were enough. Then I retched over the other side of the corridor, even before I released the overrides on the emergency lighting.

White flashes flickered across my vision for a moment, and I had to take a handful of deep breaths. After that, I looked down—wished I'd looked sooner.

The half-dead figure on the floor wore a cyb-originated

night-suit and matching goggles. The goggles hadn't helped that much because they were light-enhancers, and they're not that much good when there's no light. What bothered me most was the high thick collar and the helmet with the bulge at the back.

Despite the cyb's crushed throat and temple, his hands had begun to move, and to grasp for the holstered handgun. Good thing I was still in step-up, or I could have been dead or wounded.

"Compboost . . ." I muttered, and snapped his neck with my boot heel. Another wave of pain, nausea, and white dots washed across me, and I leaned against the corridor wall. There wasn't anything left in my gut to lose.

The man twitched one last time, but even the compboost couldn't revive someone with a smashed temple, or move the limbs of a body with a crushed spinal cord.

I staggered to the door to the lower ramps and manually locked the access from the lower levels. I didn't need any more witnesses to the carnage I was going to find elsewhere in the maintenance level.

"Crucelle, get a cleanup detail over here." I pushed the net because the repeater system in the building was dead.

"Here?"

"Power level of the admin building." I filled him in on the details.

"You can't keep this quiet, Ecktor."

"Announce a malfunction, and two unfortunate deaths from the equipment failure. I'm the only one here."

"Who's on the net?"

"Anyone who could be on this level should know better than to spread rumors." That was both statement and threat, and anyone who had the ability to infiltrate the uppernet should have understood both. Besides, anyone on that level would use net-to-net, and my concern was not letting the draff community know immediately, especially after the mess between Majer Henslom and Nislaki that I still hadn't resolved.

I left the dead cyb where he was and went to the main boards. The trail of smashed composite and plastic covers was obvious enough. So were the two dead draff techs. I had seen both before, but didn't know either the man or woman by name. The cybs still viewed the draffs as cattle, and that bothered me. They hadn't learned anything in millennia.

"Crucelle. There are three. One of theirs, and two of ours. Let Locatio know. They'll try something there tomorrow, most likely while I'm out doing the prairie dog town."

"To see if the response is the same elsewhere?"

"That's my guess."

"Mine, too. What do you want done?"

"If it's possible, I want the next one to disappear without a sign."

"We'll try." A pause followed. "It'll be another fifteen before we're there."

"That's fine. I'll do what I can."

Although it hadn't been that long since I'd done mech maintenance, I felt like I fumbled my way to finding the bypasses and getting partial power back into the building, enough for light and the basic net.

The cyb had been very crude. He'd just started smashing things, and if you smash enough things, something usually breaks, and someone investigates. That was what he, or his superiors, had had in mind. It was crude—designed to prod us—and not even designed to be successful. It was designed more to see our response, both technically and politically.

We weren't going to provide any obvious response, but the compboost would have relayed more than I would have liked.

I dropped out of step-up, trying not to shake too hard,

found some supplies, and cleaned up the personal mess I'd made, then waited until Crucelle arrived with three others. One muscular woman I didn't know stayed by the door.

His red hair highlighted Crucelle all the way down the maintenance ramp, with Gerag and Indire behind him. They carried equipment satchels and a rolled package that would turn into three opaque and grim-looking bags long enough for the bodies.

"There's a maintenance truck by the loading dock," Crucelle explained, a hint of pain in the deep green eyes. I worried that he was too sensitive, that his formality would not insulate him enough from what would ensue.

Gerag and Indire slipped past us and headed toward the mainboards.

"When you get an I.D. check, let Keiko know, and she'll notify the families—or mates."

"What about you?" asked Crucelle.

"I have to see a majer about the conduct of his marcybs."

"Lucky you. How's the satellite system?" He gestured skyward.

"Delta's still out, and Rhetoral's fuming."

"How long? Can we afford to wait?" asked Arielle over the net like the gathering storm she could be.

"They still haven't done anything, not to justify that. Do you want to destroy every demi on Old Earth?" I asked softly.

"Why are we so vulnerable that way?" mused Crucelle. "Sometimes it doesn't seem so pro-survival."

"It's been that way from The Flight. You know that as well as I do, and it's not individually pro-survival."

"Damned genes."

"We are what we are." What that was happened to be another question, and now wasn't the time to ask or try to answer it. The only problem was that there wasn't any incentive to answer it except in times of crisis.

I walked up the ramp.

The muscular demi nodded. "You want this sealed until they're done, Coordinator?"

"Yes. Until Crucelle's happy with how things look."

She nodded, and I stepped out into the main floor corridor.

Thirty draffs waited. I thought I saw Miris in the back.

"We've had a power interruption," I began, stating the obvious. "For some reason, there were some explosions, and we have a team investigating. Leader Crucelle or I will let you know when we have a better idea of exactly what happened." I hated the lie, but waited.

"How about the . . . technicians?"

"We should know shortly," I temporized. "There's at least one fatality, but I won't speculate further right now because we don't know how far the damage went."

"When was the last time this sort of incident occurred?" asked Miris from the back of the group. Trust him to ask something like that.

"At least several decades," I answered, except it was more like several dozen decades. "We'll let you know."

"Majer Henslom?" I asked Keiko on the net, glad that I didn't have to push the transmission, because I was exhausted, and my legs felt like lead as I climbed the stairs back to the office.

"He sent a messenger to indicate that he could be found at the residence bloc." Her response was acid-tinged.

"Insolence to provoke a response which they can then use as a self-justifying pretext to apply massive force to us." I paused. "Pass all of this on to the Committee, and make sure Elanstan and Rhetoral know, and K'gaio, Locatio—they'll try something there—and Crucelle and Arielle. Don't hit Crucelle until he finishes down below."

Keiko had some cheese and crackers laid out on a platter in the middle of the big desk when I reached the third floor. Beside the platter was a mug of high energy concentrate.

"Eat something before you go. You haven't eaten since before dawn."

"How do you know?" I snapped.

She just looked at me—black on gray—and I had to grin. Then I ate some crackers, and took a slow swallow from the mug. The concentrate tasted like acidified mud, except mud tasted better because it was buffered. I didn't quite gulp my way through it all, but there wasn't anything left before long.

"Thank you," I admitted.

"You're welcome, Coordinator."

I glanced out the windows. High hazy clouds were beginning to form, a sign that the weather would change again, probably with snow in a day or two.

"Now to see Majer Henslom." Not that I wanted to, but, if I saw him, I could restrict the insolence to a present issue and make myself the focus, rather than requiring him to assault someone else.

I decided to dramatize the issue more and pulled off my plain leather working jacket and replaced it with Arielle's black cloak.

"Good luck," offered Keiko as I stepped out of the office.

"If I don't get shot on the spot, that will be luck enough."

"Stop trying to avoid doing your comptime." But her smile was little more than perfunctory and revealed more than it concealed.

Even I didn't want to avoid it that much.

There were still draffs milling around on the lower level when I went down, but no one asked me anything more. They looked, but they knew I'd said what I was going to say. That was the way it was.

Outside, I didn't need to close the cloak, not with the

calm and the slight warming. I walked eastward, taking another look at the statue of the unknown draff caught in the mindblaze.

"Neither to threaten nor to destroy in anticipation." The credo drawn from the Construct made life difficult at times like these, damned difficult.

"Of those to whom much is given is much required." Those were Morgen's words, her way of accepting the Construct, words taken from something much older.

I shook my head and kept walking.

With my net full out, I could sense the transmissions as soon as I was in sight of the residence bloc. I almost wished I hadn't worn the black cloak, but part of the job of Coordinator was being the most visible target. That supposedly allowed everyone else to get on with the work. I hoped it worked that way, but I had my doubts.

". . . demi on the way . . . moving quickly. The one in that black cloak. He's alone."

"Majer . . . the demi's headed in . . ."

"I'll go out and greet him."

As the transmissions promised, Henslom came out of the residence bloc to greet me. "Coordinator."

"Majer Henslom. I understand you've been having discipline problems with your troops."

"I don't know of any."

"Oh?" I paused. "Then you *ordered* your marcyb to strike Nislaki this morning?"

"I don't recall issuing any such order." Henslom's eyes narrowed with the lie. Either he had, or one of the junior marcyb officers had forced the attack on Nislaki. The marcyb couldn't have made such a statement unaided.

"Then, if you didn't order it, you must have a discipline problem—unless, of course, your standing orders permit the abuse of bystanders." I smiled. "They don't, do they?"

Henslom stood silently for a moment, but he didn't use his net.

I waited.

"You know, honored Coordinator, I do believe I understand the reasons for The Flight somewhat more personally." He still smiled, thinking he had deceived me.

"Perhaps you do. Now . . . about your discipline problem. I believe Nislaki would accept a written apology from you, since you are the responsible party, and I would suggest that the guilty party be returned to his ship—immediately. If you have a problem with scheduling a lander, we would be more than happy to supply transportation."

The majer was seething. That I could tell, but he also didn't have the backing of his superiors—not yet. And moving one marcyb body wouldn't change a thing. My intuit senses all said that now was not the time to acknowledge the cybs' accomplishments with their troops.

I'd also have to be careful not to venture anywhere near the line of fire of the marcyb squad that would be accompanying Kemra and the naturalist the next morning. Another worry, as if I weren't piling them up quickly enough already.

With a nod, I turned and walked away, ignoring the side-transmissions of the junior officers.

". . . arrogant bastard . . ."

". . . coldcock him or shred him . . . were the majer . . ."

The cybs hadn't changed, not a bit, and I had to be the one to inherit the legacy of Wayneclint's partial clemency. Lucky me.

I pulsed Keiko.

"Yes, ser?"

"I've changed my mind. Give Majer Henslom maps for the Aquarius/Severe Wash—and don't bother with a screamer."

"Are you sure?"

"He couldn't see the sun on Mercury's dayside with a ten-meter telescope."

"As you wish, Coordinator." Keiko disagreed with my decision, but that was why I was Coordinator. Besides, marcybs weren't draffs.

Miris was doubtless waiting, and who knew what else. I kept walking.

The draff representative was waiting, but he was alone, for which I was thankful.

I gestured toward the office. "Would you like anything to drink, Representative Miris?"

"No, thank you, Coordinator." His voice was a pleasant bass.

Keiko closed the door behind us with enough of a gentle thud to ensure that Miris knew the door was shut.

Miris turned one of the green chairs so that it faced the desk directly, and then sat on the edge, not quite so stiffly as Majer Henslom had. "Your aide told you my purpose."

"You believe letting the cybs land on Old Earth violates the understanding behind the Construct."

"That's a fair summary. The incident this morning"—he stroked the dark beard—"seems to prove that the cybs haven't changed since The Flight. What do you think?" His eyes were dark and intent. Why he hadn't opted for demi training I didn't understand, but that had been his choice.

"What I *think* isn't the question under the Construct," I pointed out. "I cannot strike in anticipation, nor can I offer threats. I also can't bar any visitor from Old Earth merely because I mistrust him or her."

"I thought that would be what you said." He smiled, faintly. "How do you plan to protect the locials?"

"We are implementing contingency plans." I shrugged. "It might not hurt to have people review emergency evacuation routes."

Miris nodded. "So you will destroy them."

"I could not predict any action on those lines. I am still working quite hard under the Construct—"

Miris laughed. "You're amusing, Coordinator. They picked you because you're crazy enough to bend the Construct without breaking it. What you did to that cyb agent—I do have access to some things as the locial draff representative—was as close to a threat to them as possible even under your interpretations. And they chose not to see it."

"Perhaps they will. I can't sign death warrants for most of the demis by taking any further action now."

"Your people took it too far. Encoding passive resistance genetically, even into all the draffs . . . that was suicide."

"No. Preemptive warfare nearly destroyed Old Earth and has annihilated several of the former colonies. The Construct works. It has a high price, but it works."

"For you."

"It works for you. That's why everyone got the mods. Do you want to be turned into the equivalent of marcybs?"

Miris stood. "I didn't expect much more, but you know we're concerned." He walked toward the door.

"I know. I'm concerned, too." I stood.

"For what it may be worth, Coordinator, I'd rather have you behind that desk than anyone else." The draff rep paused, his hand on the door frame. "Try not to wait until the de-energizers are slagging the place, though."

"I have to try not to let it get that far."

He nodded and opened the door. He nodded to Keiko on his way to the stairs.

How long could I afford to wait before officially deciding that Majer Henslom wouldn't issue an apology or "act" on the morning's "incident" with Nislaki? A day? Two?

I shook my head. I needed to link with Locatio and see if we could figure out a better strategy for Ellay.

Outside the office, Keiko frowned, but said nothing as I walked to the window and looked down at the park and the winter-browned grass.

<<< XVIII

The navigator·stretched out on the narrow couch in the small cabin with the temp-controlled-wall colors, waiting for the net conference. One hand brushed back sandy hair, and she frowned as the chime rang, both in her head and on the invisible speaker beside the door.

"Commander's conference," announced MYL-ERA. "Report."

"Kemra," the nav announced, waiting as the others reported.

"All on net," MYL-ERA announced.

"Subcommander Kemra. You spent time on the previous day with the demi planetary coordinator." Gibreal's words were cold-forged.

"My report is on the net. I'd be happy to answer questions."

"You indicated the probability of higher technology. On what do you base that?"

"As I indicated . . ." the cybnav paused, "an array of subtle signs. . . ."

"No weapons, no systems that produce miraculous results?" Gorum's words dripped with acid, hissing as they fell upon the net.

"Item one," snapped Kemra. "Houses that have remained intact for five millennia, perhaps longer—yet no sign of such structures outside one area of designated ruins. Item two: instantaneous communications that I could barely sense but not even analyze basics. Some transmissions were not even detectable. Item three: none of the draffs live outside the locial areas. Item four: the extraordinarily stable and long-lived culture. Item five: the ability to respond to our arrival within hours. Item six: a functioning satellite planetary navigation system. Item seven—do I have to go on?"

"Does anyone else have something more *concrete* to support the subcommander's listing?" asked Gorum, words now coated so thickly with honey that several anonymous gagging sounds permeated the net.

"Gorum . . . your agent in the Deseret locial was neutralized," announced Gibreal. "Despite the fact that he was a trained systems technician, the entire locial control detected his entry and isolated him in one structure before he could accomplish more than minor damage." Gibreal paused. "The last impulses from the compboost indicate that he was killed by the demi Coordinator—by hand. Their draff commnets have only indicated a maintenance failure, and no one questions it." Gibreal's words got harder. "Systems?"

"Yes, ser?"

"What's your success in tapping their nets and links?"

"The same as the subcommander's. To date we've been unable to tap anything except the draff public comm freqs and the totally open-weave transportation traffic net, and that's designed to be penetrated on the top level. We can't go below that."

"Why not?"

"We don't know. If we knew . . ."

"What's stopping you?"

"First, the frequencies shift continuously, and they're entwined multiples to begin with. Second, it's all encrypted, and even the encryption changes continuously. We can't even figure out the basis of the encryption, and that's with the combined analytics of the entire fleet.

Third, from what we've tapped on the transport traffic control net, they're using a proprietary data compression module."

"You're saying that they're better cybs than we are."

A withering silence froze the net.

"Yes, ser."

"Honesty's cold comfort, Systems."

"Yes, ser."

"Let's just fry the bastards and go home," snapped Gorum.

"Bad idea," the nav found herself replying.

"That was one of the mission goals, wasn't it?"

"I don't dispute that," answered Kemra. "But think about our welcome. No medical quarantine, no tests— just an offering of food and drink and some general information."

"So?"

"Don't you see? This people's actions bespeak a form and depth of confidence—or arrogance—that suggests we'd better be careful."

"The ancient Mandi thought their empire was the center of the universe, and they had more culture and sophistication than the Anglas. The Mandi went down under the bigger guns. I'd suggest we use the guns and forget about culture," said Gorum.

"Is the marine commander correct, MYL-ERA?" asked Gibreal.

"Yes, Commander. We can blast anything on the planet at present. There are no defense screens in place. Interrogative objective?" MYL-ERA's tone was cool, carrying the sense of stale refrigerant.

The cybnav gagged, but kept that feeling clear of the net.

"The cities—those minuscule energy concentrations that wouldn't be villages on Gates—after one or two go, they'll agree," insisted Weapons.

"Observational and behavioral profiles indicate that

analysis is flawed." The sensed odor of refrigerant chilled the net more with MYL-ERA's response.

"Explicate."

"Old Earth has nothing Gates needs—except the technology in those cities. To date, no cybsenser can penetrate that technology, and the probabilities remain that effective use of that technology is unlikely without demi help, specifically the help of the ones called comps. The comps refuse to assist, and the draffs know nothing. The draffs appear restricted to the locials, but the demis appear to be able to live anywhere. The death of the last agent indicates that any isolated cyb can be killed without triggering the sensis."

"Get to the point."

A net-sense of an old-human shrug followed. "Destroying the cities will hurt the draffs, but not the demis. The probability approaches unity that one or more technological replication stations exist in locations unknown and unsensible by our equipment."

"Frug . . ." muttered Gorum. "You're saying that we can't force them, and we can't destroy them. So exactly what are we supposed to do?"

"If they were confident of destroying us or could do so or wanted to," answered Gibreal, "they would already have acted. So we have nothing to lose by waiting and seeing what else we can discover while we amass the energy stores necessary for our primary mission.

"For now, the nav will return planetside, with the naturalist, and attempt to use her influence with the demi Coordinator to gain greater advantages, such as the key to the main demi systems." After a pause, Gibreal added, "We will continue the power-up."

<<< **XIX**

I actually had my flitter secured below the locial tower before Lieza and the magshuttle drifted in, or before the cyb lander had thundered out of the gray sky and rumbled down the strip.

I checked the knife and slugthrower on opposite sides of my belt and then sealed the flitter. As I walked toward the magshuttle through the unsettled air that mixed comparative warmth and chill, Keiko caught me on the net.

"Coordinator?"

"Yes, Keiko? What's the status on Delta?"

"K'gaio isn't happy about your cannibalizing equipment from three locials, but she's not complaining too loudly. Elanstan thinks that they might have the station operational in two to three days."

"That's too long."

"That's what it will take." She paused only minutely before she added, "That's not why I linked. The cybs are headed out along the lower Aquarius trail."

"With Majer Henslom?" I glanced toward the north. Was there a hint of distant clouds?

"Yes, ser."

"Good. I'd like them to get a solid feel for Old Earth."

"You still don't want a screamer?"

"They're big boys," I pointed out.

"Yes, ser." Her disapproval—black on black—was clear. She still thought I was wrong, and maybe I was, but I didn't see any changes in the cyb attitude toward us, and without any changes, they were still going to try to wipe out us demis, seize our technology, enslave the draffs, and claim it was all justified by The Flight.

She also thought I was bending the Construct, and perhaps I was doing that, too, but the Construct didn't say anything about having to protect people from the ecosystem or the environment. It just said you couldn't provoke, threaten, or take the first step in a destructive action, no matter what the result *might* be. It also said, both fortunately and unfortunately, that you could not act contrary to the Power Paradigms. That precluded moral compromises, which was what most aggressors demanded. Working within those parameters was almost impossible—and sometimes it had proved so. That's why more than half the eleven historical Coordinators hadn't survived their charges.

I stopped by the base of the tower and waited for Lieza to float-taxi the shuttle to the area just north of the tower. While it might have been a quarter of the size of the cyb troop landers—not that I'd seen any cyb landers other than troop landers—the magshuttle was still big enough to make a flattened maize cake out of a careless Coordinator.

We still don't believe in all the excessive warning and safety devices that were another contributing factor that led to the SoshWars. Personally, I thought that attribution was just Masc propaganda, since men tend to be more careless. But we have so little left from that time that it's hard to say what happened. We do know that when safety devices exceed five percent of a device's resource contribution or weight, then there's either a fault in the design or in the operator, or both. Basically, if you can't operate well-designed equipment without safeties on safeties on safeties, you shouldn't be trying it.

I waited until the magshuttle settled onto the permacrete and the hatch door slid open, then climbed up out of the light swirling winds and poked my head into the cockpit area.

"You cut things close, Coordinator," said Lieza. "There's a big storm coming in from the north. Won't get where we're going until late in the day." She paused. "Do you really want to see a prairie dog town?"

"The cyb navigator and naturalist do."

"You didn't discourage them?" The redhead glanced at the screens and then back at me. "Their lander's on final."

"I don't have to, under the Construct."

"You're as bad as a cybschemer."

"I appreciate the compliment."

"I didn't quite mean it that way."

"I know," I told her. "I know. I'm going to meet our friends." I ducked out of the cockpit, stepped out onto the permacrete, and walked northward to where the lander would stop.

The permacrete vibrated as the cyb lander rolled off the strip and turned back north toward the tower.

After it came to a halt, the olive-black metal ramp whined down, and Subcommander Kemra and a thinner and taller man descended. Both wore informal greens under the heavy brownish-green winter jackets. Kemra wore the gold starburst of a subcommander on her collars. Her companion wore no rank insignia.

"Greetings," I offered.

"Hello." Kemra gestured to the brown-haired and gangly man. "Viedras is our naturalist."

I bowed slightly.

"I appreciate the opportunity," Viedras offered, his words spaced deliberately.

Two cyb officers appeared—one beside Viedras and one beside Kemra.

"Force Leader Babbege and Subleader Cherle." Kemra inclined her head to each in turn. Babbege was a whip-corded woman a centimeter or two taller than I was, while Cherle was a block of a man more Kemra's height. Both had the typical flat-eyed look of cyb soldiers.

On the permacrete behind them stood the cyb squad, each cyb with a rifle.

"I notice you are carrying a weapon," observed Babbege.

"Around the prairie dog towns, that's generally a good idea," I admitted. "Rifle slugthrowers for your troops should be sufficient."

"Ah . . ." began Viedras. "According to the older references, prairie dogs were a unique species of rodent. . . ."

"They're still unique, and they're still rodents, but their teeth are razor sharp, and they mass ten to fifteen kilos each. Some of the males are bigger." I glanced toward the magshuttle, then toward Kemra. "Ready, Subcommander?"

"A fifteen kilo rodent?" asked Viedras.

"Yes."

"You wanted to see them, Viedras," Kemra added. "We won't see them from here." Her eyes passed over me as though I didn't exist.

So I was in the middle of the procession to the magshuttle, behind Kemra and Viedras and followed by the marcybs.

The dozen marcybs took the rear seats in the shuttle, two abreast, and the two officers sat down in front of them, leaving several seats between the soldiers and Kemra, Viedras, and me. I half-wished I were in the cockpit, but my job was guide and host.

"Ready, Coordinator?" asked Lieza, looking back through the open hatch.

"Lift off," I said aloud.

Unlike the initial pressed-back acceleration of the cyb lander, the magshuttle's departure was smoother and more gradual. Our seats weren't quite as comfortable as the officers' seats in the cyb lander, but a lot more so than the troop seats.

"I suppose we'd better go over the background of the prairie dogs," I began after Lieza had leveled off and headed the magshuttle northeast.

"That might be a good idea." Kemra's words were cold.

I couldn't blame her for her anger at discovering prairie dogs weren't just rodents, but far larger than their ancestors. The cybs needed to see the town firsthand, and giving the entire story first might well have violated the Construct, if it were construed as a threat, as well as discouraged them from seeing what they needed to see. Besides, the prairie dogs were cute-*looking* huge rodents.

"As I indicated, the prairie dogs are genetic descendants of the original rodents of the same name. Their mass is also somewhere in the neighborhood of fifty to a hundred times that of their ancestors."

"How is that possible?" asked Viedras.

"They're mammals, and we theorize that they're offshoots of survivors of the Thimeser virus."

"You mentioned the virus earlier," said Kemra. "What exactly was it?"

"A further modification of the immune-system related diseases that preceded the SoshWars," I explained. "Something triggered more massive modifications in the Chaos Years, and in some species there were deliberate DNA modifications. That's how we ended up with, we think, the vorpals and the kalirams—among other things." I cleared my throat, trying not to think about the cybs being led along the Aquarius trail by Majer Henslom. "Anyway, some of the results bred true, and the prairie dogs almost overran the higher plains for a time before the ecosystem reached a balance. Their aggressiveness is generally restricted to their perceived territory, except in the breeding seasons, or when a member of the family screams for help. This is not breeding season, but we'll have to be careful.

They look like big furry toys. They're not. They can be very dangerous."

"What do they eat?" asked Viedras.

"Like us, they're omnivores. They're pretty good mousers or ratters. They're good at finding desert prawns in the hot weather, and they can take on most snakes. They also like cactus fruits, seeds, berries. . . ." I shrugged. "They can eat and digest the Degen plains olives."

"You say they're dangerous. Why?"

I thought I'd explained, but I expanded. "They're communal. Once they're threatened, you may find most of the guard males and females chasing you, and they're quicker than they look and their teeth are sharp. If you don't get into their territory, except close to breeding times, they'll just watch."

"How far back have they been breeding true?"

"We don't have records that far. Some time after the Chaos Years and The Flight. The original progenitors started east of the mountains, actually in the area near the Cherkrik ruins, and they've spread east and west from there."

Most of Viedras's questions I could answer. Some I couldn't. I had no idea of the differences in genetic structure from the original and extinct prairie dogs. There wasn't any way to compare since we didn't have any verifiable genetic material from the original species.

Kemra half-listened and half-looked at the destination screen on the bulkhead before her.

Lieza interrupted the questioning. "We're starting down, Coordinator."

I sat back and took a deep breath. Viedras shifted his weight in the seat, but I didn't look in his direction. I didn't want to answer more questions at that point.

Lieza set the lander down on hard and flat ground almost eight hundred meters north of the newest hummocks.

"Why did you set down so far away?" asked Viedras, with a touch of a whine, as he stepped down into the high grass. Some naturalist he was, but maybe he'd been in low ship-gee for too long.

"If we set down closer to the perimeter, we'd wait longer for them to return to their normal guard status. Also, the north side has the newer burrows, and that makes it easier to calculate the territoriality line." I surveyed the expanse of grass that separated us from the town.

Even from more than a half a klick away, the embanked mounds that constituted the prairie dog burrows were impressive, rising clear of the chest-high grasses. Viedras walked slightly ahead and to my left, pausing every few meters to use the recording device/scanner he carried. Kemra was to his left. Half the marcybs were on the left flank, with Babbege—the others on the right, with Cherle.

As we neared the town, I kept scanning for other predators, but could sense none. I pulsed Lieza. "Do you have the scanners on?"

"Do kalirams have hoofs?"

"And?"

"It's clean. We made enough noise to clear out any vorpals anyway. Too flat for kalirams."

Viedras paused and bent down to inspect something. "Hmmmm."

We waited. Then he straightened as if he hadn't stopped at all and continued scanning or recording.

From a hundred meters, the burrows were more impressive, rising two and a half meters and forming an undulating rampart.

When we reached seventy meters, I motioned for the line to halt.

The outliers were sitting on the corner burrows, perched on their hind legs as I guess prairie dogs had from the beginning. Their well-groomed brown fur glistened even under the gray light of the oncoming storm. Their heads swiveled in quick, jerky movements, taking in the grass-lands around their town.

"They are attractive animals," murmured Kemra.

At least she hadn't called them cute.

There was a single eagle circling under the high gray clouds, but one eagle wasn't a danger, except to a pup, and there wouldn't be any small pups loose this late in the year.

Farther to the west, the clouds were darker, lower, and headed our way—the storm Lieza had mentioned.

I gestured. "There's an outlier—a guard, if you will, at each corner of the town. You can't see the one in the center of the town, but there's one burrow that's higher, and there's another young male there."

"Are these guards always male?" Viedras asked, looking up from his equipment.

"No. About two thirds are male, but some are female, probably those females who won't breed in the year ahead, or maybe those who haven't, or can't, and have to provide some service to the community."

"You don't know?" Viedras sounded both whiny and incredulous.

"No. We don't. We know that the female guards don't have children and aren't associated with them, but to find out more requires tagging or something like that, and there's not much point in disrupting things when the system's in balance."

Viedras and Kemra exchanged one of those glances that indicated that I just didn't understand. They were right; I didn't understand why they were so dense. Trying to refine some knowledge is arrogance, not scholarship. Did it really matter, unless we were trying to manipulate the environment? So much of the ancients' knowledge was developed either to enhance their manipulations of the environment or in a belated attempt to undo the messes they had created. We worked to avoid either.

Viedras took another step forward. "I just need a little better angle."

I calculated. "Don't go any closer."

To his right, Kemra looked at me and stopped.

"Don't be silly. None of them are closer than fifty meters." Viedras took another step, and then another. "And I need to get closer."

"Viedras!" I yelled, but it was too late.

He took the fourth step toward the burrows and across that invisible line that marked the rodents' territory.

EEEEeeeeeeecchhhh!

Virtually simultaneously with the high-pitched call almost two dozen furry figures charged out of burrows, three out of hidden tunnels within a dozen meters of the naturalist.

"Fire at will!" I snapped at Babbege.

The force leader gaped at me.

"Fire at will! Shoot!" I repeated.

"Fire at will!" Kemra repeated my command.

Viedras kept taking images or whatever, backing away from the charging prairie dogs, stumbling as he retreated.

I had my slugthrower out. So did Kemra.

We both fired at the four dogs shrieking and bounding toward the naturalist. It's always amazing how quickly they move. I got one, then another, before they got too close.

Then I stepped-up my system and *moved,* drawing the knife as I blurred toward the two remaining dogs.

One almost clawed me, but the razor blade took his paw. I snap-kicked through its neck, and took out the second with the blade.

The two marcybs on the end went down under five of the furry prairie dogs. One staggered up, snapping rodent necks, and bleeding from a dozen deep claw marks. The other didn't.

Before I could get there, the rest of the prairie dogs were either dead, or had retreated.

Viedras stood, motionless.

Kemra scanned the area, slugthrower ready.

I bent over the fallen cyb, but there wasn't anything I could do. A claw had severed his carotid artery like a blade, and there was blood just about everywhere.

The force leader was using some sort of field dressings on the other wounded cyb.

Two other cybs, blank-eyed, picked up the body as I stood up and relaxed my system into normal speed. As usual, my muscles hurt. But my guts were stable. Prairie dogs weren't highly intelligent, an artificial distinction perhaps, but one for which I was grateful. I cleaned the blade as well as I could on the grass and replaced it in the sheathe.

"Let's go," I snapped. The scent of blood would draw the smaller brown centipedes, smaller only by comparison to the reds which could reach three quarters of a meter, and then the prairie falcons would get into the act, along with the rest of the scavengers. There wouldn't be a trace of blood or bone within a day. "We need to get back to the shuttle."

For once, no one said anything, but only for a minute or two.

"Those things are vicious." Viedras turned and glanced back at the prairie dog town, although the bodies were lost in the grass. "Why don't you get rid of them?"

"They wouldn't have been vicious, if you'd listened to me."

"But . . . I didn't know."

I wondered how many times throughout history someone had explained not listening the same way. I wasn't ready to fight that battle, not at the moment. My legs were shaky and still recovering from step-up.

"In a way, that kind of thinking is what led to their development," I explained as I turned back toward the shuttle. "There was a vacant niche, and they took it. They're not terribly dangerous outside their own territory."

Kemra looked at the northernmost line of hummocks. "They look like they're capable of expanding their territory rather quickly."

I pointed to the east, toward grass-covered mounds beyond the hummocks. "That was their last expansion, probably a decade ago."

"You had to cull them?" asked Viedras, still not understanding.

"No. Things are in balance. The vorpals did that."

"The nasty giant fox-like things? They hunt the prairie dogs?" asked Kemra.

"It's not that simple, but yes."

"I think a pack of those prairie things—sorry, I don't think of them as dogs—could stand off a bunch of vorpals." Kemra glanced from the burrows to me.

"They could, right now. But this is lean territory. It takes about a quarter of a hectare to support one prairie dog, and they won't build more than eight hummock-burrows in one hectare. The burrows are expansive for a few animals. You can see that." I shrugged. The conclusion was obvious, but it took Viedras a minute to get the point.

"They get too spread out to defend the perimeter against marauders?"

I nodded. "The towns migrate around their range, but never get much bigger."

"Little fish have bigger fish to eat them. I understand that," said Kemra. "But what keeps the vorpals in check?"

"Food, each other, scavengers, centipedes, scorpion packs, kalirams, mostly. Some desperate cougars." I kept walking quickly, following the cybs carrying their dead companion, and listening, scanning. I pulsed Lieza. "Get ready for lift-off. One dead marcyb. One pretty slashed up. Territoriality problem. Viedras didn't listen to me. Would you let Keiko know?"

"Stet, Coordinator." Lieza was all business.

"Do I want to know about the scavengers and kalirams?" asked Kemra.

"The kalirams stay in the rocky parts of the mountains. They're killer sheep that became omnivores with a preference for meat. They prey mainly on the deer, but anything will do, and they don't like humans or vorpals much."

"What else . . . never mind." She broke off as we neared the shuttle.

Lieza had converted two of the couches into flat pallets, and the cyb officers stretched the wounded cyb on one. The wounded marcyb still hadn't said much of anything, and her eyes were the same flat brown, as if nothing had happened. I suspected the dead cyb's eyes would have looked just the same, but I didn't check and repressed a shiver.

"There will be a medical team waiting," Lieza announced. "Settle in. We're lifting."

The door had barely clicked up into place when the shuttle eased skyward.

Kemra looked at the screen, and I didn't feel like talking. They still didn't seem to understand. After losing a trooper and facing the prairie dogs, they failed to see what Old Earth had become.

We were still a few minutes out of Parwon when Keiko came across the net. "Coordinator. Majer Henslom was here. He took five squads on the upper Aquarius trail. The vorpals got nearly a dozen. He's looking for your head."

"He won't get it. Besides, he'll have to stand in line, the way things are going."

"I warned you." She projected darkness with her words.

"You did. I'll keep you posted. Or Lieza will, if Henslom does get my head."

"Thanks," interjected the pilot, her words ironic on the net.

"I have this feeling that a lot's going on above us," Kemra said. "You people have a high net, don't you."

"High?"

"I can sense something, but that's all."

"Like you, we use nets for some things," I admitted. "I was telling the pilot that a lot of people were standing in line for my head at the moment."

Kemra shook her head. She opened her mouth as if to say something.

I looked at her, and she shut it.

Viedras was studying the equipment he'd used, or reviewing the results. His lips were pursed, and I wondered if he'd caught my sped-up movements.

As Keiko warned me, two more marcyb officers were waiting at the local tower when we set down. One was Majer Henslom. The other was a force leader. The force leader's left arm was heavily bandaged and splinted.

Kemra followed me out of the shuttle. So did Viedras, Babbege, and Cherle. Babbege turned and helped get the wounded cyb into the emergency medical wagon, then climbed in with her.

"Coordinator?" asked Henslom, his voice cool.

Kemra looked from Henslom to me and back again.

"Yes?" I waited, and the medical car whined away toward the center of the local.

"You seem to have a local wildlife problem. Or you used local wildlife to ambush my troops. Or both."

"What happened?" I asked.

"You certainly must know. You obviously set it up."

I looked straight into those flat eyes. "I set up nothing. After our meeting yesterday, in fact, I decided against setting up anything. All I did was refuse to warn or protect you. You don't seem to understand. Old Earth has become a dangerous place."

Henslom took a step forward.

"Halt!" snapped Kemra.

"I would not have thought you would take the side of the locals," said the majer.

"I'm not. I'm keeping you from committing suicide."

For the first time, Henslom's eyes showed confusion.

Kemra used their local net to add, "He's the one who took out your agent bare-handed in the dark. I watched him destroy four of those vicious dogs in seconds. You'd last about three instants."

"Him? Politicos don't fight," Henslom flashed back.

"They do here," came the boosted response.

I kept my face expressionless.

Henslom swallowed.

Then Kemra spoke. "I believe the majer was not prepared to find our ancestral home so . . . violent."

"Living here continues to be a struggle." My words were true, although I doubted the true nature of the struggle would ever be obvious to them. "At every turn, I have tried to let you see matters as they are, and yet you have persisted in seeing them as you wished. Yesterday, I decided against continuing any special protections."

"Warning is a special protection?"

"One reason Old Earth collapsed was that our ancestors refused to live in balance with the ecology and that they forced incredible diversions of resources to create a luxurious lifestyle and to protect themselves from what they conceived of as the slightest chance of harm." I turned to Kemra. "The subcommander has seen the ruins. This continent was filled with hundreds of areas such as those. When the earth had the chance to redress the balance, it did. We try to live with it, rather than force even greater changes."

"You can't tell me you live with things like those . . . those . . . predators," said Henslom.

"No. You're right. We avoid where they live, and we

don't build close to them, and they generally hunt away from the locials. But we also don't go out and kill them just because one sometimes kills a draff or a child."

"You'd let a child near them?"

"I wouldn't. I never did. Some people are stupid. We don't regulate stupidity. You protect it, and it breeds."

They all looked horrified, even Kemra.

"You people don't listen," I snapped. "I told Viedras to stop. I warned you all that, once you crossed the territorial border of the prairie dogs, they became aggressive. He told me not to be silly, and he crossed that line. We got away with one dead cyb, and some nasty slashes. It didn't have to happen, but you thought you knew better. That's a form of stupidity—or arrogance." I turned to Henslom. "You didn't ask us about whether it was safe to take your troops out of the local. You told us that was what you were doing. Your assumption was that Old Earth is perfectly safe unless you're warned. Is deep space safe? Would you drop into the sun's photosphere because no one warned you it would incinerate you? Nothing is perfectly safe. We don't provide warning signs to protect you from yourselves. Try to remember that." I was treading close to the edge of the Construct, possibly too close, but I had to try.

"Thank you, Coordinator. Thank you so very much," was all Henslom had to say, and he was still seething inside, and he hadn't heard a word I said. He turned and walked quickly toward the shuttle that waited to take him into Parwon center.

I wanted to kick him. He was denser than collapsed depleted uranium. Why did he think that, when he was on a mission to slag Old Earth, I should be going out of my way to protect him? He couldn't even see that by not protecting him, I was trying to let him see reality enough for him to make an intelligent choice, to avoid stupidity.

The others turned toward the cyb lander, all except for

Kemra, who waited, then asked, "Why are you so angry? You weren't hurt. You're upset with us, yet you have no reason to be pleased with our arrival."

"Any form of stupidity and unnecessary death bothers me, and it really upsets me when people refuse to see what is."

She frowned, then asked more quietly, "The vorpals, the prairie dogs—are they why the draffs don't live away from the locials?" The wind, colder than when we had left, blew her short and sandy hair forward to touch the edge of her cheeks, softening the hard planes of her face.

"Some of the reasons," I said. "The bears have lost their fear of humans, and the cougars never had much. That doesn't count the scorpion packs, the centipedes, or the rattlers, except they've always been dangerous, except now they rattle after they strike, instead of before."

"How can you demis live out there?" She gestured in the general direction of our—my—house.

"We can generally sense most of them. We do have ways of protecting ourselves, as you saw, but those with children must be exceedingly careful. Most of the predators zero in on any human child."

"Then why . . ."

"It's hard to fight danger if you don't grow up to recognize it." And besides, we weren't about to give up Old Earth to the predators. "As I said, and, as no one heard, we won't coddle stupidity among ourselves." I stopped again. "You saw those palaces in the ruins. That was stupidity, too, incredible, arrogant stupidity. The first demis isolated themselves in luxury behind an impenetrable wall. Look what happened. We can't do that. We have to stay in touch with our bodies and our world. No isolation on pristine nets."

She shook her head.

I wanted to say more, but the Construct is strong within us—even within me, grieving and confused as I was.

Behind her, the snow swirled toward the north end of the field like a dark curtain falling across the piñons, and I knew I'd have to hurry if I didn't want to be caught in Parwon for the night.

A single flake of snow caught on her hair, and one image superimposed itself on another, and the words came to mind, unbidden:

> ". . . for whitest flakes will gown my grace,
> and jewels of ice will frame my face. . . ."

I looked away and swallowed. After I moment, I pulled myself together.

"You actually looked human for a moment, Coordinator Ecktor."

"We're all human . . . if we choose to be." That was the best I could do, and it wasn't enough.

She shook her head again. "We've seen your view of Old Earth. Perhaps you should visit us."

"Perhaps." Anything but another Jykserian episode. If a visit to hell would help, I'd go, just so long as I didn't have to threaten or make the first strike. "Perhaps."

"I'll be in touch."

Then she was gone, and I walked through the flurries to the flitter.

<<< XX

The snow had begun to fall sometime in the night, and by the time I rose, in the grayness before true dawn, it was more than ankle deep. Ankle deep and powdery, the kind that came out of the north, lasting and cold, falling in a fog-like curtain.

When the kettle began to whistle, I filled the dark green pot with boiling water and dropped the tea caddy inside. Yslena had made the pot and sent it, three years or so earlier. Looking at the dark green curved sides of the pot, I realized I needed to link with her before long—but with the time differential, she was asleep.

While the tea steeped, I toasted some bread—the heavy kind, because I've never been good at making the light kind. Morgen had been, but everything I get involved with turns out heavy, including bread.

It was the last loaf I had in the keeper, and that meant either using comptime credits or making bread. I still had plenty of preserves, and I slathered them across the two slices of toast. A chunk of cheese, more ripe than I would have liked, and a bowl of dried pear slices completed breakfast, and I sat down to eat, my eyes lifting to the window.

The piñons on the edges of the ridge were concealed by the falling snow, but neither Swift-Fall-Hunter nor the raven were likely to be perched there in the storm. The sambur never browsed higher than halfway up the slopes, either.

After finishing the pear slices and cheese, I took a long swallow of tea, then held the mug with both hands under my chin and let steam and spice of tea, bergamot-scented, wreathe my face. After I finished, I set the heavy green mug on the table and looked back to the window and the falling snow. My fingers found their way to the adiamante oval on the table—still smooth, heavy, and nonreactive.

Adiamante—useless for anything except defense, unable to argue, unable to threaten. Were we the adiamante of the universe?

Idly, I wondered if the prairie dogs in their hummocks thought about cold or snow. Unlike eagles or the less force-evolved species such as cougars and bears, the prairie dogs and vorpals and kalirams were harder to read, more difficult to gain a sense of their presence and purpose. Another evolutionary adaptation?

After setting down the adiamante on the table, I swallowed the last of the tea and headed for the shower. Hot showers helped remove the chill from bones and soul.

After showering, I pulled on heavy running trousers, shirt, boots, and a jacket—plus one of the sheath knives—and stepped outside where the snow kept falling.

With a deep breath, I headed westward, boots dropping near-silently into the growing white powder as I tried to maintain a quick and even pace despite the uncertain footing. Was that life—trying to maintain the pace despite the treacherous ground across which we had to move? Was it all in vain? I shouldn't have been so desperately lyrical because that lyricism called up other lyricism.

> ". . . and words we whispered flamed in vain
> against Old Earth's last reign and rain. . . ."

Except that I was running through snow, not rain, avoiding sagebrush, cedars, junipers, and rocks half-hidden by snow. I almost wished I'd find a vorpal, but they never showed up when I was angry enough—or stupidly desperate enough—to take one on.

I pushed my thoughts in other directions.

Dialogue one: Had it been fair to let Henslom's cybs be killed by the vorpals? No . . . but wouldn't it have been less fair to delude them by protecting them? Or was that a rationalization?

I reached the end of the ridge and headed downhill, more to the south this time, away from the meleysen groves. For whatever reason, the orangish smell was more pronounced and close to obnoxious when light snow was falling.

Dialogue two: Why are we trapped by the Construct, like mutants trapped by the meleysens? Because we had no choice left except to subject ourselves to it. Unthinking aggression was genetically positive for clawing humanity to the top of the ecological totem pole, except that it ended up destroying that totem pole. With high technology, strike-first aggression proved unworkable. At last count, our infrequent interstellar surveys had proven that. Three more planets were uninhabited and uninhabitable. Why couldn't the cybs see? Was it because their whole logic structure was either-or, on-off, one-two?

The snow continued to fall, and my steps slowed as I trotted uphill once again, senses alert for possible predators, hand straying to the hilt of the sharp knife at my belt.

<<< XXI

What about that shuttle system operating between the locials and the asteroid stations around the planet? Or the spacing of those stations? Those nickel-iron hunks are positioned in almost symmetrical stable orbits," observed Gibreal.

"Each is also generating a magnetic field now, except for one, and they're sending a lot of equipment there," added Kemra. "They weren't building fields before, even if they use a lot of equipment that taps the planetary fields."

"What are they up to?" asked Weapons. "You've spent more time with them than anyone."

Kemra did not answer.

"All their shuttlecraft in use tap the magnetic fields, more efficiently than our magboosts," admitted Gorum, "but that sort of system is almost useless for warcraft. The fields fluctuate, and some planets and systems have comparatively minuscule fields."

"Just hit them and get it over with," interjected Weapons. The image of a lightning bolt flashed across the net.

"There's something we're missing," mused the navigator. "Something obvious. I could feel a tremendous frustration from their Coordinator."

"Oh . . . you're definitely doing your job, then. . . ." An undulating female figure, overripe and nude, paraded the netline, but through a signature filter.

"Sanitize it," snapped Gibreal.

The figure vanished.

"Explain, nav," the commander added.

"I've reported on the wildlife and the marcyb casualties, but their Coordinator was furious—the first time I've seen that from any of them—when he talked about our not seeing and listening. And there was a plea there, too."

"Spare us?" suggested Gorum. "Please don't roll over us?"

"No. More like spare *us*—us the cybs, I mean. It was almost as though he were pleading for us not to be stupid enough to destroy ourselves."

"That is interesting, if true." Gibreal's words were almost distant. "I have trouble believing that, but perhaps you'd better investigate more. We have a day or two more before we're ready."

"Something else disturbs me," added the nav. "Except for the nontalking heads, the ruins at Cherkrik, and the Great Wall—there's nothing left. Think about it. More than ten millennia of building things, and there are less than a dozen remnants on an entire planet?"

"They didn't take care of things," snapped Weapons.

"There were once pyramids on several continents built of hard stone that massed more than some fleets. If they'd just neglected them, they'd still be there. Or there would be some remnants. There aren't."

"So they went around destroying their heritage," pointed out Gibreal. "That's certainly not new, especially if they wanted to rewrite history. Peoples everywhere have eradicated the unpleasant past. These demis are just the first to have both the will, the technology, and the time to do so successfully."

"Then why the Hyberniums? Those scenes do not paint them as exactly good people. And the Coordinator went out of his way to show me those luxurious palaces of the old-time demis and to point out the problems they had caused. None of them live like that now."

"That's so they can claim they're honest. A partial truth to varnish over their guilt."

"I don't think so," mused the nav, the odor of libraries and ancient books overlaid with the bright light of laboratories. "I think it's all a way of subtly warning us."

"That's idiotic," countered Gorum. "Why don't they just tell us that if we don't get out of their heavens they'll destroy us? Because they can't."

"That is not a verifiable proposition," interjected MYL-ERA.

"The power build-up isn't quite complete," said Gibreal. "Do you suppose we could provide them with a warning of sorts?"

"What do you have in mind, ser?" asked Ideomineo.

"Such as?" followed the cybnav.

"Perhaps a demonstration might be in order for your demi friend, Kemra. Some moon-polishing, perhaps, in a remote area clearly visible from earth."

The image of ancient door creaking open filled the net, with a darkness oozing forth.

"Sanitize it," grumbled Gibreal.

The cybnav's lips clamped together.

<<< **XXII**

THE CYB'S TALE

Scan the files of old, and praise the copper wires that preceded the net and the fibrelines. Scan the tale of half-Jack, the father of cybs, cyb before cybs. The tale is ancient, from before The Flight, from before the SoshWars, but true for all its age and obscurity.

After Ibmer made the first cyb, there was Jack, and he was a hardcopy programmer, of that ancient cult that bears the same resemblance to cybs as alchemists did to chemists. In those names, without the clarity of identity, all humans were of the single undifferentiated type, and they all had many names. Jack's name was Jackson Green Crossfield, and he was a times-removed ancestor of Greencross. That is another story.

From the beginning, Jack marveled at the crystalline clarity of the logic, that binary clarity of yes or no, on or off. No analog shades of gray for Jack, disciple of forgotten Bebege, just black and white, on and off.

But what could he do? He was flesh and blood, and the mechcybs of his youth were metal and plastic and composite. To bridge that gap was seen as less possible than reaching the distant stars. The early mechcybs had no souls and died when the power failed. They had no scanners, and no will.

But Jack worked with a graphite stick and electroplastic discs and all the tools of the ancient age to reduce the illogic of human thought to the single-valued logic that admits of no indecision.

While Jack struggled with his task, the mechcybs that had been the size of a starlander shrank to the size of a travel case, and Jack acquired one, and he began to program, shrinking his long chains and intricate punch cards, for those came before the commandlines, into shorter and shorter phrases. The punchcards were replaced with circular plastic discs and then with logic magbubbles.

Jack created new languages, Basek, and Gummaul, and Fortable, and Debasted, and all of those that preceded mechlink and have been lost in the dead circuits of the past. And he used those languages to refine the crystalline clarity of logic, to turn the one-two, on-off, into a pattern that could not fail. A pattern that could not be changed by the ephemeral flow of hormonal secretions, or the instinctive and unreasoned reaction to a hot wind or the scent of flowers extracted and sprayed across exposed flesh.

The work was arduous, and Jack's limbs weakened. He built himself a chair that would carry him anywhere, and neural jacks in his hands to supplant the rigors of the keyboard. And he continued to refine the cybmech languages, and to create ever more simply complex logic operators.

When his heart would pump no more, he had a mechheart installed; and the heart was monitored by the lines that linked to his weak organic nerves. And when his lungs failed, he replaced them with blowers that were crosslinked to his second cybself.

As his organic body disintegrated, he struggled to replicate his thoughts in the arcane and antique crystals of the ancients—to transfer his thoughts, his knowledge, and his understanding of the clarity of one-two, on-off. As his synapses would hold no more and began to leak their bytes, he replicated them and transferred them into his second cybself, a cybmech with multi-redundant circuits, and replicating and recharging power sources hidden deep within the recesses of OldCity. Jack called that second self halfJack.

When the transfer was complete, his old body sighed

once and then no more, and in time, it was rendered unto ashes, and a metal plate placed upon a wall, and a few humans looked and left.

Within those recesses, his thoughts net-linked with the mechcyb, and the patterns flickered through the matrices and the soul crystals, and halfJack woke, and said, "I am halfJack, and more than Jack ever was."

And so it was, for Jack had never run the net-lines, or multilinked, or uploaded or downloaded, or duped and cross-checked. All of these and more could halfJack do, and he did, serving and sustaining even to the times of Greencross.

To this day, we honor halfJack, the first cyb, the cyb who ensured that logic was logic and not emotion, cyb before there were cybs.

<<< XXIII

After another shower—to wash off the sweat of a too-long run and take away the chill of snow and soul—I looked in the mirror, wondering if I'd find a thatch of silver hair, bloodshot watery eyes with bags beneath, sunken cheeks, and yellowed teeth. I didn't. The short hair was still black, the eyes green, the cheeks red from the weather, and all my teeth were still there. The circles under my bloodshot eyes hadn't been there a year earlier, and neither had the lines in my forehead. I rubbed my fingers along the jawline, but the muscles seemed firm. I'd opted against a beard and never regretted it, even when Diogen had made them the fashion for a time a decade or so back.

I showered and dressed in black trousers and shirt— more suitable for appearing behind the wide desk of the

Coordinator than were the running clothes—then poured a last cup of lukewarm tea from the green pot.

Outside the wind was rising, and the snow had stopped falling. The sky showed patches of cold china blue to the north, with clouds swift-scudding southward. I peered out the western window. The piñons remained snow-covered, and Swift-Fall-Hunter perched or circled skies elsewhere.

Finally, I sat at the table and tried the longlink.

Surprisingly, Yslena was available. Often she was out of link range, working with her team on reef restoration.

"Father! Are you all right?" I could picture the quizzical frown above the flashing green eyes. The eyes were mine; almost every other physical feature had come from Morgen—the sandy hair, the higher than average cheekbones, the almost elfin jawline, the wiry figure.

"Relatively."

"You're tired. You always say 'relatively' when you don't want to admit things aren't going well."

I could sense the concern, some concern anyway, and pulsed back the answer. "It is tiring, especially when you're dealing with people who see nothing and don't want to. I understand the Construct, and I know it works, but at times I just want to tell the cybs that what they're doing will end up killing a whole lot of us and just about all of them. But if I do that, then they'll get even nastier, and so will the results." I shook my head, even though she couldn't see that. "So I keep showing them Old Earth and hoping they'll learn something."

"And they don't do they?" my daughter responded softly. "It must be bad, if they asked you to be Coordinator."

"Any time we need a Coordinator, it's bad," I admitted, then asked, "How are you doing?"

"Tired, but it's a good kind of tired, from hard work and lots of exercise. It's rewarding and frustrating. The ecochain of the sea was bent, but not totally wiped out the way it happened on land. We don't have anything developing like vorpals. Of course, sharks were already like that, but they're not as bright."

"Not nearly, from what you've said," I interjected, half-amazed at the calm competence that had once been a laughing child, who had dodged behind trees and rocks while one of us had scanned the undergrowth and hillsides.

"The cetaceans treat them like stunted children, but they don't tease them, and they do have a function."

"So do the vorpals," I said dryly.

"It's not the same." She laughed. "You know all that already. Why am I telling you?"

"I like to hear you talk," I answered, and I did like to hear from her, but she was also sticking to the facts because it was easier. Talking to Yslena was hard, always had been, and that was probably because she took after me, without a deep emote sense. Non-emote intuits always have trouble that way, unless they're linked to someone like her mother, who linked us both. Then, suddenly, we'd lost that link.

"The reef work is so tedious. I won't live to see whether what we've done really works, and it won't even be obvious to my great-grandchildren. That assumes I ever find anyone and that we get around to children."

"You will," I assured her. "You will." Yslena had always had trouble reaching out, just as I had, but now that Morgen was gone, what choice did I have? "It takes time."

"And luck. You practically ran into mother with a flitter before you two noticed each other."

"I wouldn't suggest anything quite so drastic." My fingers stroked the chunk of adiamante. Sometimes I felt as distant as the untouchable niellen darkness it held.

"I'm glad you linked," she offered. "But it worries me. You never do it unless there's something important."

"I was thinking about you."

After a silence, she asked, "Do you think I ought to come home? I've got more than enough of a balance. I'd never use what I have in years."

"No," I said quickly, too quickly. "I'd rather . . . I mean, you . . ." What could I say? She was safer there, far safer, yet I didn't want to act the over-protective parent.

"Oh, father . . ." Her words were soft. "I think I understand, and I won't embarrass you, and I'm glad you care. Are you sure?"

"I'm sure. I'd like to see you, but now's not the time. Being Coordinator is going to keep me busy for the next few days, maybe longer. After that . . . well . . . then we can see. Maybe I can come see your reef."

"There's not that much to see. I mean, there's plenty to see, but you can't really tell what we've been doing."

"I understand. That's like most solid accomplishments." What I said was true, and I meant it, but even as I said the banal words, I wanted to say more, and didn't.

"It doesn't feel all that solid. Designing and planting coral to replace those that the hothousers' tides destroyed feels like trying to build a house with sand on sand."

"I know. I know. At times, everything feels that way." I paused. "That sounds patronizing, and I don't mean it that way." My fingers tightened around the small chunk of adiamante.

"I understand, father. I know what you mean. That's only sometimes. Other times, like when I glide after the orcas, everything feels so . . . so interconnected and right."

"Those are times to hold on to." I hadn't had many of those lately, but I remembered them, like the last words of Morgan's soulsong: . . . *our joys will last the endless years.*

"I try to," pulsed back Yslena.

"Good." I tried to convey the sense of a smile.

"Father . . . I'm supposed to be at the dock before long, and I'm not like you. I can't hold netlinks in my mind and do three other things." There was a pause. "I could come home any time."

"I know, and I'm glad to know that. I'd feel a lot better if we held off on that, sweetheart."

"I just wanted you to know."

"Thank you. Take care of yourself in that big deep ocean." That big deep ocean and its ancient god that erased all of the land that it could.

"Oh, father, I will. You take care of yourself."

After I dropped the link, I took a sip of the tea, but it was cold and flat. Cold and unsatisfying, like a lot of things recently. Like the Construct, the Power Paradigms, and links with my daughter that weren't quite what either of us needed or wanted.

With a look at the adiamante that lay wrapped in its niellen depths on the table, I stood and walked to the sink where I dumped out the cold tea and washed both pot and cup and racked them. Then I stepped back to the wide window and studied the view to the west.

In the clearing air over the valley immediately west of the house soared a winged shape. I studied the eagle until I was sure it was Swift-Fall-Hunter, and a smile came to my lips.

Then I headed out to start up the flitter and to fly north to the chaos that awaited.

<<< XXIV

The sun was struggling through the parting clouds, and with the snow, had turned the flitter trip up the valley to Parwon into a flight over sparkling white, white so fresh that I could see no tracks, not even in the valleys. The only signs of motion were the hot mists simmering up off the scattered meleysen groves like silver fog rising into the light.

A light layer of fog rose from the locial landing strip as I turned the flitter onto its final approach. I got a couple of warning blips from the traffic control system, and that showed how distracted I was. Most of the time, I could set the flitter down without even a flicker.

"Coordinator?"

Keiko's netcall meant more trouble, but that wasn't unexpected. It was close to mid-morning, and I'd run and linked with Yslena, and all that time the cybs and the Construct had been battling each other.

"Yes, Keiko?" I began to button up the flitter.

"There's a ground shuttle awaiting you."

"Why?"

"Kaluna is out here, and he's angry."

Kaluna? Who was Kaluna?

"The draff—his mate was the one the cyb attacked," Keiko prompted.

"And he saw the same cyb, right?"

"How did you guess?" My assistant's question was barely that, more of a dark acknowledgment.

"I'm naturally brilliant."

That brought a snort from my aide.

I walked across the damp permacrete toward the waiting groundshuttle. Dvorrak gestured through the open door, and I waved back. "What else has happened?" I asked Keiko on the net. "I'm not here at the crack of dawn—"

"You are never here at the crack of dawn. I am. That's so you don't have to be. That's also why you already owe a lifetime of compensatory service."

"Don't remind me." I stepped into the shuttle and sat down. "I'm in the groundshuttle, and we're headed your way."

Dvorrak closed the door, and we whined toward the admin building.

I hadn't even reached Keiko when Kaluna bounded across the carpet toward me.

"That same cyb—he still is here."

I forced a smile. "Then we will have to remove him." I paused. "Did Nislaki ever receive any apology?"

"Apology? We heard nothing."

I nodded and pulsed Keiko on the net. "Keiko . . . I'll need a restraint squad. Say ten. Black uniforms with stunners and slugthrowers. Have them meet me at the statue in a quarter stan. Then a magshuttle. Is Lieza available? If not, someone else with that level of experience."

"Is that all?"

"The shuttle should be float-tied right above the open space south of the residential bloc. That way, the marcyb is stunned, webbed—"

"You want a web-restraint unit, too?"

"Sorry. Yes. Anyway, I want that poor construct webbed and enroute straight to their flagship. I'll have to do it."

Kaluna's eyes flicked back and forth between us—between two silent demis in black.

"Next, we'll need to know which marcyb and where he is." I turned to Kaluna. "Would you recognize this marcyb? They all look similar."

"Yes." Kaluna's voice was hard and certain.

I went back on the net. "Crucelle?"

"He's out, Ecktor," answered Arielle.

"Do you have images of the marcybs in the residence bloc? Ones you can put on the mechcyb system?"

"Of course. When do you need them? Is this about that assault?"

"How did you guess? You calculated?"

"It wasn't hard," she pulsed back dryly, the storm currents swirling around her even over the net. "We've tentatively identified him, and I'll put that image first. Give us a few minutes."

"Keiko," I said aloud. "In a few minutes, Arielle will have the images on the console system. Have Kaluna identify him, and then make up a profile, such as you can, for me."

I looked directly at Kaluna. "I promised I would take care of this, and I will. It will take a few minutes to organize."

"A few minutes?" he asked.

"You have to identify the cyb, and I have to gather the restraint squad and the necessary equipment." I also had to put on the silly black cloak and dig out some armament—a stunner and a knife. The cybs knew I could use the knife. I gestured for Kaluna to join Keiko before her console while I went back into my office to change my heavy jacket for the damned cloak.

"Ecktor!" Locatio whined in on the uppernet before I even reached my desk.

I needed not to talk to him in the worst way, but when you're caught on net, there's not much escape.

"You'll have to make it quick. I'm in the middle of another mess here."

"You were right. They sent two agents—one into the power complex, the other into admin."

"Did you get them?"

"Without a casualty—except them, of course."

"Good. Make sure no one else knows. Destroy *everything,* and act as if nothing happened. They'll try again within twenty-four hours, probably with much larger teams. Be ready."

"Is that all?"

"I'll link with you later and explain this mess. You might also have an incident where a cyb assaults a draff, unless it's happened already."

"Not yet."

"If it does, let me or Keiko know. Request an apology from the cyb officer in charge and request immediate evacuation of the guilty cyb. Then wait until you link with me. All right? I've got to move."

I broke the connection, pulled on the cloak, and checked the knife and stunner that had been laid out on the desk for me.

The net wavered as the magshuttle arrived, and I took a deep breath and stepped out of the office.

"When the ice falls . . ." Keiko suggested verbally, dark eyes even more somber, but that was the way I felt as well.

"Exactly," I answered.

"Here's the profile . . . and his probable location, based on his present ENF I.D." She gave me a hard copy, and then opened the net file.

I closed my eyes and let it infeed. It's less distracting if you aren't looking at something.

"All the cybs are in the bloc now," Keiko added. "There's one squad exercising on the east lawn."

"That will make things interesting."

Kaluna didn't even move as I walked down the steps.

There were ten draffs and a squad leader waiting at the foot of the stairs, all in the black uniforms. The blond draff on the end carried a web-restraint thrower. Another dozen admin types peered from various doors, waiting and watching.

"I'm Lictaer, Coordinator," announced the wiry restraint squad leader with a smile.

"Ecktor will do. We're headed for the south residential bloc."

"What do you want from us?" she asked.

"Just to be there, and look impressive, I hope. I'll need a marcyb trussed and webbed for effect, and delivery to the Vereal Fleet."

Her eyebrows lifted.

"I'm doing the delivery."

"Yes, ser."

They followed, and, once outside, I tried the net. "Magshuttle, this is Ecktor." The shuttle floated on its field lines just south of the admin building, above the park to the west of the statue of the unknown draff.

"Coordinator, this is Borin. Interrogative instructions."

"Head for the south residence bloc, but stay above the open area to the east of the bloc until I tell you to land. You should have enough clearance."

"That's affirmative, ser. I can put it in there. There's room for a couple of shuttles."

"Good. I'm headed there now."

The black-clad squad followed me, almost soundlessly, all the way to the south residence bloc. There were two squads going through an exercise routine on the now flattened and trampled grass as we walked up. A junior force leader, not any of the two I'd met, stepped forward to greet me.

"Ser?"

"I'm looking for a marcyb." I stepped past him and scanned those in the loose ranks. None of the profiles matched.

"I'm sorry, ser, but I'll have to ask you—"

I turned and looked at him. "You can follow me if you wish." I smiled, almost hoping he'd attack.

He didn't, instead fumbling a transmission through his net. "Majer, there's some local here, looking for a particular marcyb."

I walked into the building and went up the central stairs and down the corridor to the left. A second officer, subforce leader, appeared. I stepped around him.

He grabbed my shoulder, and I went into step-up. I was sloppy, and it took three blows and a netboost to incapacitate him. I eased his unconscious form to the polished marble floor. A pounding headache would be his biggest problem when he woke.

Staying in step-up, I went through the fourth door on the left. There were three marcybs in the room. I pulled the middle one right off his bunk before the others could initially react, but some officer got a command line in, and the two started to move. Rather than fight, I yanked the one into the hall and shut the door, then moved down the hall to the stairs. The cyb thrashed, but I overrode the commands and put him out, and lugged him down the steps. I was going to hurt all over before I was done.

Majer Henslom, cold-eyed as ever, waited right outside at the main entrance. He held a slugthrower pointed at my midsection. "I see you don't respect privacy or hospitality, Coordinator."

The ten restraint squad members and Lictaer had their stunner trained on the three officers on the lawn, and on the majer.

"Go step-up, and stun the majer if I signal," I pulsed to Lictaer.

"Stet," came the tight response.

"If I recall correctly," I responded verbally to Henslom, forcing my words into the normal patterns that seemed so slow, "this cyb assaulted an innocent woman. He was to be removed, and that's exactly what I am doing, since you chose not to."

Another command went skyward. "Bring the shuttle down."

Henslom wavered at the whine of the shuttle, but his eyes didn't leave me. I was slightly hampered with one arm full of inert cyb, but my perceptions remained fixed on his arm and the hand that held the slugthrower. I did shift the cyb so I could drop him instantly.

"I am returning him to your fleet. That's all. He's unconscious." I smiled. "Now . . . if you want to oppose that action, say so."

"Could I stop you? Really?" asked Henslom. He was

trying to be polite, but the muscular tension bulged all over him. Still, he wasn't stupid.

"No."

"Even with the slugger?"

"That's right."

I could see the tightening in his arm and hand, but in step-up my free hand was faster, and the angle gave me leverage. Enough so that the single shot went into the ground beside the stone walk. Enough so that I broke two of Henslom's fingers and probably sprained his wrist. I'd have bruises on my hands later.

"Web the marcyb!" I snapped at Lictaer. Since we were both in step-up, no one else seemed to move before I'd tossed the slugthrower into the flower bed three meters to the right.

Henslom's mouth hung open as he staggered back, watching the web wrap around the marcyb.

"Don't move!" I snapped at the officers. "Not a millimeter!"

They didn't, not even Henslom.

"The fleet will fry your forsaken Old Earth," he muttered under his breath, and I still couldn't answer him. Damn the Construct! Damn the neurogenetic genetic programming!

"I would suggest you think about that very strongly," was the best I could do.

As the shuttle settled into one corner of the wide lawn, I picked up the webbed marcyb and turned to Henslom, who was trembling in rage. "I would suggest that you not attempt to take things out on any more innocents. I would also suggest you report to your superiors before you act on your rage."

"You are so helpful, Coordinator. So very helpful." Each word was bitten off in cold rage.

"I try, Majer. Just listen and watch, and you might learn something."

All the cybs remained frozen as I lifted the webbed marine one-handed and walked to the shuttle. Even in boost and step-up those thirty meters were hard. After setting him inside on the floor, I pulsed to Lictaer.

"Let's load up."

"Yes, ser." No questions, just repeated orders to her squad, and within instants they were inside. The cybs on the trampled lawn looked stunned, blank, as if a ruisine had become a rhion.

My next orders went to Borin. "We'll set the squad down in the park west of the admin building. Then we'll lift for orbit. The Vereal flag."

"Yes, ser." Borin's eyes widened, but that was all, as he eased the shuttle upward and to the west with barely a shiver.

"Lictaer," I said aloud for the benefit of her squad, although she had doubtless caught the net instructions. "We'll be putting you down west of the admin building. I'd appreciate it if you'd clear the area and post a guard on the building."

"Yes, ser." She offered a quick and grim smile.

I dropped onto the vacant second's couch and let Borin pilot the magshuttle across the park.

A few murmurs came from the restraint squad crowded into the shuttle.

". . . can't believe how he disarmed that cyb . . ."

". . . see now how they forced The Flight . . ."

"Quiet," ordered Lictaer. "Once we clear the shuttle, Heulin, you, Gersner, and Felin hold the south ports. Jinser . . ." She detailed the guard assignments for the admin building.

I scanned the known Vereal frequencies, but could pick up nothing.

"Coming down, ser," Borin reported.

"Get ready to disembark!" ordered Lictaer.

Borin eased the shuttle down so that it did not quite touch the grass, and Lictaer's squad hustled out.

The dark-eyed Lictaer looked at me from the ground. "You're sure you don't need us?"

"Not here. But it wouldn't hurt to bring up another squad and strengthen the guards around the admin building for a few hours. Just in case I'm wrong."

"We can do that, ser." She nodded. "Is that all?"

"For now. We need to lift clear."

With a wave she moved back and motioned to the restraint squad. They headed east across the browned grass as we lifted away. I was in the second's couch before the hatch was fully closed, fastening the restraints.

"Ecktor! You're insane!" Crucelle screamed in on the uppernet even before the shuttle door sealed. "They'll fry half the local."

"Good! Then you and K'gaio can activate the system before we lose forty percent of our population."

A moment of stillness crossed the netweb.

"You are insane. . . ." Crucelle net-murmured again, his formality and concern warring within him.

"No," answered another person—Arielle. "He's acting within the Construct, barely, and hoping to force them to break it, and you know why, Crucelle. It won't work. The cybs won't react that way because they'll understand that's what Ecktor wants, and they'll back away from it."

If she were right, anything I did was wrong. If I followed the traditional Construct pattern, we'd lose half the planet. If I bent the Construct, the cybs would still wait to attack in force, and we'd lose half the planet.

"I hope you're right," offered Crucelle.

"We'd do better if I'm wrong, dear." Her transmission went directly to me. "Sorry, Ecktor."

So was I.

"Home in on the cyb fleet," I told Borin, "the flagship if you can pick it out."

"Yes, ser. We've got them plotted." His eyes tightened, and I was pressed back into the couch as the shuttle accelerated.

I linked back into the uppernet, with a full override, with alarm, for K'gaio.

"That much noise was not necessary, Ecktor." Her net voice was the same smooth and oiled tone as always.

"I'm headed for the *Gibson,* the cyb's flagship." I explained the events of the day. ". . . that means that, if we get blasted or fried, you're Coordinator. It also means they've broken the Construct. Under any definition, murder of a planetary executive in an unarmed shuttlecraft is an act of aggression."

"You really do hate them, don't you?" she asked.

"No. I don't hate them at all. Except for being stupid," I added. "At times, I hate the Construct. I hate a situation where thousands or millions have to die before we can act."

"So . . ." There was a pause. "I have to admire you, Ecktor, but it won't work. They'll be so impressed by your effrontery that they'll accept the insult, and we'll be right where we were." She actually let some feeling enter the words.

"I have to try."

"I'll stand by, but I'm not holding my breath."

A momentary hiss, and the net was clear again.

I looked at the trussed and flat-eyed figure in the back of the passenger space, then toward Borin. "I can drop you off, Borin. I'm qualified—"

"No, ser. This is my job."

I slumped into the second pilot's couch. "Then I'm going to rest until we're close to the cybs."

He was smooth, and I actually dozed for a time, while my body tried to recover from the strains I'd already put on it. My hands and arms were beginning to ache, as I had known they would.

"We're closing, ser."

I stretched and sat up, too quickly, and bounced against the couch restraints in the infinitesimal gravity. After getting my mass and inertia under control, I checked the screens, but the oval shapes that were the cyb ships were more visible by their darkness than by their energy emissions. With their adiamante hulls, they were dark blots against the stars, with occasional energy bursts that represented comm exchanges between ships.

"I'll handle comm, Borin."

"Fine by me, ser. Tell me what you want."

I cleared my throat, then backtracked the burst frequencies the cybs had been using.

"Cyb-ship *Gibson,* this is Magshuttle Prime, bearing Old Earth Coordinator Ecktor. We are unarmed, and we are approaching to deliver a passenger. The passenger is one of your troopers who has violated Old Earth codes."

"Approaching craft, please say again. Please say again."

I repeated the whole spiel.

After a long pause, there was a burst of static, then a response. "Magshuttle Prime, you are cleared to lock one. Lock one will flash a green light . . . a green light. If you are not optically equipped, please inform."

"We've got it, Coordinator," flicked Borin.

"We have the green light. Commencing approach to lock one this time."

As we neared, the shuttle seemed like an ant at the base of the Barrier, lost against the featureless black that seemed to stretch forever in all directions, although the hull itself was slightly more than two klicks in length and a third of that in girth.

The open floor in lock one was big enough to engulf a dozen of our shuttles, and the screens showed three of the big cyb landers tucked in the back end.

"All the way in, ser?" asked Borin.

"All the way. It doesn't matter if the rhion eats you whole or merely chomps off your head."

He laughed nervously, but slipped the shuttle into the middle of the space. The ship's gravity seemed to be about point three, and I wondered how much power they spent just maintaining that.

When the hissing and steaming fog settled and the lock registered full pressure, I slid open the hatch and stepped into the chill, carrying the trussed marcyb one-handed. In the low grav, it wasn't that much of a strain, and I wanted the effect.

A muscular and tall cyb officer stepped forward—Commander Gorum. Behind him was a full squad of armed marcybs.

"I'm Commander Gorum." Gorum's voice was harsh, and his unspoken net-commands reverberated through the huge docking lock. "Stand easy. . . . Don't shoot unless he reaches for a weapon. Stand easy."

"I recall, Commander. I appreciated meeting you at the Hybernium. I'm returning one of your marcybs. He assaulted a woman two days ago, and I asked Majer Henslom to have him returned to his ship. The majer saw fit to ignore that request. I don't know if the *Gibson* is where he belongs, but I'm sure you can work out the details." I set the trussed figure on the cold deck. He'd probably get frostbite, but I wasn't feeling charitable. Then, I bowed. "I trust you'll take care of it, and, with your permission, we'll be departing."

I turned and walked back toward the open hatch of the magshuttle.

"Stand . . . easy . . ." reverberated Gorum's net-commands.

After stepping back into the shuttle, I triggered the hatch. "Ask for permission to depart."

"Yes, ser," answered Borin. "Vereal flag *Gibson,* this is Magshuttle Prime. Ready for departure this time."

"Wait one, MagPrime."

"They're clearing the lock, ser," Borin reported, as though he couldn't believe it.

K'gaio had been right, and I was both relieved and disappointed. Following the Construct wasn't easy, even when bending it.

"Evacuating lock, MagPrime. Please wait for clearance before lifting. Please wait for clearance before lifting."

"Stet, *Gibson*. Standing by for clearance. Standing by for clearance." Sweat poured down poor Borin's face.

"Don't worry. They'll let us clear. They don't know why, but they will."

"Lock doors are full open. You are cleared to lift. Maintain headway only until you clear the doors. Headway only."

"Stet."

The shuttle eased up and out into the darkness beyond the *Gibson,* away from the adiamante wall that held inconceivable power and hatred.

Borin kept sweating until we were nearly two hundred klicks from the *Gibson*.

"They're going to hate you, ser," he finally offered, after wiping the dampness from his face yet another time.

"They already do. They hate all of us." I yawned and stretched back out on the couch, fastening the restraints.

It was mid-afternoon when Borin approached the park. I'd used the net to check with Crucelle, but nothing had happened since I'd left, except a considerable increase in transmissions between the cyb ships and between their portable net units in Parwon and Ellay.

"Thank you," I told Borin as I waited by the shuttle hatch.

"You're welcome. It was an interesting day, Coordinator."

I wouldn't have used that word, but I nodded, and stepped out onto the browning grass. Borin was actually hovering a quarter meter off the ground. He was good. That took some skill.

I waved, and the door slid shut, and the shuttle lifted.

Miris stood by the west door to the admin building. Behind him stood five armed restraint squad members. I turned to one. "Any problems?"

"Not yet, Coordinator."

"Good."

"Impressive, Coordinator."

"Thank you, Miris."

"I meant it. You actually delivered the marcyb to their flagship?"

"What else could I do?" My eyes caught his.

He looked away. His eyes stayed on my back all the way up the stairs, but the waiting area was empty, except for Keiko. She stood as I approached, smoothing the dark gray vest.

"Did you have to do it yourself?"

"It was cheaper that way." And it was.

"I hope so. Arielle reported that the upsurge in message traffic indicates a greater probability of hostility."

I shook my head, then reached back and massaged my slightly sore neck. "They have to come up with a logical analysis. I *might* have gotten Elanstan some extra time."

"There are cheese and fruit on your desk. I assume you didn't have time to eat?"

"No." I smiled. "Thank you."

"We can't have a Coordinator with thinking impaired by low blood sugar."

I was probably impaired in all too many other ways, but I didn't protest. I just thanked her again and went into the office and ate everything on the tray.

Then I began to study the hard copy material neatly stacked and waiting for me. After three sheets, I reached for the linkboost. As it slipped in, my eyes dropped from the eastern peaks to the desk and the three hard copy sheets that showed the projected peaking of the cyb fleet's power reserves within twenty-four hours.

"Elanstan?" I asked.

"She's on Delta," Rhetoral explained.

"How long before Delta's functional? We're running out of time."

"Do you think your 'incident' shortened that time?" His words weren't quite a question.

"Arielle and I think it probably added a day, but their message traffic is way up."

"Another two days, Ecktor, that's all we need," pleaded Rhetoral. Elanstan wouldn't plead, which was exactly why Rhetoral was on the uppernet with me. She could have linked almost as easily from Delta station.

"All I can promise is one. We might get two days or a week, but one is all I can promise."

"Try for two." Rhetoral's words were ragged, and I knew they'd both been pushing themselves to the limit, but the universe doesn't much care how hard you've worked. Neither do your enemies.

"I'm trying to avoid using the system, but so far, as the saying goes, 'There are none so blind as will not see.' "

"Can't you bend the Construct?" asked Rhetoral. "You are the Coordinator."

"I've already bent it in so many directions that, if I survive this mess, I'll owe a century of comptime." My guts twisted at the exaggeration, and I added, "Not that much, but it *feels* like that much."

"They really don't want to see?"

"They're still hanging on to their yes-no, on-off, single-value, linear logic."

"But they built that fleet."

"Their ancestors also built much of what made us what we are, and then turned their back on the implications of what they'd created. Remember?" I took a deep breath. "Do what you can. I'll keep trying, but after tomorrow, I may need the entire system on line at any instant. Any instant," I emphasized.

"I know you're trying, but . . ."

"Give my best to Elanstan." I knew she was listening in, but I was being polite about it. "We couldn't have two better people there." I meant it. Not only were their self-concepts sword and shield, but their actions matched those concepts. I wasn't about to try and define mine . . . not after all I'd done.

"Thanks. I'd rather be anywhere but here—except where you are, Ecktor."

"Thanks to you, too."

He laughed and was gone offnet.

As the linkboost declined, I could sense a pulse from Keiko.

"Yes, Keiko? I'm off the link with Ell Control."

"Ser . . . Crucelle and Arielle are here."

"They can come in." I hoisted myself out of the green swivel and walked toward the door, which opened before I got within three meters.

Crucelle and Arielle stepped in, and they both looked the way Rhetoral had sounded, with circles darker than mine under their eyes, and deep lines across their foreheads, and eyes that held bloody spiderwebs. Crucelle closed the door behind them, and they slumped into the green chairs. I was left with the long green couch. So I sat there.

Arielle and Crucelle exchanged glances. Neither spoke.

"You see?" she finally said. "If you'd pleaded or stalled or ignored them, they would have tried something else. Now, they're confused."

"How confused?" I asked.

"Not confused enough. In twenty-four hours they'll be angry, so angry that they'll be able to override the implications of what you did."

Another stretch of silence filled the big office. Outside the trees wavered in the wind.

"I take it that your team hasn't made the best of progress on repeating 'the planet of death' approach to the cybs?" I finally asked.

Arielle's dark eyes smoldered, and I was glad I'd never been attracted to her except as a friend.

"It's not going to work, not exactly," Crucelle said. His green eyes betrayed the pain his efforts had caused him. "We can't touch the marcybs, and very few of the cyb officers are in range." He shifted his weight in the chair.

The sky over the eastern peaks remained cold china blue, and the tops of the trees swayed even more in the wind. All the open water, except for fast-running streams, had frozen, and even the streams had ice on the banks where the spray had frozen.

"Go on." Somehow, I'd intuited that something like this would turn up.

Arielle crossed her ankles, then uncrossed them.

Crucelle scratched the back of his head and frowned before continuing. "They've made some changes in the marcybs' genetic codes. Without some sophisticated hardware I can theoretically design, we can't set up electroneural resonance there. Not the way we did with the Jykserians or any of the others. And that hardware would take months or years to build."

"So we're back to the satellite system?" That didn't surprise me, and in some ways I was just as glad that we couldn't create large-scale mindblazes. The thought had bothered me. Supposedly, death is death, but burning out someone's neural system through sympathetic harmonic resonance is incredibly painful—both to the net generator and to the victims, except it had been fatal to virtually all the victims in the case of the Jykserians and only about twenty percent of the operators.

"There's another problem," pointed out Arielle. "A longer-term one that could be worse than this little fleet. The changes they've made to the marcybs are an easy piece of genetic engineering so far as any human-related genetic engineering is easy. They could do that to any egg or sperm, and it's only got to be on one side. Then, they'd be like us, except . . ."

"We'd have no crossovers and no leverage?"

She nodded.

"And they would probably be able to hold up under the mindblaze parameters with around a thirty-five percent mortality—on either end," added Crucelle.

That would effectively neutralize our abilities, and unlike the cybs, we no longer had war fleets—and, under the Construct, no way to build them. If we did, we repeated the errors of the Rebuilt Hegemony, with all the deaths that had caused and the millennia of recovery necessary, assuming we could withstand such a societal trauma a second time. And if we didn't, we could expect ever larger cyb fleets, to the point where Old Earth would be obliterated or forced to build war fleets.

"You seem to be telling me that the physical destruction of the cyb fleet is an absolute imperative."

"I don't know about absolute," hedged the redhead.

"It's the optimal outcome in ninety-four percent of possible logical consistent alternities," declared his dark-haired and dark-eyed soulmate.

"How about the six percent?" I asked.

"For reasons unknown, the cybs withhold an attack: point two percent. The cybs discover and embrace the Construct and Power Paradigms: one percent. They discover the Construct and Power Paradigms, realize their danger, and retreat and regroup for a later and more massive assault: two point eight percent. Unquantified alternatives: two percent."

If Arielle were correct—and, unfortunately, she usually was—we had about as much chance of avoiding all-out conflict as a six-legged jackrabbit had of escaping a meleysen grove. Little or none.

"Me . . . I liked the unquantified options," I quipped.

Arielle didn't smile, although Crucelle offered a faint twist of his lips for a moment.

"That's all we have," Crucelle said, after the silence stretched out and out.

"I can't ask you to give me what you don't have," I responded. "You need to get some rest."

"What are you going to do?" asked Arielle.

"Stall, hope, and try to make some unquantified alternity work out while preparing for the worst."

Crucelle shook his head and stood. "Better you than us."

Arielle still smoldered, like the storm-tossed darkangel she was, all the way out of the office. She hadn't liked my flippancy about her comps and analyses, but with her accuracy record, flippancy was all I had.

I left the office door ajar and walked right up to the south window and looked into the distance that held the house, wondering if three days or a week hence would find everything black glass.

Despite the triple panes, the cold radiated off the glass, and I shivered.

"Coordinator?" Keiko used the net to knock at the edge of my concentration. "Your too-friendly cyb subcommander is on the broadcast line. She wants to know if you'd be interested in visiting the *Gibson* tomorrow. They have a demonstration planned, and she indicated you might be interested. She emphasized that the demonstration did not involve inhabited physical locales. They'll drop a lander for you."

That figured. There was no way they wanted one of our ships near theirs again, especially after my exploits. Going on their lander didn't matter. If it came to that, I was expendable. Coordinators were far more expendable than dozens of locials, and a demonstration that was explained as not involving inhabited physical locales sounded like a threat. Oh, well, a threat involved delay.

"Do you intend to go?" Keiko pulsed.

"Certainly. Why not?" After what I'd just learned . . . why not? That might buy Rhetoral the day he and Elanstan, and all of us, needed. Anyway, logic said that, short of the all-out conflict between the defense system and the cyb fleet, things couldn't get that much worse— except I felt they could . . . and would.

"Such an optimist. I'll confirm the time, and let you know." Keiko dropped offline, and I looked back at the eastern peaks and the cold, china blue sky that had replaced the morning clouds: a china blue that concealed twelve adiamante hulls and a satellite defense system that hadn't been used or fully tested in centuries—and one station that hadn't been functional in a millennium.

Lovely job, Coordinator.

<<< XXV

Looking through the wide south window didn't help my sense of foreboding. The china blue sky and the cold wind that tossed the tops of the cedars and piñons from side to side told my body to shiver, warm as I felt physically.

"The subcommander will pick you up at the locial strip at 1000 tomorrow," Keiko informed me through the local net. "Are you ready for this . . . visit?"

"No. I don't happen to know what I've forgotten, but let me think about it."

"If the cybs decide to relieve you of your responsibilities—and I'm not sure how far you'd go to avoid that comptime, Coordinator—what happens next?"

"K'gaio gets the job."

"Lucky woman." A faint hiss announced Keiko's drop from the net.

Late as it was getting, there was yet another task for the Coordinator, one I didn't relish at all, but since I had agreed to visit the cyb fleet the next morning, I had to check the alternative control center for the defense net.

"Keiko, will you find Dorgan and Wiane? Have them meet me on the upper maintenance level in ten minutes."

"This isn't optional, I take it?"

"No. Coordinator's priority."

"It's getting late."

"I'm late in getting organized, but I'm not used to this. It's only been centuries since someone had to deal with potentially hostile interstellar visitors. Most of my predecessors didn't survive long enough to leave instructions."

"I'll get them." She left the local net with the equivalent of a sigh.

Another thought occurred to me, and I linked to the uppernet.

"K'gaio? This is Ecktor."

"What can I do?" She pulsed back even, oiled words, despite the fact that it had to be just before dawn where she was.

"Tomorrow, I'm paying a courtesy visit to the *Gibson,* the cyb flagship. In a little while, I'll be checking out the alternative systems. You should be available tomorrow, and you might want to be near the local alternative systems center."

"That would be advisable, Ecktor. I will do so, and I appreciate the warning. Good night."

That was as close to an admission that she had been sleeping as I would ever get.

Keiko turned in her chair as I stepped out of the Coordinator's office. "They're waiting below."

"I'll be quite a while."

"Checking out the alternative systems could take some

time," she agreed, proving she had been on uppernet. "And it was wise to inform K'gaio."

"I'm glad you think so. What else should I do?"

"If I were Coordinator, while I happened to be in the alternative system control center, I might check out the defense system nodes."

I'd thought of that, but I just nodded, then grinned and went down the steps to the maintenance level where Dorgan and Wiane waited.

"Good afternoon, Coordinator." Dorgan was thin-faced, dark-skinned, and had thin brown hair shorter than my too-short thatch.

Wiane inclined her head. She was round-faced, solemn-eyed, and willowy.

"Let's go." I headed through the heavy maintenance door and down the ramp.

They followed, and two ramps down, I opened the door to the lower power board area, stepped inside, and closed the door behind them.

"The boards are fine, Coordinator," Dorgan said.

"I know that. We're going for a bullet shuttle ride."

Dorgan swallowed and looked at Wiane. "Are things that serious?"

"The other day, one of the cyb troopers slugged a woman and told her she was useless draff baggage. Since then the situation has gotten worse. The cybs visited both the Cherkrik ruins and a prairie dog town, where they disregarded territoriality. That got one marcyb killed. I had to kill four of the rodents. The cybs claimed it was my fault, essentially, because I had only warned them twice."

"Hmmmm," was all Dorgan said.

"Under the circumstances, I'd like to take a good solid look at the equipment. I hope we won't need it, but if we do, I'm not going to have much time."

Dorgan rubbed his temples. Wiane pursed her lips as I led the way to the concealed staircase and used the Coordinator's codes to unlock the door. I could have used maintenance codes—I'd done work there, but the Coordinator's codes seemed more appropriate.

From the third sublevel, the three of us walked down the steps to the platform. The bullet shuttles glistened under the glowstrips, silver quarrels in their induction notches, ready to be fired toward the control center ten klicks east. Each of the bullets to the alternative control center was short, less than ten meters long, with seven pairs of seats. The bullets to the locial receiving areas were far larger, and far more numerous.

After palming the lockplate on the lead bullet and waiting for the door to whine open, I stepped inside and sat in the right-hand seat. Dorgan and Wiane sat behind me, leaving the left-hand front seat empty.

The ten klick trip took three minutes, almost exactly.

The platform at the other end was empty, silent, and gray. Despite the continual maintenance, the spotless composite walls oozed age—unsurprising, since this particular center had been built nearly twelve centuries earlier. The equipment all worked. I knew. I'd worked on some of it over the years—almost as high a comptime rate as satellite maintenance, and not nearly so dangerous, but requiring an even higher degree of accuracy.

The solid door at the top of the stairs was sealed. This time it took the Coordinator's codes. It could be opened with three separate maintenance codes, which, with three of us, would have posed no problem, but again, using the Coordinator's access seemed more fitting.

The blast door whispered open.

"Activate standby," I pulsed, and the glowstrips turned blackness into warm sunlight, powered by the standby fusactor.

Inside the door was the alternate control center: nothing very impressive, just a handful of hard-wired consoles supported by an independent power system in the sublevels below the equipment. The whole center, except for the bullet tunnel and the access tunnel to the comm grids, which could double as another exit, was surrounded with adiamante.

There were four other centers, scattered around the globe. Any one could handle the defense net, if necessary, but since no one could use the net unless the Construct were violated, conflicts weren't a problem. In those circumstances, no one really wanted my job, including me.

My feet hurt, and I dropped into the main control chair. "Power."

I waited as the other fusactors below came on line, one after another. Dorgan and Wiane looked from me to the boards and back to me as the power built.

Finally, after ten minutes, I slipped into and through the maintenance net for a status report before I opened the system and began the checks.

The status line was green.

"Dorgan, would you cross-check the power system after me, and note any discrepancies?"

"Yes, ser."

I turned to Wiane. "After we're powered up, I'm going into the link relays and the grids. I need you to follow the draw-downs in diagnostics. I assume you know what to look for?"

"Yes, ser. Any disconnects or lags, mostly."

First I went through all the power diagnostics, then pulsed Dorgan, and could feel him on the power systems as I crossed subsystems. Once I called on the net for a test, I had to be quick. So I ran through the maintenance routines again, concentrating on the power to the nodes. The node check showed a few more abnormalities than recorded in the annual test nine months earlier, but well within the statistically insignificant, and with that many potential links and the demi level of tension about the cybs, what else could I have expected?

Next came the pulse tests on node loading, and after that, I tried the node links myself—three times.

The first time was smooth: minor electric currents ran through me, but that invisible link to the big magfield was clear. The second time, in another node, the minor jolts ran down my spine. The third time I never really got to the field, and my eyes and spine burned.

Then, I just sat in the center chair and shivered for a while, letting Dorgan and Wiane run through the diagnostics.

Wiane's eyes unglazed first, and she looked at me. "That last link, ser, you shivered the whole field."

"I know. What about the draw-downs?"

"I couldn't find any. The net's clean."

I hoped so. Then I shivered again. I should have stopped with two node links, but, as Morgen had pointed out so often, I had a tendency to overreach myself.

At that point, Dorgan blinked and turned his head to me. "Power checks clear, ser."

"Fine." I waited another few minutes before I tried to stand. A few white spots flickered in front of my eyes, but disappeared. I walked slowly to the door to the center, then waited for them to leave.

Outside the door above the shuttle platform, I cleared my throat, then flicked the net-command. "Stand by, one red." That left two fusactors up, and the center powered at low-level, until countermanded. It also meant only a few minutes before the center was essentially functional because I wanted to keep the lags short. I had the strong feeling that, when the cybs moved, we'd have little enough time.

Powering the center fully would, unfortunately, trigger too much mistrust among the demis because most would have noted the continual power on the uppernet—the power required for the defense netlinks. And that much mistrust would have been a Construct violation on our part—meaning that if I tried to use the net subsequently, it would crash, leaving us with little or no protection. Even my brief test probably had some of the purists muttering about mistrust and nursing headaches.

My head ached with theirs, and I made my way down to the bullet slowly. Dorgan and Wiane followed.

"Do you have any ideas how soon the cybs might act?" Dorgan finally asked. He was more restrained than most would have been.

"I'm intuiting that we have twenty-four hours." I gave a half-shrug as I climbed into the bullet. "Maybe more, and there's a slight chance that they'll leave us alone."

"How slight?" asked Wiane. "You left the center on high standby."

"Very slight. But several have pointed out that I could be wrong." I leaned back in the bullet seat.

"I hope so, Coordinator." She paused as the doors closed. "But we have a Coordinator, and they're cybs, and that combination doesn't look good."

I thought so, too, but I just closed my eyes for the ride back to the admin building. No flitter trip back to the house this night—just a bunk in the transient area. I'd thought that might happen sooner or later; I did have a spare set of blacks and some sanitary necessities stashed in the office, and I was glad I did.

I also needed to eat. I just hoped Locatio didn't have any more problems—and that no one else did, either.

<<< XXVI

You let them toss a webbed marcyb through the locks?" asked Weapons, his question reverberating along the net-lines.

"Outside of blasting their shuttle, what would you have suggested?" asked Ideomineo. "Or would you have had me blast their planetary Coordinator? That wouldn't set well anywhere, not when he arrived in an unarmed shuttle."

"The effrontery . . . the gall . . ." Gorum's words hissed and spat fire through the net.

"Also, the stupidity," snapped Weapons. "Marcybs aren't much more than constructs."

"Why don't you think, Weapons?" suggested Ideomineo. "Don't you think the demi Coordinator knows that?"

"What are you suggesting, Exec?" asked Gibreal, his words cool against the residual fire of Gorum's outburst.

"This was the same demi who was on the prairie creature expedition. There he was angry at Viedras and the nav. Today he didn't show much interest in the marine officers, and he treated the marcybs like valued machinery. Here on the ship he was matter-of-fact."

"Then why would he care about a single marcyb?" questioned Gibreal. "He'd have to know that Henslom was the responsible one." A barrier blocked any further questioning, as if the fleet commander were holding back information.

"What else could you tell us, ser?" asked Gorum too politely, with honey wrapped around the acid of yet unpulsed words.

"I think we should hear the rest of the Exec's analysis, especially since the nav is already headed planetside."

The image of wiggling hips crossed the net.

"Sanitize," ordered Ideomineo in a weary tone. He waited for the image to fade. "From Majer Henslom's report, this kidnapping and return was staged," he continued after a pause. "Black uniforms, a public grab, and an immediate shuttle lift—what does that suggest?"

"Go on."

"I submit that there are certain political realities that

the Coordinator must observe. He knows that the marcybs are one step above constructs, but the draffs don't. That means that the demis are in some way beholden. Or that their power over the draffs is limited."

"So we ought to just flatten them," Weapons suggested.

"Something else interesting just came from Majer Ysslop," interjected Gibreal. "As instructed, she sent a two-agent team to attack the major power and systems centers of the Ellay local. Both agents vanished after inflicting minor damage. Their links were severed, and not even their imbedded tracers seem to have survived."

"The demis were ready. They were just waiting," riposted Weapons. "We shouldn't give them any warning."

"We're missing something," suggested Ideomineo.

"Maybe there aren't that many demis," suggested Gorum. "Individually, they're extremely powerful, but perhaps there aren't more than a few hundred on the whole planet."

"Analysis is flawed," clipped MYL-ERA. "Energy-web analytics would indicate between one and three million demis."

"That still means the draffs are eighty to ninety percent of the population."

"Let's see what happens to their Coordinator after he views our little demonstration," suggested Gibreal. "He may become more cooperative. If not, well, then we shall proceed."

<<< **XXVII**

Despite another light dusting of snow the night before, the sky was cold and bright blue when, at 0950 Deseret local time, I stood underneath the white spire of the tower, watching as the black cyb lander rumbled up. A chill wind blew out of the northwest, gusting and carrying wisps of snow across the landing strip.

At 0955 the ramp dropped, and Subcommander Kemra stepped onto it, walked halfway down, and gestured toward me brusquely.

"They're here," I pulsed on the net to Keiko. "If anything happens . . ."

"I know," my aide responded, "K'gaio gets the enviable job of Coordinator. She'll create more problems than you have, and that's saying a great deal."

"I appreciate your backhanded confidence in me, too."

"Someone has to put things in perspective."

I waved back at Kemra and walked toward the dull black lander that radiated a faint odor of hot composite and metal.

The cyb subcommander looked down at me, green eyes cool and level.

"Greetings," I said.

"I'm here to convey you to a demonstration." Kemra remained at the top of the lander's ramp.

"You wish you weren't," I observed, not moving.

"That's right."

"Why?"

"That doesn't matter. Are you ready?"

"It does matter. If you're angry because you said that I had reasons for my actions, and you were disregarded by your peers and superiors, I apologize. If you're angry because I refuse to fit your expectations, I don't."

"You are difficult." Her words remained flat, cold.

"I try to be honest, and honesty is frowned on in most cultures because it's too hard on people's egos, and that creates tensions that most societies cannot handle."

The cold wind rippled through her sandy hair, and the cold green eyes remained fixed on me. "You demis are different?"

"We try."

"So you're honest? I find that rather hard to believe."

"No human is totally honest. Our egos can't take that kind of honesty. I know that I tend to be slightly self-pitying, that I have an exaggerated sense of self-importance, and that I equate physical conditioning with superiority. That's the tip of the iceberg, but if someone told me those things, I'd be angry."

"You do take yourself seriously." A trace of a smile flitted at the corners of her mouth.

"So do you."

The smile vanished.

"See what I mean?"

She shook her head. "We need to go—if you're still interested."

"Is the subject of this demonstration a secret?"

"Only until it's over."

"We don't much care for alterations to Old Earth." I glanced up at the fifteen-meter-high cyb lander, and its winged black lifting body.

"We've gathered that." She half turned, then paused. "Why did you bring that marcyb back to the *Gibson?*"

"There wasn't a single reason. A sense of responsibility, a need to affirm that injustice cannot be imposed at the focal point of a laser or de-energizer or particle beam. Some anger. Some frustration. Some male egotism."

"Is that all?"

"Probably not."

"You never answer anything completely."

"That's because there are no complete answers, except death, and that's one I'd rather avoid."

She walked up the ramp past the pilot I'd met before. I shrugged and followed, nodding to Kessek as I stepped past him. He did not nod back.

The ramp rumbled upward before I reached the left-

hand forward officers' couch. Kemra sat down and slipped
her harness into place without looking toward me.

"Ready for liftoff, Kessek," Kemra pulsed to the pilot.

"Stet."

I pulled the restraint harness around me and leaned
back in the supple black couch. A residual stiffness permeated too many muscles, and my hands remained sore,
but they hadn't bruised—not yet. Still a trace shaky from
my tests on the alternative control center the night before,
I took a slow, deep breath to help relax myself. The lander
had no scent of use except ozone and hot metal and oil—
as if it had carried few troops or passengers indeed. After
a second deep breath, I closed my eyes.

Kessek turned the lander into liftoff position, and we
began to accelerate down the strip.

The entire liftoff and the climb to orbit were at full
power, clearly to test me in some way, since there were several scanners focused in my direction.

As Kessek finally cut back on the acceleration, and
comparative quiet filled the cabin, Kemra looked at me,
then away.

"Coordinator!" Keiko honed in on the uppernet. "Nearly
a dozen cyb agents attacked the power, admin, and distribution nexi in Ellay. Locatio reports that they destroyed
them all, but that there were several draff fatalities."

Another presence lurked behind her on the net.

"Do what we did in Deseret. Have the deaths reported
as caused by massive systems failures. But announce that
the cause of the failures has yet to be fully determined."

"Ecktor!" whined in Locatio. "People are going to
know."

"That's fine. I don't want anything outside the direct
nets. The hard nets, the screen news—anything the cybs
can access—there I want the official line. Ysslop may try
again. Bring in more demi squads. I want the cyb agents
to keep disappearing, like into a black hole."

"Ecktor . . ."

"That's it." I closed off my net access for a few moments and waited, held in place by the couch restraints. My stomach felt unsettled in the virtual null gee.

"He used something there, Subcommander," Kessek pulsed to Kemra on the cyb net. "We couldn't even record it."

"You aren't quite as honest as you'd like me to believe," Kemra began, turning in the couch to face me.

"In what way?"

"You seem able to use some sort of net to penetrate even a lander hull, and you're carrying no noticeable equipment. That's rather deceptive."

I laughed. "Since when is not announcing all of one's abilities deceptive? Would you care to describe *all* of your abilities, including personal and sexual attributes?"

She flushed, then glared.

I ignored her reaction. "Somehow, you people seem to think that we're supposed to parade all our talents, technology, and ability for you to analyze, in order for you to decide whether you can get away with either attacking or attempting to conquer us—or trying to steal knowledge. And if we don't cooperate, we're deceptive?" I laughed again.

"I told Henslom you were a dangerous man. I think I underestimated you." Her words were thoughtful in the comparative silence of our approach to the cyb fleet.

"How is Majer Henslom?"

"He's angry, extraordinarily angry."

"I can see how that might be. He's been deceived into believing that no one would or could stand up to him."

"How many demis are there like you?"

"Exactly like me? None. With roughly the same level of ability . . . I'd say a quarter of a million."

There was silence.

"He's lying . . . he has to be," pulsed Kessek.

"How would you define 'roughly'?" she pursued.

"In quantifiable terms . . . within five percent on any measurable ability, and within one percent overall."

Silence.

"Then why are you Coordinator?"

"I told you. Being Coordinator exacts a high price. I have a lot less to lose than most: I'm older; my soulmate is dead; and I'm considered slightly less sane in demi terms."

"Why is being less sane an advantage?"

I was the one who paused at that, although I should have seen the line of questioning. "Self-preservation is part of sanity. I'm considered less sane because I don't value it quite so highly at this stage of my life. Besides, anyone who accepts being Coordinator in times like these probably is less sane."

"You act like you want to be a target."

"All things being equal, I'd prefer not to be one." But all things were not equal. How could I not try something that would spare hundreds of thousands, if not millions?

"You talk as if you were an old man, but you look and act as if in the prime of life. How old are you?"

"Old enough to know better." Old enough not to play word games. Old enough not to gamble with Old Earth's future with a green-eyed woman who looked faintly like Morgen.

Words we whispered flamed in vain. . . . That soulsong fragment reminded me how different Morgen and Kemra were, that Kemra represented a mere chance physical resemblance that played on my synapses.

"That's not even an incomplete answer."

"My chronological age is sixty-seven."

Her eyes didn't even flicker. "That's not ancient."

I wasn't about to tell her that too-sensitive Crucelle was close to two hundred. Instead, I glanced at the screen and the black adiamante wall that was the *Gibson.* "That was quick."

"Fleet Commander Gibreal would not wish to waste anyone's time."

The screen on the bulkhead showed the same enormous lock I had entered the day before, except it didn't seem quite so large compared to the entering cyb lander.

The lander slid into the *Gibson*'s docking bay with scarcely a clunk, and the massive lock doors slid shut like a cage closing.

"Smooth docking . . . locking . . . whatever it's called," I offered.

"You're not that much of a kaybe." Kemra almost laughed. "You're a hands-on flitter pilot."

"Kaybe?" That was the first time I'd heard that one.

"Short for keyboarder. Someone so out of touch . . ."

"I get it." Someone so out of touch they wouldn't link directly but were limited to manual dexterity in using systems and nets—a voluntary draff, of sorts. The complexity of competence, anger, and irritation continued to give me trouble reading her, but I was comp-intuit, not an emote or empath.

I emulated Kemra's example and unfastened the restraints and eased myself up, swinging out of the restraints in the low gee and toward Kemra. I found myself close to her, within perhaps two dozen centimeters, and I realized something else. She didn't have much of a body-scent-image—just the faintest whiff of a soap, and a scent-suppressant. I frowned. The scent suppression was another oddity. I'd wondered what had been wrong when she'd stood close to me in the Cherkrik ruins, but I hadn't identified it. Were they all like that, disassociating themselves from the smells of the world around them?

"Lock's pressurized," announced Kessek. "Hold for the heat burst."

A superheated air-steam mixture disrupted the lock momentarily, but brought the ambient lock temperature up a good two hundred degrees absolute. Then the lander's ramp rumbled down, and a wave of polar air engulfed us.

"You'll get a quick tour before the demonstration, but we'll have to hurry," Kemra said.

That was ominous. A tour before the demonstration meant no one expected me to be friendly afterwards.

The *Gibson*'s gravity remained at what seemed around point three earth norm, and my legs had a tendency to bound as we crossed the lock. The two unused landers remained at the far end of the lock, shrouded in a frost that boiled off them. The chill of the deck seeped through my boots despite their thick soles and the insulation over the metalite composite. My heavy steps echoed off the composite deck covering, the sounds lost in the huge cavern.

The lock chamber itself must have been five hundred meters long and nearly fifty high. Just refilling the space after docking had to require an enormous expenditure of mass and energy—an incredible waste.

"Potlatch and status symbol," I murmured. "Throwaway power." Had they built the hull first and then just filled it as they saw fit? Just to have built some of the most massive vessels in millennia?

The faintest of scanner energies passed over me, pulling my image onto the shipnet—the open net that I could easily access enough to see my own image and that of Kemra walking across the enormous lock. Just an average dark-haired man and a slender sandy-haired woman—cyb officer, I corrected myself.

A guard of twenty-four marcybs in formal green uniforms waited by the exit hatch—a dozen on each side.

"Such formality," I murmured.

"Planetary executives do rate an honor guard."

The marcybs remained rigid as we passed. I wanted to yell something like "at ease" or "fire on deck." I didn't, just nodded, still disconcerted at the hypocrisy of the honor guard and at seeing my own image appearing on the shipnet.

We stepped through the hatch into a central hexagonal passageway, the corners between each surface filled with a thin glowstrip, the raised edges on each side of the glowstrip containing handholds for null gee operations. The side that comprised the "ceiling" was not a walking surface, but a ladder with rungs nearly eight meters long, supported at the ends and at two meter intervals in the middle.

"I'd hate to have to climb this." I forced my face to remain calm as I heard my own words cross the net.

"So far no one has, but the designers insisted." She gestured. "We'll head aft."

"Why a hexagonal corridor?" I disconnected from the shipnet I wasn't even supposed to notice, trying to remind myself that everything I said, everything I did, would be recorded and used. The slight delay in following both Kemra and the net was scrambling my senses, and I didn't need scrambled senses.

"The whole ship's set up that way. It works better with adiamante, the designers found. That's the official reason, anyway."

I hadn't thought that adiamante had a hexagonal bias, but I certainly didn't know. We had used it only sparingly and, alternate control centers excepted, hadn't done much with it in the last millennium except to deconstruct it, and that had been well before my time.

The corridor, although apparently one of the main fore-and-aft passages, was empty except for us. I didn't like that either. On a ship that carried thousands, that was another unhealthy sign.

Kemra walk-bounded aft, and I struggled to keep up with her in the light grav.

"How do you keep in shape?" I asked.

"Stay at home in low gee, you mean? The senior officers' quarters are high gee. The troopers have to make up for it with exercise, but they have the time, and we don't."

That made a strange sort of sense. Before I said more, we were at the hydroponic bays, somewhere near midships. No matter what anyone says about synthesis, repeated chem-synthesis doesn't work, and the systems lose vitamins and trace elements, or concentrate them inappropriately. Even the cybs had to grow some food. Or chose to. With the *Gibson*'s size, they could have carried a few decades of dehydrated food, even for the thousand or so the ship seemed to carry.

After looking at the long rows of greenery, hundreds of meters long, I turned to Kemra. "How many levels here?"

"Eight."

"Eight levels . . ." I mused half-aloud. Eight levels, each hundreds of meters long and stretching possibly the entire width of the ship. "You don't really need these, not for the crew the ship carries."

"It depends on what you mean by need. We can recycle everything through here, and everyone feels better." She offered a wry grin. "People trust plants more than machines."

Maybe the cybs did have a less crystalline side.

Next we turned off the main corridor into a narrower hexagonal passage, with doors every few meters. The single narrow corridor stretched more than three hundred meters to a distant and sealed hatch.

"These quarters belong to the troopers staying on Old Earth," Kemra explained. She pressed a lockplate on the side of the nearest door.

I glanced inside—four bunks, chairs, a vision screen on the blank forward wall and jacks for headsets of some sort. The walls were a pale green plastic-like finish, and an open door led to a fresher.

"All like this?" I asked.

Kemra crossed the passage and pushed another plate,

and I looked again at a mirror duplicate of the first empty room. The rooms reminded me of the descriptions of ancient monastical cells.

"I just wanted you to see." She retraced her steps to the main corridor, and we continued aft. "This whole section here is for troopers."

I calculated as we walked. Even on one level, there had to be room for more than five hundred marcybs—6,000 at a minimum on the twelve ships, 18,000 if the quarters stretched up even three levels, and more than 50,000 if six levels.

"Did you really think you'd need fifty thousand troopers for broken-down Old Earth?" I asked.

"Gorum thought fifty thousand was too few, but feeding large forces you may not need takes power and storage space."

Maybe they did need those huge hydroponic systems.

After that, another four hundred meters aft of the marcyb quarters—another four hundred meters unmarked with side hatches or doors—we stepped through two heavy open hatches. Even before I stepped through the hatches, I could sense the energy swirls.

"The power section. I'm sure you can sense the fluxes."

"It must be difficult for your shipnet."

"It's not a problem anymore. The initial engineering was difficult."

Once again, we were talking around issues, she because she wished to reveal nothing when every word was being monitored, and I because . . . I wasn't sure. Personal cowardice? Fear that revealing capabilities would push me too far beyond the envelope of the Construct?

"It won't hurt to show you a single module." Kemra guided me to another interior hatch lock and we stepped up to a small oblong armaglass window. There wasn't that much to see through the armaglass—just an insulated oblong fifty meters on a side with supercon cabling exiting into a conduit. Each side of the composite oblong contained another lock-type door, probably double or triple thickness, and everything was gray, gray, and gray. Even the light seemed gray.

"Each module is self-contained," Kemra pointed out, "and the flow conduits are independently channeled. Any single module can handle the ship's housekeeping."

"But not ops or weapons or drive systems."

"No."

"How many modules?" I asked idly.

"Enough."

From the power flows I sensed, I figured between twenty and thirty—twenty or thirty far larger than anything on Old Earth not connected to the defense net. "I'm sure."

Further aft were the drive systems, but I didn't see them. As we returned to the main corridor, Kemra just pointed, "There's the drive section, but we need to get forward now."

"Demonstration time?"

"It will be before long."

We turned forward. As we left the power section, well before the marcyb dormitories, Kemra paused. "I forgot. There's one other thing. This way."

She led me down a side corridor—the whole ship seemed like a maze, comprised of adiamante walls and composite supports and corridors. She coded the lockplate of another hatch, and I picked up the codes, not that they'd be particularly useful.

"This is lock two."

In the massive multi-level lock were twenty craft the size of a large magshuttle.

"Armed scouts." Kemra pointed to the nearest. "Each one carries a full range of weapons."

I waited to hear how extensive that range of weapons was, but she seemed unlikely to elaborate.

"Antimatter pellets, tach-heads—that sort of thing?" I asked.

"Standard weapons," she answered.

In short, at least as nasty as I'd predicted—not that the scouts mattered that much, since launching them, in my view, would also negate restrictions on me under the Construct. In a way, seeing the scouts was beneficial, since it clarified that any hostile action was backed with impressive force. That would negate any restrictions on response, assuming we could create an effective response. I hoped Elanstan and Rhetoral—ancient shield and longsword— were managing to rebuild poor defunct Delta station.

"What do you think?" asked Kemra.

"About the same as before," I admitted. "Your fleet represents the greatest concentration of force since the Rebuilt Hegemony."

"Greater than the forces of Old Earth?" A faintly amused smile crossed her lips and vanished.

"Greater than any fleets we have, since we don't have any."

"You didn't answer my question."

"There isn't an answer. You have a fleet. We don't. We have a few interstellar ships, and a planet, and you could inflict great damage. If you tried, we would attempt to stop that. If we were successful, then you would have no fleet. If not, we'd probably have no planet, or one that's not inhabitable. At this time, I am hoping that it does not become an issue of force. Everyone loses in those circumstances."

"Can't you give me a straight answer?" The green eyes flashed at me.

"I can't answer you the way you want me to," I finally said. "I'm doing what I can."

"All right. I shouldn't have pushed." Her voice sounded resigned, and I wished I could have said more.

She gestured, and I followed her forward, silently, for several hundred meters more down the still empty corridor. Why didn't they want me to see anyone? Or didn't they want the ship's personnel to see me and learn we still looked and acted human? Except they had me on the net, and that didn't make sense. What wasn't I seeing? Were personal meetings hard on the average cyb because they were shielded by their nets and preferred to avoid most personal meetings? Were the corridors empty not by order, but by choice?

Abruptly, Kemra opened a side hatch, and bounded down it. I hurried to catch up and half stumbled, half tumbled through a wave of energy where the ship's air vibrated around me—some type of magnetic imaging probe being focused. It took every bit of effort to keep walking, holding on to the faith that it wasn't in the cybs' interest to destroy or neutralize me—yet.

The feeling passed as we walked past an open hatch with a double lock, and I wanted to smile. I'd just walked through a medical scanner. That was all, and the results wouldn't offer much. All the normal human organs were of the usual sizes and in the usual places. So were the muscles, although a detailed enough analysis might show some deviation from the historical norms in the composition of fast- and slow-twitch muscles and the muscle density.

As for nerve cells—that would take a high-powered autopsy, and I wasn't ready to provide the specimens for such an analysis, not voluntarily.

"You need to see the control center." Kemra guided me into another narrow passageway that headed forward again. We paused at another armored hatch, and at this one I caught both codes and the message she pulsed. "Kemra, with the demi. Screen guard."

"Cleared to enter. Guards up," came the response.

The entire center area was girded with adiamante, except for the two locks outlined in energy. Impressive as it was in one way, it was idiotic in another, since anything powerful enough to penetrate the ship's outer adiamante hull would be powerful enough to destroy the thinner interior shell around the control center.

"This is the control center."

"Navigation and control center?" I asked, since the arrayed consoles weren't that much to look at: two dozen specialized navigation screens, most of them untended, displaying various representations of the solar system, beneath a sweeping visual screen that showed the earth spread out against the black and the moon to the right edge. Half the console outputs were blackened, screen-guarded against the dangerous demi. I held back a snort.

Five cybs in green singlesuits tended the front line of consoles. None looked up, but they didn't have to, since they were on the shipnet that had displayed my every move since I'd entered the *Gibson*.

The room held the contradictory impressions of newness and age, and the faintest scents of ozone and oil. While the cybs might erase their own scent-images, they couldn't erase those of their machines. I wanted to laugh at the idea that their machines were more human than they were, and that laugh wanting to break out showed the stress pounding down on me.

The thirty-meter-square center held no weapons or sensor inputs, and it was clear I wasn't going to be allowed anywhere near the operations or weapons centers—or whatever combined center held them both.

My eyes went to the twenty-meter-wide visual screen, and I frowned. Although the scale was difficult to determine, the *Gibson* appeared to be moving away from Old Earth and toward Luna.

I moistened my lips.

"We need to go."

After a last look at the wide screen—and the *Gibson* was indeed headed toward Luna—I followed Kemra out of the nav-control center.

"You've seen some of the ship. What do you think?"

"It's an impressive vessel, as I said before." I was impressed in spite of my secondhand recollection—pulled through the databases at Parwon—of the battlecruisers of the Rebuilt Hegemony. The old Hegemony battlecruisers had carried a few more destructive tools, but the *Gibson* had more than enough gadgetry and power to turn the country around far too large a number of locials into black glass or the equivalent.

"We hoped you would find it so." She stopped at a silver-rimmed hatch, and pulsed a signal, coded, while sending a message on the shipnet. "There's one last stop we need to make before the demonstration." The hatch slid open, and she gestured for me to enter.

The room was large for a starship—say half the size of my expansive Coordinator's office—and it held one console with an array of screens I couldn't see centered on one seat. Three empty blue chairs faced the console. A hawk-nosed officer with eight-pointed stars on the collars of his green uniform tunic sat behind the console. His faded and piercing blue eyes followed me into the office/command center.

"This is Fleet Commander Gibreal."

The hawk-nosed commander nodded, but said nothing. He didn't smell either, except of unbridled power.

The incipient energy fluxes around the walls indicated that the ship's systems were focused on and around me—quite a compliment, that they thought I could be that dangerous.

"I'm pleased to meet you, Commander." I didn't attempt to infiltrate the ship's system through the netlinks I'd unraveled. First, it wouldn't do any good, since someone, presumably the weapons officer, had a hard lock on the surveillance and power. Second, it would only make things worse.

"Sit down," Gibreal said, brushing aside my pleasantries, and pointing to the chair on the right side of the console. "I've read this *Paradigms* document. How can you make something like this work?"

"You can't," I explained as I sat. "There's no way to *make* any society work over the long run."

Kemra sat in the left-hand chair and nodded, ever so slightly, but Gibreal just frowned.

"Every society is based on trust and self-restraint. We encourage both, and we remove those who cannot or will not exercise them."

"Power-based, then . . ." muttered Gibreal, his eyes straying to the console, then snapping back to focus on me.

"Not exactly. We also penalize the use of power, even for good. Because I've been Coordinator, I'll spend years at relatively hard labor, working off that debt."

The sensors trained on me were trying to read and determine my degree of truthfulness. I'd already resolved to be truthful, but I had the feeling that truthfulness would only be read as deception if the results didn't agree with the cybs' preconceived perceptions.

"And you accepted the position? Why?"

"Someone had to, and the cost to me was somewhat less than others."

"I've read those principles. They're all so general. How can you possibly make them work? You talk of forbearance, but everyone has a different idea of what forbearing is. And trust? How can you define it or codify it?" Gibreal watched me like the hawk he resembled.

"We don't. When you have to codify values, you've lost them. Every written definition creates more exceptions, more chance of mistrust, and more opportunities for the untrustworthy to hide behind words and legalisms. Some historians theorize that the SoshWars were caused by the ancient clan of lawyers."

"Too many legalities aren't good," Gibreal admitted in a mild tone, "but to blame unrest and warfare on lawyers or programmers—they also codify . . . that seems excessive."

Kemra's eyes flicked from one of us to the other, and back again.

"I wasn't alive back then," I conceded, "but I don't think so. If a society agrees that theft is not acceptable, then theft is not acceptable. Now, let's say that an apple falls from my neighbor's tree and rolls into my yard. Is it theft if I eat it? Probably not, and no sensible individual would argue about a single apple or even a few. When a lawyer writes down and codifies theft as not including fallen apples that roll away, then that creates the opportunity for some untrustworthy individual to shake apples from a tree onto a slanting ramp that carries them off the property. Then that untrustworthy individual can claim he did not steal the apples—not according to the law."

"No one would do that."

I just smiled. "Before the SoshWars, people did exactly that sort of thing."

Gibreal stared at me, almost unbelievingly. It was an expression I was getting to know too well. Then he asked, "What can you do to stop us?"

"We hope that you'll see that there's no point in attacking Old Earth. We don't threaten you, and we haven't been interested in territorial expansion for a long time."

"That's not the question."

"No. It's not. The question is whether you can get away with revenge for being thwarted millennia ago."

Kemra's mouth opened fractionally, then shut, but I'd had to follow intuition. Gibreal was too sharp for my second-rate logic.

"If you would follow Subcommander Kemra to the observation room, our demonstration is about to begin." Gibreal stood as if I hadn't spoken at all. He hadn't really heard a word. All he'd wanted to do was to evaluate me as though I were his personal opponent.

The observation room was just that—a small room with three wall-sized screens and a dozen black padded chairs. The heavy shielding was clearly designed to keep cybs or me or both from interfering with operations. If I'd wished, I could have created some difficulties, but not before the energy weapons in the shield emplacements had made even more difficulty for me.

Luna now filled two-thirds of the center screen, and a growing sense of horror bubbled up within me as I settled into one of the center chairs. Kemra sat two chairs away. No one else entered the room.

"Five minutes until commencement of demonstration. Five minutes," came the human voice of MYL-ERA from the hidden speakers.

"What are you planning?"

"No more than others have done," Kemra answered crisply. "No more than you."

How did one answer that?

"Demonstration commencing in three minutes. Three minutes."

Luna had ceased to grow in the screen and now filled almost the entire focus, blotched in white and black, the terminator splitting the moon's image into a third of darkness and two-thirds of silvered light.

The cybnet whined and strained, and a prickling burning feeling ran through the cyb-limbo that was neither underweb nor overspace, yet which bore some elements of each. The power concentrations that poured from the linked fusactors into the magbottle focus were already twisting space itself, and sending harmonics through the overweb.

For millennia the wave of disruption that was building would cross the galaxy, puzzling future astronomers— those that captured or recorded it. More than a few demis—me included—would have splitting headaches before long.

I watched the screen, as I had been directed, although I could have caught and held the images in my mind as easily.

"Demonstration commencing."

Still, the energies built in the magbottle for a moment longer before they lashed outward, downward at the satellite below.

For long instants, nothing happened.

For minutes, nothing occurred. Nothing. One untutored in physics or deep-space might assume that, when enough energy to power half a mid-tech planet poured from an adiamante hull toward the moon, some visible sign might immediately appear. That assumption would be wrong.

The first sign was mist rising from the moon, though it was not mist, but vaporized rock and associated gases. I rubbed my forehead, trying to handle the distortions created by that much power, trying to shield my mind against the knives of power and the implications for the Construct.

Even the *Gibson* shuddered the entire length of its klicks-long hull as the energy poured forth . . . and forth.

Kemra's eyes flicked from me to the screen and back again.

That mist of vaporized rock and metal, lunar north of the ancient linear induction accelerator, widened and rose and shimmered.

The *Gibson* shivered, wrenching underweb and overspace, overloading low nets and shutting down the internal public net.

A smoother oval began to appear, ringed in darker material, peering through the fog of vaporized rock, growing larger with each gigajoule per nanosecond.

After a quarter hour, a molten eye peered from old Luna.

How wide was the new sea, the new crater? Two hundred klicks? Three hundred? It didn't matter. The baleful reddish glint to the polished surface would give the moon the look of a bloodshot eye staring down at Old Earth—at least when the new crater hardened and was fully sunlit.

The old god Lyr didn't operate on Luna, where the seas were dust and rock, but was a god of Old Earth, as my mother had said.

I closed my eyes for a time, not that there was much else I could do in response to the threat and the incredible waste of power used to deliver it. Knives stabbed through my skull.

When I reopened my eyes, still watering, the diminishing disc of the moon indicated that the *Gibson* was rejoining the rest of the fleet off Old Earth—the next target for the massive particle beams and the still-unused de-energizers that had to lurk within the adiamante hull that surrounded me like a niellen cage.

I studied the screen for a moment longer, taking in the polished orb-within-an-orb that was clearly meant as a reminder that the power of the cybs was not to be disregarded.

It might prove a different reminder, one I could do without. The cybs' reliance on physical might was a problem, a problem bigger than it had ever been for our ancestors. It would be difficult—if not impossible—to reason with hate-fired anger supported by a faith in the idea that physical force able to rearrange the appearance of a solar system was the best manner in which to resolve all problems.

I tried not to take too deep a breath, knowing that Kemra would misunderstand, but the power of both the cybs' hatred and that concentrated particle beam had reverberated through me—and both had hurt. My head and tense muscles ached, and I sat in the chair for a time, wrestling with my self-system, and gathering myself together.

Finally, I stood.

"I trust that the demonstration is concluded." My head still hurt, and I massaged my temples with the fingers of my right hand.

"That was the demonstration," Kemra said.

I wanted to say something, but what could I say at that moment? So I asked, "Now what?"

"That's all." Her voice held a hint of disappointment, as though I should have said or done something, but I didn't, and she touched the access plate.

The door opened.

Gorum was waiting outside the observation room, smiling. "What did you think of our little demonstration, Coordinator?"

I pushed back simultaneous waves of anger and sadness and met his eyes full. "It was an impressive display of brute power, Commander. I doubt the like of it has been attempted or seen since the high point of the Rebuilt Hegemony."

"It would seem the Coordinator was impressed," Gorum noted to Kemra.

"When the Rebuilt Hegemony did something similar at Al-Moratoros," I added, keeping my voice dispassionate, "it was the beginning of its end."

"That's an odd sort of threat, if it's a threat," said Gorum.

"It's an observation. We don't threaten. We can't threaten." That was as far as I could push it, and I looked at Kemra. "If you would be so kind as to return me to Deseret . . ."

". . . got to him finally," gloated Gorum on the shipnet. "He admitted they don't have the power to threaten."

"He didn't mean it that way, Commander." Kemra's pulsed response was pushed away before she finished.

I turned in the direction of lock one, and Kemra bounded to catch me. We continued aft for several moments before she spoke. "Why didn't you tell him what you said wasn't an admission of weakness?"

"Because that would have made it a threat."

"I don't understand you demis. A warship boils a hole in your moon, and you say nothing. Why not?"

"As I told Gorum, we once boiled away the entire surface of another world's moon. What could I say? That it was wrong? That we're still paying for it? That any people who does that will eventually pay for it?"

"You just threatened. Why didn't you tell Gorum that?"

"It isn't a threat, and I didn't tell him, and he didn't hear what I said," I answered tiredly. "Remember Viedras and the prairie dogs? I told Viedras to stop. It wasn't a threat; it was an observation."

Kemra halted at the heavy hatch to lock one, slipping onto shipnet and coding her entry. I waited.

The first hatch opened, and we stepped through. As it closed, the second one opened, and we walked through it and across the open space of lock one toward the waiting shuttle. No marcybs remained to pipe me off the *Gibson.*

"An observation? Explain that, if you would." Kemra's voice contained both anger and bewilderment.

I shrugged, and nearly lost my balance in the low gee. "It's simple. Using that much power results in one of two things. Either those against whom you use it retaliate with greater power, or they don't. In the first case, the result is obvious. In the second case, what happens is that so much power translates into inner arrogance within the society, and for a number of well-documented and intricate reasons I won't try to explain in detail, leads to the destruction of that society's power. That's what happened to the Rebuilt Hegemony, and quite a few other societies."

"You're impossible and patronizing," she snapped. "You won't explain because you can't. It's just some magic that you believe, and think everyone else should believe." Kemra stopped at the foot of the lander ramp.

I lurched to avoid running into her.

"Well, can you explain this mumbo-jumbo magic?"

"Not in your terms."

"In yours then."

I looked at the lander looming above us in the chill of lock one, then at Kemra's eyes, even more chill than the air around me. "Power attracts those who are corrupt. A society that can destroy a moon or a continent or boil a hole in a satellite that will last for millions of years offers immense power. That power attracts and creates equally great corruption. No society has ever lasted in the form that exercised such power because that much power is far more attractive to its members than the moral restraint necessary to maintain a functioning society. That's because no society can continue when every member insists on receiving back more than he or she contributed. The exercise of power requires that those in power receive much more than they contribute, and that means all too many others feel cheated, and fewer and fewer will abide by society's rules."

Kemra shook her head. "You're incredibly naive. For all your brilliance, you are so naive. Most members of any society couldn't even understand what you're talking about. And they wouldn't care."

"No," I said slowly. "They couldn't say what I said. But they feel it, and care, and they act upon it. I gave you your answer. Could we leave?" I'd given them clue after clue, answer after answer, and they wouldn't listen. They couldn't listen.

"Yes, we can leave." She turned angrily.

I followed more slowly and strapped into the couch silently.

Neither of us said anything until Kessek had the shuttle well clear of the *Gibson*.

As we sat in our separate couches in the lander, Kemra

turned toward me and asked bluntly, "Why didn't you clone her?"

"Who?" I was still trying to figure out a better explanation for why successful use of massive force would destroy the cybs—if we didn't first.

"Your soulmate. What was her name? Did you have children?"

"Morgen." I paused as the lander's attitude jets fired once, twice. "I thought we were talking about why excessive use of force—"

"We won't ever agree on the use of force," Kemra said in exasperation. "Let's keep it simple. Maybe I can understand this on a personal basis. First, children. Did you have any?"

"We have a daughter. She's grown—a marine biologist."

"Does she have children?"

"No. What does this have to do with—"

"Just a minute. I'm getting there. Why didn't you clone Morgen and just feed her mind to the clone?"

I tried not to wince, but the wrongness of that ripped at me. I swallowed and finally answered. "It would have been wrong."

"You . . . a demi? You—of those who once imposed your concepts of right on the galaxy? You worry about right and wrong?"

"Strangely enough, yes." I laughed, and did not conceal the bitterness. "Cloning would not have worked. An exact clone would have died soon from the same causes—"

"How? That sort of death is an interaction between genetic predilections and environment."

"Exactly. Could I doom a duplicate Morgen to a duplicate death?"

"You wouldn't have to replicate all the environmental factors. Why, with all your great knowledge of anatomy and physiology, couldn't you recreate her without the defects?" Kemra's tone was not quite sarcastic.

"Even if we managed to remove just one critical strand from the DNA subhelices—and could find just the one—don't you see? Morgen was a demi, and so am I. Her clone"—I shivered—"would be also."

Kemra looked blank as the shuttle bucked slightly at the first hint of the upper atmosphere.

"Would it be fair to make that new person conform to the lines of Morgen's life? And, as I mentioned, since humans are whole-body people, how would it even be possible? We can't cram a lifetime of experience into a few years. Look! Morgen would still be dead. You can't duplicate people that way. So I'd have a clone that was almost Morgen, but I would have gone through her death once, and, since that would change me, then nothing would be the same, and that new person would be tied to a life where nothing was quite the same or quite right, without really having chosen it herself." I winced again at the inherent wrongness of it all.

Her eyes widened slightly as if trying to grasp something, and not quite reaching it.

"You don't understand, do you?" I took a deep breath. "That's something you've never understood, part of the gulf that separates us."

Kemra turned cold again, and her eyes were hard and chill as ice three.

"Humans are whole-body creatures. Every physical and emotional impact modifies both body and the brain—merely scanning the brain and duplicating the mental images doesn't do it. That's why you all have to stay close to your nets—because unanchored mental images don't retain well."

"Coordinator, are you all right?" Keiko snapped through the uppernet, cutting through my concentration, which was wavering anyway after the headaches created by the *Gibson*'s particle beam.

"I'm fine," I lied. "Any problems?"

"Besides half the locials screaming about the cybs boiling a hole in the moon? No. No problems at all."

"Good. I'll be there as soon as I land."

"Or Locatio gibbering about the cybs in Ellay being ready to fry his locial?"

"They won't, but if they start, that breaks the Construct, and he can do as he pleases." I rubbed my forehead. Things were going to get worse, much worse. "There wasn't anyone or anything damaged on Luna, was there?"

"Some items shifted in the north depot. That was it. They chose an abandoned area."

That figured. They seemed to have some understanding of what would break the Construct without understanding the implications at all.

"There will be a groundshuttle waiting," Keiko promised. "Take it."

I would. What else could I do?

"I'll ignore that," Kemra snapped through my confusion, responding to my observation before the high speed net-exchange.

"Unanchored mental images?" I stumbled, trying to pick up the threads of my thoughts. "Why? Why do you all deny whole-body reality?"

Kessek flared the lander, slowing the monster as it dropped toward Parwon.

"We don't deny it. But it warps true logic. What is true is true, whether your body feels that way or not."

I shrugged. "That's accurate enough, but you don't resolve logic-body conflicts by ignoring your body, but rather by integrating thought and body."

"We do. We integrate bodily inputs into the nets, and we identify bodily biasing factors to ensure that they don't create emotional biases to true logical solutions."

"That doesn't work," I said tiredly, knowing the words were wrong as I spoke them, but trying to juggle too many variables and worries wasn't making clear thought any easier or more logical, and I was trying to be logical when I was half intuit, and it wasn't working.

"You have enough answers for why nothing can be done," Kemra said brightly, every word forced. "You can't or won't say anything that will stop the Vereal fleet. You couldn't or wouldn't do anything that would have saved your beloved Morgen. You don't have any descendants, and you probably won't, and you can't explain any of this. So what can you do?"

I wished I knew. I just sat there as the lander rumbled to a halt a hundred meters north of the Deseret tower.

"That's a good question," I said into the abrupt stillness as Kessek killed the rumbling engines. "I don't have a good answer, except that I know that not every question can be resolved through the application of better and better technology and more and more power." I released the harness and sat up in the supple officers' couch. "I know what is right and what is not, and I know that you can't explain that understanding in hard, bright, logical, and correct words that fit every circumstance, because you can't separate words from life and expect them to hold their full meaning."

"More magic," Kemra said, her voice as tired as I felt.

The heavy ramp whined down onto the permacrete.

"If that's how you feel, that's all it will be." I stood on legs that felt all too shaky.

"You'll turn . . . never mind." She shut her mouth as I stumbled down the ramp, but she never left her couch.

The ramp rose as I walked toward the tower, rubbing my forehead and blotting back the tears caused by the continuing headache and the cold wind out of the north.

As the lander rumbled back down the strip, I took a last look toward the black monster before walking toward the groundshuttle.

None there were so blind as would not see, and never

had that been so true, I felt. Then, that had probably been exactly how my eleven predecessors had felt.

Such a comforting thought. Six of them hadn't even survived their office as Coordinator.

Dvorrak waved, and I walked toward his groundshuttle as the cyb craft rumbled back down the locial strip, lifting toward orbit.

<<< XXVIII

THE STORY THE DEMI TOLD

The man with the silver hair, and a uncle or ancient he must have been, he sat in the corner of the room, a real room, not a space in a net or a cybfile, but an inn of stone and wood and tile. In that corner of the curved wall that formed the back of the public room, the man leaned against the back of the stool, and listened he did as the soft rain of the centuries fell outside.

The warriors, and warriors they were, would have called him old, for his hair was silvered and short, not long and dark and flowing, nor bound in silver or gold like that of a warrior, and he drank juice of the apple, not the beer of a true man or the lager of a hero or the poteen of a rebel. Nor did he have the arms of Cuchulain, nor the clear eyes of the Sons of Miled, nor the ice-edged thoughts of a Gates, nor the iron face of a Wayneclint, nor the stout heart of the true hero who would right all wrongs with a sharp blade and a strong shield. And his face was smooth as a child's, and beardless.

Sat there he did as though he belonged there, and each man thought he was the uncle of another, for he was too old to be of them and too young to be a father of any, and each knew the fathers of the others.

Cuchulain, he of the black shield and the hard, hard-headed sword, he told of the War of Words, and the quarrel over the Champion's Portion, and he laughed, as the heroes do, even at Uath the Stranger, who had carried his cut-off head under his arm, and at how Conall Cearnach fled from Uath.

Laegaire lifted his mighty mug, and quaffed it, and sure it was more than a barrel he quaffed, for his thirst was mighty, as he told of the tale of how Conchubar ordered Cathbad the druid into spelling pale and beautiful Deirdre into her journey through the strange sea to her death, and of the deaths of the sons of Usnach, the three fairest heroes who had each killed more than three hundreds apiece of Conchubar's warriors.

Those in the public room laughed and cheered, all but the old and silver-haired man in the back corner, who sat on the stool with the back, for he had not the thews of Cuchulain, nor of Laegaire, nor even Levarcham. His face was pale and thin and unlined.

Each hero had a tale, of the old days, and of how he had routed and killed, and set things to right, sometimes to right the right that the hero before him had righted. The newer heroes, like halfJack and Greencross, told the same tales, save that they used the knives of fire and the lightnings wrested from the sky. But they too had slain to put things right, and their minds were like the thews of Cuchulain, iron-hard and merciless in their pursuit of their righteousness.

In the end, only the old man had not spoken, and the lamps dimmed, and Cuchulain, being a hero and most courteous, turned to the silver-haired man.

"Surely, old man, you must have a story, of the times when you—"

"Or those who you knew," added Laegaire, he of the mighty spears, who had slain many in righteous war and who doubted that the old man had ever lifted a blade in anger or in defense.

"Or those who knew of others who knew," continued Greencross, with the black smile that all drew back from.

"—when you," continued Cuchulain, for he, as did all heroes, presented himself as noble and courteous in speech and demeanor, "saw a hero do some wondrous deed."

"Hmmm." And the little old man, he hmmed and he hawed, and he hmmed some more until Cuchulain was nigh ready to cast him out into the cold, for all that Cuchulain was noble and honorable and a right hero among heroes.

"No," said the old man. "I knew some they called heroes, such as they were. Men with great swords and great spears and great thirsts, such as Fergus, and Conchubar. Such as Conall and Cormac. Men who could grasp the fires of the sun and the knives of the storm. Men such as Wayneclint and Gates. Yet never saw I a mighty or a wondrous deed. Aye, I saw slaying, and killing, and bulls that furrowed and bellowed and burst their hearts. I saw cloaks that concealed broken hearts, and heroes who laid down with many a willing maid and then killed all who defamed her. I saw a man who thought like an engine of iron and tried to starve his betters and their children, even while he would not add a copper to the wages of a working draff. But wondrous deeds, those I never saw."

"Never?" asked Laegaire in spite of himself and his wishing to set the old man out in the cold himself, though he never would, being a right noble hero, and only of a mind to lift his blade when it was right and proper, such as to determine who was fit to have the Champion's Portion, or to ensure that Ulster and not Leinster or Munster received the Brown Bull.

"Never?" asked Greencross, his smile growing so black that Cormac edged away from him.

"Aye," answered the old man, yet again ignoring in his speech the courtesy that befit the heroes he addressed. "I saw men slaughter children, for that they might grow to avenge their dead fathers. I saw children who had escaped such slaughter grown to manhood and become heroes in order that they might slaughter other children to revenge their own dear dead fathers, and, in truth, that was what they did. And I saw the great Greencross lying once with a smile on his dead face in the ashes of Hughst with the stench of death sweeping from the seas. But wondrous deeds, those I never saw."

"An old man ye may be," said Cuchulain, "but a hero is a hero, and all the world needs Ireland's heroes. Aye, all the world needs heroes, for who will lift his blade for right, if there be no heroes, dear fellow? I say this on the cloak of the sea, on the floor of time, and by the words of the Dagda."

"All the world needs heroes," repeated Greencross, and halfJack echoed his words. "For there are those who say there are no heroes, and without heroes there are no dreams."

"Aye," replied the old man a last time. "Aye, the world in all its woe, it needs heroes, heroes like Ireland's heroes. It needs men who will lift mighty blades and make the three barren hills three hundred. It needs heroes who will fight and die over who shall receive the Champion's Portion, and women, proud women, who will die for love of their heroes, who die, like Emer, when their hero's light is extinguished. Aye, the world needs heroes like those cut from the mold of the Celts, who will fight and die to decide which child is born and which is not. Aye, the world needs heroes. It must have its heroes to kill scores upon scores that the handful who remain shall be free. It must have its heroes to turn the plains to ashes so that, after the long winter, the grasses will be sweet for roe and bison."

Young Cuchulain raised himself out of his stool, lifting his body clear with the strength of forearms like oaks that have withstood the gales and the years, and he walked toward the old man, his booted feet shivering the very stones where he walked, his eyes sun-bright with the certainty of youth, his mouth red like the blood he would spill, his spirit clear and firm.

The pale and smooth-faced old man spoke once again. "Yes, there must be heroes. Heroes to fight over which circuit is mightier. To fight over which dying truth shall die last. Heroes to hammer the stars into dust with the fire of suns cast against shields of adiamante. And then to weep in sadness when the last lights die, moaning because there are no wrongs left to right."

And young Cuchulain, he bit through his tongue, and the blood flowed, before he spoke again.

"And we will settle this outside, old man, for I say that there must be heroes, as the Champion's Portion is mine, and that truth is worth fighting over, and that you lie, and that you are coward and a craven and all manner of ill-spirited cur. You understand not, dear, how the world must have its heroes, and it's out in the chill we'll be settling this."

"I would prefer, young Cuchulain," answered the old man, slipping out of the stool in a fashion spritely enough for an old man, but commonplace enough compared to the grace of young Cuchulain. "I would prefer . . ."

"He would prefer," said Laegaire, and his ruby-red lips curled as only a hero's can curl, his voice gentle and singing like the great harp of Tara. "He would prefer . . ."

". . . not to leave this place. After all, I make no claim to be anything, and I have not for a long time, and I am not a hero. Besides, it's wet and cold out there, a fit place for a hero, but not for anyone else."

Young Cuchulain, towering like a black oak over the old man, lifted his mighty fists, and he said, "Ah, my dear, and is that the way you should have it? No, my dear, I'm a-fearing for your health, for you are no hero, and out into the cold you shall go, whether liking or not that you will be."

The old man, he stepped right up to Cuchulain, and that little old silver-haired man, without a word, he took his elbow, and it struck poor Cuchulain in the throat, so he could speak not a word, nor breathe, nor gasp. And Cuchulain the hero, with those mighty hands, he reached for the little old man, but did the evil creature stand still like a hero or a man? He did not. He took his iron-toed boots and he stove in Cuchulain's knees, one by one. And as young Cuchulain lay there on the floor, the little old man broke his neck with those selfsame boots.

Laegaire, he rose up like thunder, and he grabbed for the little man. For the silver-haired fellow scarce came to his chin, and the little old man, he didn't even run, but let Laegaire grasp him.

Then Laegaire, he gasped, and he grunted, and he fell on the floor, and his body was gutted like a hog from his manhood nigh unto his breastbone, and his bowels they spilled over the floor.

The little old man, he bowed his head to the rest, and he nodded, polite and courteous as you please, and he said, "Heroes, they don't grow old, and they don't grow smart, and we've had enough of them, and I bid you all good day."

Then he bowed to them all, and he walked out into the cold, and when Conall, who had followed him, came back, his eyes were black, and he sat at the rail, and not a word would come from the hero's mouth, save one, and that was a name.

That name was all Conall would ever say about the old man who was the only one who had brought down the mighty Cuchulain with but bare hands and his boots. Conall said it but once, and then he walked back out into the cold and the damp, and he never returned to the pub-

lic house. Nor did Cuchulain nor Laegaire, for all that
they had been raised before.

You must decide for yourself, but what Conall did not
say, what he could not say, was that when he followed the
man with the hair like the silver of the sea in the sunset,
that man put his feet upon the puddles in the street and
left no steps in the mud that remained. The old man spoke
not after he left the public house, but, as he passed the
guest house of the locial, the sole cyb from Al-Moratoros
turned white, and the thinking machine in the cyb's hand
sparked fire and died, and the draffs in the upper streets
that led to the hills bowed, their eyes dark, and their
thoughts deep within their skulls.

<<< **XXIX**

The cybs only understand power," Dvorrak had observed
as his groundshuttle had carried me around the lanes and
finally down Jung toward the admin building.

Dvorrak was wrong. The problem with the cybs was
that they had no understanding of power beyond creating
physical power. Most conquerors and would-be conquerors didn't, and that was why so many empires failed
and why so many bureaucracies endured.

The sun was touching the western hills when I stepped
out of the groundshuttle at the admin building, but a
handful of restraint squad members, boosted by an equal
number of demis in restraint squad blacks, still guarded
the building.

"Good afternoon," said Lictaer.

"I hope you got some rest."

"Yes, ser. More than you."

"Some days the vorpals eat well," I answered.

No one cracked a smile, not even me, and I hurried up to my office where Miris stood outside.

"He's been here for over an hour," Keiko pulsed at me, "but Crucelle and Arielle are already inside. That was so he wouldn't pester them."

Miris stepped toward me. "Coordinator?"

"Yes, Miris? There's not much I can say at the moment, except that I saw the cybs' demonstration. So far as I know, there was no damage to any installations or people."

"Have you checked?" he asked sarcastically.

"Yes. I'm being cautious."

"Yes, you are, Coordinator. You're being very cautious." He inclined his head. "I understand you have an important meeting. I may talk to you after that."

"If I have anything to add, Miris, I'll be happy to tell you."

"Thank you." He nodded and hurried down the steps.

"Was that wise?" Keiko was back in total black. I couldn't blame her. That was the way I felt.

"Probably not. Someone wise wouldn't have taken this job."

Both Crucelle and Arielle were watching as I entered the Coordinator's office, but they waited until I closed the door.

"Particle beam?" Crucelle asked, his green eyes resigned.

"That or something close enough that there's no difference." I rubbed my forehead. Despite my best efforts, my head ached, and my sinuses throbbed.

Arielle remained a dark and swirling storm, but silent.

K'gaio and Locatio were hovering on the net, which was one reason Crucelle had spoken aloud.

"Is it a Construct violation?" Crucelle asked.

"You could call it either way, but I don't think so."

"Then it's not. You're the Coordinator." The redhead

paused, then added, "Let's go to net conference with Locatio and K'gaio."

"Do you term this a Construct violation?" was K'gaio's
first statement.

"No."

"Turning a chunk of Luna into a polished mirror—an
eye staring down on Old Earth, certainly meets the terms
of the Construct," insisted Locatio.

"They didn't damage any installations there. We don't
have many except the depots, anyway. They didn't even
touch the old accelerator," mused Crucelle.

"Next time, they'll smash everything at once," Locatio
warned.

"Arielle?" I asked.

"They'll send an ultimatum asking for full access to all
demi technology. The demand will insist that such technology is due them as reparations for the great harm
wrought upon their ancestors."

"That follows my intuition," offered K'gaio. "I'd hoped
to be comped wrong. Will they act before an ultimatum?"

"No. They have to prove to themselves that they acted
in accord with their view of justice. We must be offered a
chance to right the wrong we inflicted upon them centuries ago. Only if we refuse can they act."

"The demands will be impossible, then," predicted
K'gaio.

"That's my calculation." Was there lightning crackling
behind Arielle's words?

"Why can't we term this Lunar incident a Construct violation?" asked Locatio again. "Why do we have to wait
and get fried by them?"

"What do you calculate, Arielle?" I asked.

"If we term this a Construct violation, the probabilities
increase by seventy percent that we will see marked numbers of mistrust cases within two years. Within a century,
the growth of those cases will render our present structure

impossible. Also, terming it a violation will reduce the effectiveness of the defense net by ten to fifteen percent."

"How do we know?" asked Locatio.

"We don't, not absolutely, but I'm willing to *trust* Arielle," I said. Not trusting her judgment and talent was just another form of hair splitting.

"So we wait until they unleash an attack, and then we try to squash them before too many millions of demis and draffs die? Is that what you want, Ecktor?" Locatio had begun to whine again, and the tone, even through the net, grated on my sensibilities.

"It's not what I *want,* and you know that. Also, even more demis will die from the stress if we use the Lunar incident as a Construct violation. Just because you can handle that doesn't mean everyone can."

"Ecktor is Coordinator," K'gaio offered in her polished tone. "That's his decision, unless you want to ask for his removal."

"No, no, no. But I can ask, can't I?"

"I, for one, need to continue working on liocial hardening and evacuation," responded K'gaio. "It might be well for you to do the same, Locatio. You have sent such a recommendation to other liocials, have you not, Ecktor?"

"Several days ago, with a follow-up yesterday."

"I doubt another is necessary, not now. Good morning, or good night to you." A momentary hiss filled the net as K'gaio dropped from the uppernet.

"Good night," echoed Locatio.

The three of us in the office exchanged glances in the gathering gloom.

"You two need to get some rest," I suggested.

"So do you," answered Arielle, her dark eyes dark-circled. "Tomorrow will bring the ultimatum, and the day after . . ."

"You're sure?"

She smiled bitterly. So did Crucelle—bitterly and pain-fully.

"Sorry."

"You can hope, Ecktor."

As they left, I studied the deepening purple and pink over the western hills, taking in the view. One way or an-other, that view would be gone in two days—unless the cybs broke their patterns, or we broke ours. Breaking ours would destroy us. Breaking theirs would save them, if they would but see it. I shook my head. Kemra had an inkling. Perhaps the cybs' computer system could compute it. No one else seemed likely even to look.

The sky darkened more, and I finally walked out.

Keiko had blanked the console she didn't need, but had waited. "Miris is downstairs."

"I promised I'd talk to him. Then I'll try to get some rest."

"Do." With that, she was gone, another dark presence. Were we all dark presences, all of us history-laden demis. I shook my head. Crucelle was warmth and life—and what was happening fell twice as heavily on him.

I waited until I heard her steps on the polished wood of the lowest hall before starting down.

Miris was waiting. Otherwise, the inside of the wide entry area was empty. The restraint squad still guarded the doors. The draff rep looked at me. "Boiling a hole in the moon isn't a violation of the Construct?"

"It probably is. But it's questionable enough that taking it as such will cause enormous problems."

He scratched his head, like an ancient advocate in one of the sealed pub-dramas in the archives. "Let me get this straight. If you take this as a violation, and act before they do, thereby reducing casualties, we'll face some disturbing consequences at some point in the future. If you let them turn that demon beam on all of us, you demis will die with clear consciences, is that it?"

He was almost right. So I had to put it clearly, knowing he wouldn't like it. "The cost of *acting* before they do will be no society on Old Earth in one hundred years, and millions of deaths over the next millennia. The cost of reacting will probably be millions of deaths now, but a stable and functioning society with all damage restored a decade or two or five from now."

Miris actually swallowed. "I appreciate your honesty. How certain are you of the accuracy of those predictions?"

"According to our best comp, the acting-first prediction is over ninety percent accurate, although the timetable for societal dissolution is not. It could begin in ten years, but no later than one hundred fifty. The death cost of the reacting prediction ranges from one half million to two-and-one-half million, with an error range of ten percent, depending on the cyb timing. The accuracy of a stable society exceeds ninety-five percent, but the physical recovery period could vary considerably."

"It seems as though we lose either way."

"Not if the basic moral principle remains the survival of a society with maximum permissible ranges of choice and minimal internal violence."

The draff representative worried his upper lip with his teeth. I wished I could offer more reassurance, rather than a tight smile. I walked into the evening, wishing I had Morgen to go home to, to talk to, to hold.

In the growing darkness, the wind was stiff and cold, and the moon glared down with her bloodshot eye, down at me. I hunched into my jacket and kept walking.

<<< XXX

The ultimatum is enroute, carried by Majer Henslom," announced Gibreal across the shipnet.

"Not our nav?" The anonymous question was followed by the image of wiggling hips, which vanished before any tracer could follow.

The crackle and hiss of lightning across the net followed immediately.

"What will they do?" asked the envoff in the stillness. "The demis, I mean?"

"It doesn't matter," gloated Weapons. "They turn over Old Earth to us, or we turn it over on them. It's their choice."

"Let's have a systems assessment," suggested Ideomineo. "MYL-ERA, report on demi subject."

"Probabilities approach unity that all statements made by the demi subject were accurate," reported MYL-ERA.

"What about his statement about there being a quarter of a million demis with his abilities?" asked Kemra.

"I've analyzed that statement. That wasn't what he said," pointed out Gorum. "He said that there were a quarter million with abilities within five percent of his and an overall average of within one percent. But the actual potential of mental abilities are better measured on a log-based system. After all, we share more than ninety percent of the same chromosomes with primates."

"Oh . . ."

"Exactly. He told the absolute truth, but, in practical terms, there could be only a handful of demis who match him."

"They don't need many with that comm system," Kemra pointed out. "They can respond more quickly than we can."

"They don't need many to hold their society together, but they're already having problems against an outside threat."

"Would you classify Majer Ysslop's efforts within their Ellay locial as internal?" asked the executive officer, his words as calm as the summer seas of Gates.

"The demi society is highly effective against small numbers of those who would disrupt it from on Old Earth itself," responded MYL-ERA.

"There's something else that doesn't go with that," pointed out the envoff. "The Coordinator is putting on a show for the draffs. He's restricted the information on the destruction of our agent teams, and, even knowing that the marcybs were only slightly above constructs, made that gesture of returning Henslom's puppet. If there were hundreds of thousands of powerful demis, he wouldn't have to act that way."

"They still have the satellite systems," pointed out the nav.

"That's fine, but how can they protect a hundred of those locials with only twelve low-powered asteroid systems?" pressed Gorum.

"Report on demis' satellite system," ordered Ideomineo.

"Data on the asteroid satellite system is incomplete and inconclusive," replied MYL-ERA. "All locational systems are now functional. They allow accurate navigation down to point one meter in non-clouded areas and point two meter in weather-obscured areas. Surface temperature of asteroid stations continues to rise. That temperature rise is at variance with perceived technology and observed power sources."

"Could they be heat leaks because the engineering

is deficient or because the systems are so old?" asked
Weapons.

"The probability that the engineering is deficient is less
than two percent. The probability that the temperature
variances have been caused by heat leaks is approximately
twenty-one percent."

"Other probabilities?" asked Gorum.

"The highest probability, at twenty-four percent, is that
of shielded power sources. The tertiary probability, at
nineteen percent, is surface anomalies created by the moving and positioning of the asteroids. Other probabilities
sum at approximately thirty-five percent." The probability
listing flashed to the net-conference members.

"I worry about those shielded power sources. Can you
quantify that, Systems?" requested Ideomineo.

"Based on specifications on file, heat leakage caused by
shielded systems would indicate between one and two additional standard-capacity, weapons-level fusactors on
each station."

"That's nothing to worry about," laughed Weapons.

"What is the probability that such shielded systems, if
they exist," Ideomineo pushed on, "have greater power
outputs than postulated?"

"No information exists on which further quantification
or speculation could be based."

"So we have a twenty-five percent probability that the
demis have more power on their stations than represented,
and if so, that power ranges from the capability of half of
one fleet ship to an unknown upper limit?" asked Kemra.

"That is correct," answered MYL-ERA.

"What is the probability that the upper limit exceeds
the capability of one ship?"

"There is no way to quantify that."

"If they had that much power, they wouldn't be tiptoe-
ing around," summed up Gorum.

A sense of assent filled the net.

"Report on demi belief and principle structure," Ideomineo continued.

"Based on the data observed, and assuming the factual accuracy of the historical events recorded in system databanks, the demis have evolved a working social system."

"We knew that," came a mutter across the net.

"That assumption is not verifiable," replied MYL-ERA. "The demis represented that they had a working system based on certain principles. Observation was necessary to verify such representation."

"What else did the system verify?"

"There appears to be social or other constraints against violence and against making threats."

"Hold it," interrupted Gorum. "That demi assaulted Majer Henslom. He killed a bunch of rodents without blinking, and killed an agent. Others killed almost a dozen agents."

"In all instances, violence was instigated before the demis took action," reported MYL-ERA coldly.

"That's a distinction without a difference, it seems to me," offered the fleet commander. "They can and have brought force to bear. That they wait until another commits to action doesn't convey any particular moral virtue, and it can be a tactical weakness—especially in the face of overwhelming force." He paused, then asked, "Will these demis wait to strike until after we do?"

"The probability of demi action preceding Vereal Fleet action is too close to nonexistent to calculate in statistical terms."

"Then, why bother with the ultimatum?" asked Gorum.

"Because I'd rather ensure that I cover every possibility. Would you like to report to CybCen that you'd slagged Old Earth without trying for the technology peacefully?"

After a moment, Gibreal added, "That is all."

<<< **XXXI**

The next morning was sunny, unlike my mood, with a brisk wind swirling leftover snow across the lanes and creating a chill that left the tips of my ears fighting frostbite. I was late, and I should have stayed in Parwon, and even a quick-paced walk from the flitter and the locial tower to the admin building didn't improve my sense of foreboding, not when Keiko had warned me on the net about a large envelope left early by Majer Henslom.

"Majer Henslom and several marcybs arrived with a large envelope for you. It has the new agreement between the Vereal Union and Old Earth," Keiko had reported over the net as soon as I'd touched down with the flitter. She added cynically, "The majer smiled a lot."

"I'll bet." Another gust of cold, cold wind brought water to my eyes, and a memory of a warmer season.

> ". . . golden autumn that will see no spring,
> for whitest flakes will gown my grace,
> and jewels of ice will frame my face."

I'd have felt better with Morgen to talk to, to help, but all I had was memory and a soulsong to help me with our ancient cousins from across the stars, cousins so willful they could not see. Cousins even more willful than the ancient heroes my mother had bequeathed to me.

In effect, the cybs had ignored Kemra's ruins tour, the episodes with the prairie dog town, and my disarming of Major Henslom and returning his marcyb. Instead of analyzing the situation, they'd just boiled a new sea in Luna and suggested that they could turn a good chunk of Old Earth into a polished replica of Al-Moratoros. As usual, they'd missed the point, almost as if on purpose.

I kept walking, my legs moving close to a run in my anger.

In the park, the statue of the mindblazed draff gazed into the empty sky, another symbol ignored by the cybs. There were no monuments to military glory on Old Earth, no statues of conquering heroes or deceased politicians, and the cybs never asked why. They didn't ask why we preserved ruins or placed a Hybernium and a statue of a draff in agony in every locial, and they didn't listen when told.

As I slowed my walk outside the admin building, I nodded to the restraint squad. There were several nods in return, and a few "good mornings."

"Good morning," I answered, although I wondered exactly how good it was going to be, with the envelope waiting for me. Wiping my forehead, I climbed the steps more deliberately.

"Crucelle, Arielle, K'gaio, Locatio—not to mention every locial rep who's awake—want to know what the cybs want," Keiko informed me, her face almost as dark as the dark brown she wore. "And Miris has been up here three times."

Her console was empty.

"It's on your desk—unopened, for my own protection."

"I should have deputed you to open it." I forced a grin.

"There isn't enough comptime credit in the universe to get me to do that."

Keiko's assessment was about the same as mine. My only question was what kind of ultimatum the envelope contained, and how it was structured.

She closed the door behind me, probably because Miris was scrambling up the steps to accost me.

I forced myself to hang up the winter jacket before going to the desk. Even standing behind my desk, I took a last look out across the park, knowing that everything was going to change and that I could do nothing about it, that everything I had tried had failed.

The pale brown envelope lying in the center of the Coordinator's desk was roughly twenty by thirty centimeters. I lifted it, trying to weigh it, but it didn't seem that heavy, and I guessed that the contents contained probably less than a dozen sheets.

"Ecktor?" pulsed Crucelle.

"I haven't opened it. It doesn't feel good, but I'll let you know."

With a faint net hiss, he was gone.

I broke the antique wax-like seal and opened the flap. There were two documents inside. The text of the first was succinct.

> If the government of Old Earth, as represented by the Planetary Coordinator, does not accept the full terms of the attached Agreement within twenty-four hours local time, or less, if deemed necessary by me, the forces of the Union of Vereal Systems will immediately apply Provision six.

That concise statement was signed by one Mathre C. Gibreal, Commanding, First Fleet, Union of Vereal Systems.

I didn't want to look at the next document, the one entitled: "Agreement between the Peoples of Old Earth and the Union of Vereal Systems." But I picked it up and began to read the words on the parchment-like paper. Parchment was definitely suitable, since the text of the Agreement was modeled on something as antique as what it was printed upon.

> When a people has been grievously wronged, deprived of home, hearth, liberty, and free pursuit of

happiness and destiny, its first duty is to ensure that such basic human rights are restored to all its members and to establish in the course of their reestablishment the protections of such rights. They have the manifest right and duty to redress any and all conditions which led to past oppressions and injustices. Such a duty requires that all prudent steps be taken to ensure that the perpetrators of such injustices never have the ability, the technology, nor the means of transportation to pose a threat to those the perpetrators once wronged.

Therefore, under the terms of the charter of the Union of Vereal Systems, any permanent agreement between the people of Old Earth and the Union of Vereal Systems shall incorporate the following provisions, as a minimal condition for the continued physical survival of Old Earth's peoples:

PROVISION THE FIRST:
The peoples of Old Earth shall provide at all times and in all places complete and open access to all communications systems, protocols, and associated technology, technical documentation, and systems design.

PROVISION THE SECOND:
The appropriate authorities of the Union of Vereal Systems shall supervise and ensure the deactivation and destruction of all satellite systems massing greater than 100 kilograms.

PROVISION THE THIRD:
The peoples of Old Earth shall surrender to the authority of the Union of Vereal Systems all air-

craft and spacecraft with a design capacity of greater than ten occupants.

PROVISION THE FOURTH:

To ensure that the conditions and tyranny which created the great human disaster known as The Flight are never reestablished, the peoples of Old Earth, under the supervision of appropriate authority of the Union of Vereal Systems, shall sterilize all adults classified as "demis" so that such adults are incapable of reproduction. Further, any child born subsequent to this provision, upon reaching physical maturity and being classified as a demi, shall also be so sterilized.

PROVISION THE FIFTH:

The peoples of Old Earth shall form a planetary government representing the draff population, provided that the actions of such a government shall be subject to review by the appropriate governing authorities of the Union of Vereal Systems. Provided further, such actions by the government of Old Earth may be modified and/or supplemented by the reviewing authority, and such revisions or supplemental laws will supercede any existing laws or policies.

PROVISION THE SIXTH:

Failure to adhere strictly to the provisions of this Agreement will subject Old Earth and its peoples to the full might and authority of the Union of Vereal Systems.

The so-called Agreement was worse than I'd anticipated, and I wondered if it had been drafted even before the cyb fleet had left Gates.

I pulsed Crucelle and Arielle, then K'gaio and Locatio,

knowing that even on uppernet, quite a few others would tap in.

"How bad?" Crucelle asked.

"It starts with a demand for total control of our nets and comm systems and gets worse."

"How much worse?" inquired Arielle, her thoughts cool, collected. Yet stormlike power swirled behind the coolness.

"Destruction of the satellite system, destruction of any mass transport not under cyb control, and complete sterilization of all demis for eternity."

Crucelle laughed. "No, they haven't changed. Not at all. Not even after all the blatant examples you threw in their faces."

"What do you propose, Coordinator?" Even under stress, even in the middle of her night, K'gaio's words were like water-polished stones.

"We'll need a conference."

"A conference? For what?" demanded Locatio. "What they've asked is absurd, impossible . . ."

"We need a conference. We have twenty-three hours or less in which to accept or face the force of their fleet."

"But . . ."

"We need a conference, and I will be setting it up. Also, evacuation requests are to be disseminated in all locials immediately. Try to evacuate everyone, except for essential personnel, and complete all subsurface hardening. No final hardening yet, but get those evacuation requests out in the locials—all of them." I paused. "Also, make sure all the magshuttles have pilots and are ready to be lifted into projected blast-free zones."

"You're pushing it," Crucelle protested. "That's going to hurt some—"

"Not so much as getting vaporized, burned, irradiated, or cut down with slugthrowers is going to hurt the draffs. And we'll need every shuttle we can get later."

"His intuition has been as accurate as Arielle's calculations," interjected Keiko, one of the first times she had presumed on a member of the representative committee.

"I defer," Crucelle said, a bitter edge to his words. "I defer to the Coordinator."

"But," protested Locatio, virtually simultaneously. "Even thinking about that . . . now . . . without overt violence. I've got a headache, and some of my team's already non-functional from what you've done, Ecktor."

"I understand," I admitted. If Locatio or the Consensus knew what I were planning, more than a few would be non-functional, and Locatio had been one of the more aggressive ones. That was why Coordinators were necessary. "But—protecting people is part of the Construct, and so long as the evacuations are by the bullet lines, and not visible, that won't violate the Construct by encouraging cyb violence. They can't be encouraged by what they can't see."

"The receiving areas will be cramped."

"Very cramped," I agreed. "Most people would rather be cramped than dead. Wouldn't you? I'm sorry. That wasn't appropriate," I said, realizing that a significant fraction of the Consensus would probably die under the backlash, and that I could be one of them. So could Locatio.

"The Coordinator has called for a conference," added K'gaio. "That seems reasonable. We have little time; so let us not quibble. Please keep us informed, Coordinator." She left the net with a crisp click, making her point.

"Crucelle, if you would join me? Arielle?"

Then I left the net. Secure as I felt the net was, some things were best left undone in public.

"Keiko, see if the cybs will send two people down here to discuss this monstrosity, but don't call it that. Tell them we're convening a conference and will reply within the deadline."

"Two?"

"I want Subcommander Kemra, and Officer Mylera."

"Mylera?"

"She's actually a construct that represents organic subjective input to the cyb fleet's net systems. I'm not supposed to know that. You can also say that Commander Gorum would be welcome, but I'm sure they'll say he's not available."

"You're sure of that?"

"Very sure." I paused. "Have a groundshuttle waiting for the subcommander—that's if they agree to send her. We won't have much time."

"You're sure of that, too?"

"Yes." I was even more certain that we were running out of time.

<<< **XXXII**

The demi Coordinator asked for the nav? And you let her go?" asked Ideomineo.

"No." Gibreal laughed, and ice pellets flicked across the net. "I ordered her to go, with Majer Henslom and another marcyb detachment for her protection."

"You calculated that she may have developed some reciprocal attraction to the demi?" responded the Executive Officer. "What about Henslom?"

"Henslom? He has already been discredited by the demi, and his usefulness is limited. He either redeems himself or he doesn't."

"I suppose you feel the same way about Majer Ysslop?" Ideomineo's tone blew like a dry wind across the private link.

"I respect Majer Ysslop, unlike Henslom. I respect her so much that I have given her a most difficult assignment."

"So . . . the most senior women in the fleet are on Old Earth? In the case of Ysslop, you fear her, and in the case of Kemra you're angry that she spurned you for the demi."

"His physical attraction to her is minimal, if existent, but he is extremely persuasive, and I've been troubled by the direction of her recent observations."

"You fear contamination."

"Hardly. But there's no reason to protect it. This way, the demis will feel they are shielded during their so-called conference. They will not agree, and they are attempting to stall matters while readying their defenses. So we will strike before they expect it."

"That analysis is flawed," announced MYL-ERA. "Observations reveal no statistically significant changes in energy flows or activities of any installations."

"So much the better," laughed Gibreal. "Fewer will escape."

<<< **XXXIII**

I glanced out the window, noting that the groups of people heading for the admin building were relatively evenly spaced. Some hunched down against the wind. A tall dark youngster smiled broadly and waved up at the building, although the angle of the sunlight on the windows probably precluded him from seeing me clearly. Two girls looked furtively toward the heavens, and one shook her head. If I strained, I could hear a dull murmuring from the lower floors.

Still waiting for Crucelle and Arielle, I used the net to review the locial status, including the performance of the bullet shuttles to the evacuation/receiving areas, and how the locial hardening was coming. Then I linked to the Deseret receiving area.

"Seborne? This is Coordinator Ecktor. What's your status?"

"We're at about thirty percent already."

I'd hoped for more, but that wasn't bad. "Good. Any problems?"

"Not yet."

After that, I uplinked to Ell Prime.

"Yes, Ecktor?" Elanstan sounded exhausted, even over the net.

"How are things going?"

"All the inlink nodes are operational; Delta is operating, but at about ninety percent efficiency. We can bring everything on line in less than five standard minutes."

"That's about what you'll have. I'd estimate that the cybs will begin whatever they have in mind in no less than one stan, and no more than three."

"Frig. . . ." came Rhetoral's mutter. "You couldn't get them to see?"

"Rhetoral," Elanstan added, "they couldn't see after they destroyed most of Old Earth the first time. Why would they see now?"

"The Construct?" asked Rhetoral.

"I've bent the Construct to the point that some members of the Consensus committee are experiencing ethic-backlash. I've ordered dissemination of locial evacuation requests."

"Are the draffs listening?" asked Elanstan.

"There's already steady traffic here. So far there hasn't been any problem with the bullet shuttles."

"No substitute for technology in a crisis," said Rhetoral ironically. "Wouldn't the cybs be surprised to hear that?"

"They don't think much of our technology, or that we have much besides a superior net capability." I paused. "I'll let you know."

"Stet, Ecktor," Elanstan closed, adding sardonically, "Coordinator Ecktor."

A rap on the door alerted me.

"Come in."

Both Arielle and Crucelle stepped inside. Both looked haggard, and both had dark circles under their eyes.

"Do you really need us?" asked Arielle.

"Not for long." I gestured to the chairs. "Sit down." I dropped onto the couch.

Arielle paced to the window; Crucelle slumped into the green chair nearest the desk. Then Arielle turned. "Go on."

"It's simple. First, what have I missed?"

"You called us here for that?"

"You wanted me to ask that on an open net? Even uppernet?"

"The man has a point, darkangel." Crucelle gave a tired grin. "I can't think of anything major. We'll have cybs to clean up on the ground, and that could get messy unless you issue heavy arms to the restraint squads."

I hadn't thought of that, and I pulsed that request to Keiko for her to implement in my name.

"That's going to shock a few souls," she pulsed back.

"Everything I do is shocking people."

"You'd better alert Elanstan and Rhetoral to the possibility of a suicide translation," suggested Arielle. "That's only a five percent probability, and it won't work unless the cybs try it on full power at the beginning. Elanstan should focus on the acceleration. It would take flexing the whole net to stop that much adiamante."

I winced.

"It's a low probability, but you asked," she pointed out, waiting as I went uppernet again.

"Already?" asked Elanstan. "We're—"

"No. Not yet," I pulsed calmly. "Arielle made a point about the cybs," I explained.

"We can run a series and have Fynert monitor it," Elanstan said. "I hope they don't try it."

"It's very low probability, but . . ." I paused. "That's it." After breaking off, I looked at Arielle. She was still at the window, looking at us half the time, and half the time out at the continuing, if thinning, lines of draffs.

Keiko knocked on the door that wasn't quite closed and edged her head inside, breaking the silence. "Neither Officer Mylera nor Commander Gorum are available, but the cybs are sending Subcommander Kemra. She's expendable, obviously," Keiko announced from the door to the Coordinator's office. "Why did you ask for her?"

"I had to ask for someone to give the illusion that we were considering their terms. That way, when they launch a 'surprise' attack—"

"You know, Coordinator, you would have made a good cyb. You're about as devious as possible for a demi. Every day, I see why the Consensus picked you." She laughed, flashing those white teeth. "I can also see that you'll deserve every year of comptime you get. It'll take that long to straighten you out."

There was another reason why I'd asked for either Kemra or the construct Mylera. If we survived the confrontation, we needed someone comparatively objective to take back the message to the Vereal Union, but I didn't mention that to Keiko. She just would have accused me of greater deviousness.

"I like you, too, Keiko. Do we have a timetable for their landing?"

"Fynert just netflashed an estimate of less than an hour. Three of those landers left their fleet."

"They'll be loaded with marcybs—and weapons."

"If you could prove that they—"

"Who's the devious one now?" I asked. "Don't answer that. Oh, everyone will scream, but inform all the locial reps that final emergency evacuation—that means them and everyone who's left—could come at any time, and that I expect them to be monitoring the net continually for the next twenty-four hours."

"Only twenty-four?"

"I'd guess about two stans," I said bluntly, glad I hadn't put that on the net.

"You are an optimist." She pursed her lips. "I'd better get busy. Some of them are hard to get—even now." She closed the door and left me standing by the wide desk.

From the green chair, Crucelle laughed once, softly. "You do have a way with people, Ecktor."

"He's too directly truthful," said Arielle from the west end of the south window where she had been studying the steady lines of draffs heading to the building. "Even after all these generations . . ." Her eyes focused on me. "There's probably something else we've all missed. There usually is. I can't calculate it."

"All right," I conceded. "You two had better head out to the command center. You're coordinating the ground-side links to the system, aren't you?"

"Crucelle is. I help."

"If we get there before the cybs strike," Crucelle said tiredly, using his arms to pull himself out of the chair. "Right now, Liseal is on the links." He paused. "Did you really need us here?"

I shrugged. "I was glad for Arielle's suggestions, and she might have come up with something even more critical. Also, I really wouldn't have wanted Arielle's observations open-net. There's still the possibility that they've cracked the systems."

"Even if they had," Arielle retorted, following Crucelle toward the door, "they're too arrogant to listen."

"I'm sorry. You're probably right. Even Coordinators make mistakes." I thought for a moment. "Especially Coordinators."

"You're allowed a few," Crucelle said.

"You'll leapfrog the links with Liseal?"

Arielle nodded as if that were obvious. "And we'll have the center up for you."

"It's been on standby, one red, since the day before yesterday," I added.

"You have been busy." Then with a warm parting smile, one that included the green eyes that cared too much, he added, "Take care, Ecktor."

"You, too."

After they left, I paced to the wide southern window and looked out over the park. In the southwest corner, two children in heavy brown coats ran ahead of their parents, going in circles around two cedars until they both flopped on the brown grass on their backs, laughing. Their mother and father gestured, and the four walked up the pathway to the admin building, to the bullet shuttles that waited well below ground level.

Parwon had twenty stations, and I only hoped I'd acted soon enough, because it would take a minimum of one and a half stans to clear the locial, although I doubted that everyone would heed the evacuation request. We didn't command, even in matters of life and death, and there are always those people who know better.

Everything was working, smoothly, and that bothered me. No one was linking in, and all systems were functioning. I shouldn't have even thought that, because the net crackled.

"Ecktor!" whined Locatio. "There's a cyb lander setting down here."

"Are they unloading anything, or using weapons?"

"Not yet."

"Good. Let me or Keiko and K'gaio know if they do. The minute they do, in the present situation, that's enough to go to emergency final evacuation and complete hardening. You don't need me for that—but let me know if you can."

"I certainly will."

I knew he would.

"There are three cyb landers down," Keiko announced through the net. "One at Ellay and two here."

"One of those here will have the cyb subcommander, and all of them will be packed with troops." I took a deep breath.

"Majer Henslom was waiting for them."

"Have they unloaded anyone?"

"No one except the subcommander. She's in the ground-craft on her way here. Henslom's on one of their shuttles."

"Good. The moment anything that looks like a weapon appears, flash me."

"Yes, ser."

While I waited, trying to figure out what I had missed—and there was sure to be something—I linked to the defense net node. The electroneural shock shivered through me, and I almost had to put out a hand to the window to keep from losing my balance.

"This is the defense node. Please withdraw until notified."

I withdrew and looked back down at the park and the walkway. The number of draffs entering the building had slowed to a few scattered handfuls.

"The groundshuttle is outside, Coordinator," Keiko informed me.

"Thank you." After a last look at the piñons and the single bare cottonwood, I walked toward the door.

It opened before I reached it, and Kemra strode into the Coordinator's office.

"Greetings," I offered.

"You've sealed my death, as well as your own," snapped the subcommander. "Why did you need me? No fancy words, if you please, honored planetary Coordinator."

"To give the impression that we're buying time and to obtain you as a witness."

"A witness?"

I shrugged. "Your career and perhaps your life were already forfeit. That happened the minute you began to believe that something strange was going on here on Old Earth. Your compatriots don't want to believe you—or me. It's something like, 'Don't disturb my convictions with your facts.' " I gestured to the cyb Agreement that still lay on the desk, untouched since I'd read it earlier in the day. "Do you have any idea what those provisions say?"

Kemra looked at me. "Not exactly."

"Read it."

"Now?"

"Now. I'll know as soon as Henslom starts to move the troops."

She gave me a strange glance. "You don't seem worried."

"I am worried. Everyone on Old Earth is worried. Wouldn't you be? Go ahead and read it."

She picked up the Agreement and began to read. After the first paragraph, she frowned, and the frown deepened. Finally, she looked up. "The sterilization seems excessive."

"The whole document seems excessive," I answered with a forced laugh.

"What did you expect? You demis have taken over our ancient home with a form of tyranny, and you want us to just visit and leave you alone?"

"Using tyranny seems like another exaggeration," I pointed out. My guts were tightening as the time passed. I couldn't move or order a final evacuation if something didn't happen—and if it didn't happen soon, people would begin to stress out. Yet I knew it had to happen. I took a deep breath.

"No tyranny is so oppressive as a society truly based on innate ability," said Kemra, "and still you do not see that. Even your draffs have seen that."

"It doesn't work that way. Not in any society. Someone is always in control. That control may be direct or indirect, strong or weak. It may be dictatorial or representative or both, or some of each mixed with anarchy, but there will always be some form of elite. Your choices generally range from an elite based on heredity, physical strength, cunning, luck, or intelligence. What you're saying is that when it becomes clear to the less able members of a society that they will never be part of the elite, they feel oppressed, and they equate that feeling of oppression with tyranny. Here . . . there is an elite, and there's a high price for belonging to that elite. That price doesn't fall equally on every generation or even every century, but even the everyday prices are high. That's one reason for comptime."

"With all your abilities," Kemra pushed into the conversation as though she hadn't wanted to hear what I had said, "you demis believe you are the peak of human perfection—true demigods. What if there is more to human intelligence and ability than what your skills can measure?"

"That's a strange argument coming from a cyb-sense culture which bases power, position, and control of resources almost solely on the possession or demonstration of primarily mental skills."

"Coordinator! Majer Henslom has the four hundred cybs and a dozen officers from the landers marshalled up. They're armed and headed toward the locial center. One of the force leaders is marshalling those at the south residential block."

"Thanks!" I linked into the main nets, at all levels, and preempted all traffic. Coordinators get to do that. They also get to suffer the consequences. "This is Coordinator Ecktor. The Construct has been violated. Armed marcybs are attacking Deseret locial. The Construct has been violated. Complete final emergency evacuations of all locials. Complete final emergency evacuations of all locials. Complete hardening, and close down. All demis stand by for defense node activation. All demis stand by for defense node activation."

Then I pulsed to Keiko. "Emergency evacuation. Close down and head for the bullets."

Next came uppernet and Elanstan.

"Power up for immediate defense net activation. The cybs have launched a ground attack on Deseret locial. I've put out the call for node activation."

"The boards are greening," pulsed Elanstan. "We're already at twenty percent." There was a pause. "You're sure?"

"Absolutely sure. We've got armed marcybs here and in Ellay, although the Ellay troops are running slightly behind the ones here. What do you have on your screens?"

"All hulls are in full-power status, and their screens are radiating into the purple. No acceleration, and no power concentrations aft."

"Let me know if it changes. Priority override."

"Stet, Coordinator."

I dropped off that segment and repeated the evacuation notice process with the Deseret locial net. While I could have asked Keiko, when time counts, it's faster to do it yourself. Then I dropped onto the maintenance level and used the Coordinator's keys to freeze all the locial's system controls and shunt them out to the defense control center.

"Let's go!" I snapped at Kemra.

"Go?"

I took a last look, and it would indeed be a last look, out the wide windows of the Coordinator's office. Outside, the pines waved in the stiff wind, and puffy white clouds scudded toward the eastern peaks. The streets were empty, but the streets of the locials were never that crowded, and I doubted that the cybs would even bother with time-comparative scans.

"Your former compatriots are about to begin their effort to wipe out society and most technology on Old Earth." I headed for the door. "If you wish to have a momentary and firsthand view, you can certainly stay. Otherwise, I suggest you follow me."

She followed.

I took the stairs two at a time. There's a time for decorum and a time to run like a crazed vorpal's after you, except a crazed vorpal's an oxymoron. This was the time to run.

Fast as I was, the building was clear—handling the shunts had taken several minutes—all the way down to the sublevels.

From the third sublevel, we went down the concealed stairs in the back of the lower power boards. Kemra's eyes were wide, but she was breathing heavily even before we came out on the narrow platform where Keiko stood, waiting, beside the bullet shuttle cars, shimmering in the lights of the admin building's sublevels.

"Everyone else took the first bullet," my aide said.

"Good. The building looks clear. You left the doors open for the main bullets? We'll hold the power as long as we can. All systems are shunted out to the control center. Draffs?"

Keiko nodded. "We can't tell, but we estimate above ninety-five percent clear."

I touched the plate on the side of the front car. As the door slid open, I gestured to Kemra, who stood there wide-eyed. "Get in."

"You never . . ."

"Get in—unless you want to get fried when your fleet's weapons hit."

Kemra slid into the front seat and I took the seat next to her. Keiko took the one behind us.

The doors slid shut and the bullet shuttles whined forward and dropped into the dark tube. Only a faint red light illuminated the interior.

"What about all the draffs? Are you just leaving them to get incinerated?"

"No. Except for the handful necessary to maintain the locial, I had everything evacuated earlier. Didn't it seem quiet when you came in? The others left while we were discussing your ultimatum—except for a dozen or so on the bullet before us. There might be two or three techs on the ones after us, but they had warning, and I can't wait now."

I had to use the boost to get to uppernet.

"Elanstan. Status on the cybs?"

"They're easing into lower orbit, at five percent power." A flash image seared at me, and I nodded. "Power drop . . . appears to be a glide and decel. They're dropping into position. Holding now. No action yet."

I swallowed. How long would Gibreal hold his ships? How long would synchronization take? Five minutes? A stan?

"How long will it take Gibreal to synchronize the fleet once he's in lower orbit?" I asked Kemra.

"How did you—"

"How long?"

"Ten minutes, longer if he's going to use particle beams."

I went back uppernet. "The subcommander says it'll be ten. Don't be hair-trigger, but don't take that as a hard schematic."

"We understand," answered Rhetoral. "They're not stabilized in lower orbit yet, anyway."

I took a deep breath and checked the bullet. Only another minute before we slid into the control center.

I was moving as soon as the bullet's door was wide enough for me to squeeze through. At the top of the platform steps, I glanced back at the tunnel, where the blast doors remained poised to close—as were four sets along the ten-klick tunnel. Then I scrambled up the steps and through the second set of locks. I didn't look back to see if Kemra and Keiko followed. There wasn't anywhere else for them to go.

Even with most of the emergency squad in place, the control center was still stark. It wasn't designed for large numbers of people, or for long-term isolation—totally isolated, it wouldn't function for more than a few weeks. The power and ventilation were adequate for years, but the more human necessities such as food and recycling-disposal of wastes weren't integrated as totally self-contained operations.

At the center screens were Arielle and Crucelle. Neither looked up, although they had certainly felt me come in.

"Link boards?"

"Dorgan, ser." The thin-haired and thin-faced man nodded at me from the screen at the end.

"Nets?"

Wiane glanced up.

The five of us should have been able to handle the system, but in case we couldn't, there were backups—Liseal, Keiko, Dyncuun, Sebestien, Vieria, and two others from Crucelle's group that I didn't know by name.

Keiko ushered Kemra to the left rear corner of the center and half-gestured, half-pushed the subcommander into a straight-backed chair. Then Keiko took the last remaining standby screen position.

I dropped into the empty center chair in front of the representational screen that depicted Old Earth, the asteroid satellite stations, and the Vereal Union fleet—which appeared to have stabilized in something slightly closer to Old Earth than a geocentric orbit.

The locators were my first priority.

"Ecktor—you on line?" asked Rhetoral as I was verifying that the cybs had stabilized their ships.

"That's affirmative. I have the cybs stable and commencing power build-up. Do you see any acceleration? Interrogative cyb acceleration."

"That's negative."

"Hold on net."

"Holding net."

I took a deep breath, *knowing* that the cybs were about to attack, but unable to bring up the net until they did *something,* knowing that the net response would be slower than the weapons, despite all the advisories that Keiko and I had sent.

The representative screen flashed, as did red lights.

"Unidentified torps launched! Torps launched!" Rhetoral announced.

I went into the command line of uppernet. **"THE CONSTRUCT HAS BEEN VIOLATED. THE CONSTRUCT HAS BEEN VIOLATED. OLD EARTH IS UNDER ATTACK. UNDER ATTACK. STEP-UP AND LINK TO DEFENSE NET. STEP-UP AND LINK TO DEFENSE NET. URGENT! URGENT! LINK TO DEFENSE NET!"**

I set the warning to repeat at three minute intervals for fifteen minutes, but before I finished the web had begun to hum. The web hummed, and I shivered into step-up, as the glow around me—around each demi anywhere on Old Earth—built.

"It's slow!" came from Rhetoral, his words seemingly dragging out in realtime.

The locators pinpointed the maroon-dashed torp tracks, and each of the asteroid stations flared purple-white as its screens went up. Almost simultaneously defense beams slashed toward the accelerating cyb torps. Where the beams intersected a torp, a bright star flashed on the screen. Above ground each explosion would have appeared as a star-point, even in mid-day, but I hoped no one was above ground to watch, not near any locial, anyway.

Despite the defense beams, some torps in the first two waves were going to slip under the net, and there was nothing I could do about it.

"Line one—in." The equatorial defense band, glimmering purple-white, shimmered into place.

Already, I could sense minute flickers along the net,

where weaker individual demis were unable to take the strain and went down in mindblazed death.

The control center was filled with sweat and fear, but no one spoke. I continued to hold the ground focus, as Elanstan and Rhetoral held the station foci where the net energy coruscated into the planetary defense bands.

"Band one stable and holding; shifting to band two," gasped Elanstan.

"Cybs launching attack vessels. Launching attack vessels," added Rhetoral.

Maroon dots appeared—fanning out from one of the twelve adiamante hulls hanging over Old Earth.

They were idiots to try that, but they'd been idiots all along—blind idiots, and we'd all pay for it.

The lights flared red, and I could sense the particle beams.

"Line two—now!" I snapped.

"Line two—in." The second concentration of power built, eased into position along the second axis. "Running ninety percent," Elanstan sounded weak already, and that bothered me, shield as she was. Not that we had any options.

Through the net, I could sense the power building, and the storm nexi changing, and the unholy mess that would follow.

"Bands three and four!" I ordered.

"Line three—in."

"Line four—in."

The agony in their voices tore at me, but we needed the entire shield—now, and *now* almost wasn't enough as the twelve ship-powered beams slammed into the net. More flickers through the link nodes told me of hundreds more demis dying, minds and souls shredded.

I forced my thoughts and concentration back to the representative screen that showed the particle beams splashing off the enhanced magfield that was our only defense.

"Energy resonation." That went to Crucelle and Dyn-cuun, who had meshed with the older demi.

The reflected energy should have set up unfavorable wave harmonics within the cyb ships—should have—but we didn't have the scanners to verify that.

"Continue resonation."

The resonation was having another effect—shaking the attack scouts into dust and energy. I tried to block the feelings, but I still felt sorry for the doomed pilots.

"Line four at eighty percent," rasped Elanstan through the command lines.

I shunted the last section of link nodes into line four.

"Ninety-four percent." Her signal strengthened, but only slightly.

"Particle beams depowered," Rhetoral reported. The rep screen verified the cutoff, and the chill white lines that appeared next confirmed the de-energizers.

"Reflect one," I ordered, initiating the shimmer shift, taking the screen a turn underweb—not really a turn, but a fraction of a turn.

Another *clinking* shivered along the net as more souls shattered or snuffed out in mindblazed agony.

The rep screen showed another wave of heavy torps, and another line of attack scouts.

"Need net-flex," whispered Elanstan..

"NET-FLEX . . . NOW!" I ordered, and threw the focus outward for as short a snap as I could, a snap of mindlinks, boosted with pure energy, trying to shield against the agony that would follow.

On the rep screen the shield shimmered, then expanded momentarily, shivering space ever so slightly, and an energy curtain fell across the twelve adiamante hulls. The hulls held, but the cyb de-energizers flickered and stuttered.

As those beams faltered, knives slashed through my

skull, knives from the thousands of deaths that single flex had cost.

Impossibly, the cybs re-energized those beams that tore at the defense shields, and once more white lines jabbed and sucked at the silver barrier, and link nodes, one after another, snuffed black.

"Lines three and four at eighty-five percent."

"Holding." We had no more link reserves.

"Target flex, Ecktor! Target flex." Elanstan's recommendation sounded as though it had been flayed from her, but she was right.

"TARGET FLEX—MARK! NOW!"

Another massive energy boost, and the shield flexed, then narrowed into a purple shaft aimed at the cyb fleet, broad enough to cover them all.

A sunburst flared where Gamma station had been, followed by Kappa, then Beta, as each station surrendered all the power it had—and more—to throw that shaft.

As the shaft reached the first Vereal Union ship, space shivered, and so did I, as adiamante fragments sprayed space, releasing more energy.

I ignored, heart-pounding, the slumped body that had been Crucelle, as I tried to keep that energy focused into its destructive form.

A second cyb-ship went—and a third.

More figures slumped around the control center, more souls backblazed into oblivion as the shield energies coruscated across where the cyb fleet had been—and rebounded.

Elanstan and Rhetoral said nothing, screamed nothing, but their deaths were like two black arrows through me.

My skull was flayed open, my eyes were blind, streaming tears of acid burned my skin, and I sat there blind and deaf, dumb, for a time. My mouth was dry.

<<< **XXXIV**

Let's see," murmured the fleet commander. "Weapons, hold ten percent of busters. Hold ten, and release the rest."

"Ninety away, Commander."

Gibreal watched as the ninety torps with the tach-heads flashed forth. Sets of white-dashed lines flared on the screens, like ancient spiderwebs dropping down to bracket Old Earth.

"No!" protested the envoff—too late, as the cyb commander hammered her into mental jelly with his overrides.

Twelve purple-white globes flared into existence beyond Old Earth, and from each stabbed lines of purple-white fire. Where each line intersected an accelerating torp, a star-point of light, an instant mini-nova, flared.

"Helpless? Helpless demis? Hardly."

A single white-purple band appeared around the image of Old Earth held in the ops and weapons screens and in the shipnet: a band like an antique halo, except that it circled the planet beyond the atmosphere and directly above the planetary equator.

"Analyze!" snapped Weapons.

"Systems unknown," answered MYL-ERA. "Energy output equivalent to . . . ." The exact number exceeded verbal translations and was projected directly to the networkers.

". . . more than a dozen fleets . . ."

"Sanitize!" snapped Gibreal. The fleet commander scanned the screens before him in his personal command center, and those he could touch on the net, dismissed both the backup visuals cursorily, and attempted to gauge the enormous power represented by the single white-purple band that arced around the globe that was Old Earth.

More torps flared into energy, but not all of the ninety launched initially.

"Dispersal one," ordered the fleet commander.

"Dispersal one beginning," confirmed Weapons, phasing the scout launches so that only a single ship had open locks at one time.

The energy *humming* from the white-purple band around Old Earth seemed to vibrate space itself, setting up a resonance in the *Gibson* that blurred Gibreal's visual images on the net, where clarity was never lacking.

"Network at one hundred ten percent of capacity," announced MYL-ERA. "Dropping non-ops nodes."

The net resonance decreased, but a fuzzy edge remained around the net visuals, and hissing permeated every word and concept hurled along the energy channels and even along the backup fibrelines.

"Power particle beams."

At Gibreal's command, the full output of hundreds of fusactors within the adiamante hulls of the Vereal fleet transferred pure energy into a dozen lines of white hell that flared toward Old Earth.

With those energy lines appeared a second purple-white band, snapping into place at right angles to the first, so that Old Earth beneath the energy flows was divided into quarters.

Then came a third band, and a fourth, and the four bands created a shimmering haze-web behind which the planet seemed to vanish.

The concentrated energy from the twelve particle beams splashed across the shield, and with that impact, the adiamante hulls began to vibrate, to shiver as adiamante hulls had never shivered for the cybs.

"Overlap shields," ordered Gibreal. The energy shields from the twelve adiamante hulls clicked into and around each other, and the *humming* that had threatened to shake the *Gibson* into adiamante fragments and metallic dust subsided into a background whine.

"Systems at one hundred five percent," reported MYL-ERA.

"Drop habitation, all nonessentials."

"Dropping all nonessentials this time," responded MYL-ERA.

Beyond the overlapped shields, the armed scouts flared into energy and subatomic particles.

"Interrogative halt dispersal one," asked Weapons.

"Negative. We need to keep their targets spread."

"Old Earth energy expenditure on scout destruction less than one percent of fields in existence," reported MYL-ERA.

"Negative," reiterated Gibreal.

A second wave of scouts reached the barriers of the linked shields—and vanished into the growing cloud of shimmering dust and energy that flared up before the twelve adiamante hulls.

The particle beams still splashed away from the barrier that protected the planet before the Vereal ships.

In a voice as cold and hard as ice four, Gibreal ordered, "Power shift. All power to de-energizers."

Unseen beams, represented by green dashes on the visual representational screens, focused on the nexial points of the purple-white bands that shielded Old Earth from the cyb energy weapons.

The shimmering haze that shielded Old Earth shivered, vibrated, but held.

"Almost," grunted Gibreal. "Almost."

"Fire remaining busters! Now!"

The ten tach-heads mounted on subtranslation drives flashed toward Old Earth, apparently untouched.

The third wave of scouts passed the Vereal shields—and remained intact.

Then, impossibly, the shimmer-shield of Old Earth flared, flexed, and both scouts and torps were gone.

A second sun followed that flexing, a sunburst so violent that the Vereal shipnets screamed.

As the electroneural screaming dropped, and the screens cleared, Gibreal noted that the Old Earth shield flickered ever so slightly, and one of the asteroid stations had lost its shields.

"Systems, get me more power for the de-energizers. Anywhere."

"Power output is at ninety percent maximum and degrading."

"Get me power," Gibreal grunted.

"Half the crew's dead," protested Weapons. "No power, no atmospheric integrity."

"I ordered power." As his thoughts iced over the net, Gibreal slammed the overrides and smashed through the weapons officer's barriers. Weapons slumped in his couch, mind-burned, mind-numb.

All but the priority screens went dead.

"Power at ninety-two percent for three minutes."

The de-energizers stabbed and worried.

The silver shimmer-shield flickered and wavered, then flexed once more, throwing a lance of purple-white flame that seemed to climb back up the line of de-energizers.

The *Gibson* shivered once, then began to vibrate. With a shrieking hiss, the net stabbed at the cybs still conscious, and Gibreal cut his connection, his eyes burning, his fingers stabbing at the slow, hard-wired, fibreline-linked controls before him.

As the first flicker of purple stripped the fleet shields, as the first Vereal ship shuddered, shivered, and translated into energy and fist-sized globules of adiamante, a second asteroid system station flared, and a third . . . and fourth. . . .

"Depower!" Gibreal's fingers slashed at the clumsy switchplates and dials, but the lance of white-purple flame continued to climb back toward the twelve adiamante hulls.

Gibreal hit another set of switchplates, and found them powerwelded open. Finally, he cold-slammed the fusactors, and sat in the dim red light of the emergencies, waiting before the blank black screens . . . waiting, as purple fire inexorably climbed the dead pathway of the de-energizers toward the twelve dead hulls.

"Systems . . . non-functional . . . non-functional . . ." pulsed MYL-ERA, her words electronic mutters on the dying net that had once bound the *Gibson* and the eleven other ships as tightly as their adiamante hulls.

In the silence of empty space, white-purple energy consumed twelve hulls, then rebounded.

With that last pulse, the impact of the energy recoil, the global energy net shivered and fragmented. . . . Vanishing as if it had never been. . . . carrying with it the remaining asteroid stations.

Beneath the spreading cloud of adiamante fragments, and ionized atoms that had been ships' interiors and crews, a last double-handful of torps dropped toward the planet below, past the vanishing violet energy of the defense system, dropped across oceans, mountains, homing on the strongest energy sources, except for one pretargeted hill in lower Deseret, where the energy radiations were almost nil.

<<< XXXV

Finally, I managed to click out of step-up, but all I could do was stare at the representational screen of the control center.

No cyb ships—and not a single asteroid station.

My eyes and mind kept burning—burning for Crucelle, Elanstan, and Rhetoral and all those on the ell stations—and for poor unbending Arielle, who would try for the rest of her life to find rational explanations for the irrational behavior of the cybs, and for the need to apply the Power Paradigm.

"Forty-three torps under the beams. . . ." said someone.

I turned and looked at Wiane, her eyes wide with horror.

Beyond her sat the darkangel, blackness around her like a shroud, immobile.

Above us all loomed the wide representational screen, showing the approaching trails of the more than forty killer torps—the legacy of the cybs, and The Flight.

With a struggle, I accessed the locators.

"First impact at Chitta—seven standard minutes."

"Interrogative impact at Parwon."

"Nine standard minutes."

After a time, I slowly turned in the swivel. Arielle remained frozen, sitting on the eternal tile beside Crucelle's body, not touching him, just there. Kemra still sat in the straight-backed chair, eyes wide, glued on the representational screen, as though she still could not believe that the fleet of the Vereal Union—twelve impregnable adiamante hulls—had ceased to exist. Except that they hadn't just ceased to exist—across Old Earth, more than a half million demis had given their minds and lives to stop that fleet.

I looked down. My eyes burned too much to weep, but I felt that way—and insane widower that I was, I was angry.

First I pulled myself out of the swivel and eased over to Arielle. "I'm sorry," I whispered, touching her shoulder. Crucelle had wanted me to be Coordinator, and I knew why. So did she, but it didn't make it any easier.

"You did what had to be done. He wanted that. And you tried everything to make it fall on you." She shook her head. "I'll be fine. I always am."

I didn't know quite what to say, but I squeezed her shoulder. "When you want to talk . . ."

"I know."

Then I straightened and looked around the center, assessing the losses—Crucelle, Liseal, Sebestien, and Vieria—four out of ten.

"Now?" asked Wiane hoarsely.

"We wait until forty-three tach-heads turn forty-three locials into black glass, and then we clean up."

"The cybs?" asked Keiko.

I'd forgotten about that detail. "Sorry. We gather together enough restraint squad members from the holding areas and outliers and we round up the fifteen hundred leftover cybs. Then we clean up." I shrugged. "I'll lead the group here. But that will have to come later." Later, after all the immediate cleanup and relocation.

With nothing else that I could do at that moment—and I didn't want just to sit and watch the screen while locial after locial was devastated—I walked across the center toward the cyb subcommander. Kemra shrank in her chair.

"Are you happy, mighty cyb? You certainly got your vengeance. More than ten thousand of us for every dead cyb and marcyb. More before this is over."

She looked blank.

"That screen was powered not just with fusactors and

boosters and relays and nodes and links, but with the soul and mind of every adult demi on the planet."

The ground shivered then, enough that I had to reach out and steady myself on the wall, despite the shock absorbers, despite the klicks of rock above and around the center.

With the second, fainter shiver I felt, I wondered. Two torps for Parwon?

I went back to the remote scanners, throwing the image on the screen.

In the screen was the rising plume of smoke that resembled, I had been told, an ancient NorAm sombrero—that was some kind of hat used by cattle tenders back when the cattle were more plentiful than the bison.

Then the knives of the backlash hit, and most of us swayed, or worse. Someone retched, and I saw Wiane collapse, more like a faint than a mental snuffing, though.

Beside her, Dorgan paled, and his face twisted, his mind already shredding under the agonies of the few unshielded draffs dying above, of the other demis dying, and of the land itself.

Kemra looked across us, her face blank and uncomprehending, and I wanted to throttle her, except my head hurt too much to move.

Parwon was black glass, and I hoped all the draffs had left, and that the cybs hadn't, but I suspected that Henslom had had more than enough sense to move his troops away. They would have to have moved quickly, though.

When my head cleared, I pinpointed the second tachhead. I no longer had a house, just a hilltop of black glass. Apparently, the residence of the planetary Coordinator was a military target, and I wondered how many times they'd tracked my flitter just to make sure.

Better my house than a locial. How many locials were gone? How many meleysen trees and how many more centuries would it take?

On the screen, black starbursts continued to dot the image of Old Earth, but the skies were clear, clear of cyb-ships, clear of satellite asteroid stations.

"What . . ." stuttered Kemra.

"No fleet. No cybs, except you and whoever Henslom and Ysslop managed to get away from Parwon and Ellay." I nodded. "Yes, your commander nuked the locials holding his own troops."

"But how?"

I didn't feel like answering, and I had a lot to do. "You people never looked, never asked how we had managed. You never paid any attention. You're like self-indulgent children." My words snapped at her, and I should have been more patient, but with the world collapsed around us, I wasn't feeling patient. Besides, there were people hurt, dying, and dead, and I could explain later.

I dropped back into the command seat and accessed the Parwon receiving shelter through the hard-wires. With the surface destruction, all the nets, except for the emergency net, were down.

Seborne was in charge of the receiving area, working with Maris.

"This is Coordinator Ecktor. Is Seborne there?"

A dark-eyed visage on a wiry frame looked at me through the screen. "Coordinator, Seborne didn't make it." The dark eyes were bloodshot, and her face twitched.

"Lictaer." I recognized the restraint squad leader. "Are you running the receiving area?"

"No, ser. Just the console. Ferik was Seborne's assistant."

"Can you run him down?"

"Just a moment."

While I waited, I wondered just how many details had been left hanging. I wanted to take care of Henslom, but that would have to wait. Hopefully, not too long.

<<< **XXXVI**

I hated the command center: buried under klicks of rock, reinforced adiamante, and energy webs, it carried the smell of age, ozone, and death. But it was the only place left with links to the remaining locials, and we needed those links in order to allocate the transport that would relocate the draffs and the few demis in each surviving receiving area to undamaged locials.

Locatio had survived, and was still whining from the Ellay receiving area. "Ecktor, we've still got those marcybs in the canyons."

"Once you've got everything cleaned up and the survivors taken care of, go out and get them. That's what our job is." I had less and less sympathy for whining.

"Not everyone is as strong as you are," came a new voice over the hard netlink, one I didn't recognize.

"Sorry, I don't—"

"You probably wouldn't. I'm Dynise, the temporary replacement for K'gaio. I hope it's temporary."

"Temporary—probably for a decade." I was sorry to hear about K'gaio. If anyone had been strong enough to survive, I would have thought it would have been her.

"Anyway," I answered Locatio, "you're going to have to solve this one yourself. The crisis is over. Now all we have is the immediate cleanup, and after that you won't need a Coordinator."

I broke the link. For a moment, I leaned back in the command seat and closed my eyes. Yslena: I hoped she was all right, but until the nets were rebuilt, there wasn't any real way to check, and I wasn't about to preempt the emergency system for that—not when there was nothing I could do, one way or another.

The net buzzed.

"This is Ecktor."

"Dynise."

"Sorry. I didn't meant to cut you out. What can I do?"

"Actually, I was going to tell you that we've got two of the big shuttles bringing in a spare net repeater. We'll have to mount it in the open temporarily, but we'll leave the location to you."

I knew where already. "There's a flat expanse about a quarter klick east of the buried Deseret antenna grid—the elevation there's about 3,100 meters. I can have a beacon there in a stan."

"That will be fine. You won't get the repeater until tomorrow. Since we're sending shuttles for relocation, we can squeeze the equipment in with the food supplements for those we can't evacuate immediately."

After Dynise broke off, I took a deep breath. We had more than enough concentrated supplies—even sophisticated medical supplies—for the receiving areas for weeks, but the sooner people picked up their lives, the better. Those who liked the Deseret area could filter back as they could—if they liked where we decided to relocate the locial center.

In the meantime, they needed to be integrated into functioning locials elsewhere. The magshuttles were efficient, but the largest ones only carried seventy-five passengers, and most were sized for fifty or less. With three-quarters of the center population of forty locials, that worked out to five hundred to eight hundred trips per local. While there were forty-two locials whose centers were black glass, in two cases the tach-head blast force had also taken out the receiving center. We'd lost a handful of shuttles, but I was glad I'd had the majority evacuated. They were proving themselves most useful. The problem was going to be pilot fatigue, since we'd lost a lot of pilots—more than half.

More opportunities for comptime. I offered a bitter smile to the screen that showed the blackened and steaming ruins of Parwon.

"You wanted to see him. There he is." At the words, I turned in the swivel.

Kemra stood less than a meter away, flanked by a pale and still gaunt Lictaer. The demi restraint squad leader hadn't totally escaped the mindblazing backlash, and her eyes occasionally twitched. Lictaer would recover, as much as any of us would recover.

"Yes?"

"What are you going to do with me? Except have me trailed everywhere?" snapped Kemra. Her fingers strayed to the cryostasis flask and miniature powerpak at her hip. Because of her comments in the ruins, I'd approved that so that she could gather limited specimens of wildflowers outside beyond the exit tunnel. I'd hoped it would keep her out of trouble, but it looked as though I'd been wrong.

"Without a guard, I can't totally guarantee that some draff—or some demi not quite sane—won't try to take off your head. You are a cyb, and you're seen as the enemy—and quite a few people died."

"You had everything evacuated, and you demis are above violence." Her tone was cold and bitter.

"That reduced casualties, but it didn't eliminate them. We lost two receiving centers—they held 90,000 people. Forty-two locials are black glass or slag or both."

Lictaer glared at Kemra.

"And almost a million demis died in the backlash."

Kemra glanced from Lictaer to me and back.

"Do you know what it took to hold that defense net? I told you once, and it didn't seem to register."

"That was your satellite, your asteroid stations."

"They were only the nexial points and the power

sources. Every adult demi on this planet was linked into the defense system, and we lost almost half of them."

"Why was that necessary? You save the idiotic draffs, and you let yourselves die." Kemra looked at me, her eyes smoldering.

"It's simple enough. It dates to antiquity, and it's called the Iron Law of Responsibility. Those with great power must exercise equally great responsibility. Some people don't choose to. Probably half the draffs on Old Earth could be demis—"

"Thirty percent," corrected Lictaer.

"Anyway, we pay for our power and responsibility. I kept telling you that, and none of you listened. I told you in the ruins. I told you in the prairie dog town. I told you on your own ship. What does it take?" I was nearly yelling when I stopped.

"So what are you doing with me?" she asked, again not really listening.

"Send you back and hope someone listens. Send back some records of a dead fleet, and hope the message penetrates."

"Who's going to listen to dead cybs?" Kemra lashed out. "Who's going to listen to just me?"

"Who said you were the only survivor? There are several hundred marcybs and their officers running around loose. Once we take care of them, there should be a few survivors, and we'll send you all home."

I looked at Lictaer. "Take her somewhere. If you can get her to listen, be my guest. If not, just keep her safe until we can get a ship ready."

Lictaer nodded.

"You're impossible," Kemra said. "You're living in a past that never was. You don't understand life. You just don't understand."

After rubbing my forehead—I still had splitting headaches, but most demis had the same problems I did—I an-

swered tiredly. "No. You don't understand. You had every
opportunity. You didn't want to listen or see. You struck
first, and we didn't even raise a defense until after you
struck. I also might add that, if you send another fleet,
based on your past efforts, its appearance is a violation of
the Construct. In simple terms, if the next thing we see
from Gates is a fleet, we don't have to wait."

"You're hypocrites."

"No." They were the hypocrites, but arguing wasn't
going to change Kemra's mind, and there was no point in
continuing the discussion. I nodded tiredly.

"Let's go," said Lictaer.

"You live in your own dead world, with your own dead
Morgen!" Kemra lunged at me, and her fingernails sliced
at my temple.

I was tired, and Lictaer was in residual mind-shock, or
it wouldn't have happened, but that didn't matter. Kemra
only came up with skin, blood droplets, and hair before we
restrained her.

"I hate you! I hate your smugness and certainty!"

The sourness of anger, fear, hatred, and who knew what
else boiled from her, but I really didn't care at that point.

Lictaer and two others led her off, and I stared at the
screen and the ruins there for a moment. Then I rubbed
my neck and forehead. Sooner or later, I'd have to deal
with Henslom and his troops—sooner, if they felt the way
Kemra did.

The netlink buzzed for me, and I reached for the connection. I still hated the control center, but once the new
relay was installed, once I took care of the loose ends like
Henslom, once Kemra was on the ship with the others,
then I could stop being Coordinator and get out of the
center—and spend the rest of my life paying for it.

I took a deep breath.

<<< **XXXVII**

When I'd estimated two or three days before I could get things stabilized enough to go look for Henslom and his marcybs, I'd been optimistic—incredibly optimistic.

Eight days passed before we had magshuttled most of the survivors out of the holding areas and redistributed them temporarily throughout the remaining sixty-six locials.

Sixty-six locials left out of one hundred and six, and that was after we'd destroyed the entire cyb fleet and probably neutralized ninety-nine percent of its weaponry.

At least we wouldn't lack for work, not for another few decades, and not until we met another set of idiots who thought that technology meant big ships and unlimited fusion power. I just hoped that the cybs didn't try to send another fleet too soon, my brave words to Kemra notwithstanding, but building that fleet had to have cost them a lot, a whole lot.

After a week, we were down to the handfuls of demis who either had lived outside the locial or who would be the core of the reclamation. I was one of them. I liked the area, and it was solid comptime work, and no one was going to argue about where I wanted to spend years doing comptime. Besides, I had one last chore before I resigned as Coordinator—taking care of the cybs remaining in Deseret.

The rebuilt net worked, except in really low depressions or gorges, but even the complete original net had had some problems there. We'd managed to link in with the scattered demis in the area, and get a fair report on the cyb forces.

The cybs had moved away from Parwon, following the valley to the north. They'd moved upwind to higher ground, possibly to avoid residual radioactivity, although the tach-heads had been relatively clean. Parwon center was mostly black glass—between the fringe of the particle beams that had slipped under the shields, and the single tach-head that had potted the admin building—now a large and steaming crater nearly two hundred meters across. Deseret locial was going to have to be relocated, or abandoned, or something, until the area could be reclaimed—and reclamation took time: centuries, if not millennia.

The cyb forces numbered less than two hundred after blast casualties, encounters with demi families, and various local fauna. Two demi families had lost members to slugthrowers, but the casualties had been lighter than I would have expected. In a way, I suspected that the environment and the survivors would polish them off over the months, but innocents would probably be killed in the process. So we needed to do something.

Rather than indiscriminate killing, of which there had already been too much, I really just wanted to take out Henslom and his officers. Then the restraint squads could round up the marcybs with comparatively little difficulty.

Finding their general location was easy enough, and I still was Coordinator, and that meant I could commandeer a magshuttle.

We loaded on at Berkin's place. His house was fifteen klicks north of the holding areas and safely out of range of damage. His soulmate—a solid redhead—would be glad to see us leave permanently, but they'd both been most hospitable.

The magshuttle pilot was Borin. He looked at me. "Is this that same cyb majer?"

"The same Majer Henslom."

"Too bad the Construct kept you from killing him back then."

"If we didn't have a Construct, we'd be like him," I said softly.

Borin looked away. It didn't take him long to carry us another thirty klicks to the northeast where he dropped the dozen of us on a hilltop downwind of the general position of the cybs. The local demis had been helping, as they could, lead the cybs toward the northeast end of the valley that held one of the larger concentrations of vorpals in Deseret.

"What are we doing?" asked Berkin as I checked the slugthrower and knives at my belt.

"In theory, this is simple," I said. "I'm going to try to disable one of the junior officers on the flank. After that, then let's see if we can guide them close enough to the big vorpal lair. If not, take out all the officers."

"Isn't that bending the Construct?" asked Gisel.

"They broke it. Let's go."

We spread out, with Berkin, since he knew the area, leading half to the west. Gisel led the eastern group, and I moved out ahead of Gisel's group on the eastern flank.

"They're headed along the stream," pulsed Berkin.

"The whole group?"

"Yes."

I tried a nature link. Sometimes it worked. Sometimes it didn't, and sometimes it didn't help even if it did work.

First came the meleysens. Extending and concentrating gave me the sense of a low bass subsonic, and against that I could hear the *tap-thump* of the cybs' boots. At least, that was the way it felt.

Another reach and the green chewing blandness of the samburs framed the meadow to the west. That did little good, because the ruisines heard the cybs and bolted before the cybs even knew the deer had been there.

Then there was the cool black-edged probing of the

mother bear who lived above the snye beyond the meadow. I tried to reach out, to warn her, but she was shielded.

At the edge of my perceptions came in the laser hate of the vorpals, and I nodded. Henslom deserved vorpals.

I eased through the piñons and cedars, keeping out of sight, trying to track down the junior officer who held the controls of the flank marcyb squad. I recognized him—Cherle, the blocky officer who'd been on the prairie dog fiasco. He'd learned from that. All of his marcybs were fanned out in front of him.

The only sounds were those of the wind in the higher piñons, the crunch of boots on the frozen ground, and the occasional snap of a dead and dry sagebrush limb. The cold air held the scent of cybs, dried blood, and even of sweat, now that their scent-suppressants had worn off.

Cherle scanned the area in all directions, his head swiveling, his eyes intent. Because the area, like much of Deseret, consisted of open ground, sagebrush, cedars, and piñons, all irregularly spaced, it took me nearly a stan to get within a few meters.

Then I went into step-up, and crossed the few meters between us. Cherle's head jerked, and he swung the slug-rifle, but I was inside it, and moving too quickly, and too angrily. For a moment, I thought I'd struck too hard, but then he shivered, and tried to break away. My fingers tightened around his neck, and I pulse-blocked, letting him slump in a heap on the hard ground beside a cedar.

"Stay," I ordered the silent squad, overriding his own repeater, before easing back uphill after the main body. "Guard Cherle." They stayed.

"Cherle! Report! Report! Why aren't you following? What do you mean by telling them to guard you?" Henslom's transmissions burned from his repeater. "Babbege? Can you raise Cherle?"

"That's negative, ser."

"Friggin' demis. May get us, but I'll kill as many of the bastards as I can."

Babbege, sensibly, did not comment.

"I'm going in," I pulsed.

"Ser?" asked Gisel.

"I'm going to get him mad enough to chase me where I want him to go."

"You'll do anything to avoid comptime," noted a familiar voice across the net—Keiko's.

"I still love you, too." With that I slipped back north and west until I could target Henslom's repeater, still a half-klick away, but that was more than close enough.

I tried to reach out, and got something else, practically at my feet—another small oval of adiamante, lying on the ground less than a meter away. Was it a remnant of the cyb fleet? One of the chunks still falling?

For some reason I didn't have time to fathom, I tucked the black oval into my jacket pocket, then edged sideways across the hill toward the small meleysen grove. There, I dropped behind the north side of a solid trunk and waited.

He was with the vanguard, as I figured he'd be. When he was at one hundred fifty meters, I rammed the signal through his own repeater. "Henslom, you're a miserable excuse for a soldier, and an even worse cyb."

Henslom's head swiveled from side to side.

"You couldn't destroy a single demi with a whole fleet."

Terrible in his cold anger, Henslom lifted the slugger, and I could see the flexsplints on his fingers. Then the bullets stitched through the meleysen trees like the ancient killer bees, the scent of orange raining down with the tattered leaves.

Behind the lower trunk, behind a meter of heart-solid wood, I waited, just as any demi would wait, calculating, triangulating as Henslom moved from ninety-one point three meters south southwest to eighty-one point five me-

ters west south west. His breath rasped through his en-
larged pharynx, as his crude selfnet revved his metabolism.

"You're still a poor excuse for a soldier, Majer," I called.
"Even if you had all your fingers."

A jay chittered in the pines beyond the meleysen grove,
and the slugger flicked that way.

RRRRRRRRrrrrrrrr. . . .

The roar and the stream of composite left feathers,
silver-blue, drifting down with pine branch fragments.
Henslom moved to seventy-five point four meters south of
where I was. His squad followed, dragged by the commands over his repeater.

"They'll all be in range before long," Gisel pulsed from
southeast of where I waited behind the meleysen grove,
trying to ignore the sickly orangish scent that dropped
around me.

"How close are they to those vorpals?"

"We're all only about half a klick." A pause followed.
"I'd rather not . . ."

"Take out one or two of the marcybs on your side—
with a lot of blood. Then get out of there. Let the vorpals
find them."

"That's hard on the vorpals."

"They'll survive."

A handful of shots echoed to the south and east of me.

Then the marcybs' sluggers roared again, and pine needles carpeted the paths that Henslom's squads had blown
through the piñons.

"Gisel?" I pulsed, waiting for a lagged response.

"Fine. Just being careful."

"Get out of there."

"Almost clear." A pause followed. "I'm over the ridge,
and I'm moving, ser. So are the vorpals."

"Henslom, you're going to lose every last one of your
marcybs, and you're going to die here on Old Earth."

Another blast truncated a pair of piñons, and more silver-blue feathers floated down with the green needles.

Henslom turned north, until he was almost looking at the grove where I waited, his slugthrower traversing a narrow arc.

The scent of piñon drifted on the wind to me, and so did the hint of blood, a hint of blood that would travel farther downwind to the vorpals.

"Berkin? Can you wound a couple over there—without getting seen?"

"Easy."

"Do it."

Another few shots rang out, and Henslom's head swiveled west.

I could sense the ferity of the vorpals, and much as I would have liked to see Henslom's reaction, I slowly eased back and then east.

"Another volley, Berkin."

"You've got it, Coordinator."

Henslom swiveled toward the west. I slipped over a ridge line and began to run. "Draw back! Now! Regroup at the dropout point, and watch out for vorpals."

"Stet."

"Stet."

We didn't have to worry. Drawn by the commotion and the scent and feel of blood, the vorpals slipped silently from their lair beyond the snye and surged downhill toward the unknowing cybs, much more willing to take on cybs than demis.

For a time, there were only the sounds of the wind and muted bootsteps on hard ground.

Then, an unwary marcyb went down with her throat slashed by the sharp incisors, even before her body could react. Two others went down before the sluggers roared again.

"Get them! Fire at will!" snapped Henslom.

Slugthrowers rumbled in panic, and marcybs went down, but not the vorpals, which dodged through the cedars and the piñons faster than the cybs' reflexes could react.

"Keep pulling back," I ordered. "We'll wait."

Cherle was almost awake when I got there.

I took his repeater from him, used it again to put his squad in combat sleep, and took the time to tie him up thoroughly. Then we waited.

Before too long, the pines, the cedars were silent again, except for the cold north wind and too many disgusting sounds from the vorpals. I would have liked to have seen Henslom's face, but it wasn't worth the risk.

Gisel and his squad joined me, and we hiked a circular route back to the pickup point where Borin picked up the dozen of us, six dazed marcybs, and subleader Cherle.

I stuffed Cherle and the marcybs in the back seat.

"Cheer up," I told Cherle. "You get to go home."

He didn't answer, just looked at the magshuttle floor, mumbling, "Don't understand . . . just don't understand. . . ."

When we landed at Berkin's to the south, the black clouds massed over the seared earth and black glass that had been Parwon.

A series of golden streaks flashed across the sky—more adiamante fragments coming to rest—hard memories of harder choices. My fingers went to the fragment in my jacket pocket for a moment, slipping around that smoothness that was neither hot nor cold.

And because the Consensus Committee had resolved that the crisis wasn't over, and that Old Earth still needed a Coordinator, I was still stuck with the need to go back to the command center with its odors of ozone, metal, and death.

<<< **XXXVIII**

As planetary Coordinator, I had to go to Klamat as part of the ceremony that would send the cybs back to Gates. So I trudged out into the dawn, and waited on the *de facto* landing pad east of the end of the escape tunnel. I stood in the chill and the wind, wearing the damned black cloak that Arielle had made, even though it reminded me of Crucelle—and Elanstan and Rhetoral—the dagger, shield, and sword who had led the many who had given all to defend us . . . and the Construct. The occasion demanded the cloak, if only for me, and its personal symbolism. I'd also brought the chunk of adiamante I'd picked up in hunting down the last cybs. That seemed fitting, somehow.

Behind me straggled Lictaer, Arielle, the six nameless marcybs, Cherle, and Kemra.

Before the sun cleared the eastern peaks, one of the large magfield shuttles hummed out of the gray sky. The door slid open. I stepped inside and peered forward, recognizing a familiar face under short red hair—Lieza.

"I'm glad you made it," I told her.

"Thank you. Be nice when things settle down." Her eyes were tired, ringed with black.

I sat down in the right front seat. Arielle sat across from me.

"How are you?"

"Fine." Arielle paused. "Not now, please."

I deferred. Grieving was harder and longer for the ratcomps, for the logical, because loss is neither rational nor logical.

The magshuttle's door slid shut after Lictaer settled the cybs into the rear seats.

"We're lifting," Lieza announced.

As the shuttle lifted and banked toward the northwest, I leaned back in the seat and closed my eyes, feeling guilty for being merely tired after seeing Lieza's face.

My eyes didn't stay closed that long, because someone moved up next to me. I opened my eyes, trying not to sigh.

Kemra stood there in her smudged and wrinkled green uniform. "I'd like to apologize." Her eyes dropped, then lifted to mine.

I sat there waiting. Behind Kemra watched Arielle, the hooded darkangel.

"There's . . . what else can I say? We didn't know. I didn't want to know." The green eyes dropped again, and she swayed as the shuttle eased out of the wide turn.

What could I say? That I'd practically screamed at them? It wouldn't do any good to hammer that farther. I rummaged in my trouser pocket and pulled out the adiamante. "You might take this with you." I handed Kemra the fragment of adiamante. "It's one of the hull fragments."

"I've never seen a piece this small." Her voice was neutral.

"Old Earth is covered with fragments of adiamante," I answered. "Until you came, I hadn't realized how many there are. The meleysens can't break them down. Nothing, except the interior of a sun, can change them."

"Or your defense net," she added.

"That's a high price," I pointed out. "But one we'll pay if necessary. We hope it's never necessary again." I sighed. "It will be, but not against you and your people, I trust."

She looked at the adiamante. "I'll try."

"That's all any of us can do." I looked at her.

She looked back, finally saying, "I am sorry. It doesn't mean much, and I can see how much you tried."

"Think about the adiamante." I was too tired to say much more. "It says more than I can." And it did—the hardest manmade substance, and it couldn't stand up to the souls of human beings.

I closed my eyes, and Kemra eased back to her seat in the rear of the shuttle, Arielle's eyes on her the entire way. I wouldn't have wanted that, but Kemra deserved that and more, probably.

As ceremonies go, the one in Klamat wasn't particularly impressive, but some events must be finished, and ceremonies are one of the few ways societies can observe endings. So a dozen of us, me and eleven members of the Consensus Committee, stood facing the cybs, with netimagers focused on us and upon the dozen or so marcybs and the three surviving officers—Kemra, Cherle, and a subforcer from the cyb group that had attacked Ellay.

As Coordinator, I had to do the speaking, and as at the Hybernium so comparatively few days earlier, I didn't want to.

"We are sending you home to Gates, and we're providing a ship as a symbol of trust. That is because the key to the universe, the key to survival, is trust. Trust is acting in good faith when you have no reason so to act. Trust is refraining from attacking an enemy first, no matter what the cost. Why is that wise? Because once any person or society strikes first, that action sows the seeds of corruption. Logic, even pure cyb logic, is formidable enough that it can justify any action, no matter how base or corrupt, as necessary to survival.

"Physical survival is not enough, not for either a person or a society. A society's principles must also survive, and if you betray your principles for physical survival, then you have doomed your offspring and your society. Principles can be improved, and we have slowly changed ours for what we believe to be the better, but they should never be changed or discarded for short-term expediency. No matter what the price, we must do what is right, and part of what is right is trust.

"The second key is mutual respect, within a society, and without. We have not threatened Gates since its establishment, and will not—unless Gates proves itself meriting mistrust. We hope not, but, as you have seen, we can and will act, and we will pay the price.

"We respect the integrity of Gates, and leave you to choose your own principles and destiny—provided you respect ours. Fail to respect others, and you are doomed—one way or the other."

I stopped. What else could I say? Then I added, "Convey this to your people. As invaders, as conquerors, you are unwelcome anywhere. As individuals, as visitors, as friends, you are welcome on Old Earth."

That really was it.

Dynise had dug up a decent hornist, and the hornist played something that brought tears to the eyes of Cherle and a couple of the marcybs, and it was over.

As the shuttle carrying the cybs up to the starship opened its hatch, Kemra crossed the permacrete toward me. I stiffened. What else did she have to say?

"Reasonable or not, Coordinator, you're harder than adiamante," Kemra said, her words coming from her mind, not her mouth, for the first time, and with a hint of warmth I had not seen in any of the cybs. Had not seen—or had not been there? "Not harder," she corrected, "stronger." She displayed the black oval I'd given her.

With that single net contact, I knew. . . . But she continued, the words screen clear and rushing at me, hiding one truth behind all the meaning they conveyed. "I don't know that any of us could bear the power and the pain . . ." she shook her head, "or would want to."

I thought of the million dead: not more than a handful of demis from the cyb-sluggers or other technological gadgets; of the 100,000 draffs blasted by tach-heads; of

Elanstan, Rhetoral, Crucelle, Dorgan. . . . My list would have been long.

"Old Earth really is the Planet of Death. . . . The legends were right . . . but, it's also the planet of life. I have the wildflowers, and we can replicate them—all of them."

"I wish you well." Each word was hard, because I understood what she had not said. What I knew and would not say, for there was no reason to, was that she would carry my child: strange enough since I had never touched her, nor she me, except once, when she had scratched me, deeply enough to draw cell samples—enough for DNA replication, though I doubted that had been her exact intention.

"You, too, Coordinator." She offered a formal smile, inclined her head, and turned. I watched her climb into the shuttle. In her hand was an oval of adiamante, a reminder that even the hardest substance in the universe can fail.

For all our nets, for all our communications, humans—cybs or demis—are aliens, aliens to each other, and to the universe, and that is why we must trust.

I watched, standing beside the white tower that was the image of the one that had stood in Parwon, a tower that was now melted white and black glass rising at the edge of steaming ruins.

The hatch slid shut, and Kemra was gone, and so were the cybs, and so was the conflict—until the next set of aliens.

Why do we wait? How could we do otherwise?

I shook my head. There was rebuilding to do—we'd need another asteroid satellite defense net, and that meant moving another dozen or more nickel-iron asteroids into the ell spaces. Given the amount of coercion I'd employed as Coordinator, I was going to be busy at that, and satellite development and maintenance for a long, long, time—maybe the rest of my life.

The cybs—or someone—would be back, but it would

be long enough that the next time it would be someone else's problem.

Arielle looked toward me, and I pulsed at her. "Not for a moment."

I walked up the permacrete to the north, into the wind, away from the others. There was one other thing that I'd put off too long. A locial landing strip wasn't perfect, but nowhere would ever be perfect. I took a deep breath and pushed out a tentative pulse on the shaky, but now-functioning uppernet.

"Yslena?"

"Father! You're there!"

"Not exactly. I'm temporarily in Klamat."

"Oh . . . the send-off for the cybs. I should have guessed. I should have watched."

"Nothing exciting. I gave a short sermon on trust and mutual respect. A trumpet played, and they're shuttling up to the ship."

"You make it sound so unimportant."

"It is. What's important is what I've put off for too long. What I never quite said to your mother, but I didn't have to because she knew. You and I, we need the words." I paused, struggling, "I'll be going back to Deseret. There's not much left of the house, except black glass, but I'm well. Tired, but doing all right. There won't be much free time—and I owe so much comptime I'll spend the rest of my life doing tech maintenance, but that's all right. There'll be another house, in time.

"I don't have much to say, except the important thing— I love you. I always have, and I always will, and it's taken me too long to say it, because I always let your mother do it."

"I knew," she said softly.

"Knowing and hearing it are two different things, and you should hear it. That I hadn't told you was something that hit me. I was lucky. I survived and got to tell you. I might not have been." I swallowed. "Since there's no place for you to come back to, not now, I'll be coming to see your reef, and, later, you can come back to Deseret, when there's something there."

"That's not important. I'm glad you linked."

So was I. We talked more, and the rest was interesting, but the important things had been said.

After we broke the link, I stood on the permacrete as the rain filtered down like mist, and a thousand klicks southwest, Swift-Fall-Hunter circled the hilltop with the black-glass center, then swung out over the valley.

Morgen had understood; so had Crucelle; I had not, though now I did.

There was another hilltop that could—and would—bear a home, and another set of piñons to run through, and another golden eagle . . . in between the years of comptime that stretched ahead, but the work would be good.

Morgen would not be there, though I owed her more than I could ever repay, and neither would Kemra, for all that she and the cybs had forced me to return to life—but Yslena would be, and perhaps others, as the years passed. And all would add to the future.

Klicks away, somewhere, Swift-Fall-Hunter circled, and I wished him well, as I wished the cybs well—Kemra and those few others headed starward on their borrowed ship, and those who lived on Gates and elsewhere—hoping that they would learn from the events we had survived, but not counting on that either.

I only counted on today's sunlight and snow, on the rain that dampened my face.

TOR
BOOKS The Best in Science Fiction

MOTHER OF STORMS • John Barnes
From one of the hottest new nanes in SF: a shattering epic of global catastrophe, virtual reality, and human courage, in the manner of *Lucifer's Hammer*, *Neuromancer*, and *The Forge of God*.

BEYOND THE GATE • Dave Wolverton
The insectoid dronons threaten to enslave the human race in the sequel to *The Golden Queen*.

TROUBLE AND HER FRIENDS • Melissa Scott
Lambda Award-winning cyberpunk SF adventure that the *Philadelphia Inquirer* called "provocative, well-written and thoroughly entertaining."

THE GATHERING FLAME • Debra Doyle and James D. Macdonald
The Domina of Entibor obeys no law save her own.

WILDLIFE • James Patrick Kelly
"A brilliant evocation of future possibilities that establishes Kelly as a leading shaper of the genre."—*Booklist*

THE VOICES OF HEAVEN • Frederik Pohl
"A solid and engaging read from one of the genre's surest hands."—*Kirkus Reviews*

MOVING MARS • Greg Bear
The Nebula Award-winning novel of war between Earth and its colonists on Mars.

NEPTUNE CROSSING • Jeffrey A. Carver
"A roaring, cross-the-solar-system adventure of the first water."—Jack McDevitt

TOR
BOOKS The Best in Science Fiction

LIEGE-KILLER • Christopher Hinz

"*Liege-Killer* is a genuine page-turner, beautifully written and exciting from start to finish....Don't miss it."—*Locus*

HARVEST OF STARS • Poul Anderson

"A true masterpiece. An important work—not just of science fiction but of contemporary literature. Visionary and beautifully written, elegaic and transcendent, *Harvest of Stars* is the brightest star in Poul Anderson's constellation."

—Keith Ferrell, editor, *Omni*

FIREDANCE • Steven Barnes

SF adventure in 21st century California—by the co-author of *Beowulf's Children*.

ASH OCK • Christopher Hinz

"A well-handled science fiction thriller."—*Kirkus Reviews*

CALDÉ OF THE LONG SUN • Gene Wolfe

The third volume in the critically-acclaimed Book of the Long Sun.
"Dazzling."—*The New York Times*

OF TANGIBLE GHOSTS • L.E. Modesitt, Jr.

Ingenious alternate universe SF from the author of the *Recluce* fantasy series.

THE SHATTERED SPHERE • Roger MacBride Allen

The second book of the Hunted Earth continues the thrilling story that began in *The Ring of Charon*, a daringly original hard science fiction novel.

THE PRICE OF THE STARS • Debra Doyle and James D. Macdonald

Book One of the Mageworlds—the breakneck SF epic of the most brawling family in the human galaxy!